We must deal with the implications of this message—the taking of an entire city was a public act; such an act demands public justification.

How can we keep the trust of the city without breaking our sacred obligations?

Amasta's pale eyes glittered coldly. Her voice, when she spoke, was arrogant and commanding. Tegestu recognized the tone at once: her superb, cunning, ruthless mind, once presented with the problem, had found a plan worth considering.

"Bro-demmini," she said, "there is a way." Lazily, she took a drink of tea. "It will require a sacrifice—there will be killing—*but I assure you, there is a way.*"

AMBASSADOR OF PROGRESS

WALTER JON WILLIAMS

TOR

A TOM DOHERTY ASSOCIATES BOOK

AMBASSADOR OF PROGRESS

A TOR Book

Published by Tom Doherty Associates, 8-10 West 36 Street, New York, N.Y. 10018

First TOR printing: April 1984

ISBN: 812-55-789-1
CAN.ED. 812-55-790-5

Cover art by Alan Gutierrez

Printed in the United States of America

Dedicated to:
    Fred & Joan Saberhagen,
    Two wise Princes of Serendip

PROLOGUE

In a storm of rain, its brightness a steadier glow among lightning flashes, the shuttle dropped into the high pasture, scattering alarmed cattle who ran in a clatter of bells for the sheltering trees. The fires dwindled; steam rose from the field. Lightning flickered high above, in the passes. The shuttle gate opened, the ramp sliding down into the wet, fire-blackened grass. Fiona, a small figure atop her tall horse, came down the ramp, leading her pack mule, and Kira followed with her own beasts.

The rain pattered on her hood, her shoulders. Fiona turned back for a moment to wave to the figures in the yellow light of the shuttle gate: tall, broad-shouldered Tyson, beside him lithe Wenoa. Their arms were raised in farewell, and for a moment Fiona hesitated, a lump in her throat. It would be years before she saw them, if she survived to see them at all.

The ramp withdrew; the yellow rectangle of light, with its two waving silhouettes, narrowed and vanished. A siren shrieked briefly: clear the area. Fiona waited until the gate's dazzle faded from her eyes. Night vision restored, she saw Kira leading her own mule away from the shuttle, and turned to follow, shivering briefly as if shaking water from her shoulders—and as she shivered, she was suddenly conscious of the gesture and wondered what it was she was shaking off: water, the thousands of years of progress since her own world had risen from barbarism, perhaps all her life that had gone before, prelude to this . . .? She shivered, turned the horse's head, and urged it in Kira's path.

When the fires began licking once more at the grass, and the shuttle rose blinding into the sky, she did not look back. It was not as if she hadn't volunteered, after all.

Fiona and Kira had been born in a year in which it had been fashionable for parents to give their children old Terran names, names recently resurrected but which were meaningless by the standards of their own culture. The names strangely prefigured their employment, their shared interest in the old star-spanning civilization. They were cousins of a sort, and though they shared no ancestry they were nevertheless distant relations according to the complicated geneology of their homeworld. They had first met when, at fourteen or so, they'd been undergoing mountaineering training at the home of yet another distant cousin, whose cheerfully volunteered responsibility it had been to train all the family's youth in mountain reliance, and they'd been fast friends since.

During school vacations they'd been in the same class on a lot of the family projects: canal maintenance, greenhouse work, soil preservation, each piece of duty supervised by some cousin or other . . . and when it came time to choose an occupational preference prior to the investment of family money in higher education, they'd both chosen the same field that had, eventually, perhaps inevitably, led them to this midnight delivery on a high mountain pasture.

Kira was outgoing, and smiled and laughed more often even than was usual in a culture in which smiling and laughing was the norm. Fiona, who laughed less, was a more serious scholar. Both were fine athletes, both stood high in their class, and both were accepted without qualm into the program that would take them to the stars. Both survived, without difficulty, the reconstruction of certain parts of their bodies that was intended to aid them on the planet surface.

Both volunteered for the first team and because of their high aptitude were accepted, in spite of apprehension on the part of their superiors that perhaps the culture in which they were being delivered might not be as receptive to women as it might have been to men. "They've got to learn sometime," Kira had said—and then she laughed, to divert the sharp glance Tyson had given her. Tyson was brilliant but he laughed less often than almost anyone.

For three days they negotiated the mountain paths, heading always downslope, northeast. They pitched their tent in solitude, in the light of the big striped moon that dominated the night sky—their own planet didn't have a moon, and the sight was a constant reminder of the strangeness of this place—and they watched the new world carefully, trying not to be overwhelmed by the newness of it all. The gravity was lighter than what they were used to, and both the women and their animals had a tendency to skip and dance, freer of the ground than they had ever been before—but the overwhelming textures of the new world sobered Fiona quickly, and often caused Kira to frown.

The vegetation, partly composed of Terran stock, was not entirely unfamiliar, the grasses particularly; but the animals, even those which they knew—like the herds of cattle being driven to the upper pasture, or hens scuttling over the yards of huddled steadings—were products of the six thousand years of separate evolution, and while familiar in outline they were strange in color and detail. The people met on the trails seemed strange in proportion, longer-limbed, taller, weirdly exotic, another function of the lower gravity.

The northern hemisphere was in transition from winter to summer; the seasons were more violent here than on their arid homeworld, subject to a greater variety of change. The sudden verdure surprised them, the turf springing up suddenly, brown to green, bushes budding and leaving, the trees putting forth new shoots, small animals, sluggish with their interrupted hibernation, coming out of their burrows. As they progressed from the cool upper pastures to the lower slopes where spring was already flowering, it seemed as if the season advanced with even greater speed. It was a little frightening, this sudden burgeoning with its chaos of color, smell, and texture, surprising after two years of colorless ship-time.

The inhabitants varied: some avoided them, others, the cattlemen bringing their herds up the wide trails, offered them a place at their fires. Fiona was quick to decline, feeling a little ashamed of her cowardice, knowing she would have to deal with these people sooner or later; and Kira, though on her own she would probably have accepted, followed Fiona's lead. Other inhabitants, children mostly, were harder to avoid: they would follow their horses for miles, asking questions: Who are you? Where do you come from? Where do you go? What do you do? They gave the answers they had ready: We are Fiona and Kira. We come from across the mountains. We are heading down to the plains. We are magicians, entertainers. No, not witches: we deal only in trickery, in illusion. And what is that, little girl, you have behind your ear? The child's eyes would widen as Fiona produced her smooth plastic egg, and it would be hours before Fiona could send her home.

Yet talking with the children gave Fiona confidence; the language tapes had drilled the vocabulary and grammar into her, but there was so much that was missing: nuance, slang, dialects, homonyms, and those words that made up the bedrock of any culture, those that defined its social structure, its ideals, its metaphysics. Her language was entirely bland, schoolgirlish; there was no ethical structure behind it, no color, very little slang—and the slang she knew she was afraid to use, for fear she would get it wrong. From the children she learned much, chiefly confidence.

The fourth morning their paths separated: Kira was going due north, to the twin cities of Neda-Calacas; Fiona would continue northeast to Arrandal. There was little said, and though throughout the morning they both smiled a lot, it was without conviction. At last the moment came, and they embraced, bussed, and promised to stay in touch. Fiona thought her inner clothing and hood to a bright red color in hopes of cheering herself.

That night she joined the main road, and crossed from one world to another. She had been among mountain folk who lived in isolation, away from the main passes, and though they ostensibly owed allegiance to one lowland baron or another, each steading was in effect independent and whatever went on in the lowlands scarcely affected them. They were all poor, earning a precarious living from their mountain meadows and clearings; but on the other hand they were also left alone, and ran their own affairs.

Now, on one of the main roads over the mountains, she was continually on a path controlled by semi-independent barons, who sat above the passes in their stone fortresses like malevolent raptors waiting for prey. They had lately been tamed by the coastal city-states, who had forbidden the worst of their excesses, but still the barons ruled their subjects with a hand composed half of steel and half of cruel whimsy, and Fiona felt her heart suddenly thunder as she turned a corner in the narrow road and saw a steep-walled castle looming over her path.

She declared her occupation to the guard and paid the toll for herself and her beasts. The guard asked her to wait and howled a query up to the castle; the answer was affirmative. Fiona was requested to stay the night, amazing the baron with her wonders: in return she'd be given a warm bed, a meal, a handful of white money, and a chance to tell her life's story.

Any real magician would, of course, have accepted. There was no choice.

In the hours before her performance was scheduled to start she tried to call Kira on her spindle, hoping to hear a few words of encouragement, but there was a mountain between them and the only way to make certain of the call was to route it through the ship overhead, a tactic Fiona did not wish to use. For the first time in her life she had stage fright: the supper the kitchens provided was tempting but there was no possibility of eating more than a few bites.

Nevertheless her first performance on the planet was flawless: she gave the baron and his court minor miracles, sleight-of-hand, juggling, tricks with her special decks of cards—she'd been pleased to find they used cards here. Only at the end of her routine did she use a trick that required her home technology: standing alone in the darkened room, she raised her arms; a red fire shot from her wand, turning into a blazing dragon, breathing fire and glaring with angry yellow eyes; and then the dragon burst into flame-petal fireworks, raining incense down on the wondering faces below—it was an idea stolen from a recently-discovered piece of Terran literature, and no one here would ever recognize the source.

Fiona accepted payment and thanked milord; he brought her to his table and plied her with questions. Where was she from? What kind of name was Fiona? If she was from Khensin, why didn't she have the accent? What kind of accent was that, anyway—he couldn't quite place it. She didn't look Khemsinla; she was brown and the Khemsinla were usually fair, and taller. Fiona sensed a malevolent interest behind the questions. She fended them off, giving her prepared answers, conflicting apprehensions warring in her. Did this bearded, jowled baron, half-reclining on his settee, his eyes flickering with ill-concealed maleficence as he asked his lazy questions—did this gross brute suspect her of being a spy? If so, he would never know how close his suspicions came to the truth. There was a deeper fear, closer to the bone, that chilled her: was milord bent on rape?

Carefully her eyes flicked over the room, seeing the baron and his family sitting behind their table, the guards loafing at the doors, the guests, minor nobles and local tradesmen, talking among themselves. She could fight her way out if she had to; there were more pyrotechnics at her behest than those in her magic show; she could kill the fat baron on his couch, burn the guards to cinders, and leave the place in flames if she desired. The laws of her calling, rigid though they were, did not rule out self-defense; but she had no desire to descend to the lowlands with a reputation for slaughter at her back.

The baron asked another teasing, malevolent question, then turned to speak to his son. Minutes passed, and it became evident that milord had, like a cat distracted from a mousehole, lost interest. Her tension ebbed; she had passed her first major test. That night she blocked her door with her chest of tricks and slept comfortably enough on a straw pallet. In the morning she took her breakfast in the kitchen and continued her ride to the plains.

She found a caravan and joined it, less for the protection it offered than because it would have looked strange had she continued on alone. Six days later, having reached one of the plains cities, the end of the long caravan route, she sold her horse and mule, changed from trousers, reluctantly, to the more proper skirts, and bought passage for herself on a barge.

Stretching north to the sea were great, low, fertile flatlands, cut with interlinked waterways: massive rivers, irrigation ditches, and canals, all winding north and northeast from the mountains. By river barge she would reach her destination more swiftly than she would via the alternate course of following the winding paths that might prove flooded with the spring runoff of melting snow, crossing the rivers at the seasonal ferries, and paying the tolls imposed by the local barons.

The barge was eighty feet long, with a deep hold forward and cabins built aft; there was a giant rudder requiring two men at the tiller, and a big square sail amidships. Mules were stabled on the bow to pull the barge when the wind was not with them. Fiona took a cabin for herself, stowed her baggage, and left the barge for an inspection of the town half a mile from the landing. There were mercenary bowmen guarding the landing stage, and Fiona wanted to know why.

The landing stage and its warehouses were half a mile from the town, which was small and walled in brown stone with about thirty towers. The buildings inside the walls were mostly mud brick and stone, with a few larger, ornamented buildings utilizing half-timber construction— timber was probably rare here in the plains, having to be rafted down from the mountains, and its use in building was, Fiona assumed, a sign of wealth. There were peat-sellers moving in carts from door to door, showing what the inhabitants burned in their fireplaces and ovens instead of the wood they probably couldn't afford.

The place seemed moderately prosperous: there was no overcrowding, no obvious poverty. There were a few modest temples to the local gods, and these seemed clean and in good repair. In one corner of the town was a stone castle with a round keep; there were mercenary cavalry moving in and out, as well as local town militia. The walls showed sign of having been recently put into repair. The flags flying over them were dark and tattered.

She stepped outside the gate opposite the river and instantly walked into misery. Outside clustered the huts and dugouts of a half-starved population: men and women old before their time, toothless crones with their begging bowls stretched out on the ends of arms like sticks, children with swollen bellies. Fiona recognized rickettsia, scurvy, infections that she could not give name to . . . the town, she saw, made some effort to feed them. Men in livery were moving from one point to another, delivering food and castoff clothing, probably less for compassionate reasons than to give the objects of their charity the strength and means to move elsewhere. There was a black market in the camp of the starving ones, slick, quick-eyed men, a little better fed than the rest, profiting from their fellows' desperation.

She had never seen anything like it before, and though she knew it was an inevitable consequence of this planet's level of technology, the knowledge had never actually prepared her for the actual sight of it. The scene, and of course the smell, were overwhelming. The sound was worst of all, somehow, for there was no sound, nothing but the whisper of ragged tents in the wind, the toothless mumble of a hag over her begging-bowl, the whimper of a dying child—such silence, compared to the bustle of the landing stage and the town. The silence of despair, of an entire population conserving their strength because they knew there was no place to go, no home for them, no hope. . . .

Fiona spoke to one of the men in livery and inquired. There had been a war, he said, between two of the neighboring barons, squabbling over a fertile province that each coveted: as a result the place had been made a wasteland, and the hopeless refugees had come here. They had arrived over the course of the winter, and the bones of those who hadn't made it were still lying huddled by the trails.

That, she saw, was why the castle had been repaired: the local lord might find himself dragged into the conflict, and even if he avoided that he might have thousands more refugees dumped in his lap when the warfare heated up again in the spring. He was trying to be humane, Fiona thought, but he was looking to his security and probably cursing his choices. If more refugees came he might have to seal his gates, care for his own people, and let those outside starve; or he might simply slaughter them lest they turn brigand.

There was nothing Fiona could do for them, nothing perhaps but aid an individual, a child . . . Fiona dropped some change into the bowl of a slack-eyed woman who was nursing a child at her shrunken breast. The woman's thanks were mumbled; her eyes scarcely brightened at the sight of the money, though it should have been enough to keep her and her child for a week. It had come too late, Fiona thought; the woman might not have the energy left to be able to process food into nourishment for her child.

Fiona fled back to the barge and cursed herself for cowardice.

She spent one night on the barge before the craft was scheduled to head downstream to the city of Arrandal, her destination. During the night the hold was loaded with local produce, the harvested winter crop, and with blocks of grey, hard stone, products of the local quarries. In the hours before departure she saw her first Brodaini: tall, disdainful men and women, their long hair arranged in elaborate ringlets and lovelocks, all bearing armor and weapons both alike in their clean, symmetrical beauty and their utilitarian, deadly purpose—elegantly crafted stuff, the armor a functional mixture of brigandine and plate, the hilts of the swords elaborately carved and inlaid with precious metal. Each carried a ten-foot spear on which a long, sharp, wickedly-curved sword blade glittered.

They were by far the tallest people on the boat: the smallest stood a head taller than Fiona. In addition to the stature that was their inherited due, Fiona knew they ate a special diet, one her ship's computers had calculated would produce muscle and weight without adding more than a healthy amount of fat.

The demeanor of the Brodaini, their reserved physical presence, each movement controlled with the careful economy of the trained athlete, set them off completely from the hurried bustle of the landing stage. The four Brodaini, two men and two women, took cabins on the port side and remained in them until the barge raised its creaking yard, sheeted the patched square sail, and cast off. Afterwards, from time to time, Fiona saw them, always together, always distant, standing apart from the others on the deck. They did not take their meals with the rest due to their special diet.

She would have to study this people, she knew, and she watched them when she could. It was curious, a warrior race that gave equal status to their women, who were presumably less proficient at war. There would be reason for such an anomaly, she thought; she hoped she would be able to find it.

It was a leisurely, sunny journey to the city; although it rained occasionally, the showers were scarcely of long enough duration to more than temporarily discomfort the deck passengers who slept on the forward hatches. Fiona grew to recognize most of her fellow passengers: the children who played on the hatch covers, the elderly, dyspeptic merchant who lived in the next cabin and who spent each night lecturing his companion, a tolerant nephew, in a

whining, querulous voice. The crew of the barge belonged
to a single family: there was a husband and wife, five
children, a brother and sister-in-law just starting life together,
and a toothless granny.

Fiona spent her time watching the passengers and crew,
watching the bank of the river and seeing the new world
revealing itself around each bend, the planet called *Echidne*
in the old star charts of the Terrans, *Demro* in the Abessas
language spoken on the plain and in Arrandal. *Achadan* by
the Brodaini, who had come across the ocean from the
north. On the banks of the river Fiona could see square
fields newly-planted, men and women working on the
levees and dykes, villages clustered on high ground safe
from spring floods, frequent towers and castles occupied
by the feudal aristocracy. The barons didn't dare charge
tariffs on the river traffic; they knew it would only bring
the power of Arrandal on them, a fleet of river-craft full of
plundering mercenaries, Brodaini engineers, deissin over-
seers. It had happened before: every so often Fiona saw
torn curtain walls and shattered keeps, massive ruins that
loomed above the river and bore eloquent witness to the
power of the North.

That power came from city-states which, lying on the
coast of a great northern sea, had in the last century been
expanding their influence. The largest social units on this
part of the planet, they controlled trade on the rivers and
the sea and had been encroaching on the feudal privileges
of the southern barons, regularizing their quarrels, stabiliz-
ing political relationships. They were not doing it for the
sake of peace and amity, Fiona assumed; she knew that
trade required stable borders and an orderly flow of season
commerce, and that the big cities thrived on merchant
traffic. They were the source of stability on a chaotic
continent; their trade networks extended far abroad, and
from there any new idea or any useful innovation would

be sure to spread quickly. They had even formed a federation of sorts, carving out areas of influence and trade, attempting to dominate any competition: the federation had a curious name, *Elva vor Denorru-Dorsu,* the Alliance of/for Community of Interests, its name alone proclaiming a certain sophistication. Of the cities, Fiona's destination, Arrandal, seemed to be the largest—her ship's cameras and computers approximated half a million people within its walls and suburbs—and was probably the most influential.

Much of the cities' expansion had come in the last twenty years, since they'd formed the league between themselves and started importing Brodaini soldiers from across the sea. The Brodaini had brought military knowledge the cities lacked and a brand of professionalism the mercenaries and city militia had never known: and after the first baronial keeps had come crashing into ruin the other feudal lords had seen reason.

The broad outline Fiona knew, and some of the details. For two years her ship had been in stationary orbit above this land, sending down robot spies, driving electronic spikes into roofbeams to pick up audio and video. Computers had analyzed the languages; cameras had mercilessly scanned the interiors of native buildings, public rooms, secret chambers; spikes had driven themselves into the roof-beams of schoolhouses, watching over the students as they bent over their lessons; the writing had been learned, analyzed, and fed into the tapes that in turn had been fed into Fiona's mind. Fiona knew as much about the culture she was entering as any outlander could.

Much of her knowledge, of course, lacked clarity. She knew names for things she had never seen; she knew it was insulting and vulgar to call someone a *scottu,* but had no idea why. Worse of all were the noumena, the words expressing the concepts by which the culture defined itself, the world it saw, the sociological universe into which each individual fit himself . . . The noumena expressed not thought or action but concepts untranslatable into Fiona's own language, understandable only from context if at all.

The noumena beat at Fiona's brain, demanding understanding: she had absorbed two languages, Abessas and Gostu, the language of the locals and of the military Brodaini; and they warred in her mind, mutually contradictory when they were not being maddeningly vague. *Demmin,* a Gostu word: it translated as "honor," but why was "honor" inadequate? There were other contexts where "honor" had not seemed to work, contexts involving correctness, initiative, advantage, esteem, place, self-worth. *Hostu,* another Gostu word, seemed to have two referents in Fiona's own language, "stasis" one, "perfection" the other. Was stasis necessary for perfection in Brodaini society? Or was the word a homonym? Or was there a larger meaning encompassing both these definitions, the meaning incomprehensible to the literal-minded language computer on board the mother ship?

Abessas was a little better; she understood the wide-travelled, practical merchant culture better than she did the military caste of the Brodaini, but the words still had implications that puzzled her. The most-used term of respect, the equivalent of "mister," was *cenors-stannan,* literally "most fortunate," but there was a subtle emphasis on the word *stannan* that seemed to imply that "fortune" was to be taken more as an indicator of wealth than of luck, though, as in Fiona's own language, it contained both meanings.

There were dozens of noumena in each language, stumbling blocks that hampered her mastery of the tongues. For everyday use she did well enough; but did not her mission demand utter confidence, perhaps even eloquence? Her lack of fluency, her lack of understanding, fretted her as the days went by and Arrandal approached.

One afternoon of brilliant sun she sat forward on the hatches, watching as a landing-stage approached and the crew competently set about the process of getting the clumsy barge to the pier while the passengers tried simultaneously to watch the sights and keep out of the way. A crowd of townsmen gathered on the wharf. The tillermen, because of the cabin built forward of their station, could not see forward, so the grandmother stood up on the roof of the cabin barking orders. The pier approached. The square sail came down on the run, startled passengers jumping clear, and a bowman, with a show-off grin, roped a bollard on the first try. Passengers tailed onto the line and the barge was hauled to its place on the wharf. A family leaped aboard to welcome some long-absent relatives; the bowman was bursting with profane orders to get a hatch raised; and suddenly alarms were buzzing.

Fiona blinked in surprise and glanced around in apprehension at the electronic roar, then saw no one else had heard it: it was her private signal. Her baggage was being tampered with.

Certain of her nerves had been rewired to permit this. She alternately prolated and oblated the muscles of her left forearm, which shut off the alarm and allowed her to think. Unnoticed in the bustle, unknown to anyone present, she slipped through the crowd to her cabin door, pulled her hood over her head and face, prepared herself mentally for violence, and snatched open the door.

Two young men, deck passengers for the last two days, were wrestling with one of her two chests, the one that contained her magic show and her offplanet technology. The other chest, which contained her clothing, was already upended and its contents scattered. No doubt the thieves intended, if they found anything valuable, to walk off the barge with it in the general confusion of landing, but the fact they hadn't stationed a lookout spoke for their amateurishness, and, unknown to them, it was going to take a more forceful technology than this world had ever possessed to open the chest.

They were amateurs at violence as well. Fiona, though unblooded, was not. Her training in self-defense had been thorough; certain pre-programmed reactions were triggered automatically as the nearest thief, his eyes wide at the sight of her smooth, blank-featured face mask, came for her with the dagger he'd been using on the chest's offplanet lock.

He came up from the deck, the knife rising with him, striking for her belly to rip up to the lungs and heart. Fiona let the knife do its worst, ignoring it; the badly-tempered blade shattered on her privy-coat and in the meantime a strike with stiffened knuckles had crushed the thief's windpipe. He staggered, clawing at his throat, the remains of his dagger clattering to the deck; Fiona's booted foot lashed out, doubling the other thief over as he stood. She reached for him, twisting his arm back before he could draw a weapon; she snapped the arm and threw him into the bulkhead in the same movement.

There was a sudden stillness, an end to motion. The dying thief had fallen half out of the cabin, thrashing as he strangled. The other lay crumpled against the bulkhead, too terrified to move. Fiona pulled her hood back and began to gulp air, feeling the thunder of her heart begin to slow as the crisis-reaction passed, as passengers and crew began to gather in silence at the door. She clasped her hands, trying to restrain the instincts that had been built into her, that were clamoring for her to attack once more, lunging at the astonished crowd outside the cabin door.

The passengers parted and two Brodaini, the two women, came striding arrogantly into view. One of them stationed herself at the door as a guard—no amateurs, these—and the other looked at Fiona with appraising pale eyes.

"What occurred?" she said in badly-accented Abessas.

"These men are thieves, ban-demmin," Fiona answered in the Brodaini's own tongue, aware her voice was uncontrolled, near breaking. "I caught them in my cabin, trying to loot my possessions."

"Indeed," said the Brodaini. Her eyes had widened slightly at Fiona's use of her own language, including the honorific ban-demmin, "honored" or "respected," one of the word-combinations most often used in Gostu polite adddress. A non-Brodainu who spoke the language was fairly rare; rarer still, presumably, was a woman who, slight though she was, could crush two bigger men in such fashion that neither had a chance to cry out.

The Brodainu's eyes cut to the man sprawled in the doorway. The man's limbs, deprived of oxygen, were beginning to convulse; there was foam on his lips, and his broken windpipe rattled as his lungs tried frantically to draw air. With a strangely withdrawn tenderness—there was compassion in the Brodainu's look, but it was almost an unearthly compassion, like a painted angel or saint—the warrior drew her straight, double-edged sword and drove the point into the thief's heart. Fiona felt as if her own heart had stopped; she wrung her hands—oddly the only gesture that seemed possible—and tried to control the feeling of horror and the simultaneous mad impulse, triggered by the unsheathing of weapons, that urged her to strike out against danger.

Fiona gulped air, trying to stabilize her own body's reactions. She knew what the Brodainu had done; it was the mardan-clannu, the "thrust of mercy" delivered to end a man's suffering. It had been a gesture of compassion after all; there was a certain perverse honor conferred with the act, in that the Brodainu had considered the thief's suffering worth noticing. The warrior cleared her sword, cleaned it on the victim's body, and returned it to its scabbard.

"He will not distract us further," she said. "We Brodaini have power of justice on the river; the other will be turned over to the city authorities. You are most fortunate, ilean. You bore no weapon?"

"No. I do not carry weapons."

The Brodainu nodded, appraising. As far as Fiona knew there was no system of weaponless combat practiced here; the most evolved combat technique was Brodaini, and appeared to concentrate on disarming attackers in order to turn their own weapons against them. Fiona had made an impression on the Brodainu's mind; it might not be a favorable one. A deadly woman, claiming to be a conjuror, speaking Gostu and travelling downriver to Arrandal . . . the Brodaini, guardians of Arrandal's peace, might wonder if she were a fugitive from foreign justice, or worse a spy or assassin. At any rate, worth further study.

The two male Brodaini arrived, keeping the crowd back from the cabin door. The Brodainu who had spoken to Fiona gave a few clipped orders—it appeared she was senior—and the body was carried from the cabin. The second thief was urgently picked up from the floor—he yelped, cradling his broken arm—and was led out by two silent warriors to meet whatever penalty, presumably death in some form, was demanded by local justice. The pale-eyed Brodainu bent to pick up the broken dagger from the cabin deck. She held up the pieces.

"This was the thief's, ilean?"

"Yes."

The warrior looked at the badly-forged shards with the distaste of the connoisseur for the third-rate, then bowed and left the cabin. The other woman Brodainu looked briefly at Fiona—her face was scarred, the nose once broken—and then bowed and followed. Outside there was a quick flash of spinning sun-struck metal as the dagger shards were scaled out into the river. Two of the boatmen approached, buckets and rags ready to clean up the blood, looking at Fiona apprehensively.

"Go ahead. Clean," she told them, and she bent to pick up her scattered clothing and stuff it in her trunk; then she hauled both trunks to their places beneath her bunk and sat down on the thin mattress while the crewmen busied themselves. She drew her knees up protectively. Her hands were no longer trembling, but she clasped the edge of the bunk, white-knuckled, and when the crewmen finished and turned to glance at her, something in her look made them hurry silently from the room, closing the door behind them.

Until now, until she had seen the young thief spasming on the deck, she had not really believed it, this new existence. She was in a feudal, violent world; if she was to fulfill her mission, she would have to become a part of it.

Perhaps the thing that frightened her most was the possibility that she already had.

Only a few days of her journey remained. Abessas and Gostu beat at her brain; she could feel herself submerging into their assumptions, many of which her old life told her were wrong, and in the conflicts between noumena—she felt herself drowning. The intensity of the world around her was terrifying, the native plants burgeoning, the strange, antique mode of transportation that daily grew more familiar, the tall, oddly-proportioned people with their rude, confident assumptions about the world and their place in it. . . . Her own body horrified her: had this hand killed? Had this foot lashed out to cripple? The privy-coat she wore under her blouse and skirts, shaped like a hooded undergarment, supple and soft to the touch but with an intrinsic, invisible awareness of its own that made it capable of repelling any weapon the planet was likely to develop for the next few hundred centuries, began to weigh on her shoulders. She knew it was a hallucination, a trick of the mind that made the privy-coat feel as heavy as Brodaini armor, but still she felt it bearing down on her, a reminder of the violent world she'd entered.

She made nightly reports to her superiors on the spindle she concealed in her magic chest. The reports mentioned little of her daily struggle to keep Echidne from over-whelming her; they stayed in the jargon she had been taught, concentrating on efforts to achieve *rapport* with the natives, to *analyze* the level of *technology* and *technological awareness.* She made notes about *proxemics,* and prac-ticed *behavior observation.* The jargon began to seem more like an alien language, something outside the reality she was dealing with—how could the disinterested, dusty words possibly describe the meaning of the place? The dictionary phrases faded in contrast to the bright, burgeon-ing world, and Fiona was filled with a fear that she was losing everything she had been; that soon her past would fade entirely, vanish into a memory that grew progres-sively less substantial. The familiar voices on the commun-icator, Tyson's gruff irony, Wenoa's calm tenor, seemed increasingly distant; their reality, even that of Tyson who had, for a time, been Fiona's lover, was slipping away. She found herself forgetting their faces, their eyes. She wished she could contact Kira without having to patch the call through the ship—Kira, she knew, would understand.

Fiona wondered if she would be able to return; perhaps she was already a creature of this planet: backward, violent, ineffably strange. Echidne, perhaps, had taken her—no, not Echidne, but Demro, or Achadan, the native names for the planet. Still, she knew the world could not have her as long as she could not comprehend it entirely as long as the noumena flailed within her skull for meaning. *Reygrin, amil-deo, dine,* Abessas noumena; *vail, hostu, demmin, dai-terru, demmis-dru,* mysterious words used by the Brodaini soldiers, their speech so alien it was difficult to accept it as a tongue spoken by humans.

A part of her mind insisted on understanding, but another part quailed at it, afraid that understanding would mean her absorption into the world, into its primitive horrors.

The river branched at last into its delta and the barge came to Arrandal. The mast was unstepped and the two mules unloaded and harnessed to the towlines; the barge passed beneath a water-gate, its massive porcullis hanging overhead like the teeth of a dragon about to swallow them, followed amazingly by the pale, hairy buttocks of a citizen who was crouching with his trousers about his ankles, one arm draped casually about an iron mooring-post, apparently preparing to defecate into the canal. He held off while the barge passed under him, grinning down at the surprised, upturned faces, and then went about his business.

The city began crowding close to port and starboard—tall, pinched houses, faced with stone or pastel-colored brick arranged in gay patterns, arched bridges with towpaths running cobbled beneath, tall brick smokestacks marking public baths, innumerable boats: houseboats, big deep-burdened river barges, swift, small oared galleys bearing passengers, messages, and soldiers. Teeming humanity, chiefly male, chiefly in a hurry. Their language boiled up about her.

The bowman unhitched the towing mules and draped the hawser over a bollard; another crewman lassoed a second bollard and the barge was brought to the dock, ripples of water curling from its rudder and stem. From among the swarm of urchins on the bank Fiona found two boys to carry her trunks. As she stepped off the barge she saw the eyes of the scarred Brodainu on her—thoughtful, wary eyes. Perhaps she would be followed to her inn, though not by the Brodaini themselves—they were too conspicuous, tall and armored in this throng—but by some hired boy.

Well, she was here to attract attention, after a fashion.

She stepped into the narrow streets, following the bearers.

The lanes were full of demanding humanity: hucksters, beggars, touts, hoteliers, prostitutes of both sexes, all soliciting her attention, her money, her soul. Their words clattered meaninglessly in her head; she would not pay attention. *Not yet,* she thought; she would stay herself a while longer, resisting the planet's inevitable victory for at least another day.

It was a comforting thought, she knew; but it was a lie. The planet had already taken her; perhaps it would savor her awhile, but Echidne would inevitably swallow, and Fiona would spin helplessly down its throat. . . .

1

The messenger, in his ruffled, sashed jacket, elaborately tooled boots, and short-cropped hair that allowed cup-handle ears to protrude, looked out of place in the austere audience hall, with its silent, waiting rows of Brodaini and their servants—forty men and women sitting in silence to hear the message from Acragas Necias, the Abessu-Denorru—the Community Speaker of the Arrandal assembly. The forty were present to support the dignity of Necias, since a public message from a person of authority required an audience large enough to support the sender's dignity, but probably the messenger did not appreciate the courtesy. He did not seem aware, either, of the contrast he made, elaborate and gaudy in a hall occupied otherwise by Brodaini in simple, elegant armor, and by Classani servants in quiet, dignified livery.

"Drandor Tegestu Dellila Doren y'Pranoth," the messenger began, the Gostu names rolling easily, carelessly, off his fat Abessla tongue, "salutations from the Abessu-Denorru*." His message, despite the Gostu flourishes,

*A glossary to this and other foreign terms, in both Abessas and Gostu, begins on Page 421.

was delivered in Abessas. Tegestu, though he spoke Abessas well enough, waited for his translator's version so that he could compose his answer while wondering at the message's implications.

The message was simple enough. The Abessu, Necias, requested the presence of Tegestu tomorrow at his palace, at the second hour after noon. Although couched as a request, the summons was nevertheless something approaching a command, and Tegestu had little realistic alternative but to obey.

Tegestu rarely presented himself to Necias in person, and then chiefly at carefully-scripted, ceremonial occasions, the usual traffic was by messenger. The summons, as peremptory as the flowery conventions to Abessla diplomacy permitted, bespoke a certain urgency.

Therefore news must have reached the Abessu of the revolt in the twin cities of Neda-Calacas, four days' sail to the northwest. The coup had been swift, virtually bloodless, and efficient—the hallmarks of a Brodaini conquest—and there had been no resistance after the first few hours. The city was now quiet.

Tegestu had been informed by his own spies two days ago, and very shortly thereafter by a formal message, delivered publicly by clattering horsebacked emissaries from the new rebel lord who had taken the city, Tastis—or, to use his full name, Tastis Senestu Tepesta y'Pranoth, Tegestu's kinsman and former comrade-in-arms, head of kamliss Pranoth in Neda-Calacas as Tegestu was head of kamliss Pranoth in Arrandal.

Tastis, employed with his clan, sub-clans, and dependents as a defender of the twin cities, had revolted against his lords and taken the city himself. The message to Tegestu had claimed provocation, that he had been forced by insults to his house into the choice of rebellion or of becomming ar-demmin, honorless and outcast. The message had been sent in a curious fashion, with the ban of kantu-kamliss forbidding anyone outside the kamliss Pranoth from reading the message or even discussing it. Despite the ban that commanded secrecy, however, the message had been delivered quite publicly, and Tegestu's employers, the lords of the city, were doubtless curious to know its contents, a curiosity that Tastis had no doubt anticipated when he sent the message under a ban that would forbid Tegestu from revealing it.

The message, therefore, had been sent as a provocation. To judge from the appearance of this overdressed messenger and his demand for a meeting, the provocation had succeeded.

His cousin's revolt was something Tegestu had been dreading for years. Taking employment in the great cities of the south after having been driven from their own land, the Brodaini warriors had taken with them their dependents, their customs, and their warrior way of life; they had lived for the most part in their own quarter of the city, aloof from the bustle outside; they had thrived after their fashion, and their numbers increased.

There had always been tension between the Brodaini and their new masters, and as the numbers of Brodaini had grown the level of tension had risen. The two ways of life were incompatible: one sought wealth, and the other demmin; one was boisterous and aggressive, the other reserved and deadly. Separate quarters for the Brodaini had served to lessen the tension, but there had always been the danger of insult followed by outrage. The native mercenaries which the local lords had formerly depended on had been known to revolt against their masters on occasion, and the lords of the cities had never quite been able to accept Brodaini assurances that loyalty—nartil—was a subject of near-religious devotion among the Brodaini, and that one of the vilest insults in the Gostu tongue was bearni—"mercenary." The city lords had always feared a revolt by their servants.

And now the revolt had occurred in Neda-Calacas;

Brodaini warriors were in command of the citadel, the city walls, probably the fleet. And Tastis, the rebel leader, had sent a private message to Tegestu in a very public fashion, calculated to heighten the tension between the two peoples and leading to further trouble, perhaps to further revolts. It seemed as if Tastis was aiming at a general Brodaini rebellion, and seizure of all the coastal cities.

And, as the message from the Abessu-Denorru showed, Arrandal's merchant princes were realizing their danger. Their own intelligence systems were not as efficient as Tegestu's, but it scarcely required efficiency to bring news of such a cataclysm. Necias had probably known of the revolt for at least a day, which accounted for the increased security around his palace, the citadel, and the city gates, as well as the bolstered patrols of mercenaries in the streets and the sudden alert that had set the fleet in a state of readiness. Tegestu's men had observed the city's preparations, but he had kept his own reactions limited: there was no obvious increase of security at the Brodaini keep, nothing to alarm the city lords. If there was to be provocation, it would not come from Tegestu's people.

The messenger finished his address. Tegestu waited until the translator concluded before giving his own reply. The local habit of coating even simple requests in an icing of sugary, ornamental speech, which he had initially found so irritating, had its advantages: while waiting for the lengthy translation, he could compose his own thoughts.

The most reassuring reply would be a direct one, he thought.

"Tell the Abessu-Denorru Necias that, obedient to his will, I shall present myself at his palace at the second hour," Tegestu said.

The messenger received the translation, waited for the icing, and then realized there would not be any. Brodaini prided themselves on direct, straightforward speech, and Tegestu had said all that was necessary.

"Drandor Tegestu, I will give your message to cenors-efellsan Necias," the messenger said, direct himself for once, and was shown out by a pair of Classani in livery.

Tegestu shifted himself on his hard, low stool, glancing over the stark chamber. The others were facing forward dutifully, awaiting dismissal or further orders.

"There will be a meeting of the aldran at the fifth hour," he said. "Those welldrani present in the keep will attend. Whelkran Hamila, you will see that those not present are informed."

"Aye, bro-demmin Tegestu," replied Hamila, an old, trusted soldier, renowned as a cunning tactician, a master of ambush and surprise.

"We have heard the Abessu-Denorru's request, and we shall ponder." Tegestu said. "Whelkran Cascan, you shall inform me of any changes in the city."

The small, agile chief of spies bowed.

Tegestu's eyes slid over the gathering. "Are there any questions, ban-demmini?" he asked. "Does everyone comprehend the Abessu-Denorru's request?" There were bows, a discrete rattle of armor, and no questions.

"You are dismissed. Ban-demmin Grendis, I would be obliged if you would accompany me."

"Aye, bro-demmin."

Tegestu rose from his stool, the other Brodaini and their Classini servants rose from their own places and began to file out of the chamber. Taking the arm of Grendis, his wife, Tegestu walked from the room to his own apartments, accepting the salute of the armored cathruni at the door.

Inside, his dog Yellowtooth rose from his bed to welcome him. As Tegestu bent low to greet the animal his rheumatic joints jabbed him with their delicate needles of pain. Yellowtooth was an old animal, twelve years now. His muzzle was grey with age; his eyes showed the milky white of cataract. Too old now for the hunting and chasing that had once been the hound's purpose, Yellowtooth had been moved into Tegestu's quarters and genteel retirement. Yet he scarcely showed his age at the moment, romping and frisking with Tegestu and Grendis as if he were a pup.

Tegestu straightened, shuddering with another shaft of pain from his joints. Yellowtooth followed as he and Grendis moved to their bedchamber, where Grendis silently helped him to disarm. It was a part of Brodaini formality to appear armed on all public occasions; only the ill and very elderly were excepted. Tegestu was seventy-one and the burden of the armor wearied him, but he was not willing to proclaim himself elderly just yet. He exercised daily to keep fit; he could still handle a weapon, and only he, and perhaps Grendis, knew how much his rheumatic body pained him, and how far the lifetime of warfare, the accumulation of scars and broken limbs, the constant campaigning in bad weather and sleeping on the ground, had advanced in its progress to drag him down.

Husband and wife disarmed, placing their armor on the mannequins that stood in the alcove devoted to personal weaponry. Dressed in tunic, trousers, and slippers they called for tea, and Tegestu stretched out on his mattress, face down, letting relief swim slowly into his limbs. Yellowtooth, with a grateful wheeze, lay down at his feet. Grendis reached out to touch with practiced fingers the back of his neck, massaging the tense muscles, the callused tissue that only partly protected the flesh that bore the weight of the armor straps. Tegestu sighed as he felt the fingers releasing his muscles, the tension draining away. Grendis knew his body well.

They were of an age, Tegestu and his wife; they had been betrothed at the age of nine, married at fifteen—that had been in the old keep at Remolina. The turrets had been decked with flags, Brodaini in gleaming white armor had marshalled in their ranks to celebrate the wedding of a young Brodainu of kamliss Pranoth to a Brodainu of kamliss Dantu, a middle-level marriage of two promising offspring who, in time, might become whelkrani, commanders of at least a hundred soldiers, or, if they were lucky and had survived to an old and honored age, might be elected to the aldran, the body of elders who governed the clans. No one had expected, on that summery day with the elite of two kamlissi gathered in their numbers, that twenty winters hence Remolina would be wasted, the curtain walls razed and the keep torn open to the sky; that Tegestu and Grendis, born to the middle ranks, would have become senior commanders as those above were slain; that they would each be elected to the aldran before they were thirty-five; or that Tegestu, before he was forty, would be elected drandor, the head of kamliss Pranoth in exile. In another generation the very name of Remolina would be forgotten except as a footnote in some Brodaini history, a speck on some mouldering map that had once marked a provincial capital sacked and burned by the winning side in a continent-wide civil war.

There was little that had not changed for the young man and woman who had been married that day fifty-six years before. They had shared much: campaigns, wounds, the loss of four children who had died in their youth of accidents and battles on land and sea, the loss of another child, a girl, wounded in the head and made simple until she died later, absently drowning herself in a well. Yes, Grendis' fingers had learned his body well: here was the scar along his ribs from the time when he'd been unhorsed in a swarm of spearmen; here the knot on his shoulder from the mace of the warrior she had in turn pierced with her sword; here was the silvery, puckered scar of the assassin's arrow that had drilled through his lung and almost ended his life. She had nursed him through the subsequent fever, the wasting; she had cooked the food on which he'd regained his strength and stood over his mattress to make certain he'd eat it. He'd been lucky that time, and in more ways than one: the assassination attempt had come during a winter truce; otherwise he would probably have been out in the field and Grendis would have been unable to supervise his recovery.

Grendis' hand slid down his lower back. There had been an injury there once, a riding accident, and sometimes the muscles knotted as if to guard against another sprain. He felt them relax. The body was scarred, but still in service; it was good for another five years, if war or assassination or illness didn't cut him short.

The tea arrived, carried by Thesau, Tegestu's Classanu servant, a companion of forty years and more. Thesau bowed to place the tray on the table by the bed and turned to Tegestu with an expression of concern on his kindly face. "Bro-demmin," he asked, "shall I send for the masseurs?"

"Nay, ilean Thesau," said Tegestu. "Ban-demmin Grendis knows these lean bones better than the masseurs. You may call for musicians to play in the next room."

"Aye, bro-demmin," Thesau bowed and left the apartment. In a few moments there was a rustle of drapery in the next chamber, followed by quiet tuning; then the throb of the bohau and the strum of the tedec began to filter into the room. Tegestu began to smell the warm aroma of fragrant tea. One of their house cats came to join him on his mattress, curling up near his head and accompanying the instruments with its purrs.

Tegestu sighed, then rolled upright on the bed, crossing his legs. Grendis put her hand on his arm; there was a lazy, contented smile on her face. He kissed her and then served her a glass of tea, highly sweetened as she preferred it. Another little moment of peace, snatched from the encompassing arms of duty and war, one of a thousand such moments they had shared and learned to cherish, moments seized during the breaks of marches, in the pre-dawn quiet before battle, in the lulls between official duties. Grendis sipped her tea calmly; Tegestu poured the steaming beverage into his own glass and drank it black, the tea's aroma tickling his nose.

The music gently infiltrated from the next room. Tegestu reached out to take her hand; she smiled at his touch and clasped the scarred fingers. Tegestu remembered a poem she had written him once, and given to him just before he'd ridden from Connu Keep, his own tower on the edge of the sea. She'd been carrying their third child, but even so had been delegated to hold their home against any attack; the lines she'd written were direct in the manner of Brodaini speech, yet with a formal elegance and an eloquent sentiment.

I shall seek your shadow before distant watchfires
As I gaze into the hearthfires of home;
Your far-off footfalls, your remote voice
Shall I hear in the wind that sighs in the crenels.
I shall ward your back from danger;
I shall keep safe our Connu Keep.

Grendis had kept Connu, kept it until the survivors of kamliss Pranoth had left their native land forever and scattered in service to the lords of another continent, as if they were no better than bearni. . . .

Tegestu's hand tightened at the bitter memory; Grendis looked up sharply, then reached out to touch his temple with cool fingers.

"Peace," she said. "Peace. The world rolls on its path, and you are not required to make it so. Peace."

He accepted the touch, closing his eyes, feeling the warmth of the tea lulling him. Feeling Grendis' touch, hearing the bohau and tedec playing in intricate duet, sensing the warmness of his animals and scenting the fragrance of the tea, it was possible to think himself back at Connu Keep, its round towers perched above the blue harbor and the walled town, all now occupied by strangers, enemies of twenty years . . . Grendis' hand caressed his long, white, intricately-curled hair.

Savor the pleasure while it lasts, he thought drowsily; abdicate for a few minutes the demands of responsibility. Seek hostu; seek peace, a glimpse of vail. *I shall ward your back from danger,* Grendis had promised; she had kept the promise, kept it for over fifty years, and with that he had more than reason enough to be content.

2

The welldrani—"elders," the term used to describe anyone, old or young, who sat on the aldran, the council that ruled the Brodaini families in Arrandal—had filed into their places, sitting in disciplined silence of the low stools that surrounded the polished, mosaic central table. Tegestu, armored once more, his badges of rank and clan blazoned on his surcoat, waited in an anteroom, receiving a briefing from Cascan, the head of his cambrani, his corps of spies.

Cascan was a young man for his position, in his mid-forties only, having risen in rank as he had demonstrated his ability to penetrate the alien labyrinths of the new continent; he was small and slight, quick, with an actor's plastic face and a versatile, mimic's voice. He belonged to kamliss Tosta, one of the smaller clans that had attached itself to Tegestu's exiles for its own safety. As a small kamliss, Tosta had depended on espionage and cunning rather than military power, and since the emigration from their homeland, their training programs, both in spying and in countering spies, had proved most useful. Tegestu had rarely found Cascan's estimates to be wrong.

"Our inquiries upriver show that the refugee situation is worsening," Cascan said. "I have received information that Baron Wollas of Cavasto will send a deputation to the Denorru-Deissin asking them to use their influence to end the war, or at least to help settle the refugees elsewhere. Other lords may join in the request; in the event of refusal they may ask for Brodaini to assist in the keeping of order."

Tegestu nodded. "And the situation in Arrandal?"

"The fleet is still on alert, bro-demmin," said Cascan. "There is heightened security at the city gates, allegedly because of an influx of illegal refugees. A new battalion of bearni have been moved into the citadel. The situation seems to be easing somewhat: orders to discontinue the patrolling on the streets and canals were given two hours ago." Two hours: that would have been in response to Tegestu's answer to Necias. Good: the Abeissu was trying to keep things from exploding.

"Our people have been given orders not to leave the keep on missions not absolutely necessary, and when they leave to travel in pairs," Cascan continued, "if there is any attempt to recall outlying garrisons of bearni to increase the forces in the city, our pickets on the roads will let us know of it. Garrisons on the islands are another problem; our marine pickets are limited in resource, and it is possible for an island garrison to sail into sight of our keep before we'd see it."

"That should be corrected, ban-demmin," Tegestu said. Cascan bowed hastily.

"Aye, bro-demmin. Boats can be purchased or rented, but the lords of the city will know of it."

"Buy boats through some of your agents that have been posing as locals, or as recent immigrants," Tegestu said. "We may risk exposing some of our men, but anything threatening our security is vital; we must know where those island garrisons are."

"Aye, bro-demmin."

There was an uneasy silence: it was clear from his tone that Cascan did not relish risking his agents. Tegestu spoke.

"News from Neda-Calacas?" he asked. "Has anything changed? Any sign that Tastis is moving?"

"All reports indicate only that he is securing his own position as master of the cities and sending out messengers to the other cities of the Elva. We do not know what these messages contain, but we're certain that Necias received one this afternoon." -

"Doubtless," said Tegestu, "Necias will inform me of what *he* wishes *us* to know at our meeting tomorrow. Is it possible, ban-demmin Cascan, that *you* can inform me of all the rest tomorrow morning?"

Cascan's eyes flickered in the dim lamplight. There was hesitation in his voice. "Frankly, bro-demmin, there is not enough time. Success is possible, even likely; but if exposure or capture resulted, there could be embarrassment."

"Yes-s," Tegestu said, frowning. Considering the situation, one of his agents unmasked or even captured might prove too great a provocation. "I agree with you, ban-demmin," he said, to Cascan's evident relief. "Your judgement is sound."

"Many thanks, bro-demmin." Cascan bowed.

"All of these matters can safely be brought before the aldran," Tegestu said. "If that is all, ban-demmin, we may proceed to the council."

Cascan frowned. "Bro-demmin, there is another matter," he said. "It may be trivial; I don't know whether it is even a matter worthy of your notice."

Tegestu looked at him impatiently. "Speak, ban-demmin."

"Bro-demmin, we have under surveillance a woman encountered on a river barge heading from Cavasto to Arrandal. *
She—" He frowned, shaking his head. "This is what does not make sense. She claims to be a conjuror from Khemsin,

but her accent is not Khemsinla—we asked a Khemsinla to listen to her speech to make sure, and he confirms she is not a countrywoman. She speaks Gostu, also with an accent hard to place. She carries no weapons, but on the barge she killed a man, a thief trying to loot her cabin, and disabled another, apparently barehanded.''

Tegestu absorbed the information impassively. ''If she were a spy,'' he said, ''she would know better than to kill a man, or to speak Gostu within hearing of our people. It would have been easy enough to raise an outcry on the barge and catch the thieves that way. Unless . . .'' Tegestu hesitated while the mental mosaic resolved itself, then continued. ''Unless the thieves discovered something she was unwilling to allow anyone else to see, and she was forced to kill hastily.''

''Beg pardon, bro-demmin, but why didn't she kill both of them?'' Cascan said. ''It seems to have been well within her powers.''

Tegestu received this logical objection with a scowl of chagrin. ''Of course, of course,'' he muttered. ''You were right to bring this to me. I don't think we need to bring the matter before the aldran just yet. In the meantime keep her under surveillance, and I think it might be best if her baggage were searched. She might be what she says; perhaps it's merely a matter of a pair of incompetent thieves and a lucky blow. But there's too great a chance she is a provocateur sent by Tastis to take any chances. Has she been observed making any contacts?''

''Many. During the five days she's been in the city, she's purchased a street performer's license and entertains daily in the public squares and markets.'' Cascan smiled admiringly. ''Her performance is quite remarkable; she's well on her way to becoming a sensation. I've seen her myself, and it's certainly unlike anything this city has ever seen. Naturally,'' he said, nodding, ''she's had casual contact with hundreds. She's accepted a few offers to perform privately in the palaces of the deissin, and we have no way of knowing what information would have been exchanged there.''

Tegestu considered for a moment. This was sounding more and more like a strange set of coincidences; but still, if she were a spy, operating under the cover of a travelling conjuror would be almost perfect, and would allow her to contact her fellow agents with ease. It would not be wise to take a chance. ''Continue surveillance,'' he said. ''Not too elaborate; if she's good she'll see it. Perhaps,'' he smiled, ''she will accept an invitation to perform for us one evening.''

''You won't be disappointed in that case, bro-demmin,'' Cascan said. ''No matter what she turns out to be, she's a splendid entertainer.'' He bowed, and Tegestu wondered whether his whelkran of spies had a gleam of triumph in his eye. Perhaps Cascan had wanted him to be intrigued— otherwise why bring up the matter in the first place? But no: with Tastis in revolt and the local forces on alert, the situation was serious; Cascan would have kept any frivolous matters out of their conference. His raising the issue at all meant that he was puzzled. The conjuror was certainly something out of the ordinary, yet she was not following any of the normal patterns expected of a spy. It was almost as if she intended to be noticed.

Well: enough. Possibly a search of her belongings would help answer their questions.

''Precede me, ban-demmin Cascan,'' Tegestu said. Cascan bowed again and led the way past two saluting cathruni to the meeting of the aldran.

The welldrani rose as Tegestu entered; he and Cascan bowed politely as they took their places. Then all bowed to the household armor—the heavy, quaint, and ornate armor worn by the founders of each of their kamlissi many centuries before, all since etched heavily with patterns showing gods, charms for good luck, and allegorical scenes, their lances—Brodaini had once fought entirely as heavy cavalry—set in place with clan banners draped from each lance point. Tegestu gave the signal to sit.

The room was only of modest size, with two doors, one at either end. The doors were massive, inches thick, in order to prevent any eavesdropper from being able to listen—presuming the guards allowed him to—and the room was barren of ornamentation or tapestry for much the same reason, to prevent anyone from hiding unseen and listening to things he shouldn't.

All twelve of the welldrani were present, all sitting in their armor and gleaming badges of rank except Truscatta, at eighty-one the oldest, too frail to bear arms but a man who had gained great demmin in his day. Nine men, among them Tegestu's son Acamantu, and four women, including Grendis Destu Luc y'Dantu, Tegestu's wife— and all the rest were related to Tegestu in some fashion or other, even if they belonged to different kamlissi; they were also related one to the other, the aldran being as much a family council as a council of state, even though the "family" over which they claimed authority consisted of the hundred thousand-odd Brodaini and their dependents who served the city of Arrandal.

"May your demmin ever increase, cousins," Tegestu said. The welldrani murmured the reply, and then there was silence as four of the autraldi—warrior-priests—entered to conduct the ceremonies of purification: incense was burned, a hymn was sung, the gods were invoked along with the spirits of ancestors. The autraldi bowed and withdrew, and the meeting commenced.

The first matters were trivial: supplies and fodder had to be sent to outlying garrisons; the watch list for the next month had to be made up; reports of various training programs were received and noted; passwords for the next two weeks were approved. Two youths, one from kamliss Tosta and the other from Dantu, had requested permission to fight a duel. Had they been from the same kamliss permission would not have been needed, but when the Brodaini had first come to the city Tegestu had ordered that, in order to prevent unnecessary friction between the clans, an inter-kamliss duel would require the permission of the aldran.

Apparently there was some degree of clan honor involved, for neither of the welldrani representing Tosta nor Dantu objected or required clarification. Permission was given therefore, and the nature of the insult was not inquired into. The duel would be with rhomphaia, to honorable serious wounds. Death might not necessarily result, but for the duel to be meaningful it was required to be a possibility.

Then Cascan gave his report, beginning first with the outland situation, the refugees and Baron Wollas' probable deputation, then continuing to an appreciation of the current situation in the city: the fleet on alert, heightened security at the gates, new forces in the citadel.

"Bro-demmini," old Truscatta said, "I hope we are not reacting to these moves over-slowly. It may be necessary to braid our hair."

"Braiding hair," meant war; for battle the Brodaini forsook their elaborate hairstyles and coiled their hair in braids about their heads.

"Cousins," said Tegestu, "we must move cautiously. We do not wish to provoke an attack."

"We must not be caught off guard."

"May your demmin increase, ben-demmin Truscatta," Tegestu smiled, "when were we ever lax?"

The old man, answering Tegestu's smile, bowed.

"Abessu-Denorru Necias has requested my presence tomorrow," Tegestu said, "I shall oblige. Surely distrust cannot survive such a meeting."

"The request is unusual." This came from Grendis.

"The *situation* is unusual, and not of our making," Tegestu said. "Tastis' strategy is obvious; he has sent a message under bar of kantu-kamliss, and this divides the Brodaini from the city, and Brodainu from Brodainu. We must face these provocations with calm. The Abeissu shall be satisfied.''

"It may be a trap." Grendis said. "Necias Abeissu may think to sever our head from our shoulders by taking our drandor from us.''

Tegestu turned to his wife, inwardly amused. They knew each other well, and he understood what she was doing: attempting to draw the sting from the others' objections by raising them herself. "I do not think Necias will make himself ar-demmin in such a way," he said. "Surely if he behaves dishonorably we will know how to respond.''

"But," he said, bowing toward Grendis, "the possibility must not be denied, and I would esteem it a favor if the aldran chooses from itself one to secure the keep in my absence, and take whatever steps are necessary to deal with any treachery. I regret that I must make a single restriction: the commander must be of kamliss Pranoth; otherwise there is no way of dealing with the kantu-kamliss matter.''

That went down hard, but they bowed to the necessity: Tegestu's son Acamantu was chosen as temporary drandor, and could scarcely conceal his pleasure at being chosen for such a responsibility at the extremely youthful age of thirty-nine. Tegestu repressed a smile at his son's joy. Acamantu's rapid advance had owed something initially to his parents' prominence, but Tegestu knew that for some time his promotions had been earned. He had proven a talented field commander, but his advance to high rank and promotion to the aldran had come about chiefly because he was one of the most successful of the Brodaini in dealing with the natives of the new continent; his diplomatic skills had proved considerable.

There was further discussion, speculation concerning whether Tastis would attempt to spread his rebellion by force of arms or whether he would be content to await events. Tegestu was inclined to suspect the latter: Tastis, he thought, was too clever simply to begin an outright attack on his neighbors, which would serve only to drive them together—Tastis would prefer, Tegestu thought, more indirect means of achieving his objectives. Tastis probably had dozens of spies in Arrandal, and more in the other cities of the Elva; no doubt other agents would soon join them. They would try to provoke incidents, sowing distrust between the Brodaini and their host cities, attempting to incite hatred and resentment. They would attempt to create a climate in which a general Brodaini revolt was inevitable.

Revolt. The idea was abhorrent, against nartil, the law of fealty, respect, and obligation; it was ar-demmin, acting against the honor that Brodaini society prized above life. The very fact of Tastis' rebellion was shocking, and Tegestu knew that the welldrani very much wanted to believe that it had been provoked by the merchant princes of Neda-Calacas, and that the provcation had been so bitter, so insulting, that Tastis had seen no alternative but to revolt. The other possibility was too appalling: that Tastis, supported by his aldran and his Brodaini, had simply seized power. That fear remained unvoiced by the welldrani: it would have been too disturbing even to have raised the possibility.

Tegestu tried to keep the discussion under firm control, refusing to allow speculation as to Tastis' motives. These were explained in his private communication, and that was under ban.

In the end the aldran ended its meeting unresolved, except to await events and the reports of Cascan's spies, and in the meantime to increase their security. It was an unsatisfactory meeting in many ways, not the least because the body designated to direct Brodaini affairs found itself unable to do anything except react to events rather than control them.

After the autraldi had been called back in to sing the final, ceremonial hymn—prayers to the gods were to be sung by the human voice, unadorned by instruments or any other artificial thing—the six members of the aldran not belonging to kamliss Pranoth quietly rose and left the chamber. The rest could properly deal with Tastis' message.

Sent kantu-kamliss, under the ceremonial ban that made it improper for anyone not bearing the surname of the Pranoth to read, touch, or even comment on it, the message was barred to some of Tegestu's most valuable advisors, including his wife, who though married to a Pranoth was still technically a Dantu. Also under the ban were his chief of cambrani, Cascan, and even Castu, Tegestu's dentraldu— chief priest—one of his chief supporters, and, like Cascan, a Tosta.

Nevertheless it was Castu, in his distinctive white robes, who brought Tastis' document, carrying it in its case so that his non-Pranoth hands should not defile it. It had been kept in the demmis-dru, the shrine where all treaties, wills, and secret documents were kept under the protection of the dentraldu and his autraldi, Brodaini priests who had forsaken the life of active warriors and the pursuit of demmin in order to attend their meditations, praise the gods, and guard the demmis-dru with all the considerable ferocity at their command. They had the one chief task, to guard the holiest place in the keep, and that task was pursued with singleminded fanaticism.

"Many thanks, cousin," Tegestu said as the container, a leather cylinder, was placed on the table before him. The case was heavily decorated with abstract Brodaini patterns, whorls and jagged lightning-symbols as well as the badge of the clan of Pranoth. The elaborate seals that had been placed on it in Neda-Calacas had been broken when Tegestu had first read it, and replaced by a simple white seal, dated and stamped, affixed by one of the autraldi when the document had been placed in the demmis-dru.

Castu bowed and withdrew, and Tegestu broke the seal. The vellum scroll unrolled itself heavily in his hands. Though it was not embroidered or illuminated it was a neat copy, the vertical Brodaini script executed with a careful hand within almost-invisible guidelines. There was no sign that it had been written in haste.

"Hail cousins, kamliss-Pranoth-sa-Arrandal," Tegestu read, "greetings from Tastis Senestu Tepesta y'Pranoth, drandor y kamliss-Pranoth-sa-Neda. May your demmin increase; may your arms never fail.

"Let your council witness the fact of revenge executed by kamliss-Pranoth-sa-Neda against persons who were our betrayers and secret enemies; let your witness extend to our sorrow and triumph, and to a disobedience required by self-respect.

"Understand that the leaders of Neda-Calacas were unwise in their actions and often insulting, but that, knowing they were ignorant of natril, we refrained from taking offense against ar-demmini, knowing their insults as harmless as the threats of so many cattle, or the insults of the black hangman-birds that flock in jeering numbers among the eaves of the city. Yet there came last month an insult we could not ignore: one of our own, Norvenan Tolmatus Tepesta y'Pranoth, a lady of the spear and a Brodainu of some respect, was savaged and raped by a gang of city youths. Though she fought she was overcome by numbers; despite her distress she was able to identify her attackers. Some belonged to the family of the deissu Spensas, and the rest to his household.

"Spensas, informed of our complaint, agreed to punish the attackers, but we later learned that the punishment consisted only of confinement within the deissu's palace. Upon being informed that the punishment was inadequate,

Spensas referred us to the Abessu-Denorru Nadielas, who in turn informed us that our complaint was out of order.

"At his point Norvenan fell on her sword, feeling herself ar-demmin. Shamed by this, our aldran determined to take action, and declared angu with Spensas, Nadielas, and their houses. Eight days followed the decision, our plans completed, we took the city.

"We are now in full command. Surprise was complete, and resistance insignificant. Spensas and those of his family who participated in the incident have been dying since their capture; we shall use our skills to keep them dying as long as possible. Their family has been purged; their banking house and its assets have been seized; and their goods confiscated. All shall be given to the population of the town, that all might see we acted for our demmin and not for gain.

"Nadielas Abessu-Denorru was allowed a swift death, as were certain of his supporters. The Denorru-Deissin is disbanded, and several of the bearni bands have been disarmed and dismissed from service of the city. They were not ashamed by their capture, but angered only: ar-demmin creatures indeed.

"Action was supported by the full membership of the aldran, including those who do not belong to kamliss Pranoth. We do not desire angu with the other cities; we are not dai-terru who desire merely conquest. We desired only to guard our own demmin; we shall continue to guard it.

"Witness, kamliss-Pranoth-sa-Arrandal, our action in defence of our self-respect; witness the end of Spensas and his household; witness whether it was fitting. Hail, kamliss-Pranoth-sa-Arrandal, and bear witness."

"Aiau!" breathed one of the welldrani—Amasta, and white-haired, lined, ferocious old woman who sat at the end of the table. "That was aspistu indeed. This Norvenan must have been a woman of great respect."

Aspistu—the discipline of artful and imaginative vengeance. Amasta had herself practiced aspistu in her youth: her cold, imaginative retributions, merciless and deliberate as the stalk of a giant cat, were still spoken of with respect and occasional private shivers. The idea that an entire city was taken as aspistu for a single Brodainu woman was impressive.

"Shemmina," Acamantu said quickly. Long-faced, thin and long-limbed, he echoed his father in physical caste and also in distaste of excess. "There is no demmin to be gained in revenge taken on ar-demmin beings, beings who cannot appreciate aspistu or its beauty. Simply killing them would have sufficed. Taking an entire city was excessive."

Amasta looked at Acamantu with pale, pitiless eyes. "Circumstances had to be taken into consideration," she said. "The city would not have tolerated a raid on two of its ruling families. Tastis was correct to take precautions against retaliation."

"Such precautions are irrelevant to aspistu," Acamantu said. "They reek of dai-terru; Tastis reached too high. Proper behavior would have necessitated the death of these criminals and their protectors, and then the publishing of the decision so that the population and the Denorru-Deissin could have understood. If the city chose to take offense, then any further violence would have been the fault of the city.

"In order to prevent revenge by the people of Neda-Calacas," Acamantu concluded, "Tastis has taken the city and invited revenge not only by its people, but by the other cities in the Elva."

"Cousins," said Tegestu, interrupting quietly before the disagreement could split the aldran, "we are not obliged to judge whether Tastis' action was appropriate, but only to witness it. Our duty lies in recording our notice, and in sending such to Tastis.

"Further, we must deal with the implications of this message. It was sent kantu-kamliss, that no one but Pranoth should be able with honor to read it or comment publicly on its contents. Surely this ban is inappropriate. The taking of an entire city was a public act; such an act demands public justification."

"The insult was to kamliss Pranoth," Amasta said. "Kamliss Pranoth has taken revenge. Justification of such an act is not required except to those of the kamliss concerned."

"I think, respected cousin, that bro-demmin Tegestu is correct," said Sethenthu. He was sixty-eight, bald but carefully wigged, and known as "Sethenthu the Silent" for his reserved manner: he rarely volunteered an idea or participated in an argument, but only spoke when he thought the subject needed clarification. "Your argument, cousin Amasta, is inconsistent. You defend the seizure of the city on practical grounds—very well, but since you must realize the practical consequences of this message, the potential for causing distrust between ourselves and our lords, surely you must do Tastis the honor of believing him to realize this also?"

Amasta was silent for a moment, and then bowed. "I stand corrected, bro-demmin Sethenthu. May your arm never weaken."

"This private message was sent very publicly," Tegestu said. "By messengers arriving in a dispatch boat that cleared quarantine here and the local customs, and who then hired horses and gear and paraded their Pranoth-sa-Neda banners through the streets of the city before coming to our keep. The Abessu-Denorru Necias doubtless knows the message was sent. Yet it will be a difficult matter to convince him that we cannot inform him of its contents, we who are his servants.

"Surely Tastis intended distrust between ourselves and Arrandal. The kantu-kamliss message was such that our entire Aldran might not read it; yet according to the scroll Tastis' entire aldran consented to the capture of the city, and his aldran, like ours, is composed of clans other than Pranoth. Surely Tastis intends—I will not say distrust, but certainly disunity—within our aldran. For what purpose, other than the sowing of discord, would Tastis send us such a message? And how, bro-demmin cousins, should we deal with it? How can we keep the trust of the city without breaking our sacred obligations?''

Amasta's pale eyes glittered coldly. Her voice, when she spoke, was arrogant and commanding. Tegestu recognized the tone at once: her superb, cunning, ruthless mind, once presented with the problem, had found a plan worth considering.

''Bro-demmini,'' she said, ''there is a way.'' Lazily, she took a drink of tea. ''It will require a sacrifice—there will be killing—but I assure you, there is a way.''

3

The room was small but exquisitely decorated, from the deep brown parquetry of the floor, to the lighter-colored carved panelling of the walls, to the lovely bronze shrine to the household gods that occupied the corner. The parquetry was gradually accumulating a series of scuff marks as Acragas Necias, master of the city of Arrandal, paced rapidly back and forth like an animal in its cage. He consumed tea-cakes at frequent intervals, chewing in a brisk, businesslike fashion with the few good teeth he had remaining on the right side. Tegestu was due for his audience within the half hour, and Necias knew the Brodaini chieftain would be precisely on time. He halted his pacing, irritated at his own distress. He felt he had lost cimmersan, becoming disadvantaged, and he had no clear notion of how to regain the initiative.

He was the Community Speaker of the city, Abessu-Denorru—"Abeissu" for short—and he was a man of vast wealth. Perhaps the wealthiest man in Arrandal, perhaps not: his social position required great expenditure, and those with greater acquisitiveness and fewer civic ambitions might have surpassed him. Though the Acragas family had not been prominent in his youth, he had nevertheless been nominated to the Denorru-Deissin, the nine-man oligarchy who ruled the city, at an early age, and had by now married into many of the great families of the city. He was not used to frustration, and was not bearing it well.

He was a large man, with a massive barrel chest and brawny wide-spread arms, and he was always in motion; for nearly twenty years he had run the city and its affairs, through a half-dozen successful major wars and a score of little country clashes, and in these last years he thought he had finally reached some kind of plateau of stability, that all the forces—social, economic, baronial, racial, military—were finally adding up to some kind of balance. There hadn't been a major war in ten years; trade agreements with the other Elva cities had seemed to define effectively the various areas of influence; the importation of Brodaini warriors had created a climate of military stability, with no city having the advantage of another; the outland barons were slowly being pacified. Necias had, he had thought, created a peace that might last a hundred years.

But now Neda-Calacas had burst into rebellion—worse than a rebellion, really, for revolts were frequent in the Elva cities, as houses of one faction purged those of another. This was a race war, as a minority warrior caste tried to impose its will on a much larger, sophisticated, and vastly dissimilar population.

And, of course, the revolt could spread to Arrandal. Perhaps, he thought with an angry, fatalistic despair, the astrologers had been right about a season of upheaval. Ever since the new, fixed star had appeared, apparently right overhead, the astrologers had been predicting a great change below. They were, as usual, unspecific about the exact nature of the change, but Necias had been assured it would be major, perhaps catastrophic. Necias had thanked the astrologers and gone about his own business, convinced that if they couldn't offer him practical advice there was little point to their art, and had then turned the new star to sensible advantage by offering a cash prize for anyone working out a way to navigate by it. But still, he thought grudgingly, perhaps the astrologers were right; perhaps it was all in the stars, and the sky had already proclaimed that Necias' century of peace was not to be.

He had been certain of Brodaini loyalty; he had seen it demonstrated in so many ways, including the inter-mural wars fought between the cities of the Elva, when Brodaini in the service of one city had fought Brodaini in the service of another. His policy had been based on Brodaini loyalty; his very rise to power was based on it. The knowledge, sudden and stunning, that his power may have been resting on unstable foundations had filled him with anxiety.

Necias gobbled another tea-cake, bit down hard on a bad tooth, and winced. He paused for a moment, rubbing his jaw, and pondered.

Why hadn't Tegestu reported to him the contents of the communication he'd received from the rebels? The message had been delivered publicly; Tegestu had to have known that Necias was aware of its arrival, and would be chafing to know its contents. Tegestu's uncompromisingly obedient reply to his summons was reassuring; but still there was a deep anxiety that underlay all Arrandal's relationships with its Brodaini, and not a little fear. There was something unsettling about the Brodaini, something alien and fierce—the Brodaini could explode into ruthless violence if provoked, and no one quite understood what constituted provocation.

Necias resumed his pacing, scowling as he prodded at his rotting teeth with the tip of his tongue. He was, he thought, a practical man; he had risen to power by making practical decisions. He had started as a middleman, priding himself on his contacts among the deissin and the guilds, the color gangs, the pilots' league—his name had reached its first prominence as a man who knew where a certain thing could be procured, who to go to when a certain favor needed to be asked. From that he'd gone on to a role as a power-broker, acting as middleman in the city's internal struggles, helping one faction obtain what it needed to triumph over another, collecting favors and eventually his reward. He'd been appointed to the Denorru-Deissin and given, among his other tasks, that of Chairman of the Famine Relief Fund, which had always been considered a license to embezzle and speculate with the vast stores of grain the city maintained as a bulwark against crop failure. He hadn't held the post for more than three years before the drought struck, ruining the crops across the entire continent, spelling disaster for the population of the cities . . . but then, to the astonishment of everyone, Necias had opened the granaries and fed the city for the two years the drought lasted. The grain had not, as had always happened before, trickled away into somebody's pocket, or been gambled away in speculations—it was there, where no one, not even the poor whose very lives depended on the grain's remaining where it was, had ever expected it to be.

People began to talk about Acragas Necias.

It was not that Necias was scrupulous. There had been plenty of fiddles of one sort or another with the grain supply; but there had always been ways of speculating that didn't mean the goods ever had to leave the warehouse. But he had known that a famine was about due, and that the best way to make a name for himself was to do the unexpected and feed the population.

After that he'd used his popularity to become the leader of the city's war party, and after importing the first Brodaini from the north had forced a declaration against Neda-Calacas, at the time the most powerful city on the continent; and Tegestu had beaten them on land and sea. By the time

Neda-Calacas tried again two years later, Necias had imported more Brodaini and the twin cities had been crushed so thoroughly they still hadn't recovered. After that there had been a purge of the city deissin, and Necias' faction had emerged as victors; Necias had been made Abessu-Denorru, had launched more wars with more Brodaini, had beaten Cartenas and Prypas and a dozen barons, and he'd revived an old moribund alliance against the barons, the Elva vor Denorru-Dorsu, and turned it into an alliance of all the city-states, and he'd made himself chairman of it.

It hadn't, he thought, been as difficult as it might have seemed. He'd simply had to reason with people, and point out that their path of advantage lay alongside his own. He believed firmly that if one simply made it obvious to people the course that would bring them advantage and profit, they would eventually follow it. He was, he would point out, a practical man, and he made a point of appealing to the practical side of others.

But that course, he knew, could not be taken with Brodaini. There was a grim kind of practicality about them, to be sure, but it couldn't be counted on. Their allegiance was not to profit, or even to cimmersan, but to a warriors' code that made no sense at all—even, Necias suspected, to the Brodaini themselves.

He remembered the horrid experience he had trying to learn Gostu. Tegestu had given him a Classanu tutor and he'd met with the man daily for three months, only to be confronted each time with the same illogical, imponderable, impenetrable language. "Beg pardon, cenors-stannan," the tutor would always correct, "but you must remember, the indirect object is always placed before the direct object. You cannot place it before the verb, as you can in Abessas, but only before the direct object." *But why?* Necias would howl in desperation, flogging his brains in frustration and wondering why the Brodaini couldn't simply decline their nouns like civilized, sensible people and stuff them into the sentence wherever there seemed room for them. In the end he'd had to give it up, concluding that Gostu was simply the impractical language of an impractical people, and rely on translators who were paid to understand such madness.

But even through a translator Necias could not talk to Brodaini as he was accustomed to talking to others; he had to feel his way carefully, making certain not to inadvertently offend one of their strange codes of conduct and cause insult. He could not appeal to their practical nature, because often the practical course was denied to them by their beliefs—which, fortunately, at least allowed utter practicality in war.

The Abessla and the Brodaini had always had to be wary of one another; and in Arrandal Necias had tried to minimize the chances of collision by giving the Brodaini possession of what was, in effect, a city-within-a-city, the former Old Quarter, with their own keep. There Brodaini law prevailed, and their oddness, their impractical ferocity, was masked.

But Tastis' Brodaini had also had their own quarter in Neda-Calacas, newly-built by the Neda Denorru-Deissin outside the former city walls. Yet Tastis and his warriors had boiled out of it, taking both cities, and at a seemingly trivial slight. Did they seriously think that some woman's distress was justification for the capture of the twin cities, the interruption of commerce, the execution of an entire household, and almost certainly general war within the Elva? Such was the justifiction offered by Tastis in the communication that had arrived just yesterday, along with a bland, badly-stated wish for peace and normalization. Was Tastis serious in his wishes: was he really that imbecile, to think that the other cities of the Elva would tolerate a coup by Brodaini? By flenssin, mercenaries?—for the Brodaini were certainly mercenaries, even if they insisted they weren't.

Necias' fevered pacing was interrupted by a scratching at his door. He gave the door an annoyed glance.

"Who is it?"

"Luco. I brought fresh tea." The answer brought an unconscious smile to Necias' lips.

"Come in." The girl slipped in, carrying a brass teapot and fragile silver cups balanced on a tray; she gave Necias a brief, dazzling smile, carried the tray to the low inlaid table set between Necias' settee and Tegestu's low stool, and set the tray down.

"Thank you," Necias said. "You might ask the servants to bring glasses for the tea. Brodaini prefer to drink tea from glasses."

"Do they? I'm sorry." She was a slim, delicate, pale-gold creature, his newest wife, the daughter of his old friend and ally Fastias Castas. She straightened and walked to him, reaching out to brush an imaginary bit of fluff from his broad shoulders. "I'll bring some myself," she said.

"You couldn't have known, hey?" She leaned forward, her cheek on his doublet-front. He touched her hair, smelling the perfume rising from her. She hugged his massive body and Necias felt, in spite of his anxiety, his response beginning to stir.

"Can't I stay?" she asked. "I've never seen a Brodainu scottu."

He frowned. She was insecure, new to the partillo and her sister-wives, uncertain of her place; he seemed to have to reassure her constantly.

"Brito is hostess, you know that," he said. "And don't call a Brodainu a scottu, it's impolite."

"Yes, Necias," she said, with a petulant sigh.

"You can watch Tegestu enter the audience chamber from the balcony of the partillo." His arms went around her. "It'll be politics, anyway," he said. "Boring for you, hey?"

She raised her head, straining up on her toes to kiss him. There was longing in the kiss, and desire; he responded instinctively, giving her the reassurance she wanted. The reassurance went both ways, he knew; he was over twice her age and it was gratifying to know he was himself still desirable.

Luco's green eyes slid deliberately to the settee by the table.

Perhaps he allowed her too much, he thought; he was scheduled to sleep with Argo that night, and she would be right to resent . . .

He wondered if there was time. Luco's face was flushed; her hands slid over his doublet as she took pleasure in the power she had to arouse him. Necias decided there was time.

His burly arms swept her from the floor; she laughed, her arms going around his neck. There was a childish pleasure in her laugh, and a childish kind of triumph. He bore her to the settee, burying his face between her neck and shoulder, inhaling the perfume of her pale hair. She was perfectly shameless, his latest wife, afraid of nothing, daring convention. He adored her fearlessness, recognizing something of his own younger self in it, but he recognized as well the danger of her, that he might all too easily let this become obsession, forgetting his other wives, his many responsibilities—yet the knowledge of the danger was itself arousing. Luco had given him much when she'd entered his life: a sense of youthfulness he had largely forgotten, the sense that every day held adventures, that every change was not an ominous portent of decay. Certain conventions could be sacrificed for this.

But not all. Brito, his first and senior wife, would still play hostess to Tegestu. It was not to be forgotten that he owed her as much, if not more.

*   *   *

The palace of Acragas Necias sprawled over most of a city block in one of the newer quarters of the city, with a water gate that permitted access by the Acragas merchant fleet to the warehouses that fronted the canal. The bulk of the palace was constructed of the grey stone brought from inland and then fronted with brick. The brick was chiefly a dull red, but was patterned with sun-yellow and pale blue in geometric designs: Arrandal was famous for its brickmakers and the best was displayed in the Acragas palace, the patterns complimenting the architecture, accenting and commending the design, pleasing but not dominating the eye. Chimneys, twisted and ornamented, curled skyward; stone beasts, both natural and mythological, peered from the gables and gutters and the panes of glass cast inward light that was stained with the colors of the rainbow. Nine hundred people lived within its sprawling confines: the Acragas family, their servants, employees, and guests; fifteen hundred worked daily within its walls.

Tēgestu and his small escort were led from the water gate through courtyards of increasing size, each guarded by a brick-fronted tower, each decorated with carvings of stone and embellished with ornate clocks. The palace as it stood was not defensible against a skilled force—Brodaini could take it in an afternoon—but it was proof against the usual threat, a city mob, and a few weeks' work could transform it into a respectable fortress. The outer layers were guarded by flenssin, mercenaries in gaily-colored, arrogant costumes that contrasted vastly with the tall, brawny Brodaini in their simple, purposeful military dress. The inner courts were guarded by junior members of the Acragas family who had the duty in rotation; their armor fit badly and their stance as they carried their pikes and great two-handed swords was awkward.

Word of Tēgestu's prompt arrival had been passed ahead, and Necias was there to welcome him in the vast audience hall, his clothes adjusted and the crumbs of tea-cakes brushed

from his doublet-front. Necias glanced up at the balcony of
the partillo, seeing five of his six surviving wives leaning
over the rail, including Luco in her green gown. He seemed
to sense a flash of indignation in Luco's eyes at being
dismissed to the company of her sister-wives, and he
smiled a satisfied smile at the remembrance of pleasure.
Then the trumpet calls began, sweet, ornamented, echoing
from the high groined ceiling, and the Brodaini delegation
strode in.

Necias had cleared most of the usual loiterers and petitioners from the hall as a compliment to Tegestu; there
were a few high-ranking members of beggru Acragas, the
trumpeters in their gallery, a handful of messengers, and
the guards spotted at the entrances—these, and the wives
at the partillo rail, were all. The enormous room, usually
thronged with people, was almost empty—all this in courtesy to Tegestu, a symbol of the Brodainu's importance in
that Necias had cleared away his other business.

Despite the years of cooperation between them and a
frequent exchange of messages, requests, and commands,
Necias saw Tegestu only rarely in person, and then chiefly
on ceremonial occasions. Their tasks had been carefully
delineated: Necias concerned himself with broader policy,
and Tegestu with military security. The Brodainu rarely
had reason to leave his keep, and Necias had less reason to
enter the Brodaini quarter—perhaps because of this, perhaps because of the special tension between them, Necias
felt an increasing apprehension as Tegestu approached. He
felt, with a certain awful clarity, the fact of the Brodainu's
alienness, his utter lack of civilization, his fanatic contempt
of life. Tegestu was old, over seventy, thin and seemingly
frail; yet he walked with rigid, disciplined martial vigor;
his belt weapons rode easily at his side, where he could
snatch them at need. The lack of ornament in his dress and
armor spoke of an overwhelming concern for the functional,

with which the elaborately curled, dressed ringlets of his white hair contrasted weirdly—to Necias an almost psychotic contradiction. The alert, arrogant, expressionless countenance the Brodaini assumed in public—the mouth tightened to a grim line, eyes intent and restless, head held high—seemed, for a frightening instant, the face of a dangerous madman, a murderous fanatic and a conscience-less killer.

No. Necias thought, rejecting the fear. *Tegestu is no less human for all his strangeness. I can comprehend him if I try.*

And then the Brodaini were across the long hallway, the trumpets were crying their final triplets, and the five warriors came down to one knee and bowed their ringleted heads.

"Rise, friend Tegestu. Rise all, loyal friends," Necias said. He had always been embarrassed by the Brodaini insistence of rendering him homage, as if he were some half-civilized baron from the outback receiving a delegation of his shepherds, but he knew they thought it necessary and he'd long ago resigned himself to the sneers of his political enemies—"old Necias preening himself among his worshipping flenssin." His usual style was to receive his visitors in one of the smaller anterooms, rise from amid his staff of secretaries and mounds of papers to give the visitor a roaring embrace, and then carry on his business while coping with a good many interruptions—but the Brodaini expected something more formal, if not majestic.

Do the Brodaini greet visitors with trumpets? Necias suddenly wondered. Or do they use them only in war? Do they call their vassals "friend?" Have I been offending them all these years without knowing it, skating on the edge of their tolerance?

The thoughts brought a hesitation to his usual decisive, noisy manner. "Come, Tegestu," he said. "You and I must speak, hey. Your men, ah . . ." He slowed as he observed that one of the Brodaini was female. "Your soldiers will be entertained here. Ahastinas," he turned to his steward, "call the musicians for our guests."

"Thank you, cenors-stannan," Tegestu said, and bowed. Necias gestured to his secretary and interpreter, the poet Caltias Campas, a tall dark man with a cynical smile and a way with the ladies, and led Tegestu into an anteroom, hearing behind him the rattle of armor that marked another obeisance. He had probably just been rude again.

He opened the four-inch-thick door and led his party inside. Brito, standing by the teapot, curtsied as her husband and Tegestu entered. Necias nodded abstractedly in reply, and then to everyone else's surprise Tegestu dropped to one knee in a bow fully as elaborate as that he'd given Necias.

Fortunately Brito responded well. "Rise, enventan, you do me too much honor," she said. "Would you like some tea, my lord, or cakes? We know Brodaini prefer a special diet; these are made to a Brodaini recipe." Necias looked at Brito with relief as Tegestu clanked to his feet. Luco would have smiled, giggled probably, but would never have recovered as swiftly. Brito was his cenors-censto, his most honored wife and official hostess; she was also his first wife, and had shared with him the long rise to power, and many of his confidences. She was a thin, hard, plain-faced woman of sixty, two years older than he; she possessed a cunning on which Necias had learned to rely, and an anildas, a desire for display and property, that would have done credit to a man.

"Cenors-stannan does me too much honor," Brito said again, correcting him gracefully as she poured tea into a glass. Cenors-stannan was a masculine appellation—Necias remembered, from his attempt to learn Gostu, that Tegestu's language did not distinguish between the sexes in regard to titles, but rather between degrees of respect.

"I am stansisso Brito, if you please," Brito said. "Will you take honey or sugar?"

"No, thank you, stansisso Brito," Tegestu said formally, with a bow.

They took their tea and sat, Necias semi-reclined on his settee, bolstered by soft cushions, Tegestu lowering himself onto one of the small, three-legged stools the Brodaini seemed to prefer—because they were so uncomfortable, Necias had thought at first; but then he realized that however uncomfortable they were, for a man wearing a full suit of armor to sit on anything else might be positively painful.

Campas, the poet, sat in a stiffbacked chair that had wide arms on which he propped his pen and pad. He dressed strikingly in black, his clothing unornamented, presumably the better to stand out in a crowd. Despite his affectations Necias had employed him for ten years now, since he was a youngster, for Campas was a brilliant linguist who, at Necias' bidding, had first lived among the Brodaini to learn their tongue and ways, and had done so with considerable success.

Brito placed a plate of tea-cakes by each elbow and quietly slid from the room after assuring that, if anything were needed, they should simply ring. Tegestu almost jumped up again for a formal bow, but Necias saw Campas make a quick gesture that halted the impulse, and Tegestu simply bowed from his seated position.

"My friend," Necias said, after a brief silence in which he waited for Tegestu to volunteer to speak, "I have received a communication from Neda-Calacas. I require your assistance."

"Cenors-efellsan," Tegestu said, "I shall help where I can."

Campas' pen scratched on his pad as he kept the minutes in shorthand. Necias glanced at him, then at Tegestu. He knew the Brodaini preferred direct speech, and he usually tried to provide it—he was known as a direct man anyway, for an Arrandalla—but there was a question that demanded an answer, and the question was ugly: "Tegestu, under what circumstances would you kill me and take the city?" He would have come to the question indirectly; and even then he might be giving deadly insult.

"Campas, read the letter," Necias said. They would start with the text and go on from there.

Campas produced a ribboned scroll and read it aloud. There was little detail concerning the actual capture of the twin cities; the rape of Norvenan and Nedielas' failure to provide satisfaction was given as a justification; most of the message seemed to be a plainly-stated wish for amity between the cities, mixed with a formal application for Neda-Calacas to be allowed to remain in the Elva vor Denorru-Dorsu.

"A bad style, on the whole," Campas volunteered, rolling up the scroll. "There are a few minor grammatical errors characteristic of the Brodaini. While it is possible that this was written by a very literal-minded scribe to a Brodainu's dictation, the evidence suggests it was written by Brodainu. Very little care appears to have been taken in its style or its calligraphy; and that would suggest it was written in haste, or by someone unfamiliar with Abessla writing."

"Thank you, Campas," Necias said. He reached for a tea-cake and nibbled it gingerly, wary of his teeth, again waiting for Tegestu to volunteer information; when Tegestu did not, Necias finished his cake and spoke.

"Tegestu, this communication is quite extraordinary. What has happened in Neda-Calacas is without precedent." Necias groped for a way to approach the problem, his thoughts spiraling into one another. *Under what circumstances would you take the city?*

"Is this possible, Tegestu?" he asked. "Did Tastis take Neda-Calacas because one of his women was attacked?"

There was a moment of silence. Campas' pen stood poised for the reply. "It is possible," Tegestu said. He spoke Abessas with slow precision. "It is the reason Tastis has given you. He is a clever man. He would not give a frivolous reason for this kind of behavior."

Necias' head spun. A city for a woman—for some insignificant mercenary female. *I can understand this,* he thought insistently.

"I have been assured—I have always assumed," he began uncertainly, "that Brodaini loyalty was unconditional. That obedience was a hallmark of the Brodaini character." Tegestu's eyes blazed, and Necias almost stopped. He felt the touch of fear on his heart. *I am insulting him, even with this indirection!* he thought. But he had to know.

"How can this be, friend Tegestu? I do not understand. I wish to understand."

"You are our canlan, our lord," Tegestu said. His glare was fierce, aroused. "We obey you."

"Tegestu, understand me!" Necias said. "I am not questioning your loyalty. I wish to know how such a thing can be. How can a people so devoted to loyalty rise against their, their canlani?"

Tegestu paused, his eyes falling, his frown tightening. "We obey nartil, Abeissu Necias," he said. "It is our law: it demands obedience and respect. We serve our lord, and he aids us by giving us a place, by making it possible for us to exist, for allowing us to care for our dependents. Do you understand me, cenors-efellsan?"

"Yes, my friend." Nodding. "I understand this."

"But nartil is not simply obedience. It is respect. It cannot go one way only. We obey and respect our lord, but he must respect us, as we respect our servants. If our lord does not hear our just requests, if he treats us as if we were ar-demmin—I am sorry, but there is no word for this in your language—then he has violated nartil. He has not fulfilled his obligations."

"Ah," Necias said. "It is like a contract. You are saying that Neda-Calacas did not fulfill the terms of its contract with Tastis, hey?"

"It is not a contract. It is nartil."

Necias looked helplessly at Campas for assistance. Campas' pen halted on its pad.

"Cenors-stannan, perhaps we ought simply to accept that Neda-Calacas did not live up to its obligations," Campas said, "and that Tastis saw this as justification for rebellion."

"Is this understanding acceptable to you, Tegestu?" Necias said.

"I understand this as approximation," Tegestu said. "It will suffice for present understanding. I wish to correct a statement you made earlier; it is not *I* who claim Neda-Calacas failed in its obligations; I do not know this. Tastis claims it, in his message."

Necias blinked. "Very well," he said. The point seemed insignificant, but Tegestu seemed to be attaching an importance to it. Was Tegestu disassociating himself from Tastis' actions? He made a mental note to ask Campas afterwards.

"Is it possible," he began again, "for Brodaini to take offense at their lords' actions, and to attack them without warning? Without a notice to the effect they were displeased?"

Tegestu's answering silence was prolonged, and then he turned to Campas and spat out rapid-fire Gostu until Campas waved his hands helplessly to signal the Brodainu to slow down. Tegestu began again, Campas nodding, his pen scratching on the pad as he made notes. He turned to Necias.

"Cenors-stannan," he said, "it seems there is an aesthetic principle involved."

"*A what?*"

Campas smiled apologetically. "An aesthetic principle, cenors-stannan. It is called *aspistu*—I do not understand it entirely, but it is quite important in Brodaini society. Much of their literature, or what passes for literature, concerns it. Aspistu is revenge considered as art. Imagination and appropriateness are major considerations—for a small insult a small revenge; a large insult demands a revenge of large proportions, inflicted with suitable imagination.

"Tastis' revolt has to be considered in the light of aspistu," Campas said, "much in the same way as a poem's tone and approach must be compared with its subject matter."

"If Tastis rebelled for the reasons he claimed," Tegestu added, breaking in abruptly, "then it was for aspistu. His people were grossly insulted, or so he claims; a great aspistu was necessary."

"If it is aspistu," Campas said, "then the question becomes aesthetic, not political: was the aspistu satisfying, was it appropriate?"

"My question wasn't an aesthetic one," Necias, "but it seems I've been answered. Brodaini can, it seems, revolt against their lords."

"Insult is given," Tegestu said ponderously. "Aspistu is necessary. Aspistu takes many forms. The question becomes one of appropriateness."

"Aspistu may involve informing the victim in advance, or it may not," Campas said. "Whether or not to do so is a matter of artistic judgement."

The words spun like falling leaves in Necias' mind, circling in the wind, never alighting. He was close to despair. What kind of beasts had he allowed into his city, when he had permitted the Brodaini to come in their tens of thousands? A people who murdered their overlords and called it art?

"To clarify," he said, trying not to show the desperation he felt, "once insult is given, all bets are off, hey? The insulted party can be attacked without warning."

"The insult would have to be great," Tegestu said. "It would have to be . . . noticed."

"I think I see what the drandor means," Campas interjected. "There are people who are beneath notice—their insults are also beneath notice."

"This is true, ilean," Tegestu said. His tone was satisfied.

"And Tastis' rebellion?" Necias asked, still seeking clarification. "Was it good aspistu or not? Was the thing justified?"

"Justified is not the point," Tegestu said. "It is not a moral issue. It is or is not *appropriate*."

"Very well. Was Tastis' action appropriate?"

Tegestu was silent for a long time, his white head bowed, his eyes narrowed as he concentrated. Campas' recording pen scratched on for a moment and then stopped. Tegestu looked up.

"I do not have enough information to make that judgement," he said.

"I understand," Necias said, not understanding at all. Was Tegestu simply refusing to commit himself, or was it truly an issue on which he did not have information?

"Tastis has rebelled, hey," Necias went on. "He has done so—we are told—for reasons which our people find difficult to understand. I can say with perfect confidence that Neda-Calacas will be expelled from the Elva, and that the cities of the Elva may take military action, either together or unilaterally."

Tegestu nodded, silent. Necias continued.

"Friend Tegestu, we do not know the Brodaini well; there is a great deal my people do not understand. You may be uncertain about us as well, about our motives, our intentions. In this situation there must be trust, there must be openness. My friend, this question is not meant to offend; and if there is offense I apologize sincerely. But I must ask: would the Brodaini of Arrandal, if the decision were taken, hesitate in fighting Tastis' people?"

The fanatic gleam returned to Tegestu's eyes, and Necias shivered. The Brodainu's voice, when it came, was cold, matter-of-fact, as if he were stating simple facts to a child of slow understanding.

"You are our canlan. We are Brodaini. We serve."

Necias drew a long breath. Brodaini had fought Brodaini before, in the service of the cities; it seemed as if they would fight one another again. Necias felt his anxiety ebbing.

"Tegestu," he said, beginning once again. "We know you have received a message from Tastis."

"We have, cenors-efellsan."

"The minds of this city would be greatly relieved should you inform us of its contents."

"Cenors-efellsan, I cannot," Tegestu said. Necias leaned back, surprised.

"Tegestu, I am your canlan," he protested. "Why should I not be told?"

Tegestu's distress was plain to see, even through the arrogant mask of Brodaini bore in public. He turned to Campas and spoke quickly in his own tongue. Campas listened, clearly surprised, and then turned to Necias.

"Cenors-efellsan, it seems the message was sent with certain restrictions," he said. "The restrictions are called kantu-kamliss, a rather archaic custom, I gather, but still respected. The point of them is this: anyone not of his clan, his kamliss, may not touch the message or know of its contents. It is a clan matter only; it is a disgrace to kamliss Pranoth should anyone defile the message—there is a religious element involved here, too, some manner of taboo."

"But I—I am their lord," Necias protested.

"You are not kamliss Pranoth," Campas said. He shrugged wryly, and suddenly Necias wondered: Do Brodaini shrug? I've never seen it. Do they even have a different language of gesture?

"It seems, cenors-stannan," Campas said, "that Tastis has taken the matter out of your jurisdiction."

Necias turned to Tegestu, bewildered. "You may not discuss this? Not even *discuss* it?"

Tegestu bowed; he held himself low while he spoke. "That is true, cenors-stannan. I regret it." He rose, and for a moment Necias was looking again into those cold, fanatic eyes. Tegestu's speech was slow and deliberate.

"Our reply to Tastis will be sent tomorrow," Tegestu said. "Due to the unsettled conditions, two copies will be sent, together with copies of the original message. One answer will go by despatch boat, three Brodaini plus crew; another will go by land, with three Brodaini to guard it. Both," Tegestu said very clearly, "will leave tomorrow at noon."

Necias absorbed Tegestu's sacrifice with awed silence: despite his shock, his mind worked swiftly on the implications of Tegestu's announcement. The message carried by land would be the one intercepted, Necias thought quickly; the waterborne one might go in the drink. Of course there would have to be no survivors; he'd send twenty mercenaries at least.

"Thank you, my friend," he said; he heard his speech coming out thickly, slow to recover from the shock. "I am happy to have achieved this, this communication with you. Shall I ring for more tea?"

"Thank you, cenors-efellsan," Tegestu said, and bowed again. There was triumph in those cold, glittering eyes.

As Brito entered and poured the tea, Necias' thoughts ran uncontrolled. The man is surely mad, he thought. He will tell those soldiers to go, knowing they will die. All because he can't violate some ridiculous custom or other.

His eyes wandered to the bronze shrine standing in the corner.

Ai, gods, he thought. What have I let into my city?

4

There had been a small amount of strained small talk over tea, and it had been so halting that Necias wondered if the Brodaini had any small talk at all among themselves—there seemed so many taboo subjects among them. He had tried once, years ago, to speak to a Brodainu about trade—it was the usual conversation starter in Necias' circles—but the Brodainu began staring at him as if he were mad, and Necias had silenced himself before the man had taken insult. He'd learned later that Brodaini did not participate in trade agreements directly—they had a whole class of dependents for just that purpose—although they approved or disapproved of those made by their people. It appeared they considered trade itself dishonorable.

Necias had never repeated the offense.

After the second cup of tea was finished, Necias rose to escort Tegestu to his companions. Tegestu rose, turned to give elaborate thanks to Brito for the tea and cakes—Brito was flattered by the attention, and gave flustered thanks in return—and then, Campas trailing, they returned to the audience hall.

"Cenors-efellsan," Tegestu said as they walked, his eyes sliding over the room, watching the people bustling on their various errands, "if I may, I beg to mention something concerning security here. If there is to be a war with Tastis, we must realize the kind of war it is likely to be. Tastis will know he cannot fight all the cities of the Elva at once; he will try to break the Elva, or cause internal conflict in the cities."

"Yes," Necias said. "I realize that. With the message he sent you, he has already begun."

Tegestu paused, then apparently decided not to dispute Necias' analysis. "You must realize your personal danger, cenors-efellsan. There could be no provocation so great as the assassination of the Abessu-Denorru by a Brodainu. This place is too open. I would like to assign my whelkran y cathruni—my head bodyguard—to the task of guarding you, or at least to the task of conferring with your own guards. Your access should be very strictly controlled."

Necias looked at Tegestu grimly. His palace was open to almost anyone: he had always moved freely among his people, without guards, without a large entourage, and he took pride in it. The guards around the palace were chiefly for display and to prevent theft, rather than for the prevention of assassination, which was not an Arrandalla trait. Tegestu wanted him closeted away, remote like a Brodaini ruler, untouchable—and he would be surrounded by Brodaini guards, guards who could take offense and attack at the smallest slight.

"If there is a problem with your confidences," Tegestu said, seeing Necias' hestitation, "I could assign guards who do not speak Abessas."

"Later," Necias said, brushing the matter aside.

Necias said farewell to the Brodainu and his escort, going through the parting bowings and kneelings with resigned patience. As he watched the Brodaini stalk from the room, the guards at the door shifting uncomfortably as they passed, Necias sucked at his false front teeth and slowly began to absorb the implications of Tegestu's last remarks. This was not a war of city against city, or beggru against beggru; this was a war of all the Abessla against a Brodaini clan, and that was different.

He had fought wars with cities before, but the Brodaini on both sides had been directed by their native lords, and certain conventions had been in effect. Spying had been permitted; outright assassination had not. But assassination and this—what was the word?—aspistu, this imaginative revenge, were hallmarks of Brodaini wars. He *would* have to guard himself well if he were to war against Tastis, and that would, he realized with growing apprehension, probably involve accepting Brodaini protection. And that would make him even more vulnerable should Tegestu attempt a rising in Arrandal, as Tastis had in Neda.

With a sick feeling he remembered the attempted assassination twelve years before, by a deranged merchant who thought Necias had ruined him. His younger brother Castas had saved him then, intervening only to fall beneath the assassin's dagger himself while Necias, paralyzed with horror, had watched helplessly—Castas had been commemorated by a day in his honor, when all the household and much of the city honored his memory with prayers. . . . *Gods*, Necias thought, *don't let it happen again.*

"Cenors-efellsan," said a voice at this elbow. "I have arranged the program for next week, the fete."

Necias glanced sidelong at Ahastinas, his steward; when he answered his voice was brusque. "Yes? Is this necessary?"

"There are Fastias' mimes, which he has generously lent us," Ahastinas went on, blind to Necias' annoyance. "And the spectacular conjuror Fiona—"

"Fiona! What kind of name is that?" Campas interrupted, his blue eyes shining with mischief.

Ahastinas paused for a moment, flustered. "I don't

know, cenors-stannan. It's an outland name of some sort. But the conjuring tricks, ah, yes," he smiled. "They are spectacular. The woman is truly astonishing."

"A woman. It should be Fiono."

Ahastinas shrugged, unaware that he was being baited. "An outland name, cenors-stannan. And then there are our musicians, and, ah—"

"The poet Caltias Campas," said Campas, "will recite from his new *Pastoral Cantos*."

"Of course," Ahastinas said. "Beg pardon, Campas, but it escaped my memory."

"Your memory," Campas said, "is riddled, like wormwood, with the passages carved by escaping facts."

Ahastinas glared at the poet, then decided to ignore him.

"Concerning the banquet, cenors-efellsan," he began, "I think it should perhaps begin with—"

"I trust you," said Necias, "entirely in these matters."

"Thank you, cenors-efellsan." This time the steward hadn't missed the tone of dismissal. Muttering, he scurried away.

Necias, fingering his collar absently, turned to Campas. The poet was paging through his notes. Necias was blind to the merits of Campas' verse; the klossila school, with its tedious insistence on the corruption of city life and the purity of pastoral existence, had never impressed him. If the pastoral life was so glorious and pure, why were the klossila never found seeking employment as shepherds? Yet Campas was brilliant, in his way: a good linguist, an intelligent scribe, an invaluable secretary—and Necias was willing to accept the judgement of others concerning the merits of his verse, knowing that to employ a young man of such evident talent would add to his own anildas.

"Do you wish a fair copy of my notes, cenors-efellsan?" Campas asked, looking up.

"Yes. Together with any observations that may occur to

you. Do it now, while your memory is fresh; you may have the conference room if you like.''

Campas nodded, his thoughts abstracted. He plucked his pen from the inkwell at his waist and made a brief annotation.

"Campas," Necias frowned, "you know the Brodaini. At least as well any of us know them."

"I try," said Campas. "I've lived in their quarter, studying their language, their arts. There is a certain virtue in their poetry—most of it is so straightforward that it lacks the subtlety I think verse should possess, but there's a kind of formal, harsh truth to it, as there is to so much that is Brodaini."

"You've lived among them," Necias said. "You've said they've *tolerated* you. How do you think they tolerate us at all, Campas? Why haven't the Brodaini revolted elsewhere as they've revolted in Neda-Calacas? Surely we offend them often enough, even without meaning to. You've seen it, the way Tegestu turned murderous the moment I mentioned Brodaini and disloyalty in the same breath. And the rest of them—this aspistu business, all this emphasis on killing and revenge. It seems insane, completely deranged."

Campas nodded, soberly for once. "In Brodaini society they know what causes offense and what does not," he said. "Within their own society, the system works."

"But how can we avoid future revolts, if we're so constantly giving offense?" Necias repeated. "The Brodaini have been there, in Arrandal, longer than in any of the other cities. Why has there been no revolt?"

"I have a theory, cenors-efellsan," Campas said. He grinned cynically. "It will do little for our self-esteem, however."

Necias scowled. "Out with it."

"We call them Brodaini," Campas said, "but that's incorrect. The Brodaini are the warriors, the highest caste, but there are three other classes in their society, the servants, the peasants, and the tradesmen. The servants and peasants—Classani, Meningli—are thought to have honor appropriate to their station, but the tradesmen are honorless, ar-demmin. Yet here in Arrandal the Brodaini find themselves in the employ of merchants, and surrounded by commerce.''

"Yes, but it doesn't make sense," Necias said. "That should produce tension, not reduce it."

"Cenors-efellsan, you understand that we are honorless," the poet repeated. "We are nothing, we are unnoticed, nothing we do matters. The Brodaini have decided to ignore our offenses," Campas said, his grin rueful, self-mocking, "because we are so low we are beneath their notice." He gave a short, scornful laugh, and looked up at Necias. His eyes were sober, making a lie of his grin.

"It's enough to make one think," he said, "isn't it, Necias Abeissu?"

5

Fiona stood at her table in the Square of the Lancers, her hands busy with trickery. She loved this small-work, the sleight-of-hand and misdirection, all the cunning little maneuvers performed with her hands and wits alone. Her hands were good for the work: small, agile, stubby-fingered—long, "artistic" fingers would just have got in the way. It was all classic stuff, utilizing none of the alien technology she had brought with her: her mastery of it gave her a small measure of comfort that was otherwise absent. And so the Deuce of Bells leaped from the deck to the gasps of her audience; a pair of spongy balls appeared in an urchin's palm, and though she slipped for an instant at reuniting the cord cut by the militiaman's dagger she didn't think anyone had noticed.

There was tension in the city, that she knew; and before long she knew the reason why, Neda-Calacas in the hands of the Brodaini. Her thoughts had leapt to Kira, who had entered Neda-Calacas eight days before—had she known she was running into a city under occupation? She used her spindle then, routing the call through the ship, and Kira had answered. Yes, she'd reported, the cities were a little grim; but things were fairly normal, and no one showed any sign of paying any attention to her that she didn't want paid. There had been a laugh in her voice; Fiona knew her well enough to know that if she'd any forebodings the laugh wouldn't have been there. They'd exchanged jokes about the Abessla and agreed to talk again in a few days.

But the tension in Arrandal remained. The militia had increased their drill in the public squares from one day per week to three, causing grumbling among the hucksters, entertainers, and small merchants—the whores, however, were delighted. The mercenary troops were more in attendance, having been granted large cash bonuses by the city to keep them happy, and no doubt producing more joy for the whores.

The Brodaini were scarcely seen at all. Even so Fiona had noticed a certain involuntary movement on the part of the citizens, a kind of furtive look back over the shoulder at the towers of the Brodaini keep, as if at any moment a column of grim soldiery might issue forth.

Otherwise things had been going well. There had been initial expenses: a permit to perform in public, money to the local militia captain to keep disturbances and pickpockets away from her table, more money to the Blue Gang to keep the Red Gangsters away, money to the Red Gang to keep the Blue Gang ditto . . . so far as she could tell the entire city ran by open bribery. Her fellow performers, however, assured her that things were much better than in the old days, before the rise of Necias, who kept even the Color Gangs honest. And more money had been swallowed up by her indulgence at the public baths, one bath before work and another following.

Her spectacles had created a sensation; hundreds had seen the dragon illusion, the Bower of Bliss illusion, the Amil-Deo illustration. She was paid well and no longer needed to perform for the gallery, but she wanted to: it kept her sharp, it kept her in touch with the city, and it forced her to go out among the crowds instead of huddling in her room, as she wished so often to do.

She knew that her stock would fall rapidly if she performed too many spectacular miracles for the vulgar—the oligarchs wanted something exclusive, for them alone—and so in the Square of the Lancers she chiefly confined herself to the small-work she loved, with the occasional flashy trick to preserve her reputation.

Her performances in the public squares were always well attended, even on days like today when she did nothing but sleight-of-hand. And soon there would be the spectacle at the Acragas palace, where she would reveal her biggest, most spectacular, and most revealing illusion of all.

Fiona found herself dealing more easily with the people, at least on an ordinary, day-to-day basis. The uncertainties that clawed at her were still present, along with the knowledge of her own alienness, but somehow, in the everyday rush, none of that mattered so much. Most people she met she met as Fiona, the Conjuror; discussions were about fees, performances, professional secrets; and when she faced an audience during a performance, it was they who were entering her world, not the other way around. It was only occasionally that the world of Demro intruded: there was that moment, following a performance at a merchant's palace, that she was bundled into a closet by a drunken princeling, all sour breath, clumsy hands, and bad skin . . . and then it had been *he* who was given a surprise, left bent over, clutching his wounded gonads and bleeding snout while Fiona laughed and stalked away.

She gave an unconscious, wolvish smile at the memory, her hands busy with cards. It had been an unpleasant encounter, fortunately brief, and she hoped the young idiot had been taught a lesson—Fiona had learned hers, to be sure. She had enjoyed what she'd done, very thoroughly enjoyed it, and the knowledge of her own ferocity had not terrified her, as it had before. Not faced with deadly attack, she had responded in a non-murderous fashion; the knowledge that her inbuilt reflexes were capable of such discrimination was comforting.

Fiona's cards flew apart, revealing the solitary ace, and her audience burst into laughter and applause.

She was passing the hat, collecting the white money from her audience, when once again the alarm-bells began to clang in her mind. Stunned for an instant, she performed the gesture to shut off the alarms and turned to Caucas the Model-Builder, who held the next table, and asked him to look after her gear. After his nod she gathered up her skirts and bolted, leaving the surprised audience in her wake, money still jingling in their palms.

She ran flat-out, holding the brim of her cap over her eyes so as to keep it from flying off, dodging among the surprised wayfarers. There was the usual human traffic jam on the Bridge of Panandas Polloiu, navigated with much cursing in three languages, and then a quick left and a half-block run to her hostel. She was in through the common room and up the steep stairs before any of the surprised customers could look up from their suds to call their greetings; she skimmed her cap back down the stairs and clawed back to raise the hood of her privy-coat and seal it around her face.

There was a man leaning on a corridor wall: fair close-cropped hair, lantern jaw, brown, soiled leather jerkin. He stepped out to block her way. "Are you Fiona the Conjuror?" he asked loudly. "My lord Canvallas Castas would very much like to arrange . . ."

"Pardon me," Fiona said, bowing, trying to duck under his arm. He stepped back and blocked her again, the oaf.

"You don't understand. I'm talking about a commission."

She tried to step over his leg, failed. "Look here," the man said again.

Her skirts would have hampered a kick, but there was a nerve complex just under the nose and another beneath the ear: she hit them both with the edge of her hands, striking with all her strength; the man blinked and, suddenly nerveless, fell against the opposite wall, which let her dash past him and hurl herself bodily against her door.

Fiona didn't weigh much, but she was moving fast and the little hasp broke with a small metallic squeal of surprise. She tumbled in, picking herself up just in time to see someone's backside disappearing out of the window. Too late to kick it, alas, but after she rose from the floor she picked up her empty water jug and loosed it at the two grey men who had just slid down the rope to the street below. It missed, and by the time she had the champerpot elevated and ready to let fly they were well out of range. She darted back to the corridor but the lookout was also gone, replaced instead by a staring bourgeois couple whose quiet afternoon was so unaccountably disturbed by a brawl in the corridor, and by the voice of the landlady, calling out her questions as she moved her vast, arthritic bulk up the stair.

"Thieves," Fiona said briefly, undoing her hood and stripping it back off her head. The bourgeois couple looked at each other, communicating silently. She walked back into her room, aware only now of the hammering of her heart, the lungs gasping for air. She looked at the room: nothing missing, no damage. Someone had been at the lock of the chest again, but of course failed to open it. There was a small grapnel stuck in her windowsill, its cord dangling to the street. The man in the corridor had called out his warning and delayed her just long enough for the others to make their escape.

The landlady arrived, and things were made clearer. The

three had arrived that morning, asked for a room on this same floor, paid in advance. That, the fact that only one room was entered, and the sophistication of their plans, made it plain that the thieves had been professionals, and had meant only to acquire the secrets of Fiona the Conjuror.

Fiona collapsed on her narrow bed and leaned back against the wall, trying to lower her heartbeat, restore her mind to a state of calm. She waved off the repeated apologies of the landlady and urged the good woman not to call the militia. The thieves were well away by now, to be sure. Just keep an eye out for them in the future.

Now that Fiona had time to think, she didn't want them caught: that would mean execution or slavery in the mines. She didn't want to be the cause of another's death or misery—not again—particularly since these folk were obviously doing a job.

For whom? she wondered. Had those Brodaini-on-the-barge carried tales to their superiors? Were the servants of the Abessu-Denorru screening her before her appearance at the fete? That oligarch princeling, desiring revenge? Perhaps, she thought, some local conjuror was jealous and wanted to look at her tricks.

Even though it was unlikely, that was the story she'd use. "One of my professional rivals," she said. "Trying to puzzle out my illusions. Happens all the time. I'm sorry about the door and the pitcher: I'll replace both."

The landlady pooh-poohed the offer of payment and went to call her husband to replace the door hasp. From the corridor she could hear the bourgeois couple shuffling back to their suite.

Who? she wondered.

And decided it didn't matter. The point was that she was attracting attention.

And that meant she was doing her job.

6

"May your vengeance be always appropriate, bro-demmin," Cascan said. "A curious matter." Tegestu looked at him sourly, a fetid taste in his mouth. He had just returned from the inter-kamlissi duel between the boys from Tosta and Dantu, and a pointless butchery it had been. The two had hacked at each other for what seemed hours—no art, no grace, no intelligence, just two terrified fools drunk with nerves and obstinacy. They were both in the infirmary, where they'd lie useless for weeks. Perhaps they'd each lose a limb or two: rhomphaia produced hideous wounds. The distasteful sight had left a sourness in Tegestu's heart: he hated a public demonstration of idiocy, and could only be thankful his own clan had not been involved.

"Aye, ban-demmin?" Tegestu said testily. Cascan, his mobile face cast carefully in a simulation of neutrality, simply bowed.

"If this is inconvenient, bro-demmin . . ." he began, but Tegestu cut him off with a shake of the head.

"Speak, Cascan," he said, and then added, "If it's

important." The spy's plots-within-plots were not, at the moment. to his taste.

"Perhaps it's not," Cascan admitted. "It involves that conjuror woman I told you about, Fiona—the outlander?"

"I recall the report," Tegestu said. "What of her?"

"Obedient to your will, I had three of my men endeavor to search her room while she was out. There was also a young woman watching her performance in the Square of the Lancers, ready to alert our people if she showed sign of packing up her equipment and returning to her room."

Through Cascan's careful mask Tegestu detected a trace of apology, and decided to cut straight to the source. "It went wrong?" he asked.

"My sorrows, bro-demmin, it did," Cascan said, bowing again.

"Will we have to get our people out of prison?" Tegestu asked. Going to Necias to interview with a magistrate on a matter like this was a humiliation he did not desire.

"Nay," Cascan said, seeming a bit startled at the idea, and at Tegestu's sharpness. "Our people all got away. But *how* the thing went wrong is what is curious."

Tegestu tried to control his impatience. Cascan was trying to intrigue him, but what he most wanted now was to get out of his armor and take a warm bath to wash the smell of butchery off him. Those boys had been a disgrace. Even now, at his age, he could have carved either one of them like a slab of beef.

"Accompany me to the Blue Scroll Chamber," he said finally, bowing to the necessity. "I hope you have time for tea."

"I am honored, bro-demmin," Cascan said. They walked across the courtyard, Cascan staying a pace behind as was proper, narrating as he went. "The woman had a pair of trunks and a satchel. The satchel was mostly empty, but apparently she'd carried food in it, as there was some bread there, and dried meat wrapped in a kind of nose paper. One of the trunks contained nothing but clothing and a box of modest jewelry—no weapons, no false bottoms, nothing suspicious.

"But the other trunk, bro-demmin, that was the curious thing—to begin with, it had some kind of outlander lock that our folk hadn't encountered before. Couldn't cope with it."

"Has their training been neglected, ban-demmin?" Tegestu asked. He let Cascan chew on the question while he received the salutes of the cathruni at the postern and walked with long, impatient strides to the Blue Scroll Chamber. It was a small room, built as a library, its shelves lined both with scrolls and bound volumes. At one end, beneath a shrine to the household gods, rested the Blue Scroll, an epic of verse concerning an ancient war, a thousand years before, in which the Pranoth clan had been involved. This particular copy was eight hundred years old, was dedicated to the Pranoth ancestors, and was of sufficient demmin in and of itself to be considered a major religious relic. Tegestu bowed deeply to the scroll, then rang for servants and sat on a stool, his ankles crossed in front of him. Cascan bowed respectfully to the Blue Scroll— not being a Pranoth, the relic did not have as great status with him—and sat down, facing Tegestu, on a stool.

"May your demmin increase," he said. "The lock was one never before encountered, based on unknown principles; training was not a factor. No doubt our people could have conquered the lock in time, but the point is that they were not given time."

"Go on," Tegestu said. A Classanu appeared in the doorway, bowing; Tegestu ordered tea.

"The woman, Fiona, seemed somehow to be alerted," Cascan said. "Even though she was at quite some distance, in the Square of the Lancers, occupied with her performance. Our person there reports that she suddenly looked startled, put her business in the hands of one of the hucksters, and then ran for her hostel as fast as she could. Our person could not pursue without causing attraction herself, and so remained in place.

"Once back at the hostel, Fiona met our lookout in the corridor, who attempted to delay her. She struck him, stunning him momentarily, then ran for the door and broke into her room. Fortunately the lookout delayed her long enough for our people to make their escape through the window. There appears to have been no pursuit."

Tegestu frowned. "This woman. Describe her."

"Small. An inch or two over five feet. Very brown skin. Black, curly hair. Black eyes. Built rather sturdily, but not fat. Perhaps twenty-five years of age."

"And your lookout?"

"One of our best people for this kind of work," Cascan said, stroking his chin. "He's too tall, really, to be entirely inconspicuous, but he's a talented actor and mime. Twenty years of age, broad-shouldered, adept at imitating the Arrandalu."

"In his physical prime, in other words," Tegestu said. "Yet this small woman disabled him."

"A surprise attack, I believe, and—your pardon—stunned, not disabled. One does not expect violence in these situations—in fact the woman's behavior was entirely unexpected. No doubt Fiona would have had the worst of it had the fight gone on, but our person was under orders to avoid entanglements and left as discreetly as he could. The surprise, I think, was not in her combative skill—no doubt a woman travelling alone in this land of tears must have one trick or another to avoid unpleasantness—but rather the fact she was alerted at all."

They fell silent as the Classanu appeared with a small table and tea-things; she poured the fragrant tea into the clear glasses, then bowed and withdrew.

"There was no one who could have seen our people

entering, and run to give her the word?" Tegestu asked, breaking the silence.

Cascan frowned. "Our people say not," he said. "And our person in the Square reports no interruption—no one approached her, no one spoke, there were no shouts of alarm. She looked startled for a moment, then ran."

"Witchcraft?" Tegestu asked. "She is a magician, after all."

Cascan sipped his tea. "A possibility," he said, matter-of-fact. "We have our own witches, of course; we can show Fiona to them and ask what they perceive. But most likely they will want some belonging of Fiona's in order to read her aetheric emanations and that will mean another visit to her chambers."

"No," Tegestu said flatly. "Too dangerous." He fell silent for a moment, then spoke. "We have our own Classani conjurors, as well. Can they view her performance with an eye toward how they're done?"

"No doubt. Perhaps we can invite her to perform here, in our quarters, and give our witches and conjurors as much time as they need."

"Do it."

"Aye, bro-demmin. But there is another, more vital problem. Fiona," Cascan said, "is scheduled to perform before the Abessu-Denorru tomorrow night, at the fete. What if she is an assassin sent by Tastis? How can we prevent an incident?"

Tegestu tasted his tea, letting the silence broaden as he mulled on the problem. "We must certainly send a message to the Abessu-Denorru's people," he said. "Fiona should be searched before being admitted to his presence. And some of your own people, dressed and accoutred as Classani, must accompany our own party, and position themselves so as to intercept any assassination attempt on the Abessu-Denorru. The Abessu-Denorru is a brave man,"

Tegestu reflected, "who does not fully comprehend the danger he is in."

Cascan's eyes reflected approval: probably he would have recommended these steps himself. "Aye, bro-demmin," he said.

"Your best, mind," Tegestu said. "We don't want any half-trained witlings blundering in the Abessu-Denorru's presence."

"Of course not, bro-demmin."

Tegestu was about to add another admonition, but then realized it was prompted only by his own impatience and petulance, that he was still upset over the blundering duel that afternoon, and by his spies' blundering as well, if blundering it was. He changed the subject. "Any reports from Neda-Calacas?"

"Nay, bro-demmin. No change reported."

"Very well." He rose, Cascan standing with him. "You will excuse me, ban-demmin. I have a busy schedule."

"May your arm never weaken."

"May your eyes never fail you, whelkran i cambrani." He and Cascan bowed to one another, then to the Blue Scroll. Tegestu began the walk to his chambers.

Fiona, he thought. What kind of name is that? There was so much out of place concerning her, and it fretted him. Why couldn't Cascan get to the bottom of it? He snorted. Strange locks, indeed. Incompetence was far more likely.

Well, the best spies were being deployed toward Neda-Calacas. No doubt they would best serve there.

He put the conjuror from his mind. Cascan had never failed him on this kind of assignment before, and if Cascan failed—well, then there were always the witches.

7

The palace of Acragas was ablaze with light, and busy with revelers in their hundreds and servants in their thousands. It was a vast brawl of people: the oligarchs on horseback, surrounded by retainers with their torches, their women in gilded litters that glowed red in the flame; other people of importance coming by barge, the prows carved with the images of sea serpents, dragons, or the mallanto of Arrandal, the long-winged seabird with its fierce beak and wise, pale-gold eyes. It was the Fete of Pastas Netweaver, the god of judgement who had learned wisdom from the dragons of the Farthest Isles, and who, not coincidentally, was Acragas Necias' patron deity, appearing with his curragh and net-of-souls on the Acragas banner.

Fiona, with her urchin hired to help her carry her trunk of tricks, came quietly in the tradesmen's entrance, a dark cloak over her scarlet performing gown. There were Brodaini guards in addition to the militia, which surprised her, and she was further surprised by being taken aside to a small room so that her baggage and then herself could be searched. The Brodaini seemed particularly interested in her trunk and insisted on inspecting all her paraphernalia, and on her making clear the function of each device. The spindle she claimed as a musical instrument, and produced sounds from it to prove it—the rest, her various props, she claimed privileged, though she let them examine each to prove to themselves it could not be used as a weapon. Then the males left and she was forced to undress under the businesslike eyes of the two women Brodaini, who turned her gown inside out, looking for secret pockets—they found many, though none of them were yet filled with her tricks. They insisted on her stripping completely, and for a moment she felt unease as she slipped out of the privy-coat that protected her; except for her visits to the public baths, where she'd sat in a cabinet tub while hot water was poured into it by brawny women working behind the screen, it had never been removed. The Brodaini searching the garment scowled at the unfamiliar catches and the strange material, but let it pass. They even combed her hair for strangling-wires, and probed elsewhere, intimately elsewhere, looking for poison capsules. No one else seemed to have been accorded this treatment. Fiona tried to submit with a good grace. It was, after all, a sign that she'd aroused their curiosity.

Afterward they summoned a maid to help her get laced into her gown again—they didn't seem to have any experience in that area themselves—and bade her a polite farewell. The maid was young and intoxicated, though whether with wine or excitement was not apparent. Making her way to the Great Hall, Fiona passed among a glittering forest of armor, halberds, and two-handed swords.

Once inside the Great Hall of the Acragas, however, there seemed little security at all. Servants, performers, guests, all milled about attracting little attention from the Acragas militia posted about the room. Fiona went backstage to prepare her act, made all ready, and then, since she would not be on till late, stepped out to watch the crowd as they entered. The privileged guests moved to the dining room for a feast, and the rest dined informally. She supped on a surprisingly good fish-and-porridge pie, sipped her ale, and talked with a pair of jugglers who were also awaiting their cue.

Then the trumpets cried out, filling the great room to the rafters and stilling all talk, and Acragas Necias walked into the room with his train of wives and cousins. Cheers and applause drowned the trumpets. Fiona stood on a bench for her first good look at the merchant-king of Arrandal, the man who had created the Elva and brought the Brodaini from their cold and violent northern land.

He was impressive, in spite of rather than thanks to the elaborate, lace-decorated, jewelled doublet and the fur-embroidered short jacket worn over one shoulder. The clothing was far too gaudy to be in good taste, and he did not wear it comfortably—it constrained him; there was an immense vitality in the man that was not to be inhibited by mere fashion.

He was tall enough to look a tall Brodainu in the eye, broad-shouldered, and barrel-chested, and was still a powerful figure despite the great pendulous belly that was roped in, with great lack of success, by his wide belt. He walked with an assured, unconscious swagger, his first wife on one arm; she, a thin, hatchet-faced, cunning-looking woman, awkwardly matched his long-legged paces. He did not bother to match hers, but moved massively around the room at speed, bellowing greetings, laughing loudly, seeing friends across the hall and rushing to embrace them, his wife dragged along on his arm like a doll in the hands of a heedless child.

Necias' round face with its fringe of dark hair, small eyes, and multiple chins bespoke a fierce animal vitality, bold self-reliance, and a confidence that seemed near-inspiring. A perfect example, Fiona thought, of a man of this time. A self-made man, of course: the Acragas had been a minor family before Necias had made them the most influential of all.

There was a group of Brodaini that followed, their upright bearing and simple clothing and armor standing out in this mob of embroidery and jewels. There was a lot of bowing and deferring to an old grey-haired Brodainu, and suddenly Fiona realized she was looking at Tegestu, their chief—a fierce-looking fellow still, tall, lean, and broad-shouldered in his armor. He must have been a terrifying warrior in his day, Fiona thought, though now he seemed to walk carefully, and with a hint of weariness. There were a pair of older Brodaini with him, a strapping woman about Tegestu's age and another younger, though greying, man: the rest were all eagle-eyed young men, the Brodaini and their servants both, and Fiona recognized among them some of those who had searched her. The Brodaini stayed near Necias, she saw, and some of their liveried servants mixed with the oligarch's hangers-on. A sensible precaution, she thought, in this atmosphere of war: she wondered if Necias even realized such care was being taken.

Necias and his party made a circuit of the room, greeting his guests, ending up at Fiona's bench last of all. She stood to greet him, bowing with a flourish, and saw two Classani step quietly to either side of the Abessu-Denorru, ready to intercept a weapon. Necias simply nodded at her, a broad smile creasing his face, and said: "A lovely gown, young woman. Scarlet suits you. I like the hood as well. Isn't it a lovely gown, Brito?" Fiona suddenly realized that his front teeth were artificial.

"Very appropriate," said the eldest wife in an uninterested tone, and the party passed on.

Necias returned to his place, and at a signal the many lamps that lit the entire hall were all extinguished, leaving only a thousand candles flickering outside the footlights on the stage. An orchestra began to play for its gallery. The music was intricate and compelling, the bass carrying a theme forward while the alto and tenor embroidered their way around it: and then a full-voiced chorus began to sing out from above, and Fiona realized this was a hymn to the god Pastas, of how he had learned wisdom from the dragons, who had created the world and stars, and how he had eventually surpassed even the dragons in knowledge, such that he counselled the dragons against beginning their war with the great sea-demons, who had created the watery universe and the things that dwell there—a war that destroyed the world and the deep and most of mankind, that resulted in the extinction of the sea-demons and the decimation of the dragons, who now, few in number, have retired to their hidden islands and dream away the eons, leaving the universe to the gods and their pets, the humans.

Was it memory of a great catastrophe, Fiona wondered, that had prompted this myth? Were the ancestors of these people, and of Fiona herself, disguised as the wonder-working, too-wise, and dreaming dragons? Or was there simply something in the nature of humankind that demanded a catastrophe myth? Her own world had them in abundance, different in detail though somehow alike in flavor: there were always a few virtuous chosen who survived the disaster, whatever it was—here it was inundation by the sea that seemed most universal; on her own world it was a holocaust of fire.

The choral hymn slowed, then came to an end; it was followed by a clear counter-tenor, with minimal accompaniment from the orchestra, who sang bell-like praise to the god; and then the chorus and orchestra boomed back in for a splendid fortissimo finale that had the hall ringing with applause. The composer, a chinless, shock-haired wonder, came out for his bow, and Necias gave him a jewel from his finger, while many others flung him purses.

There followed a mechanical marvel, a metal mallanto

that cocked its head, raised a very real shellfish between its webbed front toes and opposable claw, and bit down with an audible crunch from the curved beak; it then spread its wings and gave a great inspiring cry while its eyes winked golden fire. More applause, and another purse from Necias for the inventor.

There were acrobats, then, and the jugglers; afterwards there was a noisy intermission followed by the poet Campas. He was about thirty, small and slightly-built, with curling dark hair worn longer than that of most of the men present. He dressed simply, in somber colors—to stand out, Fiona supposed—but there was a white scarf thrown dashingly around his neck, and he wore a multitude of rings that flashed as he turned the pages of his manuscript.

The poem was clearly a part of a larger work, written to the specifications of some poetic tradition or other, and Fiona lost interest quickly amid a hopeless array of muses, minor deities, allusions to other poems in the cycle, appearances by past poets operating under a bewildering array of pseudonyms, woebegone shepherds longing after shepherdesses of ethereal beauty and cast-iron chastity . . . and then, just as she was prepared to go to sleep for the duration, something made her sit up and take notice. His use of language was beautiful, Fiona thought, even though his subject matter was dead as the mechanical mallanto; his rhythms were perfect, his word-order exact and not over-clever, the vowel sounds ringing changes throughout the verse that echoed and sang: and sometimes, even when describing something as hackneyed as a young swain's sighs for his mistress, or the disillusioned 'prentice abandoning the corruption of the city for the blissful simplicity of a shepherd's life, he managed to introduce an invigorating breath of life into it. *This man is good,* she thought, excited, and applauded madly when he was done.

There were a pair of purses flung from the audience;

Campas picked them up, bowed again, and stepped from
the light. A fussy grey-haired man introduced the mimes
of Fastias. Fiona was next, so she slipped backstage again,
made certain she was ready, and waited for the introduction.

Backstage watching the mimes, she felt the blood pounding in her ears, and realized that, oddly, it was not fear she
felt, but simple excitement. At last these people would
know who she was, and why she had come.

She started with standard tricks, clear glass jars of water
disappearing, reappearing empty, the water itself appearing inside a cap she had acquired from a member of the
audience—good stuff, guaranteed to start the act with
laughter. There were more tricks along those lines, then
she began to cut things up and make them whole again,
and this was followed by the first major spectacle. A small
icon, the Amil-Deo, was placed on a table, and suddenly it
appeared, much enlarged, on the curtain behind her. She
could hear the audience shifting in their seats, and a
sudden murmur of astonishment: then enthralled gasps as
the Amil-Deo began to move, raising kings on high, each
more splendid than the last, before casting them down
again. When the trick faded the applause was deafening,
and she felt the thud of purses landing on the stage. She
ignored them, instead picking from her table a pair of
gleaming hollow tubes. She brandished them over her
head, feeling her back arch as she crossed them, rapping
one on the other.

"Good people, I beg your leave to tell a story," she
cried. "A story that may seem strange, a story full of
wonders, a tale that may even seem impossible." She
lowered her arms, standing plainly in front of them; she
lowered her voice as well, making them listen. "It is a
story, however, that is absolutely true." Her quiet voice,
her simple stance—it was all guileless, without artifice or
staginess, the more to convince them of her sincerity.

Fiona raised the tubes again and a white mist shot from them, spouting high into the air as her audience gasped in wonder. The fog hung between the audience and the rounded arches of the ceiling, a pale translucency that obscured the candles that flickered there; and then, as Fiona lowered the tubes and switched on her projectors, it seemed to those below as if the roof suddenly opened to reveal a cloudless, pitch-black sky, ablaze with the great glittering stars. The audience moaned in wonder.

"Behold the stars!" Fiona called. "The stars as the dragons first made them, the stars as they first glittered in the vault of the heavens on the first night of the new-born world. Here they sparkle, new-made, as they move in their courses." The stars were registered at local perspective: any navigator in the audience would have recognized them. They began to rotate, as if with the motion of the planet.

The Arrandalla were good astronomers and navigators; a hundred years ago they'd abandoned the Demro-centered concept of the universe and adopted the notion of their planet circling a star, with the laws of gravitation and planetary motion springing up a generation later, discovered simultaneously in half a dozen places. This understanding would make Fiona's explanation easier.

The stars slowed again, then stopped. The stars faded, and dawn began to blaze across the eastern sky. The sky lightened, turned to day. There was some scattered applause from people thinking it was the end of the trick.

"Let us take to ourselves the wings of the mallanto," Fiona said, stifling the applause before it could begin. "Let us take wing, and soar into the sky." And suddenly the perspective of the display changed; there was a lurching sensation, and then, coming into view, was the horizon, with Acragas' palace squatting recognizably in the foreground, the city stretching beyond, and after that the blue, gleaming water. There were cries from the audience, an audible buzz; and there was suddenly movement as a number of them bolted for the exits, making the sign against the evil eye.

The perspective swung dizzyingly as the view gyred, circling higher over the Acragas palace, catching here a glimpse of sky, of cloud, of the city walls, of the plains and rivers beyond. "Let us mount higher with the wings of the mallanto," Fiona chanted. "Let us climb into the sky and look down upon the creation of the dragons and of man."

The viewpoint looked down, at the shrunken palace and the city; and then it suddenly pulled back, the city fading away into a mosaic of brown plains, green wetlands, blue sea, all dotted with a scattering of cloud. There was a low moan from the audience, some overcome with vertigo— and there were the snowcapped peaks to the south, the greybrown land of the Brodaini, broken by mountain-teeth and the snaking white forms of glaciers, across the smoking northern sea. Still the perspective drew back until all of Demro hung in the void, snow-capped north and south, the white cloud constrasting with seas of the deepest blue, the dull-brown continents almost insignificant in the display of shocking colors. And around the glowing bluewhite globe burned the steady, suddenly nonflickering stars.

"Here we have mounted, above the world," Fiona said. "From here we can see the dragons' creation, all of Demro laid out below us. The creation of mankind, all the great cities, all the fields and nations and alliances—from here they are invisible, lost in the totality of the universe."

The perspective began to move again, Demro fading away into the midst of the stars, Demro's sun appearing in a blaze of white, both fading now with distance. "We journey now among the stars," Fiona said. "Higher even than the wings of the mallanto can take us. Here only the encompassing mind of the dragon can bring us. Demro fades to a distant speck of blue, and vanishes. Even the sun fades in the cold distance, until it is no more than a star. The dragon's dream is cold and lifeless, here in the barren spaces between the stars.''

In a slow moment the perspective changed again, rotating through 180 degrees until the viewpoint was dead ahead, the stars moving past as the simulation forged onward. This was not, Fiona knew, how the starfield moved at near-light speed—the reality was more spectacular, the stars refracting as they bent around the speeding mass of the ship—but this was straining her audience's understanding enough, without her delivering a disquisition on relativity physics.

A star moved into center view, growing brighter, its white light somehow bluer, fiercer. "Here," Fiona said, "a small star, another star of the dragons' making. But even at this immeasurable distance the dragons build true— for around this other star circles a world, another world. And it is a world where the dragons have, as here on Demro, created humanity.''

The new world appeared, a brown speck at first, hardly visible in the hard glare of the new star, then growing rapidly until it filled the display. There was much less water here, that was obvious: the brown areas greatly outnumbered the blue, and the patches of white around the poles were much smaller.

"The dragons made a harsher world here," Fiona said, "a warmer world, where water is rare, and greatly prized. Here the humans, battling the harsh conditions of the land, were forced to dig great networks of canals to water their land—not canals as they have here, to regulate the flood and speed commerce, but canals to bring water to thirsty crops." She showed her audience scenes of the other world: the great flatlands; the giant, branching canals reflecting the ruddy hues of the sky; the grey upthrust stone

of the mountains, cleft with black shadow; the deserts and
semi-deserts with their strange beasts.

"The people grew wise in the ways of their land, in the
ways of artifice. Their ambition grew, as did their
knowledge; and they yearned to move among the stars
with the wings of dragons." Here the simulation showed,
for the first time, the inhabitants of the other world: brown,
lithe, sturdy people, swift to laugh and swifter to smile,
draped in robes of bright color, moving among their low,
earth-colored houses—and Fiona's heart lurched, seeing
these carefully selected, carefully edited scenes of home.
A sudden, overwhelming yearning filled her as she viewed
this world she had so carelessly left behind, *her world,* the
world she could never expect to see again, except in these
dreams created for the enlightenment of these savages, for
if she ever returned to her homeland thousands of years
would have passed, and what she had known would be
long gone . . . She fell silent for a moment, swaying on
the stage, her prepared speech gone from her mind; but she
steeled herself, breathed carefully in and out, and then
spoke, her words coming swiftly as she tried to recover
lost ground.

"Wise they grew in the ways of alchemy, and of han-
dling metals. They harnessed the fires of the dragons.
Their priests were granted to know the stars about which
the dragons had created planets, and the planets where the
dragons had made humanity. Their alchemists wished to
know these other humans, to visit them, and to this end
they built a ship powered by dragonfire. A ship such as the
universe had not known, capable of moving between the
stars."

Here the display showed the great ship a-building on a
barren plain of the brown world—an outright lie, since the
ship had actually been built in orbit and could never taste
atmosphere, but Fiona could not expect her audience to

understand that. "The ship," she said, "was built of metal, smelted in the fire of the dragons, and was crewed by hundreds.

"But there was one problem," Fiona said. "The spaces between the stars were such that the ship would take years to complete its journey—not years only, but lifetimes. So the artificers of this world contrived to put the crew to sleep for the duration of the journey, and so built the ship that it might pilot itself, all with machinery." The simulation showed the crew in their glass-fronted coffins, moving down the rows of sleeping to a porthole that showed the stars. "And the ship rose at last, and moved among the stars with its sleeping crew," Fiona narrated, and the view showed the stars moving past, faster this time. "Years passed, and the crew slept, and the ship moved straight and true on its course, until another star approached."

The star appeared, and its blue-white planet; the viewpoint rushed downward, down through the cloud to the city of Arrandal and the palace of Necias—there were gasps from the audience as they recognized the endpoint of this journey—and then the perspective tilted up again, showing the night sky: the same night sky the simulation had shown first of all, different but in one detail.

"The ship, flying high over the land, appeared as a fixed, gleaming star," Fiona said, and there was a murmur among the crowd as the fixed star winked in the revolving heavens. "The crew of the ship rose from their beds and for two years studied the land below, before sending their people down to greet the humans, so like themselves, who lived in this strange world. But at long last the ambassadors came down from their ship, and travelled the long miles to greet you."

The vision faded, the white fog suddenly only fog, dissipating slowly in the drafts of the upper hall. And suddenly there was only Fiona, standing alone in the brightness of her scarlet gown, her hand at her throat. She raised the hand.

"From my world to yours, greetings," she said.

And the world changed.

8

In the mad pandemonium that followed, half the audience applauding, half near-riot, purses flying through the air, dozens breaking from their places to cluster up about the foreign conjuror as if she were a goddess come to earth, Necias thought quickly. He leaned toward Tegestu and bellowed: "Get her out of here! Someplace safe, and quiet!" Tegestu made a gesture and suddenly there was a wedge of Brodaini slicing through the crowd, its ardis aimed at Fiona. Necias felt the grip of Brito's hand on his arm.

"Get Campas!" she said, her eyes glittering with urgency. "Tell Campas to go with her!"

Necias nodded and roared the poet's name. There was another hand on his shoulder, a hand that glittered with rings, and Necias turned to give Campas his instructions. Campas listened with a strange, knowing, half-cynical smile, nodded, and then followed in the wake of the Brodaini. The woman was reached, cordoned off, snatched from the crowd. Classani swept through the crowd to pick up her table, her equipment, her trunk, her litter of purses.

Necias saw the bewildered, white-haired figure of his steward Ahastinas in the melee. He tried to signal Ahastinas to continue the program, but it was no use—Ahastinas was already banging his staff and shouting to no avail; the poor man was almost weeping with frustration.

Enough.

Necias lurched to his feet, climbed onto his stoutly-built settee, and cupped his hands to his mouth.

"Silence!" he roared. "Silence, all of you! *Silence!"*

That did the trick. The milling crowd grew less noisy and then stilled, staring up at him in surprise, the upturned faces demanding an explanation Necias could not provide.

"We will investigate this matter," Necias said, his voice sounding hollow in the stillness. "I'll have the heralds announce the results tomorrow. In the meantime," he said, gesturing brusquely, "the program will continue, after you return to your seats. Ahastinas, what's next on the program?"

"A new concerto by Naralidas Pastas, sir," Ahastinas quavered, and Necias clapped his hands.

"Excellent!" he bellowed. "The man's good!" He looked out at the crowd, then scowled. "Back to your seats, then, so the show can continue."

They moved, grudgingly, and Necias clambered carefully down from his perch and sat himself. Brito leaned over to whisper into his ear.

"Very well done, Necias."

"Thanks," Necias said, tugging at his ear and frowning. *Ai, gods,* he thought. What in the name of the dragons and demons did all this mean? If that girl was a charlatan he'd have the hide off her. But if she wasn't . . . no, it *had* to be trickery, or witchcraft. Had to be. The alternative was too dizzying.

As dizzying as the stars burning in the void, as dizzying as flying high above his palace on the wings of a mallanto

. . . He shook his head, clenched his fists. He'd get to the bottom of it, just wait.

There was the touch of a hand on his shoulder: Campas. "She's in the small conference room," he said. "Guards are keeping her safe. She said she'd be pleased to speak with you."

Necias tilted his head back, looking into his secretary's businesslike face. "Good," he said. "Has she said anything?"

There was an amused, smug gleam in Campas' eye. "She complimented me," he said, "on my verse." And then he frowned. "We didn't get all her gear out. Some of those people were after souvenirs."

Necias shook his head. "Couldn't be helped," he said. "Go stay with her. Don't ask any questions yet, but if she volunteers anything, write it down." He looked at the crowd, dispersing now, murmuring among themselves, still casting him looks ranging from bafflement to suspicion. "Make her comfortable, hey?" he said. "Give her anything she wants: food, drink, anything."

"Except her freedom, as I take it?" Campas asked, his tone light. Necias looked at him sharply, seeing the quick, cynical mockery in his eyes, and then gave his secretary a grin.

"Don't worry about that," he said. "She didn't cause a sensation like that just to disappear into the night, hey?" He jabbed a blunt finger into Necias' chest. "She's after something, my boy, and we'll just have to find out what it is. Cut along now."

Campas nodded and made his exit. The lights dimmed and the concerto began, but Necias found that his mind wasn't on it, and neither, he suspected, was anyone else's. The applause was desultory, the flung purses were few; and even the program's finale was a disaster. It was a one-act farce by one of the city's finer playwrights, guaran-

teed to send the audience on their way laughing, but every
joke fell flat, and the clowns sweated for every grudging
laugh. Necias was glad when it was over.

After that the dining rooms reopened for a later supper,
and the ballrooms for dancing, but Necias sent Brito to the
dining room to bring him a plate of food and a mug of
beer, dispatched his other wives and their escorts to play
hostess at the various other events, and then made his way
to the small conference room.

The conjuror Fiona was seated calmly, her hands folded
in her lap, on one of the three-legged Brodaini stools, with
Campas sitting, notes in hand, to her left. She had thrown
a grey shawl around her shoulders, and a half-drunk cup of
tea stood on a tray by her side. Fiona looked up as Necias
walked in, then rose, her skirt rustling. There was a dignity,
a gravity, in her bearing; she was, he thought, bearing
herself as an ambassador would, conscious that she was
representing not simply herself, but her people.

An "ambassador from the stars." Well, he thought,
we'll see.

"Sit," he said, waving an arm, and dropped onto his
settee. He put one of his feet up and watched Fiona as she
seated herself. Her eyes, black and calm, turned to his.
She seemed prepared to wait.

"You are comfortable?" he asked. "Would you like
another chair? Something to eat? Drink?"

"I thank you, Abessu-Denorru, but no," she said. Her
voice was self-possessed and calm, and Necias thought he
saw a hint of amusement at the corners of her mouth. Is
she amused, then? he wondered. At the fools she's made
of us with her trickery?

Necias leaned back suddenly, tapping one hand rest-
lessly on the arm of the settee as his nervous energy sought
an outlet. "What do I call you?" he asked. "Do you have
a title?"

"Not as such, no," Fiona said. "You can call me Ambassador, if you like. It's as good a description as any." Campas' pen began to scratch across his pad.

Necias frowned. "Ambassador" was a masculine noun; it didn't apply to women. But "Fiona" wasn't a standard Abessla name, with a feminine ending: it wouldn't clash quite as much with the title as, say, Luco or Brito would.

"Very well," Necias said. His hand tapped on the settee's arm twice, lightly, then he became conscious of the nervous gesture and halted it.

"You say you are from the stars," he said. "Are we to take this seriously, or was this merely a part of your act?"

"It was part of my act, yes," Fiona said. Her manner seemed a bit distracted, distanced, as if she were concentrating on choosing her words very carefully. "But I was very serious. I *am* from a star—or rather, from a planet circling another star. My planet is called Igara. You have seen the—the views of that planet I've provided." She paused, then added: "The star is visible from here. I'm not sure if your people have a name for it: I think not. But I can tell your astronomers where to find it."

Necias gave a jerk of his head. "Not necessary," he said. "One star's much the same as another."

Fiona smiled, then gave a serene nod. "Very true," she said.

What, Necias wondered, was the girl feeling? She seemed strangely relaxed in these circumstances, very cool, very loose—she ought to be keyed up, he thought. Instead it's as if she's terribly *relieved*.

There was a scratching at the door; Necias, annoyed at the interruption, barked out his query, and Brito's voice came in answer. Brito with his plate of food and mug of beer. Necias was suddenly aware of his hunger, of the cavernousness in him. This was going to be a long night: he'd need to keep alert. "Come in," he said.

Brito entered the room with a tray, plates heaped high with goose, roast pig, pickled eggs, grilled sea-rampalla, cheese. A maidservant followed with a pitcher of beer and a heavy mug. They set it down on the table in front of Necias' settee. Necias waited for the beer to be poured and then took the mug, taking a deep draught. He gestured to Fiona.

"Sure you don't want something?"

A gentle shake of the head. "No. Thank you."

"Campas?"

The poet looked at the heap of food, then nodded. "Yes. A little goose and cheese, I think."

"You," Necias said, addressing the maidservant. "Go fetch it."

"Yes, Abessu-Denorru."

The girl bobbed her goodbyes and went. Necias looked from Brito to Fiona.

"This is Brito," he said, "my cenors-censto."

"Honored," said Fiona.

"Fiona," Necias told Brito, "says she is from another planet." He picked up a slice of pig and devoured it.

"I heard," said Brito.

"We all heard," Necias nodded, beginning to enjoy himself. This was something he well understood: the complexity of negotiation, of truth-finding, here in this little, familiar room. Fiona wouldn't stand against it: he'd get the truth tonight, crack her composure somehow. He took another swallow of beer, watching the faces in the room, Fiona with her smile, Campas with his pen poised, his face set in a slight frown as if contemplating a problem, the two Brodaini guards with their elaborate hairstyles and arrogant, masklike faces.

Brito was watching Fiona closely, he saw. She was a good judge of character; he'd keep her in the room and ask her opinion later.

"Sit by me, stansisso," he said. "Keep my mug full."

"Yes, husband." Brito sat on one of the hard Brodaini stools. Necias wiped his greasy fingers on his jacket and turned his eyes to Fiona.

"Another planet." he repeated. "Can you offer any evidence?"

"I have already offered a great deal," Fiona answered promptly.

"Witchcraft, perhaps. Demralla witchcraft—it doesn't have to come from another planet."

"If you can find a local witch who can duplicate my performance, your supposition, Abessu-Denorru, can be proven. Until then, not." The conjuror's answer came pat. Necias grinned.

"You sound like you've been to Fastias' Academy of Rhetoric," he said, tugging an ear. Fiona smiled at the statement. Necias held up a finger. "But it's not my place to offer proof," he said. "That job is yours. Prove what you say—and prove it now." He lowered his voice to a menacing seriousness, fixing Fiona with his eyes, his gaze holding hers. For the first time she seemed uneasy, shifting on her seat. "Prove it," he said quietly, "or get out of my city."

There was a moment of silence in which Necias could hear the blood pounding triumphantly in his ears, and Fiona pursed her lips slightly, her black eyes turning abstractedly upward. Then she turned to Necias.

"What," she asked, "would you consider proof?"

"That's up to you," Necias said. "You claim to have come alone from some other planet—no heralds, no credentials, no escort—and of all the cities on Demro you come to mine, but you live like a spy for days before revealing yourself. I'm flattered," he said, bowing with his hand on his chest, an exaggeration of humility. "I'm flattered, but I find all this suspicious. I need more proof than you've shown so far."

Fiona held up a hand. "I understand," she said. "I can, of course, give you credentials—I can provide them tonight, if you give me leave to walk on the roof, or in some courtyard, and let me take my trunk with me." She lowered her hand, then continued: "But you misunderstand. I never said I was alone. Igara has sent ambassadors to other cities, other nations—to all the cities of the Elva, and to the Clattern i Clatterni of Gostandu. You can inquire of the other cities, if you wish."

Necias grunted in surprise and sat back in his chair. He saw the two Brodaini guards, startled enough to drop their masks for an instant, give one another alarmed glances— the Clattern i Clatterni, King of Kings, was the Brodaini princeling who had conquered their entire continent, driving Tegestu, his clan, and the other mercenary clans into exile; Necias could well understand the Brodaini being disturbed. But Necias was more appalled by another implication of what the conjuror had said.

"*All* the cities of the Elva?" he grunted in astonishment. "Including Neda-Calacas?"

Fiona nodded. "Yes. Neda-Calacas as well," she said.

"Ai, gods!" Necias leaned forward, anger filling him. "What were your people thinking of?" he demanded. "Neda-Calacas is an outlaw city, a renegade! All embassies will be withdrawn. And then the rebels will be destroyed."

Fiona looked solemnly into his eyes. "Igara has no quarrel with Neda-Calacas, or with any other city or institution. We take no sides in your wars. We will deal with anyone who will deal with us."

Necias frowned, then took a piece of grilled rampalla and gobbled it while he thought. "*Deal*," he said. "You said *deal*. What kind of deal are you after?"

"Trade," Fiona said simply. "We are interested in your people, your—your artifacts. Metalwork, painting, sculpture, your ideas, your—" She nodded to Campas. "—your poetry."

"And you will pay for this?" Necias asked, still frowning.

"In gold, if you like," Fiona said. "We have a supply. We also ask permission to make certain—suggestions and criticisms," she said. "Suggestions and criticisms that may help you, though you may feel free to disregard them if you wish. There are conditions attached to this, however—we insist that any suggestions we make be shared by all, and not benefit any one person or city."

Necias scowled and shook his head. The girl wasn't making sense. "I don't understand," he said. "What sort of suggestions are you talking about?"

"Suggestions that may alert you to possibilities of which you may not have been aware. Suggestions that may help you with, for instance, trade, or with, say, alchemical knowledge. Suggestions that may, in the end, help you to travel between the stars, as we have travelled."

Necias drained his mug and held it out to Brito to be refilled, certain there was something wrong with what he was hearing. This was ridiculous—no one offered knowledge like that free of charge.

There was a scratching at the door, and he barked out a curt order to enter. It was Luco, his youngest wife, carrying a tray. She was flushed, and her eyes were wide as she looked at Fiona; then she swallowed and turned to Necias.

"I brought Campas' tray," she said. A transparent excuse: clearly enough she'd just wanted to see the woman from another planet, and perhaps hear part of the discussion.

"Our husband sent someone else to that task," Brito said, her tone sharp. "We do not carry trays for our husband's employees."

"I'm sorry, stansisso Brito," she said, stepping into the

room, putting the tray on Campas' table. She stepped back nervously, her eyes moving from Necias to Fiona and back again, her stance awkward, unwilling to tear herself away. Necias gave her an impatient glance.

"Get out or sit down!" he snapped. "I don't care which!"

Luco jumped at his tone, flushing, then murmured, "Thank you, husband," and rushed to a settee, sitting in a rustle of skirts. Necias could feel Brito's annoyance: it was Brito who had a place here, as official hostess; Luco did not. Perhaps Brito was angry at what she might think was favoritism, but it seemed a small concession for him to make. Luco was curious, and Necias saw no reason to deny her curiosity. Let her listen, and if it would make her happy then he saw no reason to forbid her presence. Happy wives were better than unhappy ones, to be sure.

He turned his mind away from partillo matters and sipped beer while considering what Fiona had said. Suggestions, knowledge, offered by these planet-people. Offered gratis, it appeared; they even asked permission.

Well. He'd approach it one step at a time, until he saw the flaw: then he'd pounce.

"These suggestions you want to make," he said. "What kind of suggestions are you talking about?"

Fiona inclined her head. "This is a suggestion I have been authorized to make, as an example." Fiona said. "We've observed your ships. They have difficulty sailing into the wind, do they not?"

"True," Necias said impatiently. It was an elementary fact, known to all. The ships, with their square sails, could only sail efficiently downwind, though with very careful bracing and a heavy hand on the rudder a ship could be brought very slightly into the wind, though not far enough to change the basic fact that upwind sailing was unknown. The fact had brought disaster often enough—sometimes entire trading fleets were pinned on a lee shore, unable to beat away from the rocks, and were torn to pieces when their anchors dragged.

Entire trade patterns were based on these simple facts of sailing. In the spring a gentle, warm southerly wind came over the passes, and the trading cities like Arrandal, their fleets made ready over the winter, sailed north to Gostandu and the northern Elva cities, their hulls bulging with trade goods. Then, after a late-summer period of storms, a blustery, cold northern wind came down from the lands of ice, blowing the fleets back to their home ports with their foreign-made goods, accompanied by fleets from the northern Elva cities which would winter in the south until the winds changed again. In the spring and summer, ships from the north found it next to impossible to journey to the south, beating against the wind the entire way: and in the winter there was no possibility whatever of fighting the hard northern winds to travel across the seas from the south. Urgent messages that had to be sent against the wind had to be carried on oared galleys, rowing madly at a fantastic cost in rowers, who had to be paid well for their efforts.

"We can't sail into the wind," Necias said. "That's elementary. What of it?"

"We can sail into the wind," Fiona said, "on Igara."

"With dragonfire?" Necias asked. "Puffing from behind, to fill your sails?" He saw a smile flit across Campas' face as the secretary wrote down his question.

"You will have to change the style of your sails," Fiona said solemnly, refusing to rise to Necias' bait. "You will do better to have the yards of your sails—some of the sails, anyway—arranged to lie fore-and-aft on your ships rather than athwart them." She looked up at Necias, bright-eyed. "Try it, anyway. Take a small ship and experiment. I think you'll find that I'm right."

Necias's brows came together as he considered the suggestion. "I don't understand," he said. "What difference can it make? And how d'you mean, alter the yards?"

"May I have a piece of paper?" Fiona asked. "I'll illustrate."

She took pen and paper from Campas and drew some simple figures of ships as seen from the top, little wedges, with dots for masts and arcs for sails. "This is the sort of sail you use presently," she said, pointing. "Try to arrange the sails more like this. Fore-and-aft, you see?"

Necias ate bits of pork and considered. It sounded absurd to him, but if it worked—*if* it worked—as she said it would, the results would be stunning. It would be possible to get trade information across the sea, instead of having to wait half a year for the wind to change. Trade could be increased. Could be doubled, perhaps; places formerly inaccessible could be reached in all weathers. *If* the scrawls on the paper meant anything.

He'd give the orders tomorrow, to modify a small boat. What harm would it do?

"And there's nothing you ask in return for this piece of information?" Necias asked. "Nothing at all?"

There was a slight hesitation before Fiona's reply. "We intend that this knowledge be considered part of my credentials, proof that I am who I say I am. We ask nothing of you in return: only that the suggestion be distributed to Arrandal as a whole," she said, returning the pen and pad to Campas, "so that anyone who wishes can make use of it. Igara is not interested in giving information solely for the benefit of a few."

Necias nodded, frowning, wondering how slow distribution could be and still be considered distribution. If he couldn't be the sole beneficiary of this new system— assuming of course that it worked—he could certainly take a great deal of the credit to himself, by arranging to give it to the city. Likewise with any other bits of wisdom to come from the conjuror.

The time of Acragas Necias, he thought, the time when people came from the stars, and the world leaped forward. His name would never be forgotten. . . .

And then he shook the dream from his head. Not proven, he thought, nothing proven. He looked at his hand, seeing the fingers drumming on the settee arm again, and stopped himself, annoyed. There was something that didn't fit, here.

"You want to give us knowledge," he said. "And give it for free. Why?"

"It will help us to communicate with you," Fiona said, "if we share a common knowledge with your people. But understand this, please: we won't be making suggestions like this very often. This particular suggestion was just to help me prove my identity, that I am who I say I am."

"Why not simply hand out all the information you possess?" Necias demanded. "It doesn't make any sense that you're so particular."

Fiona nodded gravely. "I'm sorry, Abessu-Denorru, but it's a necessary stipulation," she said. "There are reasons for it—perhaps at another time I'll be free to tell you. But now is not the appropriate time."

Necias felt a nagging dissatisfaction. There was something wrong in what he was hearing, something beside Fiona's refusal to explain the logic behind her stipulation, but he couldn't find it. He gulped at his beer to buy a little time while he thought, his eyes scanning over those in the room, Campas with his little frown, Brito with her hard, intelligent eyes, Luco with her mouth open in an expression of reverent awe . . . the girl was staring at Fiona as if the goddess Lipanto had materialized in the room complete with dogs and horn. He scowled into his beer and then put the mug down.

"Credentials," Necias said. "You said you could provide them."

"I can send for them, if you think they'd help," she
said. "You realize why I wasn't carrying any—you couldn't
tell them from forgeries. But, as I said earlier, if you will
allow me access to the roof, or a small courtyard, I can
produce them."

"From your trunk?" Necias asked cynically; and to his
astonishment he was suddenly aware of a glare from Luco—
Luco, of all people!—who was glowering at him as if he
had just committed gross blasphemy. He stared back at
her, challenging, and she colored and dropped her eyes.

Fiona looked at her trunk on the floor, undisturbed by
Necias' sarcasm, then glanced up at Necias. "I think
you'll be satisfied as to the documents' origin," she said.
"Can you give me a place?"

"The checkered terrace," Necias said. "It's private—
just outside my own apartments." He rose from the settee,
his knees cracking; it felt good to be able to move again,
to work off the nervous agitation that was gnawing at him.

"Follow me," he said, and then gestured to the two
Brodaini guards. "Take her trunk," he said.

He could hear the sound of music and conversation from
the fete as he stepped into the corridor. He turned left,
away from it, and moved swiftly through the lantern-lit
corridors until he came to his own apartments.

Here was a broad room where he entertained private
guests, with an efficient peat-burning stove on one end and
a vast, much less efficient fireplace that burned rare and
precious wood—a display of anildas common among the
deissin—on the other. The settees were plush and comfortable; tapestries, the products of Arrandalla looms, hung
rustling on the walls, depicting important moments in the
history of Arrandal, including the victories over Neda-
Calacas and Cartenas and the formation of the Elva, all of

which featured Necias prominently; imported rugs lay on the floor three-deep, Necias' feet sinking to the ankle as he walked; there were desks and stools for clerks in case contracts had to be recorded; and there was a bronze-faced door that led to the partillo. Necias walked swiftly through the room, wishing he'd thought to bring his tray with him, then unlocked a small door and pushed out of the door into the cool night.

The checkered terrace was small, fifteen paces square, and flagged with black and white slate diamonds. Gargoyles decorated the sandstone railing that surrounded the terrace on two sides; below, to the right, the canal glittered coldly in starlight. Necias turned, puffing with the exertion of his swift pace, and saw Fiona, stepping swiftly to keep up, walk out onto the terrace, her red gown swirling about her ankles. Luco was on her heels, almost stumbling in her eagerness, with Campas, looking a bit indignant about this haste, following after, his pad jammed under his arm, his inkpot and pen balanced in his hands. Then came the two impassive Brodaini, carrying Fiona's small trunk between them—and then last of all came Brito, carrying Necias' tray, and Necias smiled and took it from her, kissing her cheek. Brito gave him a careful look.

"That conjuror is mad, Necias," she said, lowering her voice so Fiona couldn't hear. "A good witch, but mad. Mind she doesn't bewitch you."

Necias shook his head. "That's not what she's after," he said.

"What is she after, then?"

Necias looked carefully at the small woman standing alone in the center of the square. "I don't know. Yet," he said.

"Put it down over there," Fiona said, gesturing toward one of the far corners, and the Brodaini obeyed, then retired to the door. Fiona turned to the others.

"This will take a while," she informed them. "Perhaps you'd be advised to get a cloak or shawl while you wait—it's cool out here."

Necias began clearing his tray of food as he watched Fiona kneel by the trunk for the space of three minutes or so; then she closed the lid, rose, and faced them. "Now we wait," she said. "I think it would be wise if we all left the center area clear." She looked up, her eyes searching the sky. "I don't think we'll see anything," she added. "There's too much cloud tonight."

Too much cloud for her mallanto to find our city, Necias thought wryly. *That will be her excuse when nothing happens.*

Fiona walked to stand beside one of the gargoyles. She was straight as an arrow, a lone figure in her gown that seemed, in this light, the color of blood. Her eyes turned skyward every few seconds. No one spoke; only the sounds of the canal below, those and an occasional distant snatch of music carried to them by a gust of wind, broke the silence. Necias cleared his plate and began to pace, seeking an outlet for the restless energy he felt coiled inside him; he kept to the periphery of the terrace, though he knew not why.

Then Fiona cast her eyes upward suddenly, as if she'd heard something above; and Necias looked up himself, and then realized everyone was doing it. They had all heard it, whatever it was: some kind of whisper in the night, a sound somehow *unnatural,* that should not be there. Necias looked upward, feeling the strain in his neck, his eyes moving across the skyscape, the long, high chains of clouds crossing the stars, their undersides reflecting the silver moonrise. *There!* Was that a shadow crossing the clouds? No—it had gone, there was no way of telling.

But then there was a hiss of air like the sound of the north spring wind whipping through the gargoyles on the palace roof, and suddenly all the stars were blotted out. Necias staggered, thunderstruck with the sight; he heard a cry from Luco, gasps from the others, the earnest whisper of one of the Brodaini chanting something—a prayer for deliverance? A charm against witches?—in his own language.

It was a vast metal *thing,* winged, massive, delta-shaped with the blunt end forward, hovering with its outlines indistinct in the darkness—and suddenly lights stabbed out from its underside, illuminating the terrace in a harsh, merciless yellow light. Necias saw Fiona's scarlet dress flash like a blaze in the light, her arm upraised in a gesture of welcome; and then something came falling out of the dazzling light, something that thudded onto the terrace with a metallic ring.

The lights winked out, and as Necias' dazzled eyes tried to adjust to the darkness he received an impression of the winged thing vanishing into the dark, wind hissing from its wings. Nearby Necias heard the sound of a woman sobbing, then a rush of skirts, and Luco had her arms around him, pressing her cheek into his barrel chest. "It's true!" she cried. "She's from the *stars!*" Her voice was hysterical, though not, Necias realized, from fear. He recognized with surprise the touch of ecstatic, mad joy in it, the same rapture he'd heard in the voices of the priestesses of the god Plantas as they raced through the streets on their god's day, drinking their spiced liquors until they were giddy and flogging one another in their madness until their white robes were spotted with blood. He looked at Luco in shock, then forced his eyes to return to Fiona.

She had stepped into the center of the terrace, kneeling to the object that had dropped, some kind of tube of white metal that had partly crumpled with the impact. Necias lowered his eyes to watch her, his arms going around Luco as she wailed into his chest. Fiona detached one end of the tube, and with some difficulty got a rolled shape out of the crumpled form. A scroll.

Necias' mind, laboring still through the awe and surprise, began to cry aloud the opportunity. Acragas Necias, it said, founder of the Elva and the Hundred-Year Peace, the man who sponsored the star-people for the good of all Arrandal.

He would do it, he thought. His name would never be forgotten.

Fiona walked toward him, the tube clattering on the flags, offering the scroll.

"My credentials," she said.

Luco sobbed on in her ecstatic madness. He lifted his hand from her shoulder and took the scroll.

9

Fiona, yawning in her bedroom, scratched her head and opened the window overlooking the canal to bring some morning air into her small room. She was in the Acragas palace now, in a comfortable series of apartments, locked away—thank goodness—from her admirers in the city. Their early response to her appearance had been hysterical. That first day there had actually been a riot, thousands of people shouting her name, trying to storm the gates of the palace in hopes of a glimpse of her. Dozens had been trampled, two small children had died. She had, at her own insistence, appeared on the walls, hoping to calm them—the sight had been terrifying. A roaring mob, surging and eddying like the tide, reaching up to her, screaming her name, worshipping, crying, *demanding* . . . demanding things she did not understand, and could not give. A visitor from the sky, the story had spread, who would distribute wealth and happiness to all, and who had miraculous powers. A goddess, perhaps. Certainly not an ordinary mortal.

She'd told them to go, but they hadn't listened: there was

so much noise she hadn't been able to make herself heard. In the end, after they'd started piling into boats and trying to get through the water gate, Necias had the militia turned out, and they were dispersed. In the eight days since then no more mobs had appeared, but there were still far more people than normal outside the gate, many of them gazing wistfully upward; and there had been a steady line of petitioners presenting themselves, hoping to interest the starwoman in their ideas, or hoping for relief from their problems.

She was almost at the point of envying Kira. Kira had made her announcement to Neda-Calacas two days after Fiona, at a massive celebration that their new Brodaini ruler, Tastis, had proclaimed to announce his policy of normalization—which meant, apparently, that he had enough of his prospective opponents under arrest that he could afford to take most of his soldiery off the streets. Kira, speaking over the spindle, had been ecstatic about the success of Fiona's performance, and apprehensive about her own.

But the performance had gone well, and she had been invited to move into the Brodaini quarters, where servants had been provided to attend to her needs. In her case the government hadn't asked for the proof Necias had required: no atmosphere craft had descended on Tastis' keep, nor had there been mobs of hysterical people rampaging outside her doors—the Brodaini had seen to that—but instead a number of civilized meetings with Tastis and his aldran, at which they asked respectful questions and appeared impressed by her answers. She had, as agreed, given them the idea of the fore-and-aft sail, and they'd agreed to study it. Tastis, Kira had reported with surprise, was *charming*— she hadn't expected charm from a Brodainu.

So Kira was prospering, and it was Fiona who had to cope with the mobs. The worst were the cases of sickness. Desperate people, knowing they were dying, had been coming in swarms—or, most horribly, they'd brought their children for healing: mothers with pale, limp forms in their arms, weeping, shouting, pleading. . . . There had been nothing Fiona could do. The conditions of her mission forbade it. In the end she'd asked Necias to make a proclamation to the city: Fiona was not a healer, could offer no advice to the physicians and surgeons who already existed in abundance.

A lie, and a heartbreaking lie. There was so much Fiona could do even without taking up the practice of medicine: most illness here was caused by bad sanitation and bad diet, these and the nonsterile conditions of the home and the surgery . . . but such aid was forbidden, until these people came up with the notion of sterility and sanitation themselves. Then she might—*might*—be able to give them some ideas. If, in the meantime, they asked her in the right way, she could at least present them with ideas that might tend to lead them in the right direction.

To help or not to help? Every decision had implications that were terrifying, each raised another dilemma in its place. Dilemmas that she, her cohorts, and her eventual successors would live with all their working careers. "Learn," she'd been told, "to accept the conditions of these people's existence. Learn to accept the fact that most will die young, and that most will live in wretchedness their entire lives. Your duty lies not to them, but to their descendants. And to *your* descendants. Remember that."

She tried her best to remember, but their and her descendants were so far away, and the present wretchedness so apparent. . . . She tried her best not to think about it, to stay here in the Acragas palace and get as much of her work done as possible.

There had been, for example, an entire day spent training the town's watchmen and criers, plus delegates from the majority of the deissin and the deissin themselves, in her mission, her presence here. She had to be very careful in presenting herself: what she could do, what she could not. She would *not* be involved in politics; she would *not* give military advice; she would *not* act as an oracle. For the present, she announced, she wanted only to live in the city and grow acquainted with it. Afterwards, perhaps, she would be able to offer a suggestion or two.

And in the meantime the Acragas project, altering the rigging of a small coastal barge in conformity with her design, was proceeding. It had sailed up and down the harbor a few times, but there had been problems with the sheets controlling the radically new sail—it was a primitive lugsail, she noticed, not a lateen or gaffsail; her diagram could have resulted in any of the three—and there were other difficulties with staying the mast. Yet the crew were enthusiastic, and would continue working with it. Necias seemed pleased.

Fiona saw Necias every day, and he had provided her with a staff of servants who, no doubt, were instructed to spy on her as much as possible. Necias' visits were not long—there was much weighing him down now, with the preparations for war with Neda-Calacas—but he seemed genial, well-disposed toward her, and full of plans. There were also a great many social invitations, many of which had to be declined, but Fiona felt obliged to visit as many of the prominent deissin as possible; she didn't wish them to think the Acragas family was monopolizing her. She wanted to make it clear that they could have access to her, should something arise—though what that something was, neither she nor they yet had any clear idea. The lugsail idea, if it worked, was going to wreak a massive enough change in trading patterns. That change would have to be analyzed before any others were contemplated.

For the most part Fiona intended simply to talk to people. Her own servants first of all, starting with her secretary Acragas Palvas, a junior member of the Acragas family employed chiefly to write the endless numbers of replies beginning with: "The Ambassador Fiona of Igara regrets that she cannot . . ." He was an odd, awkward young man, compensating for his awkwardness by a fussy insistence on correctness. Fiona suspected that he was secretly scandalized by her. He was, she thought, doomed to this kind of role all his life: he was undistinguished except by his rigidity and punctilio, and probably was intelligent enough to know it. Perhaps, she thought, he would have been happier in the more formal, militarized society of the Brodaini, where everyone was careful to know his station and observe the forms; here among the Arrandalla he was sadly misplaced.

The others of her staff, a pair of maidservants who were also trained to act as hostesses when the situation demanded, were more forthcoming. They seemed all blushes and giggles at first, and it took some time before Fiona understood why: to these girls the idea of a woman ambassador was so unheard of it was *titillating,* a naughty joke. She was, to them, a minor indecency.

Fiona persevered: if she couldn't communicate with these two young women there was very little hope for the rest of her tasks. Gradually they opened to her; under Fiona's persistent prodding, they began to regard her less as an official and more as a woman, and subject to womanly confidences. The women of the city—those of the wealthier classes, anyway, and those who served them—lived almost entirely in their own world, carefully bordered, the world of the partillo and the servants' hall. They rarely ventured out, and never alone: there was usually an older female relative, or if wealthy enough, liveried servants, to act as chaperones.

Their world was small, closed, intimate: there were no secrets between them. Both the maidservants considered themselves lucky: they'd both come from the lower artisan classes, families of leatherworkers and furniture makers respectively; and the Acragas family had bought their contracts when they'd reached their teens. They'd received training in acting as hostesses, and each had another valuable skill: Tibro, the elder by a year, had a fine singing voice and could play the flute, while Vico, surprisingly, was literate; her older brother had taught her to read. These various abilities raised their hopes for the marriage sweepstakes. If they were very lucky, they might have hopes of becoming a junior wife of some minor deissu or other, perhaps even an Acragas; otherwise the chances were good of becoming the wife of one of the other servants, some of whom were paid very well indeed— which would mean a stable life and a steady income, revolving around the excitement of the palace. On the whole, prospects were better than if they had stayed at home, where they would most likely have been married off to craft guildsmen, comrades of their fathers and probably much older than they; the guild system kept apprentices and journeymen too poor to marry.

Tibro and Vico were remarkably frank about these matters—and what they said was common enough knowledge, anyway. The social system of Arrandal, particularly as regarded respectable partnership and marriage, revolved around money. The deissin married one another's daughters in order to keep their wealth within a limited circle, and to stabilize trading relationships. The servants, guildsmen, and small traders spent much of their lives acquiring enough capital to marry and start a family; and ambitious working girls put aside much of their own meagre pay in order to make themselves more attractive to prospective husbands.

Illicit relationships, Fiona learned, had their financial aspect as well. Rich men, in addition to their various wives, often kept mistresses, usually without any attempt at concealing them: a mistress kept in style added to one's own status, since it proved one could afford her. Fiona would very much have liked to have talked to one of these women—perhaps later, after the furor of her arrival died down, she could arrange it.

The results of all these financial constrictions on sexual passion seemed clear: large-scale, open, and more or less legal prostitution, catering to all wages and tastes; plus a large and lively literature, both of unfulfilled longing and of adultery. When Fiona asked Tibro, the vocalist, to sing some songs of the common people, she complied with a series of ballads about chaste couples who, too poor to marry, are forced to love one another from afar for years, usually with the woman trying her best to avoid marriage to an older, more suitable candidate, before finally being able to marry—or, alternately, dying before they could fulfill their love for one another. Campas' elaborate poems about shepherds and shepherdesses living their frustrating and chaste lives, Fiona thought, made a little more sense against this background.

More lively were the songs about fornication. Usually these involved a young, junior wife married to an older deissu, and who acquired a lover her own age. Universally these women seemed to come to bad ends: dying at the hands of jealous husbands, betrayed by their lovers, condemned by the law, shut up in nunneries. The deissin had an active and jealous regard for their property, among which they most certainly counted their wives.

And so the ballads painted contrary pictures: one of ideal, continent couples locked in hopeless, unfulfilled love; the other of lusty young men and women cheerfully trysting in odd corners of the palace, hiding from the watchdogs of the doddering but jealous spouse. Two views of Arrandalla society, Fiona thought, with the truth probably lurking somewhere in between.

She'd reported her conclusions to the ship, and her surreptitious recording of Tibro's ballads were on file. Artifacts of a civilization, keys to help Fiona's successors live within this culture and perhaps to comprehend it, and to provide, in some future, material for an academic thesis, "Marriage and Morality in Classical Arrandal."

None of which, of course, would help her now.

Fiona leaned out her window, seeing a swift dispatch boat skimming over the canal below, a self-important little man sitting in the sternsheets with a dispatch case. She was three storeys above the green, sluggish canal, and the fresh southerly trade wind kept the smell at bay. Across the canal was a moored barge on which an old woman was stringing laundry that she'd just washed in the filthy water. Fiona thought of typhoid and shuddered.

There was a scratching on her bedroom door, and Tibro's soft voice. Fiona called her in. "Campas is here, Ambassador," Tibro reported. "He has a message from the Abessu-Denorru."

Fiona shook the woolly morning thoughts out of her head and blinked. "Very well," she said. "Show him into the study. Offer him tea or wine if he wants it. I'll be with him directly."

Tibro bobbed and backed from the room. Fiona changed from her sleeping-caftan to one of her receiving gowns —in her own apartments she'd given up wearing her privy-coat—and combed her hair into some kind of order, then stepped out of her bedroom, down a passage, and into her private study door. Campas, dressed in a tunic of dark red with the Acragas insigne, the god Pastas, on the shoulder, rose to greet her. She waved him back to his chair and found a chair herself.

"The Abessu-Denorru regrets he will be unable to visit you today," Campas said. "He'll be busy all day reviewing the army."

"I thank the Abessu-Denorru for his courtesy," Fiona said, wondering if this was the entire message.

"He has authorized me to tell you," Campas added, "that war with Neda-Calacas will be declared officially tomorrow, which will be followed shortly thereafter by declarations from all the cities of the Elva. The fleet will sail immediately to commence a blockade, and the army will march as soon as logistical preparations are concluded, probably in a few days."

Fiona nodded. "I thank the Abeissu Necias for the information," she said.

Campas leaned forward, lowering his voice to a more intimate tone, his ringed fingers linked in front of him. "Because of the policy complications bound to arise with all the allied armies in the field," he said, "the Abessu-Denorru will be accompanying the army himself, along with Marshal Palastinas and the drandor Tegestu. He would count it a favor, Ambassador Fiona, if you would accompany him."

Fiona felt her chin jerk upward in surprise, and she deliberately paused for a second, composing her answer.

"I am surprised," she said. "Why should the Abessu-Denorru feel my presence would be of value? I can give no military advice, you know."

Before Campas could answer came a scratching at the door, followed by Tibro's entering with tea and cakes. She bobbed to both of them, poured tea in silence, and then backed from the room, leaving the door open.

There was a reason for that open door, Fiona knew, and it annoyed her. Passion was so constrained in this society that it was assumed that if an unattached man and woman were alone for more than a few seconds, nature would take its course. That the couple might deny that anything transpired was counted for little: they were alone, yes? He is a man; she is a woman—what could be more natural? The door was open, not so that Tibro could spy on them, but rather so that she could act as a discreet chaperone. Because of her own cultural antecedents the assumptions behind that open door drove Fiona to fist-clenching fury; and she was irrationally tempted to closet herself with all manner of men simply to outrage as many conventions as she could. *Let them gossip all they want,* she thought. *What does it matter to me?*

But, of course, it did matter: she was here on suffrance and could not afford to outrage local opinion, not yet—and so the door stayed open. And through the door came the sounds of Tibro's reed flute, allowing discreet conversation.

"The Abessu-Denorru wishes me to accompany the army," Fiona said. "Why?"

Campas' answer was quick. "Your people—the Igaralla, I mean—they have sent an ambassador to Neda-Calacas, yes?"

"That's true," Fiona said.

"The Igaralla are neutral in this war, you have made that clear," Campas said. "There's no other power on the continent that can make that claim. And you can communicate with your people in that, that star-ship of yours; the city walls are no barrier. It may be useful to have a neutral representative on hand—we may have to conduct negotiations regarding prisoner exchange, for example, or—eventually—for surrender. We will win, you know," Campas said, matter-of-fact. "It may take a year or two, but Neda-Calacas can't hold out against all of us."

Fiona was silent for a long moment, taken completely aback. The proposal, of course, was completely logical; she could see nothing wrong with offering the kind of assistance requested here, and there might be some interesting data coming out of the campaign—on the Brodaini, for example—but on the other hand wars had a way of involving people in unforseen ways. She decided to temporize.

"I regret I can't give an immediate answer," she said. "I'll have to communicate with my superiors." Which, to be sure, was truthful enough.

"There will be a delay of several days before the army marches," Campas said. "Will that time be sufficient?"

"I should think so."

Campas leaned back in his chair, stretching his long legs

out before him, crossing them. He looked at her with a careless smile. "You are satisfied with your conditions here?" she asked. "No problems with the staff?"

Well: the official part of the visit seemed to be over. Fiona relaxed as well, picking up her teacup. "No complaints. The embassy will have to acquire its own building sooner or later, of course," she said. "But I'm being treated very well, thank you."

"An embassy of one is unusual, here," Campas said.

"It serves two purposes," Fiona said. "A single ambassador, travelling on her own, was thought to be less threatening—we didn't want to alarm you, not with a lot of people swooping down from the sky. Also, since we had a limited number of people on our ship, and we intend to be here for a very long time, there's a problem with personnel. We have to plan far ahead, especially since we intend to have an embassy in every major country, if we can." She sipped her tea, shifting in her seat. "But I will have an assistant in a year or so, I expect. With the Abessu-Denorru's permission."

"You didn't want to alarm us, you say, with a large embassy," Campas said. "Is that why your people sent a woman?"

Bull's eye, Fiona thought with surprise. Campas was quick, quicker than she'd thought.

"That—idea had occurred to us," she said. "But not all of our ambassadors are women. It was more a matter of interest and aptitude among the candidates." This conversation was beginning to get too close to matters she preferred the Arrandalla not to know, at present; she moved swiftly to change the topic.

"Will you be going with the army, Campas?" she asked.

Campas accepted the change of topic without comment. "Alas, yes," he said with a wry grin. "I'll be with Necias in the field. They're putting me on staff, to help deal with the Brodaini.''

"The Brodaini, now—you've lived among them, haven't you?"

"Yes," Campas said noncommittally. "Necias wanted me to learn their language. A curious people."

"A violent people," Fiona said. "How do you advise an outsider, someone like myself, to deal with the Brodaini?"

Campas grinned. "Learn to apologize quickly and sincerely," he said.

Fiona smiled and spoke in Gostu. "Ban-demmin, may your arm never weaken, I intended no offense," she said, and Campas laughed—it was a genuine laugh, filling the small room, a hearty, healthy reminder that the Arrandalla laughed loudly and often, as did her own people. A needed reminder: they were all careful around her, a little in awe, their speech formal and very . . . diplomatic. She joined his laughter, achingly aware of how long it had been since she had laughed with someone.

Tibro's flute hesitated, then continued its song.

"Bro-demmin would be better," Campas said, still smiling as he settled in his chair. "More subservient."

"Not from an ambassador."

He nodded, conceding the point. There was a small silence as each waited for the other to fill it; then Fiona spoke.

"Do you know Tegestu? I've only seen him once, the night of my last performance." Campas frowned, his fingers plucking at his doublet as he considered his answer.

"I'm *acquainted* with Tegestu," he said. "I've met him many times. But I can't say I know him, no. Yet I know he's a very remarkable man."

"Remarkable? In what way?" Fiona asked. Her recorder had been turned on and was quietly collecting every word. Data, to be transcribed later: *The Brodaini, as described by an Arrandalla Observer.*

"He's very intelligent, very quick," Campas said. "And he's made the compromises necessary to live here, and made them understandable to his followers in their own terms—that's his great achievement, I think."

"Compromises?" It was easy enough to prod most people into talking about themselves, about their ideas: so it was with Campas.

"Their society is very rigid, you see," Campas said. "It doesn't take easily to compromises—Brodaini consider tradition and honor more important than life, and in one sense it would have been easier for Tegestu's people to hold their ground and be killed by the conqueror, rather than alter their way of life to take service with us. But Tegestu saw a chance to survive, and to do it with a minimum of change, and that change slowly.

"It took him time, you see. Years. He had to hold off the Clattern i Clatterni for the first of those years, while he made his deal with Necias; and then he had to make his deal with the conqueror. He would evacuate his country over a period of ten years, taking as many of his dependents as wished to go, and in the end the conqueror would have the territory without having to fight for it—with its castles intact, its fields unscorched by war. The treaty was very complex—I've seen it—but it was eventually hammered out, and both sides abided by it. Tegestu evacuated his people; the Abessu-Denorru found land for his peasants and wars for his warriors; and that created a demand among the other cities for other Brodaini.

"Tegestu was cunning in all this negotiation," Campas said; then he smiled. "Subtlety isn't supposed to be a Brodaini trait; but I think it's that they have different ways of being subtle. Tegestu would make a good deissu, crafty as he is."

"Do you like him?" Fiona asked. She found herself

genuinely curious: Campas, she thought, was a likable man. A good observer, she thought—had he been born on Igara he could have had her job, had he wanted it.

Campas thought for a moment, then shook his head. "No," he said. "I don't. I admire him, but the Brodaini are not for *liking*. There's something strange about them, so fierce and so—alien." He looked as if he were repressing a shudder. He looked up at her, speaking candidly. "Even to someone who has lived among them, like myself, they're unpredictable. We don't know what sets them off. And now Tastis has gone mad and seized an entire city." He leaned back in his chair, frowning in thought. "But that will be an end to him. The change will come too fast."

"I don't know what you mean."

Campas looked up at her quickly. "Don't you?" he asked softly. His lips twitched in a little, cynical smile, his eyes holding steadily on hers. "It's obvious," he said. "Tegestu was given the Old City here, walled off for his people; and he settled his peasants in little communities of their own guarded by Brodaini soldiers. It was to lower the incidence of contact, obviously, to minimize the shocking contrast between one people and another. But the contacts were there, unavoidably, and all Tegestu's care wouldn't keep them from happening, and once that happened his way of life was doomed. They're brave, but they don't fit in here; their way of life is too different, and our numbers are overwhelming. Whether he realized it or not—and I think he *did* realize it; he's a canny man—he was trying to keep the changes from happening so quickly that his people would be overwhelmed by them, perceive them as threats, and react violently, as Tastis has done. So that the changes would come slowly, and so that some of his way of life might be preserved—changed but not destroyed, as it will be destroyed with Tastis."

Campas leaned back in his chair, sipping his tea, his

blue eyes watching Fiona intently. "You've been asking me a lot of questions, Ambassador," he said. "Most people in your situation wouldn't bother to inquire after the opinions of a mere messenger. I wonder at your interest."

"Your question isn't very diplomatic," Fiona said.

"Neither were yours," Campas said, his face hard. "You're *studying* us, and for that reason you're interested in what we think; but you've drawn your own conclusions well ahead of time. I don't think you like us very much, but you try to be polite. I recognize what you're doing, you see." His lips twitched in a bitter smile. "I lived among the Brodaini and studied them, and I didn't like them, either." He put down his tea, then looked up, his gaze frank, and frankly hostile. "Your people are after something, and I'm not sure what it is. Not conquest—I believe you there—but it's not trade, either. You're not as disinterested as all that." He stood, looking down at Fiona with an odd mixture of puzzlement and stubbornness on his face, as if he were still trying to sort out his impressions, his conclusions. "I haven't forgotten what you said to the Abessu-Denorru, when he asked you what you wanted in return for your suggestion about the sail. We ask nothing from *you,* you said; I noticed the emphasis even if Necias didn't. But you *do* want something in the end, if not from Necias. And I wonder what that is." He shrugged. "I'm sorry if I've offended you, Ambassador. I'll remove myself." He gave an exaggerated bow. "Your servant," he said, and walked toward the door.

"Sit down," said Fiona, and when he only hesitated she repeated herself, with emphasis. *"Sit. Down."* Campas stopped, then turned and faced her, an expression of anger on his face—but then he shrugged again, smiled his cynical smile, and in the end obeyed.

Fiona looked down at her hands grasping the arms of her chair; their knuckles were white. Deliberately she relaxed her grip, relaxing as well the jaw muscles that had clenched her teeth together.

Campas looked at her expectantly.

"That was a remarkable performance, Campas," she said. "You're quite an actor, aren't you? And now I'm compelled, like you, to wonder why. What offends you, Campas? My private judgements? Why should you care at all what I think?"

"Your thoughts are of no concern," he said. "Your attitudes are. Do you think you can fool us so easily? Necias may be satisfied for the moment, but once he has a little time to think he'll begin to try to reason out what you're doing here, and he'll begin to wonder the same things I've been wondering."

"So you simply think me dishonest?" Fiona asked, frankly disbelieving. "You consider that we Igaralla have concealed motives of our own, and for that reason you choose to despise me?" She barked a short, contemptuous laugh. "Give me something better, Campas," she chided. "Someone demanding candor should be candid himself."

Campas sat silent for long seconds, his eyes burning into her. "Brito thinks you're a witch," he said. "They haven't executed witches here for a hundred years, but I think she'd see you chopped up in the public square if she could. You frighten her."

"I'm sorry for that," Fiona said. "But you're not arguing for the revival of the laws against witchcraft, I take it?"

Campas shook his head; but his fierce eyes never left her. "But you *are* a witch, you see," he said. "I'm not saying you have cast a spell over us all—it would have been better if you had: spells wear off. You've done something far worse. You've changed the world."

Fiona became aware of the silence from the other chamber, the absence of Tibro's flute. Well, she thought fiercely, let the girl listen.

"Worlds change every day," she said.

"Not like this, they don't," Campas said. "The people are intoxicated with you. *See the star woman. Hear of her wonders.* They think of you as this benevolent force, come to improve their lives. They haven't yet realized what you really mean.

"Now we know there are other worlds," he said. "Other peoples, peoples who can work wonders. And before long we will begin to measure ourselves against you. What will happen then? We do not build ships that sail between the stars; we cannot fly above the clouds; we are unable to communicate between cities in the blink of an eye. A lady walks among us, offering in her whimsical condescension 'suggestions,' little driblets of knowledge from heaven, that can turn us upside-down. Our triumphs are insignificant; our knowledge pointless. It's all been done before.

"Your spells have taken our souls, witch," Campas said, his bitterness etched on his words like acid. "You've shown us our insignificance. Our dreams have been dreamed before, and better. You've shattered us, Ambassador. We were better off before you showed us the stars."

"I don't think you're so fragile as all that, Campas," Fiona said. "I don't enjoy being a part of this poetic conceit of yours." He turned his eyes away as her shaft struck home; and then she stood up, walked briskly to the door, and caught a glimpse of Tibro, flute in hand, perched on a settee, her eyes wide with shock. The maidservant flushed. "Beg pardon, Ambassador," she stammered.

"Play," Fiona said, and then expressionlessly closed the door, putting her back against it. Let them think what they damn' well please, she thought fiercely, and then, feeling the firmness of the door against her shoulders, she spoke.

"What I'm going to say is not meant to go beyond these walls," she said. "Can I trust you not to go running off to Necias with this, like that girl out there, who is certainly going to dash off downstairs with the news that I'm a witch after all?''

"I can keep a confidence." Grudgingly. No woman had ever talked to him like this, Fiona thought. Too bad it hadn't happened before.

She walked across the room and returned to her seat. "Do you think you're the first people to have your world turned around?" she asked. "It's happened before, and it's happened worse. I've seen the history you teach your children. Five hundred years ago the Abessla were conquerors, coming over the passes from the south, weren't they? They toppled the weak Captilla kingdoms, and then the Sanniscu Empire, and the result has been five hundred years of anarchy as the successors, the barons and the cities, warred among themselves. Do you think the Captilla and Sannisla didn't have their world changed?"

"They were destroyed," Campas said. "Wiped out. You serve only to illustrate my point."

"Hardly destroyed. They still live, Campas," Fiona said. "Their kingdoms were destroyed, but the people lived under new rulers. And they *learned*, Campas. They learned from their conquerors, and their conquerors learned from them. And eventually they became a single people. Ideas may shatter, Campas, but the people survive them, if they're wise. You can't be afraid of putting aside the ideas of your youth, when you grow older—or can you?"

Campas looked at her balefully. "If these youthful ideas are all I've got," he said. "If these quaint, eccentric little concepts are all that's holding me together, I damned well resent their supercession."

"Dramatics."

He glared up at her sharply, resentful. Fiona settled into her seat, plumping up the pillow behind her, pulling her legs into the chair. "I'm going to tell you a story, Campas," she said. "Believe it a true one or not, as you please. I'm not an artist such as yourself, so forgive my crudities of phrase.''

Sardonic humor entered Campas' eyes. "Now who's being dramatic?''

Fiona grinned. "Conceded," she said. She sipped her tea—by now it was cold, but it still refreshed.

"I'll have to ask you to imagine a planet much like your own," she said. "Its name was Terra, and humans lived there from earliest times—they lived, and boon-re blessed them, such that they learned to travel among the stars. Not slowly, such as my people do it, but swiftly, in an instant. So they travelled among the stars in their fast ships, and they found many planets on which the Terralla could live. Their people came to these planets in great numbers; and they settled there and prospered. They came to my planet, Igara, and they came to yours, Campas; and they settled in both.''

Campas sat up, his eyebrows raised. "You're making a case for these people as our ancestors?" he asked.

"You're quick," Fiona said. "But I'm just telling a story, remember. I don't want to turn your fragile world upside-down again.''

Campas smiled, his smile this time self-mocking, conscious of Fiona's elaborate irony. "Very well," he said, gesturing grandly. "Please go on.''

"Thank you." The muffled sound of Tibro's flute sounded through the door. Fiona settled again into her chair, and went on. "But there was a flaw in the knowledge of the Terralla," she said. "Their method of travelling among the stars was dangerous, and they did not know it." She paused, trying to choose her words. How could she explain to this man, bright as he was, that the Terran faster-than-light ships, using their vast power to warp the fabric of space-time, had created a monumental instability in the balance of space, matter, time, reality? And that when the balance was at last overturned, the catastrophe had been sudden and swift, destroying entire planets, sending others backward and forward in time, destroying human civilization?

"Imagine that the Arrandalla build a new type of ship to sail upon the sea," Fiona said. "And that this new type of ship is very fast and successful, so that the Arrandalla expand throughout the world and become very rich, and that their knowledge increases and they become very wise. But that the means by which this ship is driven through the waves injures the ocean, so that ocean is forced to attack the ships in self-defense." She saw incomprehension in Campas' eyes and paused. "I'm sorry," she said. "I know this is difficult."

He waved a hand by his head, mimicking his own confusion. "This ship is injuring the ocean?" he asked. "Is the ocean alive, then, in this story?" Then a light of understanding entered his eyes, and he leaned forward. "Or am I not to take this literally? Is this a metaphor?"

"A metaphor," Fiona said gratefully, thankful that Campas had made that leap of understanding.

"Very well. Go on." He leaned back in his chair, his legs still thrust out before him.

"The Terralla did not entirely understand the means by which they travelled among the stars, just as your alchemists do not entirely understand why their compounds work, or do not work," she said. "Just as the alchemists might accidentally make a compound that is dangerous—that might be poison, or that might cause a fire—the Terralla did not understand that there was great danger created by their ships. They caused a great disaster, and most of the Terralla died. More than ninety-nine in a hundred were killed instantly; all their ships were destroyed: their cities were turned to ruins. Many of the survivors were driven mad by the catastrophe."

She paused, seeing an intent, intelligent comprehension on Campas' face, knowing she had him intrigued. "You may be interested to know that my people have a large literature concerning the Terralla,'' she said. ''Tragedies, many of them—they show the Terralla as wise beings descending, through fatal curiosity, to disaster. The catastrophe is presented as the inevitable result of their meddling with things they should have left alone.

''Other interpretations show the Terralla as decadent, self-indulgent sensation seekers, playing among their palaces, tempting fate for the pleasure of it. Yet others show them as immeasurably wise ancestors from whose standards of perfection we have fallen. Others just use the time of the Terralla as a background for tales of fantastic romance and adventure.'' Fiona smiled, seeing Campas nod, understanding well the matter of literary interpretation. ''Personally,'' she said, ''I think all these approaches make fine literature, but all are off the mark as far as the truth about Terra is concerned. I suspect the Terralla were much as we, that their fall was not a measure of arrogant curiosity, or of their decadence, but a measure only of their human fallibility. They fell because even though they were wise they were still human, and did not understand enough about their universe. They fell from lack of knowledge, not from too much.''

Campas nodded. ''I compliment you, Ambassador,'' he said, his tone serious. ''I didn't realize you had this gift, truly I didn't. You point your morals very elegantly. I shall have to look upon you as a rival, in future.''

Fiona looked down at her lap, strangely embarrassed by the compliment, and then shook her head. ''Your gift is poetry,'' she said. ''Mine is storytelling. Yours is the greater.''

''My compliment was sincere,'' Campas said. ''I don't flatter in these matters.'' Then he grinned. ''I can write my poetry for a hundred years, and it won't alter the world a bit—it's still valueless, as far as my masters are concerned. My chief uses are secretarial, and my poetry is useful to

Necias chiefly as a demonstration of his anildas. It enhances his esteem to have a court poet, and so he does.

"But your little stories, Ambassador—" His smile faded, replaced by sadness. He waved a gentle, admonishing finger at her. "You told one tale eight nights ago, and this old world hasn't been the same since. And I've been angry at you for it." He bowed. "Jealousy, I'm sorry to say. I apologize."

So that's what set him off, Fiona thought. He's been trying to get his poetry through their dim minds for years, and now a little foreign woman has done in a night all he's ever wanted to do.

"I haven't invalidated your verse," she said. "It's still as accomplished as ever it was."

"Just far less relevant." Lightly, but still with bitterness. His eyes rose to hers. "But you were telling me about the Terralla. What's become of them?"

"Gone, we think," Fiona said. "Terra itself disappeared in the catastrophe. And the survivors, here and there on other planets, having lost everything—well, they started over. Much of their land would not support life, at least not at first. It was a terrible existence, and only gradually did it improve. They forgot Terra and all they had been, except perhaps as a land in a legend. Their own worlds were all they knew.

"Some recovered earlier," she continued. "Their worlds had not been scarred as badly, and, when they had progressed enough to understand them, they had Terralla artifacts to help them. It was these who began to first move among the stars again, moving much more slowly this time, so as not to risk the holocaust caused by the Terralla."

"Your people," Campas said. "The Igaralla."

Fiona shook her head, and she saw surprise in Campas' eyes. "No, Campas," she said. "These were other peoples altogether—two other planets rose, simultaneously, to that position; and they began to seek out the planets the Terralla had populated, first by signalling and then by sending ships.''

"There are others, then?'' Campas asked. "Not just Demro and Igara, but others?''

"Eleven that we know of, counting your own,'' Fiona said. "My own planet, Igara, had advanced enough to understand the signals when they came—ships weren't sent to us. After that, Igara leagued with the other planets, and agreed to send out ships, as the others had done. Most of the ships found nothing—no planets at all, or worlds that were dead. My own ship was lucky.''

Fiona fell silent, seeing Campas trying to absorb the idea; there was a frown on his face, and he stared down at his boot-tip. Then his gaze rose. "It's a lot to understand, all at once.'' He shook his head. "The priests won't like it—they have their own notions of how we got here.''

"I'm not telling the priests,'' Fiona said.

"No,'' he said, with a quiet smile. "You're not.''

"I have yet to come to my moral,'' Fiona reminded him. Campas gave a short laugh.

"I forgot,'' he said. "Pray continue.''

"My point is that out of the all the descendants of the Terralla we've yet discovered, none have equalled the Terralla civilization. None as large, none as wise, none as brilliant. Whatever we've done, the Terralla have done before. Whatever discoveries we've made, the Terralla made them first. But we've found that *it's not a reason for despair!*

"The discovery that a given idea was conceived of first by someone else does not mean that the idea is false, or the conceiver a lesser being than his predecessor. The fact that two other civilizations recovered from the Terralla holocaust and began to travel among the stars some hundreds of years before Igara did—this does not make Igara false. Nor does it make your own life less, or your work.''

She leaned back in triumph, straightening her shoulders, proclaiming now with a flourish, her hands waving. "My coming hasn't invalidated your poetry, it's just put it in a different perspective. Perhaps it was a perspective that was needed."

Campas sat still for a moment, watching her with brooding eyes, and then he began to applaud, his handclaps echoing in the small room. Fiona, pleased with herself, gave him a flourishing stage bow, bending from the waist.

"Ambassador, I grovel before your eloquence," he said. "Had I such a thing as a fat purse, I would throw it. In future, I shall make a point to write for a stellar audience."

"Your servant," said Fiona.

Campas drew in his long legs and stood. "Ambassador, this was most enlightening," he said. His craggy face was serious, carefully appraising. "You've given me much to think about."

"Must you go?"

"Alas, yes," Campas said. He smiled and bowed, suddenly breezy. "Necias wants me to meet with Marshal Palastinas' staff this afternoon, to discuss logistics." His tone turned to one of dry mockery. "No doubt I shall learn a great deal about march rates, and bridging trains, and other matters of no interest whatever."

Fiona reached down to her waist to turn off her recorder— damn the ship anyway, this was none of their business— then uncoiled from her settee and rose. "Visit again, if you wish," Fiona said. "Believe it or not, I've enjoyed this talk. And I appreciate your candor . . . and your discretion."

"The pleasure was mine, as was the enlightenment," Campas said—typical Arrandalla speech, flowery and complimentary, but Fiona thought she detected a measure of sincerity. "Forgive my discourtesy, which you are so good as to call candor. I shall call again, if I can."

"I am glad to have made a friend," Fiona said. Campas

seemed startled, looking at her sharply for an instant; then he said, "Ambassador, your servant," opened the door behind him, and backed out.

Tibro was still tootling dutifully away, and Fiona, exhilaration filling her, stepped into the parlor, leaning her shoulder on the door jamb. She felt as if she had just passed a test . . . and almost certainly she just had. Campas' objections to her presence had not been unanticipated; but the man had surprised her, coming to her so quickly. Campas was surprisingly acute.

She realized suddenly that she was very hungry. Giving speeches on an empty stomach: bad for her. "Tibro, bring me luncheon," she said. The girl put down the flute.

"Yes, Ambassador."

"The white wine, I think—the gift from Fastias."

"Yes, Ambassador."

Fiona smiled as Tibro bustled out of the room: there was going to be a lot of talk downstairs. Probably it would get to Necias, eventually; and then Campas might be in for an interrogation. Well, the man was inventive: no doubt he could create a suitable story if he had to.

She frowned as she realized that Campas might simply go straight to Necias and give the Abeissu everything she'd just told him—there was certainly no proof to the contrary, nothing but her intuition that his promise to keep a confidence meant something. She had to trust someone, she thought stubbornly; she was all alone here.

Not that it much mattered. If Necias had asked the same questions, she would have told him the same story.

With, she knew, the same, appalling, inbuilt lie. The worst kind of lie, the sort that can be told while telling the most scrupulous, factual kind of truth. Campas' accusations had been far too close. We ask nothing of *you:* Campas had been perfectly right that her subtle emphasis contained an evasion, and that eventually the spacefarers from Igara would ask payment for their help. She hadn't dared answer that accusation, and so she'd turned the subject him: her story, without containing a single lie, had diverted him from the most overwhelming truth of all.

She had called Campas friend; and he'd been surprised. Could a friend conceal such a truth from a friend? No: not a truth of that sort. Not the most gigantic truth, the truth why the Igarans had so hastily begun to travel from star to star.

The meal came, and Fiona, her exhilaration fading, ate it without enthusiasm. That lie would be paid for; she knew it.

Afterwards she returned to her room, to find that Vico had quietly cleaned it in her absence. She opened her trunk to transfer the recording of Campas' visit to her larger-capacity recorder, and discovered, to her surprise, an urgent message from the ship. She frowned: this hadn't happened before. She cued the communicator. The reply was instant.

"Fiona." Tyson's voice, sounding weary, discouraged.

"Yes, Tyson."

"A problem, Fiona. Kira's dead."

And suddenly there were ridiculous tears stinging Fiona's eyes—appallingly useless, of course, no good to Kira or anybody. But still the emotional hammer came, and flattened her against the anvil; she hadn't realized that any news could strike her with such force.

Kira, laughing Kira, eager, so vibrant—now the first to pay the penalty for her idealism.

"What happened?" Fiona asked, when she had confidence her voice wouldn't crack.

The tale was one of lunacy, of bad judgement by everyone concerned.

Kira had been pleased with her reception, and treated with all courtesy—and then, last night, Tastis had struck. Brodaini had come smashing into her apartments, seizing her in her bed, dragging her down to the prison. An emissary from Tastis had given her an ultimatum: she would inform her superiors that their knowledge would be used for the benefit of Neda-Calacas alone, or her life would be forfeit.

Fiona, seeing her knuckles whiten on the spindle as she heard of the attack, was suddenly thankful Necias had insisted on such proof in her own case—if Tastis had seen that huge atmosphere craft cruising above his city, he might have thought twice about using such brutal tactics.

Kira had told them their demands were impossible, but they hadn't listened. They had simply shown her the instruments of torture available there in the dungeon, explaining their uses—and demonstrated them, in a few cases, on their other prisoners. She would have a night to think it over.

She was alone, her spindle having been confiscated; she'd taken off her privy-coat before going to bed. But the mission planners had foreseen even this; there was still a means of defense, and also of communication, both hidden beneath her own flesh. Kira had done what was necessary; she'd touched a point in her left armpit, at the soft bend of the left elbow, at another place on the wrist—that would have numbed a little area on her forearm. And then she would have begun to rub that spot with a spoon, or a piece broken off from a stool, or with her fingernail—with anything available—until the flesh was scraped away and her new communicator revealed among the bloody tissue. The ship had been contacted and the atmospheric-maneuverable shuttle sent down. While air-dropped flares lit up the sky around the city, attracting the attention of the watchers on the walls, Kira had, with a weapon hidden in her right arm, blasted her way out of prison and fought her way to the roof of the keep, where the speeding aircar dashed to meet her.

Too late. She was found dead on the roof, a Brodaini arrow in her ribs. The aircar crew burned every guard they could see and carried her body to the ship. They had been reprimanded for excessive use of violence.

Fiona, her fingers digging into her palms, repressed the urge to shriek at Tyson. Excessive use—my god! These people had purged half the great houses of the city. If she had been in the rescuers' position, looking down at Kira's body, she would have burned the entire keep down about their ears.

"New rules, Fiona," Tyson said. "Keep your privy-coat on at all times, even when sleeping. We'll want reports twice each day, instead of once."

"Of course."

"Anything to report?"

"No, nothing," she said—why couldn't they leave her alone? But then she remembered she had news after all. She rubbed her forehead, trying to clear her mind. "Oh, yes. Arrandal will declare war on Neda-Calacas tomorrow. The rest of the Elva cities will follow." *And not soon enough,* she thought savagely.

"I'm sorry, Fiona," Tyson said. "This must be a shock. She was someone very special. There will be a service for Kira tonight at the eighth hour, your time. Will you want to listen?"

"Yes. Thank you."

"We'll signal when we begin. Oh, Fiona, one thing."

"Yes?"

"This news—it brings no joy, Fiona. But don't let this overwhelm you. You won't do Kira any good by growing angry. Try to think what she would have wanted you to do."

Fiona swallowed hard. Tyson knew her well; his words were well-meaning, but also pointed.

"I'll try to remember," she said. "Thank you, Tyson."

Her numb fingers dropped the little spindle as she tried to switch it off; she cursed and kicked it across the room, knowing it would take no harm. Damn this world and its madness. These people didn't deserve Kira; they didn't deserve anything.

A sudden idea struck her, and she leaned back on her couch, considering it. Necias had asked her to accompany the army; and now the idea seemed an attractive one.

Of course the original purpose was gone. She would not be going as a neutral.

But she would see Tastis' towers fall. That would be satisfaction enough.

10

Tegestu looked at the four burn-scarred stone walls, then at the shade trees planted nearby with the fresh graves among the sod. Tastis' men had passed this way, and left their devastation behind.

"Noon meal here," he said. "There will be an hour's halt."

For the last three days he had seen much the same thing, over and over. Farmhouses burned, barns put to the torch, women outraged, animals slaughtered. Often, if the farmers hadn't been able to get to their strongholds in time, the bodies of the peasants lying amid their animals. At least here there'd been some survivors—otherwise the dead wouldn't have had burial.

It was logical, he had to admit. Tastis held the deissin and their motives in contempt: he knew they scorned demmin and cared overmuch for profit. Therefore he intended to make this war too costly for Arrandal to wage successfully—all he had to do, from his point of view, was to hold out until the deissin of the Elva realized there was no profit to be made here. And then, no doubt, they would give up and recognize his revolt as legitimate.

And so, to that end, he'd unleashed a horde of raiders into Arrandalla territory: unprincipled mercenaries for the most part, and the scum of the cities' jails, armed only with a few light weapons and fast horses. Their purpose was simple: to cause as much murder, devastation, and chaos as possible—and also to divert as many Arrandalla forces as they could.

Tastis' plan had, thus far, worked well. The slow-moving baronial forces couldn't cope with the invasion, though they helped—and of course they provided valuable garrisons in the towns and strongholds. But it was the city forces that had to chase these renegades. It was proving difficult, since it required waiting until the raiders were so burdened with loot that they were slowed down.

But, Tegestu thought, ultimately Tastis was wrong. The Arrandalla *did* possess demmin, he thought, at least demmin of a sort. Tastis' rebellion had violated what the Elva cities cherished most, their freedom from foreign domination. Tastis threatened them all, and they would not rest until the threat was ended.

Besides, Tegestu had seen the Arrandalla forces as they'd marched past those first few devastated crofts, the first butchered bodies lying in their yards . . . the Arrandalla would not forget such sights easily; their eyes had burned for revenge.

Well, Tegestu thought. Revenge they'd get, sooner or later.

He signalled for the midday halt and Thesau, mounted just behind, slid from his horse to help Tegestu from the saddle. Tegestu came wearily to the ground, pain crackling through his stiffened muscles. He gave Thesau a weary smile; but he needed Thesau to carefully support his elbow for the few long moments until he found his feet.

"There is a bench beneath the tree, bro-demmin Tegestu," Thesau said. "You can take your ease there."

"Thank you, ilean," Tegestu said. He walked deliberately through the sudden bustle of his staff dismounting, Classani servants jumping to tend the horses, his standard bearer Ghantenis raising his banner by the road so riders would know where to deliver their dispatches, messengers departing to order the column to halt. A drifting cloud of brown dust, stirred by the thousands of hooves and feet, moved over them like a pall—riding at the front of the column, they'd been ahead of the dust, but now it came looming over them, floating down to settle on their armor and banners. Tegestu came to the smooth wooden bench and sat down. He slitted his eyes against the dust as Thesau took off his helmet and coif, unlaced the quilted underpadding, then unpinned Tegestu's long grey braids and let them fall down his back. The long Brodaini hair was braided on campaign, and coiled around the top of the head: it provided extra padding for the helmet, and also helped to ward a head cut. Tegestu leaned back against the tree.

"Will you eat now, bro-demmin?" Thesau asked. Tegestu shook his head.

"Not yet, ilean. But I would like some cider, if there's some handy."

"Aye, bro-demmin." Thesau gave a commanding movement of his hand, attracting the attention of one of his younger assistants. "Cider for the drandor Tegestu!" The Classanu halted in his tracks, bowed, then ran to the little two-wheeled gigs that carried headquarters supplies.

Other members of the staff—Cascan, Acamantu, the Arrandalla poet Campas—began to gather beneath the tree, bowing, then lowering themselves to the ground near Tegestu. Tegestu began to scent, lightly through the dust, a charnel stench: those graves were shallow. Then a gust

of wind came, shifting the brown cloud, and the scent was
gone.

"Please eat, if you wish, ban-demmini," Tegestu said.
"Don't stand on courtesy." They bowed, and some called
for their servants to bring them the prepared meals that had
been packed the night before. The Classanu arrived with a
wine skin and the cider; Tegestu uncapped the skin and let
the cool liquid slide down his dust-covered throat, tasting
of last summer's apples.

There was a clatter of hooves and a group of riders came
out of the dust: Tegestu recognized Necias seated uncomfortably on a big-boned gelding—a bad rider, he had spent
most of the march seated in his covered gig, the leather
curtains drawn against the dust. Necias was accompanied
by the Marshal Palastinas, the army's commander, various
members of his staff, and the Igaran Ambassador, Fiona.
All had bandannas wrapped around their lower faces to
guard against the dust, except for Fiona, who had drawn
the hood of her undergarment around her head, enclosing
it completely, even the eyes; she looked as if she were
wearing a bleak carnival mask. Today the color of the
hood and the rest of the garment was a dark brown, several
shades darker than her skin; yesterday it had been a cheerful yellow. Tegestu wondered whether she had many such
garments, or if she could, with her offworld magic, somehow change the color of the one.

Necias dismounted heavily and began gesturing to his
people, who, Tegestu knew, would begin setting up a
pavilion in which the Abessu-Denorru, accompanied by
the Marshal and their respective staffs, would be able to
take their leisurely luncheon. The pavilion, Tegestu knew,
was a luxurious one: there were carpets, a field kitchen,
portable tables, folding chairs, a silver dinner service; it
took up three ox-wagons and required a staff of six, not
counting the teamsters. A ridiculous waste of resources
better spent in moving and feeding fighting men; but then

Tegestu's advice had not been solicited. His own equipage took up the backs of two horses, and he ate what the other Brodaini ate.

It was lucky the march to Neda-Calacas was not intended to be a fast one. They were moving deliberately, scouts always on the alert for Tastis, who had a deserved reputation for appearing where he had no right to be.

Palastinas handed his broadsword to a lacky, nodded to Necias, and then walked toward Tegestu. He was an Arrandalla, a portly, vigorous, greying man of about sixty, with a funny dab of white beard on his chin; he was both a prosperous merchant and Arrandal's most successful soldier. He and Tegestu understood one another well enough, and had fought together before: Palastinas had even learned to speak Gostu, which was more than most Arrandalla managed.

Tegestu rose from his bench and bowed, hearing the rattle of armor as the other Brodaini rose to make their respects. Palastinas waved them all back to their places.

"Don't get up, we're all old repini here," he said in Gostu—he was a hearty man, ingratiating, with no understanding of tolhostu; but Tegestu liked him nevertheless.

"Take my bench, whelkran," Tegestu said, stepping aside; but Palastinas took him by the elbow and directed him to sit:

"There's room enough for two, drandor Tegestu." They sat, and Palastinas drank deeply of the apple cider, smiled, wiped his chin, and then fixed him with a careful eye.

"News, drandor?" he asked.

It had been obvious from the beginning that such a major effort on the part of the city, and in such a cause, could have no commander but an Arrandalla: a Brodaini would not have been trusted. All Arrandal's major wars had been fought under their own commanders, those with Brodaini contingents included, though Brodaini commanders had been given independence in smaller assignments. Tegestu bore no resentment: he, and all his people, understood subordination well enough.

But the Brodaini superiority in combat, organization, and intelligence had been recognized, since Tegestu had been made chief of staff. It was his people who planned the complicated logistics for moving fifty thousand men across the four hundred miles, strewn with rivers and cut with canals, that separated the cities; it was the Brodaini who sent out the scouts, who processed the information; and if battle came about, it would be Tegestu who suggested the plan and who, assuming the plan was accepted by Palastinas, would be charged with implementing it. Palastinas would absorb much of the credit; but he was a fair-minded man, and had always given a fair share of the honor to the Brodaini in the past.

"Our scouts have gone to the border, and found nothing but this devastation," Tegestu said. "This wreckage ends at the border, and on the other side people are starving. The peasants have had all their grain taken to the city, even the seed-corn. Tastis wants us to support his people as well as our own."

Palastinas frowned. "We'll have to, I suppose," he said. "But it's for the Abessu-Denorru to decide."

Tegestu nodded, understanding: What was Necias along for, if not for Palastinas to pass on to him all the hard decisions of policy?

"There is a problem once again," Tegestu said, "with sanitation."

Palastinas grimaced. "I'll send out another general order," he said. The Arrandalla, with canals so close at hand, were used to defecating wherever they wished; and the country people, militia and mercenaries, also dropped their trousers wherever it suited them. It made a large encampment an odorous mess, and the Brodaini had, without any great success, been trying to introduce the custom of the slit trench.

"Beg pardon, Marshal, but there have been general orders before. Without any enforcement the situation will only . . ."

"Aye, aye," Palastinas said wearily, pulling his little white beard. "We'll have to start lashing the ones who don't obey, I suppose."

"I think that would be wise, Palastinas Marshal cenorsstannan," Tegestu said, satisfied. He looked up. "Another piece of news," he said. "There's been a victory over the raiders, one of their columns chopped up. It happened at Fallonito."

"Indeed?" Palastinas said. Fallonito was a small town, the center of one of the border areas that had been settled by Brodaini dependents, in this case mainly Meningli farmers, with a few Brodaini and Classani to keep order and to act as garrison. "There wasn't much of a force, was there?" Palastinas asked.

"Three Brodaini, under command of a young man, Dellila Gartanu Sepestu y'Dantu. Four Classani, and the rest Meningli," Tegestu said with pride. "They were lucky enough to have warning of the raiders' arrival. Dellila armed the entire population; knocked holes in the walls between the houses so he could move his people without exposing them, and then lay in wait for the attackers; he let them ride in, then slammed the gates behind. None got away. They counted over sixty dead, with three Meningli killed." Palastinas said *aiau* softly, impressed, and Tegestu smiled his satisfaction. "Dellila suffered eighteen wounds, but is expected to survive," he added.

"I'll send him my congratulations," said Palastinas.

"He would esteem it an honor." Tegestu uncapped the wineskin and let the sweet cider roll down his tongue, then looked at Palastinas and said, "Dellila's kin to my wife. I'll be pleased to find more important work for him, if he lives."

"It's good to have a victory over these bandits,"

Palastinas said, scowling. "It'll show what can be done, if a few men stand up to them."

If a few Brodaini *stand up to them,* Tegestu thought; but he didn't say it. Abessla could fight surprisingly well if the spirit was with them, but he suspected they couldn't have done what Dellila had done.

"Will you share our meal with us?" Tegestu asked. Palastinas laughed, then shook his head.

"I think I prefer Necias' table to the stuff you people eat on the march," he said, rising and gesturing the others to remain seated as, automatically, they rose to salute him. "There'll be a staff meeting tonight?"

"Aye. When we call a halt."

"I'll be there. Drandor. Ban-demmini." He nodded to all and began walking quickly toward the pavilion, which was staggering erect as yelling servants began pushing the center pole upward while others strained at the guy wires. Tegestu called for his meal, but paused as he heard the sound of hasty galloping coming from ahead of the column. He leaned forward to look out around the trunk of the tree and saw three swift, light horses riding breakneck toward him. The dust had settled by now and he could see their banner clearly: it was Grendis, who was chief of the scouts and often ranged ahead of the army with her riders. She reined in as she saw his own banner planted by the road, and then turned the lathered steed in. Behind her was her bannerman, then a breathless, travel-stained young man, one of her light cavalry whelkrani, a leather case containing a telescope bouncing at his side. Impatiently she pulled her helmet back off her head as she pulled the horse to a halt, then called out her message even before she dismounted.

"I think we've found Tastis!"

As he rose, leaving his untouched meal, Tegestu smiled to see Palastinas, halfway to Necias' pavilion, suddenly stop dead in his tracks and spin around, a grin of feral exultation on his face. . . .

All the staff was present, so the staff meeting was held on the spot, over luncheon in Necias' grand pavilion. Grendis presented her whelkran, who had commanded the squadron sent ranging ahead to the great bend of the East Rallandas River, the broad, sluggish band of muddy water that led north to the great salt marshes and thence to the sea. Yesterday morning he'd found the principle ford guarded by cavalry, but his scouts had infiltrated through them to find the ford blocked, heavy iron stakes planted along its bottom, the bluffs behind set with Tastis' engines, ready to fling stones down on the heads of anyone trying to force a passage. There hadn't been a sign of any large force, however, and the young man was thorough: that night he swam his horse across the river and scouted the enemy himself. Campfires, he'd reported, by the hundreds.

Assuming six people to a campfire, he said, there were at least ten thousand men on the other side of the river. Probably at least twice that, since he was sure he hadn't seen all the fires.

Smiles broke out, and relieved chattering. The whelkran, his ears burning with compliments, was dismissed.

"So: we have their force located," Palastinas said, smiling. "The riverbed fortifications won't hold us for long; we'll get across somewhere, upstream or down, once we bring the bridging train up. Someone send for it, hey?" One of his staff grinned and began a note.

Tegestu looked down at his hands, and frowned.

"Doesn't sound like Tastis," he said, aware that his voice, speaking Abessas, sounded harsh and angry. There was silence in the tent: eyes turned toward him.

"Doesn't sound like Tastis, a battle at the ford," Tegestu insisted. "I fought with him; he was one of my whelkrani, a kinsman, one of the best." He gestured with his hands, trying to emphasize his points, painfully aware of his inadequacy in the language. "He . . . he *moved*. Not like this, not behind stakes, no. Light. Quick. Attacked with surprise. Ambush. Cunning. Nothing like this, not ever." He saw the eyes of Grendis on him, comprehending. "It's not like him. There's something in this we haven't seen."

"Yes," Grendis said. "That bothered me." She looked down at the table, her brows knitted in concentration.

"Perhaps it isn't Tastis," Necias offered. His meal, half-eaten, lay before him; he made quick, impatient moves with his hands as he spoke. "Perhaps Tastis is still in the city, or out with the fleet, somewhere."

"Has other whelkrani to take care of the fleet," Tegestu said. "Is not his, his specialty. Was light cavalryman himself at first; always thinks of moving fast. Cunning is his specialty. There is a trick in this, I think."

Palastinas watched him with a grave frown, then nodded. "We must be alert." he said. "Keep our scouts busy."

"They are overburdened," said Grendis. "So many of our cavalry are chasing the raiders. We're going to lose a lot of horses if we keep running them the way we've been doing."

That, Tegestu realized, was like Tastis. Sending out the raiders, realizing that in addition to the damage and confusion he was causing the Arrandalla forces to detach a lot of valuable light cavalry to chase them down; he'd given himself a better chance at an ambush. And so he'd prepared this fixed defense at the ford, hoping to rivet his enemies' attention on that river crossing, while he did something elsewhere—but what?

"The country," he said. "We need to know the country."

"It's flat," Grendis said. "Many little canals, yes, but no obstacles till the river. A few little orchards, but no forests." No place for ambush, then. "The river twists," Grendis added, illustrating with her hands. "Slow, shallow, but footmen can only cross in this one place. Lots of woods on the river bottom. The west bank is higher than the east, Tastis has that advantage.''

"It doesn't sound," Palastinas said. "like good ambush country. Maybe that's all Tastis could do, hope to delay us at the ford. Or maybe he's hoping that we'll divide our forces in order to cross somewhere else, and he can fight us in detail.''

They looked at Tegestu for his answer, but he had none: he could only frown and shake his head. "There's more in it than we see," he said. There had been too many small frustrations, he thought; he longed for something clean and straightforward, a battle, a clear challenge. Much of the strategy of the war had been necessitated by political considerations, rather than military ones—the very choice of the country they marched through was dictated by the necessity of cutting Tastis off from such of the country barons as might support him, while Tegestu, for safety's sake, would rather have embarked the army aboard the fleet and transported it swiftly to the enemy cities by water. Instead there was this ponderous march across country, Brodaini engineers moving out ahead to bridge rivers and canals, barges having to come by water to bring the army its supplies at prearranged points. Even with all the handicaps they'd been moving quickly, but Tegestu found himself fretted by the delay. It wasn't the merging of political considerations with military . . . no, he'd had to deal with those sort of compromises all his life. It was the fact that Tastis was being given time to expand his base of power, to make some kind of accommodation with his new-taken city.

Tastis, he knew, was an intelligent man, and something of an unorthodox thinker. A generation younger than Tegestu, more flexible in adapting to this new continent. Good at improvisation. He had been valuable as an independent commander, and had always shown an ability to act on his own initiative, often with irregular forces, and to do so brilliantly: he'd always kept the enemy off-balance, uncertain how to respond. He could shine in a situation like this. The war could be a long one.

"Bro-demmin, we will keep a good watch," Grendis said. "He won't be surprising us; our riders are keeping watch."

Tegestu nodded, unhappy. Something, he thought, was missing here. He would have to hope that after he'd seen the ford the pattern would somehow would fall into place.

11

Fiona looked down at the ford, seeing the dark iron of the stakes reflected in the silver waters, an intricate, geometric certainty reflected by the eddying, shifting, fluid medium. Behind, on the bluffs overlooking the river, was a solid black line of torsion engines, ready to smash the placid water into froth at the sign of a crossing. There was an old castle there, its walls torn down, its towers gaping. The white wood of hasty repairs showed clearly. Over it floated the enemy banners, Brodaini, city, baronial, and others that were strange to the invaders, new ensigns describing the new reality in Neda-Calacas. "It won't be difficult to get around, they tell me," said Campas. "We're having boats sent round behind us by canal, then the boats get portaged over the last twenty miles, and we've got a bridge wherever we need one. The scouts are deciding where it's going to be. Somewhere near a ford that the cavalry can use, so foot and horse can cross at the same time."

She gave him a look. "You've learned a lot about this, all of a sudden," she said.

"I'm staff," he said simply. "I see most of the dispatches. And I spent an entire damn day with my eye glued to a long glass set up on a tripod, making notes about what I saw. Deadly work, I had a headache afterwards for hours."

"And Tegestu?" she asked. "Two days ago he thought it was a trap."

"He still thinks it," Campas said. "But he can't find one." He hesitated, then spoke. "I have an intuition he's right, and Grendis and Cascan agree with him, too. But none of us can see how."

Campas frowned. He glanced downriver, then over his shoulder at Necias' big pavilion. "Can we move out of sight of Necias?" he asked. "He's been inundated with dispatches from the city this morning, with barons squalling for help against the raiders—and I don't want to spend the rest of the day finding diplomatic ways to tell them no. Necias brought half his household with him—let *them* do a little work for a change."

"As you like." They turned their horses' heads downriver and moved off at a slow jog. The slope gentled down to the thick, tangled underbrush and trees that surrounded the river. They heard the sound of axes: pioneers and assistant cooks were here, getting firewood and cutting brush away in case the enemy made a sally across the river and Arrandalla forces had to be moved through the tangle in a hurry. They moved northward along the slope in silence, keeping out of the tangles.

"Have you been sleeping well?" Campas asked suddenly, turning to her.

A thrust, straight at the heart of vanity. Fiona, suddenly self conscious, glanced up at him in surprise. "Yes," she said. "Everyone sleeps well after riding horseback half the day."

"You look tired." His frowning face seemed concerned.

She shook her hair back out of her eyes. "I'm all right," she said. Not true, she knew, not entirely. It was the burden of hatred that was draining her, hatred for Kira's killers, for all that was represented by those fluttering banners on the west bank. She passed a hand over her brow. "I'm all right," she said again.

They passed out of sight of the camp, seeing two gallopers dashing toward them, each carrying a dispatch: Grendis' people, heading for the pavilion. "News," she said. He laughed.

"All I can do is offer thanks that it won't be me reading it," he said. "I appreciate your borrowing me for the afternoon."

"You're welcome."

The messengers tore past, one of them, a young woman, raising an arm in greeting as she galloped by. Fiona turned her head to look after her.

"That woman Brodainu," she said. "That's one of the things I wanted to ask you about."

"Ask. I'll tell you what I can."

"It seems unusual that the Brodaini grant women equal status—make them officers, even. It's not what I'd expect from a military culture. The Brodaini are physically large, with the women being built to scale, but they're not as strong—they can't pull a bow as far, or strike as hard with a sword."

Campas shrugged. "Our people simply think they're crazy," he said. Fiona grimaced: no culture that had survived for so many hundreds of years was crazy. Campas spoke on. "I've talked to the Brodaini; but they just say it's always been that way." He looked up at her, curious. "Do you approve?"

"It's not important whether I approve or not," Fiona said, preferring to leave that particular issue unexamined. "I—I and my people—we want to understand them, if we can. And understand the Arrandalla, as well. My questions won't offend, will they?"

"We'll see." Easily, with a shrug. "Ask what you like."

"I haven't talked to the Brodaini that often," she admitted. "For the most part they've been too busy to answer my questions. But I've been talking to the Classani, when I can."

"It didn't take you long to learn that the servants are always the best suorces of information," Campas grinned. "My congratulations."

"Thank you." A large, dull-colored bird came fluttering up from the underbrush almost under the feet of Fiona's horse; it snorted and half-reared. Fiona brought it under control, soothed the horse by stroking its neck, and then looked up at Campas.

"After the Classani got over their surprise at having their opinion solicited at all," she said, "they talked very freely. I've been trying to make sense out of what they told me. And of what the Brodaini have told me about themselves, and of what your own people have told me about them. So I thought I'd ask for you for the afternoon, to help me sort it all out."

He looked at her with a wry smile. "I once started a history of the Brodaini," he said. "The Brodaini were very much in fashion for a season or two, you see, about ten years ago. All the city fashion brats trying to dress simply, imitating their direct speech, striving to affect martial virtue. No doubt it amused the Brodaini to no end. But the fashion changed . . . and suddenly there was no audience for my history. I abandoned it, but whatever I learned is at your service, Ambassador."

"Thank you, Campas." The history was a surprise, a stroke of good luck. She rode on for a moment in silence, wondering how to begin. She'd had abstracts of the formal history the Brodaini taught their own children, of course: there was a lot of strange legend in it, gods and spirits wandering among the mortals and motivating their behavior, but there had also been large swatches of careful statistics— which lord brought how many men to which battle, that sort of thing—that seemed factual enough. There were also a great many madmen running through the histories, with nothing made of it: it was as if the Brodaini considered it a fairly usual thing to go mad, and never held it against the madman after he'd recovered his wits. It had all been difficult to untangle, particularly since the motivations of everyone in the histories had been so difficult to fathom. They went here, they did this: but why? Motivation and psychology were unknown to the Brodaini; they simply didn't bother explaining them, aside from the appearance of an occasional god or demon whispering in a warrior's ear. There was no distinction between fact, supposition, legend, and myth. The personalities had to be understood in the context of Brodaini culture, and it was a context Fiona found entirely opaque.

There were also enormous gaps. The Brodaini warriors held center stage; the Classani were occasionally given a footnote, if valiant enough; the other two classes were scarcely mentioned at all. It was not unusual, she supposed, for the ruling class to be blind to the thoughts and actions of their inferiors, but it was frustrating.

"The Brodaini," Campas said, filling the silence, "came as conquerors. They were living in the mountains to the north of their land, in the deep valleys there . . . and their gods told them to go down and conquer the flatlands and the islands, which they did, though it took them sixty years. There were a lot of revolts, of course, and the Brodaini had to be wary; their gods told them how to order society for the betterment of all, and things settled down. But after the revolts had all been put down the gods started fighting among themselves, with their Brodaini adherents battling right along. There hasn't been peace up there since."

"Yes," Fiona said. Barring the nonsense about the gods, it made sense. A poor people living on the fringes of the glaciers, looking down with envy on the more prosperous folk below. And then the climate changed, perhaps, forcing them south; or their numbers increased, demanding a migration in search of living space—and then a sixty-year war, won by the invaders thanks to the total militarization of their society and a certain technological superiority: their armored lancers, once they'd learned proper tactics, had run smash over their enemies' infantry-based armies. The numbers of Brodaini had never been very large—less than one-tenth of the entire population of the area they controlled—and their survival depended on their constant military preparedness. The class barriers would have risen in an attempt to keep arms from the conquered; the danger of revolt would have demanded constant military readiness, and a firming of the military system. And after the situation had been stabilized the military caste would have needed a justification for their existence, so they began fighting one another. Another society might have expanded outwards in search of conquest, but the Brodaini had been too inner-directed: a possible revolt of their subjects would never have been far from their minds, and they would not have dared to send a military force abroad lest their inferiors rise up while they were away. The result: a feuding upper caste obsessed with its own security and committed to maintaining a rigid class system that kept them safely on top. Anything alien, anything foreign that threatened to upset the system was an enemy: their ideal was stability, rather than evolution. Vail, in their own language, an ideal, eternal, unchanging harmony. . . .

"After that the chronicles are filled with wars to the point of tedium," Campas said. "Also geneologies: those people were always allying by marriage, but the alliances didn't always hold, so a lot of first cousins ended up giving each other the chop."

"Do you think the women would have become militarized during the conquest?" Fiona asked. "To be able to hold down the peasants while the men were off at war cutting off new bits of territory?"

Campas frowned. "I don't know. That possibility hadn't occurred to me." He gazed abstractedly northward, toward a great east-bending swoop of the river. "The idea seems reasonable," he added. "I can think of any number of Brodaini heroines who were celebrated for conducting epic defenses of their homelands while their menfolk were off fighting somewhere else."

"Do they reach as far back as the conquest?"

Campas knit his brows. "Let me think. There's Amasta Toronu y'Tosta—the Tosta family epic is about her. There *was* a big defense of the home castle against an uprising; she won by spreading plague among the attackers. Later she went mad, poisoned her husband, and started a war that ended tragically. Committed suicide in the end; there's a famous verse drama about that, all dramatic monologue, hell on the voice but a part to kill for." He looked up. "But it was the seige that made her famous. And she's from the time of the conquests. You may be right."

He looked at her with open curiosity. "Do women fight on your world, Ambassador?"

Fiona glanced away. Why was she finding it so hard to lie to this man? The answer, in all its full implications, was such that he couldn't possibly understand it in any case.

"Yes, we do," she said. "I would be thankful if you kept this private."

"Of course, Ambassador."

"We've made our weapons very small," Fiona said. "Physical strength isn't required. Anyone can carry them."

Now why had she said that? It would do nothing but raise further questions, questions that she would be bound not to answer. He couldn't possibly understand the nature or evolution of energy weapons, nor was it proper that he should. Nor the nature of war on Igara, the carefully formal dance of death between the complex, interwoven country families, the city block republics, the tenuous, infirm nations, theoretically controlling so much planet surface but with such little real power. War was real, but it was kept small; it was murderous, but in its way it was also very personal, almost intimate. And, when it happened, sudden and incredibly violent.

But Campas was apparently satisfied with her answers; he asked no more questions. Fiona glanced ahead. They had ridden upslope once more, and were on a grassy bluff overlooking the river valley. The river itself was invisible, hidden by the trees and brush covering its banks, but from the bluff she could see the dark trees winding on ahead, following the jagged course of the river. Behind she could still hear the sounds of axes.

"Shall we eat our luncheon?" she asked. Campas nodded. They dismounted, hobbled their horses, and opened Fiona's satchel: cheese, bread, fresh goat-meat, dried pears, two bottles of black beer. Fiona sat cross-legged on the ground, facing the river—it felt good to be out of skirts again—and opened her beer. Campas pointed to a smudge of dust hovering above the opposing bluff.

"Reinforcements for Tastis," he said. "Or cavalry on maneuvers. We'll be getting another galloper at the pavilion tonight to tell us which." He looked down at the beer in his hand and twisted the cork. "They've got thirty thousands of men over there. That's more than we expected—we thought he'd have to leave a larger garrison back at Neda-Calacas."

"I hadn't realized," Fiona said, "that a campaign was so slow-moving. I thought there'd be a lot of marching, a battle, and then it would be over. But nothing's happened yet, and nothing seems likely to happen for a long time; and no one seems to be concerned."

"So far as I understand it," Campas said, "we're moving slowly because we don't want to make any mistakes. We have advantage in numbers, and so long as we don't leave Tastis any openings we'll win. Plus, as time goes on, the other cities will be able to mobilize and put their own forces into the field.''

Fiona slit open a narrow loaf of bread, inserted the goat-meat and cheese, and bit down. The blandness of the food here still bothered her: the locals had little in the way of spices, and few of the spices were taken on campaign.

''You say that Brodaini women are first mentioned in the chronicles as defending their homes,'' she said.

''And as advisors. Prophets, seers, and so on. Divinely mad. Expressions of their clan's will, or their god's.''

Fiona nodded. ''When are they first mentioned as military leaders?'' she asked.

''As opposed to clan leaders?'' She nodded. ''Let me think.'' He chewed meditatively, then turned to her. ''During the time of the tyrant Grestu, about a hundred years ago. His wife was a famous general, and there were several other prominent women military leaders at the same time.''

Grestu. Fiona, searching her memory, recalled the name. Vilified by the Brodaini histories for his attempt to put all of Gostandu under his rule, but that hadn't stopped others from trying in the hundred years since. Two had succeeded, though the first of these empires had once again come to nothing on the death of the founder; the second was the man who now ruled Gostandu, the Clattern i Clatterni— ''King of Kinglets,'' as Tyson, a year or more ago, had once facetiously translated.

The shipboard computers had concluded that the northern continent had reached a level of communication, sophistication, and economic interdependence so that a centralized government had begun to be possible. But the shipboard computers had only a limited vision; their conclusions were based only on what their programming permitted them to understand—vast amounts of data were set aside, either not understood or judged irrelevant. The computers could point out large, visible trends, but lacked the capacity to interpret its own statistics. The framework in which to set the data was lacking. It was a framework Fiona was expected to help construct.

There were anomalies in any human system, serving to throw light on how they operated: the position of women in Brodaini society was one—a culture that prized combat and physical strength offering theoretical equality to those less strong was unique. If, as Fiona suspected, it were true that the women had been given military training in order to defend their homes against invasions or peasant revolts that occurred when the menfolk were away, this helped to explain a lot. The women would have to have been given civil rights in order to manage clan affairs while the men were absent; and they would have to have been given high status in order to command any defense.

The Brodaini system had been under increasing pressure for the last hundred years or more: the continent of Gostandu had been in continual war. Possibly, Fiona thought, women Brodaini had grown increasingly valuable as the wars drained the supply of men—valuable both as soldiers and as breeders of future generations of fighters: a contradictory demand, probably settled in contradictory ways, both by increasing their status and making them available as front-line soldiers, if the situation called for it.

There was a pragmatism in their deployment, however. It was obvious, simply by observing the columns of marching troops, that the Brodaini on this campaign of conquest were still overwhelmingly male, while those left in garrison were chiefly female—and though many of these were officers, they commanded Classani militia, not soldiers of their own class. Those women used as front-line troops tended to be used as light cavalry and scouts, duties better suited to the smaller physique, and also requiring a higher premium on riding ability than on physical strength. Many women were employed carrying the Brodaini sword-tipped spear, a duty requiring less physical strength than that of a bowman or swordsman. And the front ranks of the spear formations, where increased exposure required heavier armor and the demands of battle required more physical strength, were almost universally male. There were, Fiona had been told, many female cambrani and lersri—spies and assassins, professions demanding wit, stamina, and intelligence rather than strength.

There was, Fiona concluded, a strong pragmatism underlying most Brodaini decisions, a pragmatism that did not seem entirely consistent with their rigorous code of conduct. When pragmatism demanded a decision that conflicted with nartil, how was the contradiction resolved? It was a question that demanded an answer.

"Nartil," she said. "Nartil and Tolhostu. I don't understand them."

"No one does. Not outside the Brodaini world, anyway." Campas seemed amused.

"A code of behavior," she said, "expressly designed to avoid giving offense, and explicitly stating the obligations of one Brodainu to another. Supposedly all of this is clear, and there should be little room for misunderstanding. So long as everything is understood, peace is part of the natural order, and war contrary to it. But," she said, jabbing the air with her beer bottle, "the Brodaini are always fighting one another."

"So you want to know why they fight?" Campas asked. His tone was light, a little condescending. Fiona looked at him sharply.

"No," she snapped, more nettled than she would have liked to admit. "I'm not so naive as to wander about this planet like a little simpleton asking rhetorical questions about why you people fight wars. I'm not interested in giving you reign to wave your arms to the heavens and philosophize about the perversity of mankind."

"My apologies, Ambassador," Campas murmured, surprised.

"What I was wondering," Fiona want on, "was how

the Brodaini justify it to themselves. In terms of their own code of behavior.''

Campas looked dubious, frowning and rubbing his jaw. ''That's a deep question, Ambassador,'' he said. ''I would rather have answered the one I thought you had asked, in truth.''

Fiona said nothing; she sipped her beer and waited for a response.

''I don't understand nartil,'' Campas said slowly. ''And I'm not supposed to understand demmin—that's for Brodaini only. The codes are complex, and I wasn't born into that way of life, I only observe. But it seems to me that the codes are—are capable of variation.'' He looked at her, his own confusion plain. ''They're not written down, you see. They're taught by example, by tradition. There are stories that every Brodaini child is taught, to learn the nature of one particular virtue, or one particular evil. Hamila and the Redtooth Keep, for example, to learn about obedience to a superior.''

Fiona knew that story: the spikes had picked it up in many places, so many that the computers had flagged it as important. Hamila was ordered to hold a particular strong-hold with a small band; when the enemy army came Hamila's superior ordered him to withdraw, but through a bungle the order never reached Redtooth Keep: there was a gallant and ingenious defense, though in the end the defenders died. And Hamila's side, through various other blunders, lost the war.

''I know that one,'' Fiona said.

''Good: then you know it's used to teach the value of obedience,'' Campas said. ''But there are other morals to draw from it, if the storyteller is clever enough. It depends on what he wishes to emphasize. There is one long poem—there was a furor over it when it appeared, but since the author was a proven warrior it was eventually accepted—it treats Hamila quite differently. As an example of waste: brave man lost through oversight, his gallantry made pointless since his sacrifice meant nothing in the long run. The moral drawn was the value of initiative: the poet clearly thought that Hamila was a fool for staying, though he didn't quite dare to say so—but it's clear he thought Hamila should have retreated and rejoined the main army, where his skills might have been put to better use.''

Campas fell silent for a moment, trying to knit his thoughts together. ''Nartil, demmin, tolhostu . . . they're not as rigid as they seem,'' he concluded. ''The Brodaini treat them as if they were inflexible, but it's not so. They're subject to interpretation, they have different shades of meaning.''

Fiona nodded. Any code transmitted orally would prove subject to change, she thought. Human nature being what it is, any ambiguity or shade of interpretation would be exploited. But, she wondered, how was it done?

''So nartil, for example, can be used to justify an act that, on the surface, disregards the obligations of nartil?'' she asked.

''Or demmin can be invoked to justify violation of nartil, or any number of other combinations,'' Campas said. ''That's what Tastis has done—he overthrew the Nadielas coalition and claimed they'd violated a code they couldn't possibly have understood.''

That pragmatic streak, again. Tastis, once he'd decided to take Neda-Calacas, had chosen the most covert and deceptive way to go about it—his moves had been absolutely practical; but he'd found cultural justifications for everything he'd done.

''How do you think Tastis' mind worked?'' Fiona asked. ''Was he simply waiting for an excuse to take the city, and then found the justifications for his actions afterward; or do you think he was responding to circumstance?''

Campas shrugged. "Who can say? I'm not a member of his aldran."

"Your opinion, then," Fiona insisted.

Campas picked up a dried pear and began tearing at it absently, popping the bits into his mouth as he thought. When he spoke he was staring off into the valley below, abstracted. "I would say Tastis is not a simple man," he began. "I don't think his actions are that simple—I don't think *any* Brodainu is as simple as he pretends to be. There's a mingling of traditions, of codes, of practical necessities, of motivations. His laws and his motives were mixed, shall we say, as they are with us all; and it would require a god to sort them out." He turned to her with a dismissive half-smile. "I'm sorry, Ambassador. You keep asking me about things I haven't thought about. It's difficult for me to be wise on the spur of the moment."

She reached out to touch his elbow, reassuring. "Thank you, Campas," she said. "You've been helpful, truly."

He looked up at her cynically. "But you have some more questions," he said.

She drew back her arm and grinned. "Yes. I do."

Campas tilted his head back as he drained his beer, then absently tossed the empty bottle downslope. She frowned at the waste—her reflexes, born of a planet with scarcer resources, were hard to overcome. She tried to put it out of her mind.

"Go ahead," Campas said. "I'll try to summon up what wisdom I can."

"We spoke once before, you remember, about the Brodaini. And you mentioned all of the elaborate methods that Tegestu had devised to keep your people separate from his."

"Yes. I remember that conversation." He smiled ruefully. "Even the parts I wish I could forget."

Fiona smiled. "I'd like some idea," she said, "of what happens when these two people *do* meet. They must have developed some ways of working together, of getting along—otherwise Neda-Calacas would have happened everywhere.''

Campas shrugged. ''There are ways of getting along with foreigners,'' he said. ''It requires some extra effort. Extra courtesy, and extra tolerance.''

''You can make yourself understood by the Brodaini?'' she asked.

''Most of the time,'' he said. ''But, you see, nothing I say or think truly *matters* to them—I'm not Brodaini, so my opinions don't count.'' He shrugged. ''I got along better with the Classani, as you did. We understood each other better. They're warmer, more open . . . friendlier, if you like.'' He frowned, his fingers absently dismembering the pear. ''But there's a furtive quality to them I don't care for. They're too used to moving about quietly, skulking behind stairs, as if they don't want the Brodaini to notice them—they're too submissive.''

They were silent for a moment. Both, Fiona thought, had an idea of what being *noticed* by a Brodaini might consist of.

''Has that attitude changed, do you think?'' Fiona asked. ''If they don't like their masters, they can run away—If they ran away back home, they'd still be Classani, but here there's a whole new continent, with more opportunities.''

''Some do run, of course,'' Campas said. ''But not many. Most of the Brodaini and their folk haven't bothered to learn Abessas, for one thing, except maybe for a few words here and there. So if they do run they find things hard, and strange. And for the most part the Classani are well off; they live in the same conditions as the Brodaini, eat the same food—and they aren't required to do a lot of military service.'' He ate a piece of pear, then went on. ''And of course their family will have stayed behind, and these Brodaini set great store by their families. All four classes of society in a kamliss, you see, are all supposed to be one family, even if few of the lower classes are actually related to the Brodaini. Life outside would be lonely, as well as hard. It's not the Classani who run, it's the Hostli.

"They're the lowest class, the merchants, small traders, storekeepers. The most despised." He smiled. "They have the most contact with our people, acquiring supplies and the like, doing business for their kamlissi; so they've learned the language quickly. They see how much easier it would be for them outside, and many have come across."

"Has the status of the remainder improved as they've become rarer, more valuable?"

"Indeed yes," Campas said. "No more insults, no more shouldering Hostli aside on the street. The Classani feel threatened by the change." He gave her a sly look. "You've been talking to the Classani about this, haven't you?"

"Yes." She finished her beer and returned the empty bottle to the pack. "They're proud of their status, next to the Brodaini. Sometimes I have the feeling that they're more tradition-bound than the Brodaini themselves."

Campas seemed curious. "Why do you ask me, then?"

"I might be wrong. It's good to have independent confirmation."

Campas frowned, seemingly puzzled. Truth was a received thing in his culture, Fiona thought, transmitted by family, tradition, religion, personal observation; the idea that data might be assembled from different sources to create a new whole, a new truth, was foreign to him.

"And of how many people have you asked these questions?" Campas asked.

"Not many. The Classani, mostly. But I wanted to talk to someone outside their world, someone who doesn't share their . . . attitudes." She looked up at the sound of hoofbeats: a galloper was trotting north from the camp, a dispatch-case bouncing on his hip. An Arrandalla this time, tall in a plumed helmet, a case of javelins strapped to his saddle. The rider trotted past, ignoring them.

Campas was looking at her steadily. "Will you be asking the Brodaini about us?" he asked.

"I have already."

He rubbed his chin. "It's as if you don't trust your own judgement."

"I don't." She spoke quickly, trying to drive home her point. "Not in everything. I haven't known your people long enough, so I ask them to explain themselves, and I ask others—other foreigners—to explain them to me." She paused, trying to think of an example. "It's like your poetry," she said. "I admire your gift with words, your understanding of their rhythm, the way the sounds can be linked into music, all resonating, echoing one another. That much I can understand; that much I know.

"But I don't understand the subject matter. All the shepherds and shepherdesses, all the plant symbolism, all the references to other poets. I come from another place; our poetry is based on other traditions, other forms. I have to have kloss—klossalla—"

"Klossila," Campas corrected.

"Klossila. Thank you. I need to have it explained to me; I haven't lived in Arrandal long enough to understand it."

Campas, uneasy, looked down into the valley. "It's as I said before, in that other conversation," he said. "My life's work is suddenly out of date. Your people can't comprehend the form."

"There are many people on this planet," Fiona said, "who can't understand your work. Many of them in Arrandal. Why should you suddenly be concerned for the opinions of a few Igaralla?"

"Because you're the future," Campas said. His answer was prompt, though his tone was moody, uncertain; it was clear he'd been thinking this out. "A poet writes for posterity, you see—or at least he does if he has any sense of his own worth—and suddenly posterity has appeared in Arrandal, and doesn't understand my work." He looked down at his hands, then pushed them out, a gesture of denial. There was a grating desperation in his voice. "I've been forced to look at my work again, with new eyes. Your eyes. And there's so much I don't like, don't understand. It's frightening."

He looked at her suddenly, his uncertainty plain. "Your poetry—Igaralla poetry," he said. "What's it like? I'd like to know."

Fiona shook her head. "It doesn't matter," she said. "It's not written for *you,* any more than your work is written for us. It wouldn't make sense here." She paused for a moment, then added, "You can't simply adopt Igaralla forms; they're not suitable for you, and you'd just be an imitator. You have to find your own way. You don't need our approval."

He absorbed her words in silence, his hands absently plucking at the sod. When he spoke, his voice was hesitant, without assurance. "I—I've had some ideas, some words running through my head. I don't know what to make of them . . . they're not klossila, though. This is something new. A new form. Brodaini, almost, in its straightfor-wardness, but much more lyrical." He frowned. "Maybe it's time for klossila to die," he said. "It was a revolution, fifty years ago, insisting on the rights of poetry to be itself, to be independent of the popular understanding; perhaps it's moribund now." He shook his head. "I haven't written it yet. It's slow in coming."

"I would like," Fiona said, "to see your new work, if you ever write it. Not to approve or disapprove. Just to read it."

His eyes rose to hers, held them for an instant; then he nodded. "I'd like that," he said.

A possible revolution in poetry, Fiona thought. It wasn't

what she'd been sent to accomplish; but it certainly hadn't been forbidden, either. An interesting conceit, to think of herself as a muse.

She gave him a grin. "I'm done with my questions," she said. "I've got as much as I can deal with, for the moment."

Campas gave her a slow nod. "You're very welcome, Ambassador," he said. "I hope you can take me away from my dreary tasks some other time."

Fiona busied herself repacking their meal, while Campas brought the horses back. She looked down the slope, seeing the bottle Campas had thrown; and then she walked down the slope to pick it up and return it to her pack.

Old habits die hard, she thought. The bottle would be thrown on the camp rubbish heap in any case, but at least she would keep this grassy slope uncluttered, in case another couple ever came for a picnic. She laughed at the silliness of it all—a lone foreign woman, tidying up after this horde of soldiers—and then walked merrily up the slope, digging in her pack for a handful of grain, a treat for her horse.

12

Tegestu felt his muscles tighten with anger as he read the dispatch. Some of Tastis' cavalry had forded the river and circled behind him; they'd intercepted one of the trains of bridging-boats that were being carried overland to the army, chopped up the escort, and made a pyre of the boats. All this would set the river-crossing back several days, until the boats were replaced.

He looked up at the solemn faces of the staff, seeing the hesitation in their eyes, their apprehension at his sudden blaze of anger. Deliberately, disdainfully, Tegestu crumpled the dispatch one-handed and let it fall to the floor of the tent. He turned to Cascan.

"Who is this Osta Tolmatu Tosta y'Tosta?" he asked.

Cascan bowed. "My cousin, drandor Tegestu," he answered carefully. "A whelkran of two hundreds."

"Your cousin has shown himself a fool," Tegestu said. "A fool with the bad taste to survive his disgrace." Tegestu's tone grew brisk. "You will convene a kamliss court in ten days to decide his punishment. Inform him."

"Thank you, drandor Tegestu," Cascan said, relief apparent through his grave mask. The ten days' delay would allow some time for Cascan's cousin to redeem himself, traditionally by a raid, with a few friends to act as witnesses, on the enemy. If, that is, he could find any friends to accompany him on such a suicidal mission—if not, he'd have to bring back proof of his actions, usually in the form of enemy heads accompanied by rank badges. Either Osta would die on his raid or he'd bring back enough heads so that the kamliss court would not have to embarrass themselves by handing out a major reprimand: either way kamliss Tosta would avoid the major disgrace Osta might otherwise represent.

"Acamantu," Tegestu said. "You will assign someone of proven competence to guard the next bridging train."

"Aye, bro-demmin."

Tasting bile in his throat, Tegestu rose from his stool, the others rising with him, and then walked out of the staff tent toward his own. There was a skin of cider hanging from his tent pole; he pulled the cork and drank, washing away the bitter taste of anger. He had given that young cadet more leniency than he deserved, he knew: he should have had him back in camp, reprimanded publicly, and broken in ranks to a spearman; yet something had urged him to be lenient.

Perhaps, the thought came to him, because he himself had seemed unable to do anything but as Tastis wished. And in Osta's incompetence he had seen a reflection of his own.

Tegestu spat, dismissing the notion. He entered the tent and his Classani servants stripped the armor from him and dropped a robe over him, belting it; they made his cot ready, placing a pillow for his head and another for his feet.

He dismissed the Classani and lay down, feeling pleasant relief ease slowly over his limbs, wishing he'd been able to bring some of his household animals with him, cats and dogs to share his tent with himself and Grendis. He was unable to rest: thoughts of the war, of Tastis, kept tugging at his mind, demanding attention. He could feel the first feather touches of the net that surrounded him, ready to be drawn tight; but he didn't yet see the nature of the trap. He could only preach vigilance and hope that Tastis' design would make itself apparent in time.

The war news had not been good. Twelve days ago the Abessu-Denorru of Cartenas had been assassinated by a man readily identified, by his equipment, as a Brodainu, and so presumably Tastis' agent; the city was in turmoil, and there would be a delay in sending their army, though fortunately their fleet had already arrived in Arrandal. Perhaps it was lucky that Necias had chosen to accompany the army, and was now surrounded by fifty thousand bodyguards. A few days after the assassination Tastis' fleet had launched a surprise dawn attack on the fleet of Prypas that had been advancing slowly on Neda-Calacas from the west, opposite the Arrandalla army, their fleet paralleling the army that marched slowly along the shore; two dozen galleys, drawn up on the beach, had been burned, and a number of the deep-draught sailing vessels taken—but Tastis had lost some ships as well, and the raid had served only to delay matters. Arrandal's own fleet, joined now by that of Cartenas, should have arrived in the Neda-Calacas area by now, preparing a blockade. Tastis' fleet could not hope to match the united squadrons; their strike at Prypas had been all they could do.

Other good news had come. Tastis' raiders had, for the most part, been dealt with: they'd either slowed down enough to be caught by the Arrandalla pursuers, had withdrawn with their loot to neutral areas, or returned to Tastis with enemy cavalry snapping at their heels. More and more of Tegestu's light cavalry were returning to the army, improving his sight and reach.

Word had come from the northern Elva cities, brought

back.

s' pattern *not* to attack. There
le that Tegestu hadn't seen—
Cascan, and the scouts half-
information. Tastis' force had
e of Cascan's daring cambrani
o come back with careful de-

w, half Brodaini and Classani,

the other half city men and mercenaries. The city men were good, no half-trained militia among them; Tastis had taken the cream of his fighting force. He would not let them sit idly on the high back of the river, waiting for Tegestu to force a crossing on one flank or the other.

Tegestu heard the drum of hoofbeats, then the heavy tread of spurred boots entering his tent. He opened his eyes and saw Grendis, her grey braids piled high on her head. She was looking down at him with her soft affectionate eyes, plucking at the straps of her supple leather armor. She shrugged out of the cuirass, then bent to kiss him lightly; he could smell her familiar warmth through the scent of leather, animal and exercise, and he smiled.

There was excitement in her glance, and triumph. "I've found it, I think," she said. "What we've been looking for. The key to Tastis' plan."

Necias looked up at Tegestu and Grendis as they walked quickly into his pavilion, and rose hastily as they went down on one knee before him. "Canlan Necias, Grendis brings news," Tegestu said as he straightened. "We know Tastis' intentions."

Necias frowned for a moment, then turned to one of his servants. "Where's Palastinas?"

"Ah—with a hunting party, Abessu-Denorru."

Necias frowned. "Fetch him." He glanced up at the other servants. "The rest of you, get out."

They backed quickly out of the pavilion while Necias looked impatiently after them; then Necias moved across the room to the table normally used by one of his secretaries. "You have a map, I see," he said as he settled his bulk onto the settee.

"Yes." Tegestu took the rolled map from Grendis, then pinned it down on the table with inkpots and a glass of stale beer. He looked at the map with pleasure, appreciating it as a purely functional piece of design, clean and

informative. Cartography in Arrandal had been much farther advanced than in Tegestu's homeland, a result of the
need for nautical charts; but the Brodaini engineers had
learned quickly, and now produced fine, precise, and accurate works of their own. The map was of Tastis' camp, the
known elevations marked in a precise hand, banners embla-
zoned precisely to mark the tents of Tastis' commanders,
with notes as to the strength of their regiments.

Tastis' main camp wasn't directly above the ford, but
rather two miles to the southwest along the road, south of
a thin line representing an old, small canal that emptied
into the river. The purpose was clear enough: Tastis could
water his horses and men in the canal without having to
bring them to the river, within shot of Tegestu's own men;
and if the ford were threatened Tastis could get his men
across the fields to the ford speedily enough.

Tegestu put a stubby finger on the little canal. "Two of
bro-demmin Grendis' scouts," he said, "went up the canal
last night." Arrandalla men in fact, two deissins' sons in
the quest of adventure. They'd certainly found it.

"The canal has been deepened by Tastis' engineers, and
there has been a double dam constructed at the river
entrance," Tegestu said, spraying the difficult Abessla
words in his haste. "We thought they did this for the
purpose of keeping enough water in it for the horses and
men."

"All our scouts," Grendis said, "came into the camp
from the south. It's open that way. To get in from the
north they would have to sweep behind the castle fortifications and then circle well behind, then cross the canal."

"I see," Necias said.

"And then these two boys," Tegestu said, "swam across
the river last night. The dam was guarded so they went
around, then got into the canal to follow it to the enemy
camp. They wanted to steal an enemy banner, to boast to
their friends."

Necias looked up at them, bewildered. "So what did they find?" he asked.

"Barges," said Grendis.

"Many barges," Tegestu added. "Taken from the river and hidden in the canal."

"Boats," Necias repeated. He seemed bewildered. "So you found boats in the canal. Why shouldn't there be boats in a canal?"

Stumbling over the unfamiliar words in their haste, Grendis and Tegestu explained. Tastis had, of course, sent men up and down the river to destroy or confiscate every boat and barge he could to prevent Tegestu from using them to aid his crossing. But the barges hidden here, in the carefully deepened canal, suggested he was intending to use them for purposes of his own.

The deep water in the canal meant that when the dam was broken down the barges would all float effortlessly into the river on the current. Tastis' engineers could assemble them into a bridge—probably more than one bridge—in a few hours. If done at night the chances of being seen were slim, particularly since the heavy timber in the river valley would obscure the vision of anyone on the heights above; and if the cavalry forded above the bridge while the infantry crossed over the barges, Tastis could get most of his army across before dawn.

And then, Tegestu explained, there would be a smashing dawn attack on the Arrandalla camp. The defenders would be caught by surprise, with no plan of action, probably without time even to don their armor. Such of the army as survived would be driven back in disorder, delaying the campaign for months, and allowing Tastis time to move his forces against Prypas, presumably to attempt the same sort of surprise.

It had been only because two Arrandalla youth had gone in search of adventure that the barges had been discovered at all—all the safe scouting approaches were well away

from the canal. And the cavalry raid Tastis had launched
had faded away to the north, suggesting that Tastis was
hoping to draw his enemies' attention there, away from a
river crossing. It was masterful.

Tegestu felt a warm certainty filling him as he spoke.
The plan was pure Tastis: an opposed river crossing to
delay the enemy and lull them into security, a diversion to
draw attention away to the north, a sudden crossing to fall
on the enemy camp from an unexpected direction. Swift,
sudden, flexible, the attack in strength and unlooked-for.
The hallmarks of a Tastis campaign. It would have worked,
too, but for those two young scouts. And Grendis. A
seeming accident, still their escapade would never have
taken place without her insistence on finding Tastis'
intentions, trying to slip into the camp from an unusual
direction.

Tegestu glanced at Grendis, standing travel-stained on
Necias' fine carpets, feeling his heart fill with joy at the
sight of her. She had kept faith, believing Tegestu even
though there was no evidence to support him she'd kept
her scouts working night and day until, at last, the revela-
tion had come. He reached out to touch her arm; and she
glanced up at him, her eyes filled with pride.

"I'll reward those two young men," Necias was saying.
"Their fathers will be proud." He looked up at them,
pulling his lower lip. "When will the crossing be?" he
asked.

"Soon." Tegestu said. "Or he will have wasted that
cavalry raid."

"So," Necias said. "We can meet him, there on the
water's edge. Push him back."

"May your arm never weaken. Abessu-Denorru," Tegestu
said. "I would wish to let him build his bridge and bring
his army across." He saw Necias' bewilderment and allowed himself a grim, reassuring smile. "We should let
Tastis' plan take its course."

Tastis had devised such a good plan, Tegestu thought, it would be a shame to not to let him have his battle.

It was two nights later that Grendis' watchers on the riverbank brought word that the barges were moving. Tegestu, lying in the dark repose of his tent as the tedec and bohau played outside under the stars, heard the hooves of the gallopers and their whispered conversation outside the tent. He reached out to touch Grendis' arm as she lay on the next cot and felt her start as she came awake.

"The news has come," he said with quiet certainty. Comprehension came into her eyes, and she rasied a hand to touch his cheek.

"Tegestu." A world of trust in the way she said the name. *I shall ward your back from danger*, she had promised; the promise was kept still.

There was a scuffling of feet outside the tent. "Beg pardon, bro-demmini." Thesau's voice.

"Once more, my heart," Tegestu said. He kissed her hand. "I am grateful every day," he said, and bent to kiss her, his unbound hair caressing her forehead, and then rose to his feet and told those outside to enter. Thesau was there, armored already in his leather; with him were Acamantu and Cascan.

"Inform Marshal Palastinas and the Abessu-Denorru," Tegestu said, after he'd heard the news. "Then have the army called quietly to arms. No trumpets or drums—make certain of that."

"Aye, bro-demmin."

He and Grendis sat opposite one another on their cots, their knees touching, as the Classani braided their hair and coiled it carefully atop their heads. Grendis looked at him with a slight, tranquil smile, not speaking—no words were needed; it was perfectly understood, all that they meant to one another.

They stood to have their armor fitted, Grendis with her

light cavalry leather cuirass and jingling coif of chain beneath her light helmet, Tegestu in the heavier linked plates of brigandine. The Classani handed them their swords and, Tegestu in the lead, they walked out of the dark tent.

It was black. There was a glow in the west where First Moon, with her stripes of deep azure and yellow, was setting; Third Moon had risen, but he was small and provided little light.

Ghantenis, Tegestu's bannerbearer, stood outside the tent, the heavy standard folded darkly over his head, along with others of the staff and a dark mass of whelkrani, commanders of hundreds and thousands who, forewarned somehow by some uncharted sense, had known to migrate in this moment to the tent of their drandor. Tegestu received their salutes gravely. "Ban-demmini, Tastis is moving tonight," he said. "I trust his welcome is prepared?"

"Aye, bro-demmin," they chorused softly. Tegestu could see the fervid glow in their eyes, the glow that anticipated combat and rejoiced in the anticipation . . . he raised his gauntleted hands, and his limbs felt younger by twenty years.

"Blessings on you all," he said. "Go to your places. There is no need for haste. There are many hours before dawn."

They bowed again in silence, and the whelkrani dispersed, the staff standing ready beneath the folded banner. Tegestu called for the horses. There was a flurry of movement on the fringe of the group and suddenly it parted for the Abessu-Denorru, moving rapidly in the dark. Tegestu hastily went down to one knee.

"Rise, rise," Necias said hastily, and Tegestu came to his feet again. Necias seemed agitated, shifting his weight rapidly from one foot to the other; he had a coat of chain on, with one arm fully armored and the other not, as if too impatient to armor himself fully. Necias put his fists on his hips.

"Tastis is coming, hey?" he asked quickly. "You're sure about it?"

Tegestu bowed. "Is certain," he said. "He will come tonight."

Necias clapped his hands. "Good," he said heartily. "Very good. We'll beat him, hey?"

Tegestu bowed again. "Canlan, our arms are strong," he said.

"Good," repeated Necias. "I'll be ready to ride with you, as soon as my armor's strapped on." He looked at Tegestu, his eyes dark and strange. "I trust you, Tegestu," he said. He licked his lips and glanced up at the dark sky, then looked at the Brodaini faces under their tilted helms, the shadowed faces that watched him impassively. "I'm counting on you all."

The faces seemed of stone. Tegestu saw spittle on Necias' cheek. "We'll get them, hey," Necias said to the silence, clapping his hands again.

He is afraid, Tegestu realized. *He rose to power in a series of wars, but he has never been on a battlefield before. It has made him nearly witless.* The thought unnerved him, that he served a frightened man. Yet he had always known it, that Necias was not a martial man, that he had no understanding of demmin . . . he pushed the thought away, that a lord could have no demmin. He should take Necias away from here, he realized, before the others realized what they were seeing.

He took his canlan by the arm. "A word with you, Abeissu," he said, as firmly as he dared. Necias nodded quickly, and seemed eager to be led away.

"My force will move soon, canlan Necias," Tegestu said. "You wish to be with them, I know, but I think you must stay here."

"Here? In the camp?"

"Aye. With Marshal Palastinas. Here you shall see more. Out in the dark, with me, nothing. I shall send messages, you will be informed.'' He tightened his grip on Necias' arm, trying to be reassuring. "We shall break Tastis tonight, with the gods' help.''

"In the camp. Yes,'' Necias said. He nodded briskly. "That makes sense, Tegestu. Thank you.'' He tugged uncomfortably at the chain around his neck. "I'll go, then,'' he said, and clapped Tegestu on the shoulder. "I'm counting on you. Smash those rebels and we can all go home, hey?''

"No worry. We'll beat them,'' Tegestu said. He leaned closer to Necias. "Tell Marshall Palastinas I'm moving my headquarters to the old farm. He knows the one.'' Necias nodded, repeated the message in a breathless voice, and then hurried away. Tegestu knelt, feeling a stab of rheumatism as his knee touched the cold ground, then returned to the silent group of Brodaini. The horses had been brought and stood saddled and ready. Tegestu looked carefully at the faces, watching for a sign that they had recognized the Abessu-Denorru's fear, for any hint of contempt. Nothing, he thought, or they were keeping it to themselves.

His horse was brought; he put an armored foot into Thesau's cupped hands and heaved himself up into the saddle. His horse was a mature beast, gentle and understanding of his old bones; it accepted his weight without protest. He looked down at the ring of faces.

"We shall triumph tonight, of that I am certain,'' he said. "You have all done well.'' He glanced at Grendis and saw her smile; he addressed the next words to her. "You have kept faith,'' he said, "and you have made this victory possible. The gods reward you.''

They bowed in silence, the grave Brodaini response to praise; and then he signed them to mount. There was the sound of trotting hooves, and the interpreter Campas came out of the dark, looking uneasy in his unfamiliar and second-hand coat of chain. "Marshal Palastinas sent me,'' he said, speaking his easy Gostu. "He thought I might make myself useful."

"Come then," Tegestu said; he donned his helmet and led the party to the south gate of the camp, where he could see the regiments moving into position behind him: armored cavalry, spearmen, bowmen, heavily armored figures carrying rhomphaia—Brodaini, Classani, mercenaries, and the men of Arrandal, all marshalled silently between the rows of tents. Each had two strips of white wrapped around their upper arms to aid in identification—Tegestu would have preferred the forehead, but Tastis might think to use that himself, and he didn't want confusion. The soldiers had rehearsed this, yesterday in the late afternoon and again this morning: their officers should know their tasks by now.

Grendis saluted and departed, to join her squadrons, the light cavalry detailed for pursuit. Tegestu watched her go, sadness in his heart, breathing a prayer for her safety. He knew that her job exposed her to no great danger—she would only be employed when the battle was already won—but still Tegestu felt the tightness in his jaw and belly, his worry for her.

Tegestu gave a signal and the pioneers dashed out on fast horses to their marks, ready to guide the column. Then the long line of men moved out of the camp, guiding themselves by the winking shuttered lanterns of the pioneers, each of whom was standing by a stake that marked the line of march, a route carefully designed by the engineers to keep out of sight of any of Tastis' columns. A messenger came to Tegestu as they marched.

"They've completed two bridges," the young woman said, breathless from her ride. "They've got men across already, clearing brush for the others."

"Very well," Tegestu said. "Sit you down yonder, and rest your horse. Join us later."

The march went on. Tegestu and Palastinas had divided

the army between them, Tegestu taking the mobile column on its night march, Palastinas holding the fortified camp. They would crush Tastis between them as the rebels marched, strung out across country, en route to their own surprise attack.

The last stage of Tegestu's march was made dismounted, each trooper holding his horse's bridle and moving slowly, careful to avoid any sound that might alert Tastis or his men, their hands ready to clamp on their horses' muzzles in case a shifting wind brought them the scent of other horses and the beasts tried to call out in welcome.

Tegestu turned aside to a tall stone farmhouse, his new headquarters; the inhabitants, landowners owing allegiance to a baron who theoretically owed his own obedience to Neda-Calacas, were roused out of their beds by Classani and shut up in the attic. The column flowed past, down into a shallow fold in the ground that would shelter them from Tastis' eyes until the time was right. The others were disposed carefully in their own places of hiding, the pioneers leading them with colored lanterns, each lantern shuttered to beam its light only at the approaching troops.

A night attack, Tegestu knew, demanded uncommon planning; but his staff was practiced, and he himself had been over the ground yesterday and again today. He would not go out again tonight; there would be little point, and he would serve better remaining here at the headquarters where any message would reach him. And messengers began to trickle in, from the whelkrani and mercenary captains and the city soldiers, breathlessly informing him that the men were in place and ready.

"They have all reported, bro-demmin," Acamantu reported, ticking off the last messenger on his list. He looked up at his father with satisfaction.

"Very well," Tegestu said complacently. "Tell the runners to return and tell their captains there will be no action for the present. The soldiers may sleep on their arms.''

''Aye, bro-demmin.''

''And send one of our own runners to the Abessu-Denorru. Inform him that our force is in place and ready.'' He might as well ease Necias' anxiety if he could. He hoped the elderly, patient Palastinas would serve as an example for Necias; he was certain that, even if things went utterly wrong tonight, the Marshal would lean back, stroke his dainty white beard, and take it with what philosophy he could.

No more messengers would come for a while: he had no watchers near the bridges, not wanting Tastis to stumble across one of them and take alarm. Instead his scouts were disposed overlooking Tastis' likely route of march, ready to inform him when the enemy started moving. That wouldn't be for some hours yet.

For the present there was nothing to do; Tegestu asked Thesau to bring him tea and eyed a plush settee sitting comfortably in the next room. His Classani, used to his ways, brought it hastily forth, and he sat himself down, leaned against the pillows, closed his eyes, and awaited events.

He must have slept, for when he awakened the glass of tea that had been so carefully put by his hand was cold. One of Cascan's spies, her body and head shrouded in midnight black, had come in to report. ''Tastis is moving, bro-demmin,'' she said with a bow. ''My companions remain and are trying to estimate his numbers.''

''Thank you, ban-demmin,'' Tegestu said. His voice seemed cracked and dry; he had an unpleasant vision of himself sleeping with his mouth cracked open, snoring while his staff watched, and banished the thought from his mind. He sipped his tea, feeling it slide welcome and cool down his throat. ''Return to your post,'' he said; and the woman bowed and vanished, light as a cat in her tall buskins.

"Messengers to the captains," Tegestu said. "Their soldiers are to stand ready." He paused, then added as an afterthought, "And send someone to Palastinas. He will probably wish to know." And Necias as well, he thought, who would be driving his companions half-mad, fretting for more news.

The runners, each knowing his destination, slipped quickly from the house. Tegestu finished his tea and smiled. Other reports came in, telling of numbers, hasty estimates made in the dark, and of Tastis' progress. Tegestu nodded his comprehension of the picture and let his staff do the work.

He had another, fresher glass of tea, watching his people busy at their tasks, and then saw the poet Campas standing idle by the door, his hand tugging at the collar of his mail shirt where it chafed his throat. Tegestu, amused at the man's hopeless awkwardness, wondered where he'd got the old byrnie; by looks it should have been scrubbing pots in the Acragas kitchens long ago. Campas yawned, covering it with the back of his hand, turned and paced to the other end of the room, one eye cocked toward the door and any further messages.

"You seem impatient, ilean poet," Tegestu said. Campas turned to him and bowed.

"I had thought these things moved with more speed, bro-demmin," Campas said. "All these days of waiting, and now with the enemy two little hills away there is still more waiting."

"Things will move swiftly enough, by and by," Tegestu said.

Campas smiled. "I said that myself, to the Ambassador Fiona, just a few days ago," he said.

"Did you?" Tegestu said. His plans were shaping as they should; he felt in an expansive mood, rested and light-hearted. He looked up at the poet. "I haven't yet spoken with her. Do you see her often?"

"I see her daily," Campas said, tugging at his mail coat again. "I *speak* with her rarely—Necias keeps me too busy."

"And she is busy herself, asking questions of my household," Tegestu said. A wary look entered Campas' eyes.

"She wants to know your people," Campas said. "She does not mean to offend."

"To know us is not difficult," Tegestu said. "She may come and go, as any ambassador; her people are not our enemies."

"No, they are not," Campas said, seemingly relieved. He glanced toward the door as another midnight-garbed messenger came in, breathless from having run from an outpost two miles away. She stammered out her message: the enemy column, stretched out in its long line of march, lay like a strand of soft metal twixt hammer and anvil, and Tegestu had but to let the hammer fall.

Tegestu smiled, and rose slowly from the couch. "It is time to do some fighting, ban-demmini," he said, "Give out the order to advance. Send someone to Marshal Palastinas to tell him—a galloper this time, no need for discretion. Tastis will think it one of his." He glanced up at Campas. "Now you will have your wish: things will move rapidly from here."

"I understand, bro-demmin."

The messengers dashed out again, and Tegestu followed as far as the door, catching a whiff of the fragrant night air. He sensed that Campas had followed him. "I might as well go to sleep again," he remarked. "Our people have but to follow the plan. I'll only be needed if things go wrong, but I don't think they shall."

He felt a pressure in his bladder—all that tea—and stepped out into the darkness, receiving the surprised salute of some of the Classani grooms. To his left, dimly sensed, he could discern the dark shape of spearmen standing, their bladed shafts at rest in the ground before them as they stood ready, awaiting the order to move. A lovely night, he thought, to be a young spearman and stand at rest beneath the stars, breath catching in the throat in anticipation of the battle to come. Stars, dew on the grass, breath frosting in the night air, the chink of armor . . . there was a poem in that, he thought. He would try to write it tomorrow, his victory poem.

Tastis was out there, he thought. He would not miss this, he knew. He remembered his cousin, his cunning face, his agile wit. If Tastis was taken tonight, or killed, the war might well be over. But somehow he could not wish it.

He walked some distance from the farmhouse and urinated, then turned and came back. The dark form that was the bodies of spearmen heaved suddenly, the hundreds of men moving as one, sloping their pikes forward at the ready with a sound like the distant rattle of autumn twigs. Starlight glitted on the blades; and then, almost silently, the spearmen began to surge forward, moving swiftly in a compact mass, each man aligning on his file leader. He watched as they moved up the slope, their legs swishing in the grass; then they topped the rise and were gone. A poem, Tegestu thought, truly.

The bright lamps in the farmhouse dazzled him as he stepped inside, and he stood blinking in the doorway for a few moments as his staff stood ready. The force was divided into three main groups, each hidden along Tastis' line of march; each, it was hoped, would strike Tastis at more or less the same time, though that was a difficult task at night. A few minutes' difference either way would not matter.

He returned to the couch and his tea, his mind still full of the night, of the sight of those glittering blades topping the rise. The others stood by respectfully, waiting . . . and then it came, softly on the still night air, the sound of metal drumming on metal, thousands of weapons smashing on thousands of shields, helmets, pieces of armor. He saw Campas look up, a frown on his face as he tried to identify the sound; and he saw satisfaction slide into the eyes of the staff, and their triumphant smiles.

After that the messengers began to come and they were all busy. Reports were confused, not unnaturally, but they were all positive: many of the enemy had been broken at first contact, others were holding and trying to cut their way out, but were being contained. One detachment of heavy cavalry had been assigned to push its way to the bridges, cutting the enemy from retreat; this group reported an early success, but the group sent to follow, rhomphaiamen to chop their way across the bridges to the other side, with pikes to establish a secure perimeter on the west bank, reported a failure: there were steady Neda-Calacas Brodaini there, repelling any attempt to take the bridge. Tegestu would have to be satisfied with denying the enemy retreat.

A message came from Palastinas, saying that he was moving: apparently the old marshal wasn't content to sit in camp, waiting for the enemy to be driven to him; he wanted to do some driving himself. So long as the camp was garrisoned, Tegestu thought, so that enemy stragglers couldn't loot it, Palastinas' attack could do some good.

Messages came back, all reporting victory. Some of the enemy spearmen had held, their pikes forming an impenetrable ring to cavalry; but the reserve rhomphaiamen had come up, heavily armored and with their heavy sickle-blades on their short three-foot hafts, and chopped their way through the spears as they had been taught. Tegestu smiled with pride: those rhomphaia were his particular innovation, something he had introduced to kamliss Pranoth during the long civil war, to break up the enemy's invulnerable pike-hedges. They worked well, so long as the armored attackers were well trained.

Now, he thought, they were being used on their brothers, the Pranoth men on the other side. Because Tastis could not keep his allegiance. He frowned. The Brodaini in this land were so few, and now more were dying. It was best that Tastis was killed or taken; that way his people might survive.

All the messages were now of victory, of banners taken and Tastis' people fleeing, all order lost, into the trees by the river. There they were holding out: Tegestu's own soldiers lost their order trying to pursue into the thick woods, and the battle was swift and vicious. Little profit would be had, he thought, from heedless pursuit into the thickets, and he gave his one order of the fight, to sound the recall and wait for dawn.

There was not long to wait; the sky was already paling. Tegestu ordered up his horse; he left word as to where he could be found and rode out across the fields, his staff following him. The first people encountered were wounded, staggering back from the fight; and then, dark on the trampled ground, the dead. He could see how it had gone: here they had given way utterly; there some cavalry had pitched into a deep depression in the ground and came to a crashing leg-snapping halt; and here again the enemy had made a stand, beaten off Broadini spearmen, then been broken by the rhomphaiamen and died in their ranks. It had been a chaotic mess of a battle, as night fights always were, but surprise had been with Tegestu's army and the impetus had carried them through the enemy.

And then he came to the slope overlooking the river, seeing the dark woods stretched out below in shadow, with the ranks of his own men forming just below the crest of the slope. He wished it were later in the season, for then fire could be used to burn the enemy out; now there was no way but to go after them and dig them out.

He rode along the ranks, receiving the silent salutes of the Brodaini and the bellowing cheers of the city folk. He rattled off his orders swiftly, improvising, wedges of men to pierce the woods and the enemy line, then roll them up from either side. "Is there any news of Tastis?" he kept asking; but Tegestu's cousin had not been seen. His banner had not been among those taken; he and his entourage must be below, waiting in the forest with the wreck of his army.

We will not get him now, Tegestu thought, not unless his body turns up among the fallen, unnoticed. He can swim back to the friendly shore; he's a strong swimmer.

So the attack progressed. The Brodaini guard on the bridge were inundated by arrows, smashed by infantry and then cavalry, and sent reeling back; but by then enemy engineers had salvaged most of their bridges, preventing Tegestu from using them. The fight in the woods, more broken and confused than any night battle could ever be, took longer; but in the end those enemy who could swim took flight, and those who could not died or joined the long lines of prisoners toiling up the hill.

Then Palastinas and his forces arrived—they were well-marshalled and still fresh, for they'd had little to do in their sweep but run down fugitives or take in prisoners—followed by part of his staff and the Ambassador Fiona—her hood was a deep blue today, Tegestu noticed. The Marshal rode up cheerfully, waving his riding whip, and Tegestu saluted him gravely.

"The enemy are broken, but there will still be many in the wood," he said. "I would like to use your people to ferret them out; my own are done."

"Take 'em," Palastinas said with a shrug. He glanced behind him. "I've ordered the surgeons to move their field hospitals up here," he said. "That should make it easier on the wounded."

"Thank you, Marshal," Tegestu said. "That was

thoughtful.'' He looked at the faces of Palastinas' staff—young faces for the most part, not all accustomed to war, most of them curiously glancing down into the trees, seeing the bright uniforms and armor, the banners staggering through the brush. "Has the Abessu-Denorru accompanied you?'' Tegestu asked.

Palastinas smiled a private smile. "No, Drandor Tegestu, he did not,'' he said. "He started with us, but fell ill and retired to the camp.'' He leaned close to Tegestu, lowering his voice. "He was a little green, I think,'' he said privately. "He's seen heads lopped off felons and the like, but he's never seen death in such quantity before—nothing like this field.''

Tegestu gazed bleakly down into the valley, wishing he hadn't been told. The Abessu-Denorru, his canlan, afraid of a little blood. . . . Necias had always seemed a strong man, for an Abessla, unsentimental enough when ordering soldiers to do his work for him. The thought that Necias would turn ill at the sight of a massacre he had himself ordered made a black foreboding ooze slowly into Tegestu's mind.

"Not like our little Fiona, now,'' Palastinas went on, cheerful. "She's like an old campaigner—won't wear any armor, just that old robe of hers, and rode through that mess without turning a hair.'' He looked over his shoulder at the small figure of the ambassador, perched frowning on her mare with one leg crooked carelessly around the saddle horn. "I wonder if they fight wars where she comes from, hey?'' he asked.

Tegestu looked up at the brown face with its cap of dark curls, seeing Fiona looking down into the valley with the others, her eyes intent, glowing almost, her mouth tight and grim. *She's a hater*, he thought with wonder. *What's happened to make her hate them so much?*

"I don't know, Marshal,'' he said, recovering slowly from his surprise. "Perhaps we could ask.''

Palastinas sighed. "So," he said. "We have other things to think about. I've got the Bricklayers' Guild Scarlet Lights coming up behind me, and they haven't wrestled with an enemy yet—where d'you think I should send 'em?"

Tegestu turned his mind from the ambassador, then glanced down into the trees, gauging the mixed, lurching, confusing battle. "I don't know," he said. "Give me leave to think a moment."

13

Necias swirled the wine in his crystal goblet, frowning.

"Over two thousand bodies," Listas' high-pitched, annoying voice went on. "I have the precise figure here somewhere—ah. Two thousand two hundred sixty-one, so far. There will have been many undiscovered in the trees down there and many more drowned. Almost fifteen hundred wounded and captured. Eight thousand suits of armor recovered at the water's edge, abandoned when their owners swam for it. And," Listas' voice almost purred with satisfaction, "seven hundred and eighteen of the bastards captured unhurt. Ready to be delivered to your justice."

"Good." Necias said, his mind elsewhere. Listas was his son by Argo, a popeyed, neat, orderly person with a tidy clerk's mind and a grating vioce, happy in a world of numbers. He and two of Necias' other sons were supervising the army's commissary for the benefit of the House of Acragas, but Listas had been borrowed for the day to replace Campas, who was off supervising the interrogation of the surviving prisoners.

"They had thirty thousand men," Listas said, his voice

a little sharp, sensing perhaps that Necias wasn't paying attention. "That's almost one in five of their army that we've either killed or captured, plus thousands more forced to abandon their armor and swim like water-puppies. And most of their cavalry scattered, Palastinas said, rather than fighting—they'll be useless. Palastinas said that if he were Tastis he wouldn't even try to oppose our crossing the river. He said if he were Tastis he'd already be sending his baggage to the rear."

"Is that so?" Necias asked. He turned his head and looked at his son. "How many of those dead and captured were Brodaini—Tastis' own men?"

"Ah—I don't have those figures available."

Necias grunted, then turned to scowl at the crystal goblet in his hand, the dark wine swirling within. Wine the color of blood, the color that had drenched the grass that morning. Feeling bile rising in his throat, Necias put the goblet on the table and pushed it away.

Men lying in the grass, hacked up with swords and spears and those Brodaini choppers, as if a horde of apprentice butchers, unused to their craft, had been loosed on the field. And with Tastis making his escape there would be more such butchery, until the renegade was caught.

At least Tegestu had proven loyal. It had seemed suspicious to Necias that Tegestu insisted on letting Tastis' army across the river—almost as if he wanted to unite Tastis with his own Brodaini, and turn on the Arrandal men. The suspicion had grown as the hours advanced, and Necias had almost been driven mad with worry. He had the suspicion that he had said a lot of foolishness last night while he was trying to reassure himself that Tegestu and his stonefaced henchmen weren't eyeing his neck and wondering if they could hack it through with a single stroke.

Well. That worry was done with. All he had to do was treat Tegestu with respect; that was all the Brodaini wished, and not understanding that had been Nadielas' big mistake. He should be relieved, but for some reason relief hadn't come.

Necias grabbed the goblet suddenly and gulped the wine, trying not to look at it, trying not to think of those raglike bodies strewn over the fields. He put the goblet down and wiped his lips. He should write to the city to announce the victory—he should have done that first thing.

"Draft a proclamation," he said, and without waiting for Listas to collect pen and paper he began, the words rattling off his tongue without need for thought—he'd dictated proclamations before, and their composition was easy enough. "From Acragas Necias Abeissu, to the Donorru-Deissu and the people of Arrandal, Greetings. The Marshal Palastinas and I are pleased to announce a victory—make that a *brilliant* victory—over the forces of the renegade Tastis, fought on the, ah, the right bank of the East Rallandas River. In the field the Brodaini Tegestu commanded the left, and Marshal Palastinas the right. Tegestu's forces alone crushed the enemy before the right could engage. Marshal Palastinas then conducted a successful pursuit, resulting in the capture of hundreds of enemy soldiers." He saw Listas lift an eyebrow, and turned to him with a belligerent snarl.

"That's what happened, didn't it?" he demanded. "Or did I get right and left turned around?"

"I didn't say anything," Listas protested.

"Tegestu earned his praise," Necias growled. "I want to spare the city any anxiety they may feel about his loyalty. Understand?"

Listas nodded mutely. Necias turned away and held out his goblet for more wine. "White," he told the servant, and the man took the cup, bowed, and withdrew in silence. Necias resumed his dictation.

"Then add those figures of enemy dead, wounded, and captured," he said. "After that, write: A trophy will be set up on the field and dedicated by our priests, and suits of captured armor will be returned to Arrandal to be set in its palaces and temples. The city of Arrandal will be pleased to know that its forces behaved with invincible spirit, courage, and steadiness." He looked at Listas. "Got that all?"

"Yes, Father."

"Have it sent by messenger tonight." The wine cup returned and Necias took a swallow. Next would come letters to the barons owing allegiance to Neda-Calacas, urging them to open their gates to the Arrandalla army. Most of them, he suspected, would have avoided declaring for one side or the other: this battle would change that. He turned at the sound of footsteps.

"Abessu-Denorru," Campas said, walking in with his long strides. He had got rid of his coat of chain, and was back in his dark, tailored clothing. "I have a message from Tegestu. He's got news about the new bridging train, and expects to cross the river within three days."

"Good," Necias said. He knew that Tegestu's message had probably been a good deal more formal than that, and appreciated Campas' editing it to its essentials. "Sit down," he urged. "Have some supper and tell me what the drandor's been doing."

"Sleeping, mostly," Campas answered, drawing up a settee and throwing himself down on the pillows. "Went to bed after turning things over to Palastinas, then got up early this afternoon and wrote his victory poem. A nice little verse, by the way—there's an effective bit of imagery about spear-blades shining on the grass like dew." He looked up with a grin. "Shall I translate?"

"Spare me," Necias said. "I'm not interested in what Tegestu thinks is poetic." Or poems about battle, either. Spear-blades on the grass, he thought. Who was going to write a poem about all those city boys on the grass with their tripes cut out?

Campas shrugged; then he smiled, as if privately amused. "Tegestu seems to have spent most of this battle asleep," he said. "He was asleep through most of last night, until the battle actually started, and once he turned things over to Palastinas he went back to bed again. Wouldn't it be nice," Campas said, his eyes mischievous, "to be able to dream your victories the way Tegestu does?"

Necias snorted at the notion. It wasn't often that the poet dared to be so ridiculous in his presence. Campas grinned.

"I couldn't sleep a wink, myself. Couldn't understand why Tegestu and his people were taking things so calmly. I suppose it was because they knew exactly how things would go."

"Yes," Necias said. "That must have been it." That calm that he had mistaken for frigid enmity: he shuddered at the recollection, then chose to change the subject. "How many recruits from the prisoners, hey?" He had offered amnesty to any who joined—it was better than slavery in the mines or galleys until the war was over, with execution for the leaders. Campas frowned, scratching his chin.

"Not many, I'm afraid. Only a hundred or so. I was surprised, I admit—a lot of these people support Tastis."

"Eh?" asked Necias in surprise. "What d'you mean, support him?" He gestured irritably. "That man gave the chop to half the government of the city! How the hell could they support him?"

"He's got his own government now, it seems," Campas said. "He's got this Denorru-Censtassinn he's set up. And it isn't as if the last government was exactly popular."

Denorru-Censtassin, Council of the Populace. One of the little puppet-boards Tastis had set up to help him rule the city.

"Popular?" Necias grated. "What's that got to do with it?" He slammed the goblet down on the table. "Oh, yes, he's got his little puppets. So what? It's Tastis who's got the power—it's not as if these Denorrinn were anything more than a sop thrown to the city."

"Beg pardon, cenors-efellsan," Campas said regretfully. "But Tastis has been very cunning—he's given power to many who haven't had it before, and they'll not wish to give it up. Neda-Calacas is still a divided city, uncertain of its allegiance, but there are more holding to Tastis' faction than we've ever thought."

"Faction?" Necias barked, laughing. "What kind of faction can Tastis have?"

Gradually, under Campas' prodding insistence and despite Necias' reluctance to believe it, the appalling truth came out. The composition of Neda-Calacas' Denorru-Deissin had been altered: most of the deissin had been purged from its ranks, a majority of Brodaini chiefs had been added, and the name changed to Denorru-Welldrannin, Council of the Elders, the latter a term barbarously borrowed from the Gostu. This council, Tastis had proclaimed, was charged with the "guidance" of the city and its people through the troubles.

But Tastis had created another denorru, the Denorru-Censtassin, a junior council of two hundred men of the city: it was elected by all the male citizens over the age of thirty, and anyone was eligible to take a seat. This was in contrast to all precedent: the Denorru-Deissin of Arrandal, and every other city, was composed only of men of substantial wealth. The Denorru-Censtassin had a broader base, including the poor; and Tastis had actually given his new council control of most of the actual working of the civil administration, the street patrols, magistrates, prisons, and so forth.

"The city is in terror," Campas said. "Before there was no outlet for resentment against the deissin, but now Tastis allows it. Corrupt magistrates have been arrested and condemned, deissin have had their goods confiscated and distributed to the poor, usury has been outlawed."

"Ai, gods," Necias murmured. How many of his own allies in Arrandal could survive if those sort of standards were applied to them?

"He's done more," Campas explained. "He's altered the makeup of the Guilds: now there's a League of Journeymen within each Guild—policy's no longer decided simply by the Masters."

"Ai, gods," Necias said again, the full horror of this easily penetrating. The craft guilds were composed of three classes, the Apprentices, Journeymen, and Masters: always power had been held firmly by the latter. This had always been resented by the Journeymen, who were kept on low wages until a Master died and they could fill his place, at which point the Guild gave permission for the new Master to seek contracts of his own. Now, with the Journeymen taking a more active part, they could start demanding higher wages, perhaps even seeking commissions. The entire system would crumble.

"Tastis has a lot of money now," Campas explained. "He's purged some houses altogether, confiscating their goods, and he's forced other of the deissin to pay heavy fines; he's also seized direct control of some of the banks. The dole to the poor has been increased, and the rest has been used to recruit mercenaries and pay his militia. He's got a lot of volunteers for the city forces and the fleet because suddenly the volunteers are making more money than they've ever made before."

"It can't work," Necias said. "Not in the long run. It's too—too *convenient* for all these people." His mind, after recovering its shock, was beginning to work on these little pieces of information, to assemble them into a mosaic; and he thought he saw that some of the pieces wouldn't properly fit with the others.

"He'll bankrupt himself," he said. "How can he afford all those payments—to the poor, to his militia, to the mercenaries? He can't keep confiscating the wealth of the citizens, not over and over—he'll run out." He gulped wine, then held up a finger to make a point. "And he can't change the Guild system without debasing their product—it was set up to guarantee the quality of goods. With the journeymen being in competition with the masters *everyone* will lose; there'll be too much craft coming out of the city, and too much of it will be poor craft, and prices will be too low to support anyone. He's depending too much on the small traders. These little diné are too poor to control the big trading fleets the city depends on. He can make laws against usury on loans, but he can't force the lenders to make loans against their will. The money supply will dry up."

"He can keep the bankers terrified, that's how he'll do it," Campas reminded him. "This new system will keep him afloat for a few years, and that's all he cares about. If he can get a large part of the citizens to aid in the defense of their city, thinking the changes will bring them benefit, then he'll be able to hold on longer, and any troubles he has can be blamed on us."

"All the more reason to crush him now." Necias frowned. "Before his notions have a chance to spread."

Campas nodded. "Yes. Think how Tastis' ideas might sound to our own poor, to our own journeymen—and for that matter, to our mercenaries. He's paying his own a lot of bonuses. And however much the flenssin dislike the Brodaini, they respect them as fellow-soldiers; perhaps they'd rather serve soldiers than merchants."

Necias heaved himself up from his chair, rubbed his chin briskly, and began to pace. "We've got to isolate our prisoners, then," he said. He turned to Listas and prodded his chest with a stubby finger. "You," he said. "Get to Tegestu immediately and tell him to relieve the prisoners' guards with his own people. The Brodaini are to have sole custody, hey?"

"Y-yes, Father," Listas said, rising unsteadily. He rubbed

his chest where the finger had poked him, then snatched his cloak and made for the entrance to the pavilion.

"Listas!" Necias bellowed, as another thought struck him. Listas turned.

"Yes?"

"Request Tegestu to visit me at his earliest convenience." He gave a look at Campas. "I want to know what the Brodaini think of this. They might have a notion or two that we haven't thought of." He swivelled back to Listas. "Use all courtesy, mind!"

"Right away, Father," Listas said, and ran for it. Necias paced silently, his mind working doggedly on the problem of Tastis. Thank the gods Arrandal had won this battle; it would make Tastis' more faint-hearted supporters fall away and make the others, at least, glance nervously behind them, wondering what might befall them if their side lost—both sides, as all knew, could play at this game of purges. And a lot of Tastis' best troops were smashed up; that would make his militia wonder if their prowess was as great as Tastis told them it was.

There was a tramp and jingle of armor outside the pavilion, and the captain of Necias' guards entered. He was a nephew, the only son of Necias' brother Castas, who had died keeping the assassin's dagger away. He was named Acragas Necias, and was therefore referred to as Little Necias, a name Necias suspected he resented, since he was a tall, broad-shouldered man, as tall as his father.

"Drandor Tegestu," Little Necias reported, "with his retinue." Necias nodded, then stepped from behind the screens that divided his private chamber from his public one and received the Brodaini, watching as they bowed in homage. "I trust your people will make their needs known to my servants," he said as Tegestu rose. "My friend, I need to speak with you."

He told a servant to bring Tegestu a stool and then walked with him into the private chamber, seeing Campas rise and bow in the formal Brodaini way. "Tell him," he snapped at Campas; and the poet nodded and began rattling out Gostu. Tegestu listened in silence, his face impassive, his eyes slitted in thought.

"Well," Necias said when the poet was finished. "What do you make of it, hey?"

Tegestu slowly shook his head. "It is not our way. Very strange." He hesitated for a moment, then turned to Campas. "May your arm never weaken, canlan Necias, I am sorry that I do not have the words. In our own tongue, this is an-hosta, very bad. Dai-terru, to tamper this way with a governing. It breaks the lines of nartil."

Campas took a deep breath and blew his cheeks, struggling with the dismal facts of translation, then turned to Necias. "Disharmonious," he said. "Tastis has taken too much on himself, to break up authority that way. It is not the Brodaini way."

Tegestu seemed to be pondering deeply. "It is very like Tastis, this news," he said. "He has always been, ah, flexible. Thinks quickly. Ah, improvises very well. Adapts." He shook his head. "But it is not Brodaini, it is something else. A strange . . . compromise. I do not know how to think of it."

Necias pounced on Tegestu's words, harsh delight bubbling through him as he saw Tastis' weakness. "Tastis has compromised the Brodaini way, hey?" he said. "He's made too many changes, acted too quickly." He leaned closer to Tegestu, his voice eager. "Will his own people support him in all of this? Or will they think as you do?"

Tegestu paused for a moment, his deep eyes troubled. Then he looked at Necias and nodded. "Some will not approve," he said. "But Tastis must have the support of most of the aldran; otherwise he could not proceed in this at all."

"Can we work on that?" Necias asked. "Many of his, his kamlissin are divided between Neda-Calacas and

Arrandal, with the senior people in Arrandal. Can you
urge Tastis' people, the ones who think as you do, to
return to their old allegiance, to yourself and the others of
your welldran?''

"It is—I do not like to break nartil in this way,"
Tegestu said, obviously unhappy. "But it is declared angu,
there are no courtesies between such enemies. I will do
what I can."

"Good, good," Necias said, a grin curling his lips. He
reached out a hand and patted Tegestu's armored knee.
"Good man," he said. He glanced up at Campas.

"There are other holes in Tastis' armor," he said. "The
deissin and bankers aren't without influence, and the flenssin
aren't invulnerable to bribery. All we need is for a small
company to take a gate and hold it for a few minutes.
Neda-Calacas is composed of two big cities, with four
harbors between them; there are lots of places for people to
get in and out. A little prearrangement, a little gold, and
we'll have everything but the keep—maybe even that.

"But we'll have to move quickly," he added. He glanced
at Tegestu, seeing the old warrior stolid behind his frozen
mask of calculated ferocity. "We've got to get the army to
Neda-Calacas as quickly as we can—force march if we
have to. Before Tastis can arrange things to suit his convenience again."

Tegestu bowed. "It will mean being less careful," he
said, "but it can be done safely enough. Tastis' army is
not harmless, but he can't strike us hard, not without new
strength from the city. But he will raid us, Abessu-Denorru,
and there may be a few surprises."

"We'll take the risk," Necias said.

"May your arm never fail," Tegestu said, and bowed
again.

"Proclamations to the barons—we'll need those," Necias
said briskly, standing and rubbing his hands. "Tell 'em
we're here, hey, that their rights will be respected, that

Tastis is finished." He reached for the goblet and drank the last of the wine, beaming happily down at Tegestu and Campas, satisfied that things were moving his way at last, that at last, in spite of some nasty shocks, he was beginning to comprehend the flow of events. The Hundred-Year Peace, he thought; he might still be able to salvage it.

With, of course, the help of a little gold, and a little treason in the right places.

14

Tastis' forces faded from the ford an hour after Tegestu's first bridges were thrown across five miles downstream, and though Tegestu pushed Tastis hard the armies of Arrandal never managed to catch their enemy. There were, as Tegestu had predicted, raids here and there, on the baggage trains, on isolated columns; the raids were of mixed success but even at their worst did not delay the march.

Barons holed up in their strongholds were bypassed, but most threw open their gates and welcomed the Arrandalla, with varying degrees of enthusiasm, as friends. The army forged on, presumably to the barons' relief, until it came to yet another river and another castle perched on a bluff.

It was troublesome, this little outpost on the West Rallandas. Knowing that their commerce depended heavily on control of the rivers and canals, the cities had conquered and destroyed most of the baronial keeps that could threaten the flow of trade, and the rest had been reduced by treaty or garrisoned by city troops. This small castle was one of the latter.

There it perched on its rock, right at the curve of the river where it could command barge traffic, a half-bowshot from the principle ford. The West Rallandas was easier than the East; it was slower and shallower and more fordable—but the other fords were not as convenient, and so Tegestu readied his assault on the castle and called on the garrison to surrender. Even if they refused, he calculated, it would not hold for longer than three days.

If they surrendered he would grant them the honors of war, allowing them safe conduct to Neda-Calacas. If not they would be exterminated, and presumably they knew it.

An officer in charge announced that he would surrender—Tegestu's heart eased—but then produced a strange condition. He would give up the keys of the castle to none other than Tegestu Dellila Doren y'Pranoth in person, and only after being allowed to speak privately with him for the space of half an hour.

An assassin, Tegestu thought, and a clumsy one; but then the officer announced he was prepared to come unarmored and that he would willingly be searched for weapons first. Tegestu thought again. Perhaps, he concluded, this young man was a foe of Tastis; perhaps he was the one the Abessu-Denorru was looking for, the man who would open, in addition to the gates of the fort, the gates of the city.

And who was the man who made such demands? Aptan Tepesta Laches y'Pranoth, he called from the low battlements—Tegestu realized with a start that this was one of Tastis' sons. Could a son be a traitor? But neither would Tastis ask one of his heirs to draw an assassin's weapon: Aptan would be too valuable to throw away on such duty.

For a moment Tegestu considered throwing his forces against the castle now, hoping to seize Tastis' son as hostage . . . he might be worth the losses. But no, he thought; Aptan would have instructions to have one of his men hack off his head before he allowed himself to be captured. The losses would be for nothing. Curiosity gnawed at him—and of course the castle would be surrendered that much more quickly.

And so Tegestu consented. A canvas awning was set up before the castle, well out of bowshot, and the besieging army withdrew a pace. Under its shade two stools were set. The gates of the castle opened a crack and a man came out—a slender, smiling, good-natured lad, it seemed, walking with open arms to where Cascan and his cathruni waited. The search was thorough, and a little rough: when Aptan walked to his stool, his hair mussed from being unbraided to discover strangling wires, he didn't seem nearly as cheerful as when he'd first come out of the castle.

Then Tegestu came out, armored, with weapons ready to hand. His guards halting just out of earshot, he walked to the place appointed: the stools were still three paces apart. They faced one another, and then Aptan bowed.

"May your demmin ever increase, drandor Tegestu," he said. He inclined his head, his tolhostu broken by a slight, rueful smile. "My compliments on the efficiency of your cathruni."

"They know their duty, ban-demmin," Tegestu said. "Sit and deliver your message."

Aptan bowed and sat, his face still showing his small, appreciative grin. Tegestu lowered himself heavily to the stool, a shiver of pain running through the muscles of his upper thighs as, for a second only, they took his weight.

"I am charged with a kantu-kamliss matter," Aptan said, "from bro-demmin Tastis Senestu Tepesta y'Pranoth, drandor y Kamliss-Pranoth-sa-Neda, to Tegestu Dellila Doren y'Pranoth, drandor y Kamliss-Pranoth-sa-Arrandal."

Another kantu-kamliss matter, Tegestu thought sourly. The ban would keep him from reporting the substance of this conversation to Necias, which, no doubt, was what Tastis had in mind.

"Speak," Tegestu said shortly, then held up a hand.

"Confine yourself to matters relating strictly to kamliss Pranoth, however," he added. "I will not see the holy label of kantu-kamliss assigned frivolously."

Aptan, seemingly a little surprised, bowed hastily. "May your arm never fail, bro-demmin," he said, "I hope you will keep me on the right track, should I stray from it."

"I shall, ban-demmin Aptan," Tegestu said grimly. "Never fear."

Aptan sat back for a moment, apparently considering the proper opening; then he nodded, presumably to himself, and spoke. "Our kamliss," Aptan said, "is divided. Most of Pranoth serves Arrandal; the rest rules Neda and Calacas with the help of its allies. In both places, Pranoth voices are the first to speak among the Brodaini, and they speak with the greatest authority." He paused, his green eyes looking with curiosity at Tegestu as if waiting for him to agree; but Tegestu remained gravely silent. Let the boy say his piece, he thought.

"We have served the Elva cities well," Aptan said. "Our people have been loyal for twenty years, and have overlooked many insults. We Brodaini have fought one another for the benefit of these people—and our divided kamlissi have fought against one another, cousin against cousin, and now we find ourselves fighting one another again." Aptan held up a hand, leaning forward to bring himself nearer to Tegestu.

"With one exception, bro-demmin," he said. "This time Kamliss-Pranoth-sa-Neda fights for itself, not for the benefit of others who do not understand us. It grieves us to fight our cousins, whom we admire and respect, whose arm is strong and whose demmin is unblemished."

"And whose fault is this, ban-demmin?" Tegestu asked, seeing the direction this was heading. "It is not the fault of Kamliss-Pranoth-sa-Arrandal, whose demmin, as you say, is unblemished. We did not commit dai-terru by seizing an entire city and starting a general war within the Elva.

There were more proper ways to take revenge for your woman of the spear; and we of Kamliss-Pranoth-sa-Arrandal feel shame for our cousins, who have committed such an inappropriate aspistu.''

Aptan listened to this without blinking, a troubled frown on his face. ''Our aldran was convinced, bro-demmin Tegestu, that such action was necessary,'' he said, then added, ''But I was not sent to you in order to offer justification for our actions: we know our own hearts, bro-demmin, and we are convinced we were wise.''

''Speak on,'' Tegestu said: he had made his point.

''Through these events, bro-demmin, we Brodaini find ourselves with command of two foreign cities.'' Aptan went on. ''We find ourselves with hundreds of thousands of dependents, dependents strange to our ways and unlike any dependents Brodaini have ever before been obliged to care for. We are often puzzled by them, but we know they must depend on us for protection, and we intend to do our duty.''

He waited for a reply, but Tegestu gave him none despite the sarcasm that came to his mind. Aptan, apparently encouraged, flashed a nervous smile and continued.

''When we first came to this country we were refugees, and we were grateful for any opportunity to serve our new homes.'' Aptan said. ''But now it seems clear that we and the Abessla are not suited to one another. Our debts to them have been erased by twenty years of unflinching service, and it is no longer fitting that Brodaini should have such overlords, who cannot know our minds.''

''My lord Necias has offered us no insult,'' Tegestu said quickly. If this is an attempt to win me to sedition, he thought, let it end now: I will not submit to such affront. ''He has treated us with honor, and we obey him dutifully and with willing hearts.''

''Does he know demmin, then?'' Aptan asked in mock surprise. His grin broadened, his eyes winking good humor.

"Is he a martial man, this Necias whom you serve? Or is his concern only for acquiring gold and for displaying his wealth, to overawe the ignorant?"

"He is our canlan," Tegestu said. "I will not stand for this insult." But he felt Aptan's words touch home, remembering Necias' strange fright the night of the battle: no, Necias was not a martial man; he did not know demmin. It was regretful that it should be so: but the regret had to be carefully hidden away, unacknowledged.

But Necias *was* lordly enough, Tegestu thought, in his way: he recalled the conference the afternoon following the battle, Necias with his confidence restored, giving orders, making plans for the winning of the enemy cities, master of the political element. It was not a Brodaini type of authority, but it existed. Remembering this, Tegestu felt comforted.

Aptan smiled reassuringly. "Insult was not intended, bro-demmin," he said. "I did not intend to say that Necias was not a good man, by his own lights: I wished only to point out that we do not understand them, nor they us. It is best that we live apart from them, or if alongside in such a fashion that they are compelled to respect us. Now we have the opportunity."

He paused again. Tegestu kept silent, his face immobile, knowing that to even tell the boy to speak on would be to condone his premise, to acknowledge it as the basis for discussion. Even though it echoed Tegestu's unspoken thoughts, Tegestu would not allow this. Aptan spoke on, his tone assured.

"We can make Neda-Calacas Brodaini cities, bro-demmin drandor Tegestu," he said. "Those Abessla who wish to leave for elsewhere may have our permission to do so, and those Brodaini and their dependents who wish to live among their own kind can come within our walls. Kamliss Pranoth may live united once again, holding its own keep, protecting its own territory. If the cities of the Elva wish to

employ us in war, they may do so—but under our own
conditions, for our own benefit. Not to bleed for the
benefit of the deissin.''

''And what must I do to achieve this fantasy?'' Tegestu
asked, putting as much bitter sarcasm in his words as he
could. ''Betray my lords merely, and attack our comrades-
in-arms? March with my people into the walls of Neda-
Calacas, accept the authority of drandor Tastis, and be
sieged up there to die or surrender, as Tastis shall? Know
this,'' Tegestu said, raising a hand for attention. ''The
Elva will not rest until Tastis and your house are brought
down. This will take place whether or not I join you—their
numbers and power are too great, even if every Brodainu
in Abessas should join your standard. Your words are
futile, ban-demmin. The best thing for drandor Tastis would
be to surrender himself and the keys to the city, and in that
way many of his folk may be spared. Otherwise they will
not.'' Tegestu lowered his hand, seeing Aptan's eyes grow
troubled.

''This is truth I speak, ban-demmin,'' he said. ''I try to
do you service in telling you this. I hope you will give
Tastis my words, and my meaning.''

Aptan bowed, his head low, and stayed bowed down for
a long moment before rising. ''You misunderstand me,
bro-demmin,'' he said. ''My apologies for being unclear.
My message was not to offer you a place under drandor
Tastis. You are his senior, his teacher; he would not
demean you. We wish rather to offer you the city. We will
put the keys of the city in your hands, drandor bro-demmin
Tegestu, and obey without question your commands and
the commands of your aldran.''

Aiau, thought Tegestu, stunned. Through the shock, he
heard himself asking, reasonably, ''And the conditions for
this surrender?''

Aptan bowed again. His voice was plausible. ''That the

city remain yours, bro-demmin Tegestu, and that you surrender it to no other, no native canlan or lord."

For a moment Tegestu felt the world reel below his feet.
The scope of Tastis' vision was breathtaking, and his
audacity limitless. To open his gates to the Brodaini who
were his enemies, to allow himself to be put in their
power, confident that once they stood in his place they
would think as he. . . . And to dare to fulfill the exiles'
longing for a homeland—Neda-Calacas was not, and could
never be, the rock-strewn coast, the deep green dells, the
dappled whispering forests that Tegestu had known in his
northern domain: it could not bring Pranoth into being
again, for Pranoth was forever dead; but it could be
something—something of Pranoth again in the world, a
place for the young to grow in and love, to cherish and
guard as Tegestu had cherished Pranoth, something beside
the rootless service, the perpetual exile. . . .

And then the giddy spinning slowed, and Tegestu felt
his mind coping with realities again, with the must-be
instead of the dream. To accept Tastis' offer would be a
betrayal of Necias' trust, and of his own way of life: a new
Brodaini society could not be built on treachery or
disobedience. Such a beginning would curse the exiles
forever.

And then, through the dim haze of his astonishment, he
thought he saw a way. Necias would not be betrayed, but
still Pranoth might come into being, not through dai-terru
and the breaking of nartil, but in ways that would reassert
order in this chaotic situation. If only this boy proved
pliable.

"This is not a kantu-kamliss matter," Tegestu said
firmly. "This proposal does not involve our kamliss only,
but all the other kamlissi of Arrandal. If I am to consider
this, I must have permission to bring it out of Pranoth."

For a moment he saw triumph in Aptan's eyes. The boy
thinks I will accept, he thought; he has lived for too long

among these Abessla, who leap all unheeding after gold
and the promise of power.

Aptan bowed. "You are the elder, drandor bro-demmin
Tegestu," he said. "Your judgement is sounder than mine.
If you must consult your people, my fa—drandor bro-
demmin Tastis will certainly understand."

And now Tegestu himself slitted his eyes to hide his
own feeling of triumph; for his mind had embraced
possibilities, he thought, that hadn't occurred to Tastis,
and Aptan had just given him permission to break the ban
of kantu-kamliss and inform others of Tastis' offer. "Your
people," Aptan had said, not "your aldran" or "your
staff." Tegestu intended to make the most of that ambiguity.

Ah, Tastis, he thought. Cousin, you should have come
yourself. This boy has not seen enough of treachery.

"If we reach agreement on this matter," Tegestu said,
"how do you suggest we contact drandor Tastis?"

"A messenger, sent with a note under your seal, will
always find access to the city," Aptan said. "Or you can
send an embassy—we have prisoners of yours, you have
some of our people; we can discuss anything under the
guise of an exchange."

"You may say to drandor Tastis that I find his offer
interesting," Tegestu said. "That is my present answer."

"He will be pleased."

"You will surrender the fort, then?"

Aptan grinned. "I had forgot," he laughed. "Oh, aye,
we'll surrender if you grant us honors. Within the hour—
I'll beat a drum to let you know when we're coming out."

"Very well, ban-demmin," Tegestu said. "I will have a
pass ready to let you pass our pickets."

He put his hands on his knees and rose, trying not to let
Aptan see the pain that flickered through him. He bowed,
feeling his head swim, either from his sudden rising or
from the giddiness that walking so careful a line would
bring. He walked across the turf to his own lines, seeing

the tense postures of his guards relaxing as he came away from the enemy.

His staff was there, Grendis, Cascan and the others; and he saw tense curiosity in their faces. "He will surrender within the hour," he said. "Arrange to pass them through the lines." He looked at them and smiled. "I must see Necias, ban-demmini," he said. "Something interesting has occurred."

He could see their curiosity rise; but for the moment it was best that few of them knew of Tastis' offer. But Grendis, he thought, should be informed: she was cunning, and would be able to give valuable advice. "Ban-demmin Grendis, I would be honored if you would accompany me," he said, and with his wife at his side he walked to Necias' pavilion.

Necias, once told of the need for privacy, cleared the place of his hangers-on, then he offered them stools and lay down on his own settee.

"What did the man want?" he said with a scowl. Scowling, Tegestu thought, at the idea of intrigue, for that was what this was bound to be.

"He wanted," Tegestu said, enjoying the sheer drama of the situation and unable to keep the smile from his lips, "to discuss the surrender of Neda-Calacas."

He had made a bet with himself that Necias' mouth would fall open at the news. He was gratified to discover he had won his wager.

15

The ban of kantu-kamliss was broken; and Tegestu was
free to do the thing that, he had no doubt, Tastis would
never have anticipated: he would give Aptan's offer to his
canlan. Pride warmed him as he thought of Tastis' ultimate
fury, when he learned what dispositions Tegestu and Necias
together would make.

Necias called in Campas as his translator, and for twenty
minutes he listened solemnly, nodding as Tegestu made
each point, fidgeting with the rings on his stubby fingers.

"The city," Tegestu said, "will surrender to me, as
drandor of Pranoth. I am subject to you, our canlan.
Neda-Calacas will become a Brodaini state, but subject to
you and to the Denorru-Deissin of Arrandal. Tastis can be
exiled to one of the baronies, or ordered to kill himself—
whichever you prefer. In the end, I will hold Neda-Calacas
in your name, and as your perpetual ally. My people will
have a homeland in which they can settle if they desire,
but of course they will also be available to serve the cities
of the Elva, as before."

Necias lay motionless on his pillows, his small eyes

flitting from Campas to Tegestu and back again. The posture seemed odd, unnatural and disturbing: Necias was usually a physically active man, always moving, frequently pacing, his hands gesturing broadly or occupying themselves with the tea-cakes he always had placed by his elbow. Doubt began to creep into Tegestu's mind. "Tastis and his rebels," Tegestu said, trying to explain the advantages more clearly, "will be punished for their presumption. Hostu and nartil will be restored. And Neda-Calacas, instead of being your greatest rival in the Elva, will be your ally."

Necias frowned, reaching for a cup of tea; he drank slowly, staring into the dark liquid as he swirled it about the rim of the cup. Tegestu looked at Grendis in surprise. He had expected a more enthusiastic response than this: why wouldn't Necias leap at such an idea?

"This offer argues weakness, hey," Necias said finally, speaking as if he grudged every word. "Had Tastis won the battle of the ford, he would not be laying down conditions for surrender."

"That is likely, cenors-efellsan," Tegestu agreed. "He is not a man to give up his independence without reason. Had he won the battle, he would be demanding our submission, rather than offering his own."

Necias glanced at Campas again; there was some nervousness, Tegestu thought, in the look. Then he placed his teacup very carefully on his table, orienting it with a finicky carefulness that seemed unusual in him, as if he were trying to set carefully into place the elements of a puzzle; he rose from the settee and shook his head.

"Tegestu, I am aware of the magnitude of what you offer," he said, "but surely you're aware that I'll have to say no to this."

Tegestu felt his heart turn over. He could only gasp out a stunned reply. "But why, Abessu-Denorru?" he asked.

Necias began to pace, his arms folded on his massive chest; he turned and looked at Tegestu.

"The cities of the Elva cherish their independence," he said. "It's a cardinal point in all that we do. No Elva city has ever ruled another. No Elva city *will* ever rule another. For me to claim Neda-Calacas now would be to tear the Elva apart. They would all league against us. It would destroy all I've worked for." He shook his head slowly, emphatically. "I won't risk that, Tegestu. I daren't."

Tegestu glanced at Grendis in amazement, then back at Necias. "But we march *now* to take the city!" he said.

"But not to rule it," Necias corrected. "We mean to restore its native government, not impose our own. Naturally," he nodded, "our people, and the others of the Elva, will try to take what advantage we can. The city's markets will be disrupted, and we'll try to gain what we can from the disruption. Our banks will make what profit they can in loans to the new government, once it's installed." Necias waved his hands. "That's all conceded," he said. "But to rule directly, or even indirectly—it's out of the question. And to let foreigners do our ruling for us—" He hesitated for a moment, then went on. "That's impossible. I'm sorry, Tegestu. But I speak truly. I know my people."

And so the dream ends, Tegestu thought. We will remain a homeless people, wandering among strangers, until we are finally dissolved among them like a handful of salt in an ocean, losing everything that makes us ourselves.

But what made him Brodaini was also obedience, and he bowed to that. "I hear you, Abessu-Denorru," he said, sick at heart. "What answer am I to make to Tastis?"

"None at all," Necias said. "Keep him guessing as long as you can. And in the end, refer him to me." Necias smiled grimly. "That'll put an end to his hopes."

No doubt it would, Tegestu thought numbly.

"I want the army marching again once the fort surrenders," Necias said briskly, businesslike. "We've got to move swiftly, as long as Tastis sees compromise in us."

"Aye," Tegestu said. "I'll give the orders."

Necias walked back to the settee and sat down, looking with concern at Tegestu. "You understand why I have to give these orders, Tegestu?" he asked.

Tegestu nodded. "I understand."

"Very well." Necias fell silent for a moment, then licked his lips. "If there's anything your people want," he said, concern on his face. "Anything within reason, please inform me, and I'll grant it." He reached out to touch Tegestu's knee. "But not this, old friend. Not this."

Tegestu bowed, then stood. "I will transmit your orders to the army, Abessu-Denorru," he said.

Necias nodded, then turned to Campas. "No record of this, Campas," he said. "Burn your notes, and do it now. And you'll say nothing of it, ever."

Campas nodded. "As you wish, cenors-efellsan."

Tegestu knelt, then walked from the pavilion into the sun. He heard Grendis' tread behind him and turned to her, seeing her gazing at him with troubled eyes. "I didn't foresee it," he confessed. "I didn't understand Necias well enough." He laughed bitterly. "That was what I said to Aptan, that Tastis didn't understand who he was dealing with. Now my words are turned against me."

She reached up a hand to touch his cheek. "It was a bold try," she said. "Brilliant." She tried to smile encouragingly. "It wasn't your fault it failed."

Tegestu kissed the palm of her hand, then turned away, feeling the unrelenting ache of the armor on his shoulders and neck, an ache that seemed insignificant beside the one in his heart. "Can you see the orders are given?" he asked. "I would like to lie down a while, before we march."

"Aye. I'll see it's done," Grendis said. He began to walk to his small tent, trying to keep his back straight, his shoulders back. Trying to stay Brodaini to the last, even in this unhappy land of exile.

16

Fiona, standing on the siege works thrown up before the city, gazed at the walls with sullen anger, the cards flickering through her fingers as she performed tricks to calm her spirit. Snapping cards out of the deck, she looked up at the hundred eighty grey stone towers of Neda-Calacas and tried to guess on which of them Kira had died. Across the river, probably, in the Brodaini quarter of Neda, where Tastis' banners flew boldly in warm summer breeze.

For two days the army of Arrandal had been building its siege lines in front of Calacas, the easternmost of the twin cities. Neda was an older city, a capital of one of the Captilla kingdoms that had been shattered by the Abessla invasions hundreds of years before. Neda had never been taken, and marked the end-point of Abessla expansion: to end the wars, an agreement had been reached to allow the Abessla people to settle across the river and built their own city of Calacas. Gradually the people, and their cities, had become one, and the formality of purging the royal family of Neda, who had long before lost all real power to the deissin, had come late, only a hundred years before.

And now the banners of a new invader topped the walls, and the Abessla of Arrandal and Cartenas, the Captilla of Prypas, and the half-dozen other ethnic varieties that made up the rest of the Elva, were coming to take it back. The problems the siege presented were enormous, Fiona had been told. There were a quarter of a million inhabitants behind those walls—half the normal population, since many had fled or been evacuated to the islands where the Elva fleet was obliged to feed them—and the walls were massive and stout. The cities had grown in the last four hundred years, and walls had been built outward to protect them: once an outer wall was breached, there were three or four lines of inner defense, each a wall guarded by a series of interlocking canals that doubled as moats, each line marking the limits of an older, smaller city.

The army of Arrandal had settled before Calacas, the easternmost city, as Tegestu had thought it might prove easier: Neda had an additional line of defense, the new Brodaini city that had been added in the last twenty years, and built with all the craft and strength of a warrior people. Neda was unsieged at the moment—the army of Arrandal was too small to encircle both cities, straddling the Neda river, without risking having one part of it overwhelmed by an attack—but there were patrols in front of Neda day and night to discourage the enemy, and when the army of Prypas arrived in a few days the circle would be closed.

The sea route was already cut off. The united fleets of Arrandal, Cartenas, and Prypas held the islands and maintained a strict blockade, with other Elva squadrons expected daily. Tastis appeared to have realized that he could do nothing against them: his own fleet had been drawn up on the beach and short of an anchor watch appeared to be abandoned.

The cards flickered through Fiona's fingers. A pair of Brodaini engineers, mapping the area forward of the lines, looked at her with interest, then returned to their work. Fiona frowned, remembering Tyson's words as she'd spoken to him that morning.

"It's moderately interesting data you've been collecting, all that information on the mercenaries," he said. "But it's not your real work. You could have done this, and more, if you'd stayed in Arrandal."

"I was asked to come," she'd said with surprise. "You agreed that it would be a good idea to make myself useful to Necias."

"But what has he used you *for,* Fiona?" Tyson asked. "Could he be using your presence to put pressure on Tastis? Telling Tastis to go along with him, or he'll send the star people in after him?"

"That," Fiona snapped, "would imply he knows about Kira. I don't think he does. There's no evidence for what you're suggesting."

"Perhaps not." Tyson's deep voice, as always, was annoyingly calm, a Tyson-knows-best tone of voice Fiona had always thought patronizing, if not infuriating. "But unless Necias can suggest a less . . . a less *opaque* role for you here, you might suggest to him that you might do your work best in the cities."

"The army of Prypas will be here in a few days," Fiona said. "They'll be bringing another group of diplomats with them—I think I'll be able to make myself useful then."

"Keep what I've said in mind, Fiona," Tyson said, in warning tones, and she scowled at the spindle in her hands, then shut it off without saying goodbye. A petulant act; but then Tyson had done his best to be annoying and certainly deserved it.

She knew he was right, however. Her time could be better spent elsewhere. It was ridiculous to think she could remain here for long: unless Necias managed to buy open a gate some dark night, the siege might well last a year. Her hands deftly broke the deck of cards in half. She shirt—he'd been wearing it ever since the enemy battlements came in sight, but still did not look at ease in it.

"There's a problem, Ambassador," Campas said. "The Abessu-Denorru would like to see you, if it's convenient."

"Of course." She picked up her rucksack and slung it over one shoulder. "What's the nature of the problem?" she asked.

"Some strangers have arrived, with a bargeful of goods. From a country far off, to the south. Necias wonders if you might know them."

Fiona frowned. "I don't know everyone from the south, just because I travelled there."

Campas grinned. "I don't think Necias quite understands what being from another planet truly means," he said. "He just thinks it means from far away. You're from a far country; this other man is from a far country: therefore you might know one another. This man is dark, also, like you." He shrugged, and immediately winced at the chafe of the mail shirt on his neck. He sighed. "I was relaxing in Necias' bath house," he complained, "up to my neck in nice hot water, and now these people have showed up."

She followed Campas toward where Necias had pitched his pavilion on the banks of a canal, half a mile into the lines. Campas glanced over his shoulder and frowned. "Necias isn't in a good mood today," he said. "There were dispatches from the city. Some of the weavers' apprentices and journeymen rioted, burned down the workshop of Nalsas—he was a real slavedriver anyway, so it's no great loss, but the Denorru-Deissin is terrified Tastis' grey walls. Tastis had exploited the cities' weaknesses well, she thought; he had allied himself with those who had always been on the edge of power, but never had a chance to grasp it. Could it be that he was allying himself with the future? she wondered, the forces that would inevitably succeed? Fervently, she hoped not.

Campas, in answer to her question, started to shrug, remembered his mail shirt, and threw up his hands instead. "I don't know. I'm sure Tastis has agents aplenty in Arrandal—he had enough time to send them out. And he's been sending some into our camp, disguised as sutlers with goods to sell, trying to seduce the mercenaries and the soldiers, but we cut off a few heads and sent the rest packing." His voice grew reflective. "And of course we've agents aplenty in Neda-Calacas," he said, then cocked an eye at the barred enemy gates, above which a dozen heads rotted, grimacing at the besiegers, "but they have a harder time getting in and out." He grinned. "I hear you've been talking to the mercenaries," he said.

"Yes." She had assembled a lot of raw data: individuals in the mercenary companies had come from half a world away, from half a hundred nations. She frowned. "Many of them aren't very nice people."

"No. They enjoy their work too much." He paused. "Have you given up on the Brodaini, then?"

Fiona shook her head. "It's just that the mercenaries were here, and I don't know when I'll get another chance to speak to so many of them." She glanced up at the hot midsummer sun, wishing she'd thought to bring a hat.

"Your poetry goes well?" she asked.

"Well enough. I'd thought the hours on horseback would have been a good time to work out the patterns, but Necias keeps me up half the night doing his correspondence, and I use the horseback journeys to catch up on my sleep. I've learned the trick of it, and the beast keeps to the track."

He looked at her with a half smile. "But what I've done is good, yes. I'm pleased."

"I'm glad it's working. I'd like to see it."

"Not till it's done. I'm strict about that."

"I understand." They reached the pavilion, and Fiona saw at once the strangers outside. There were half a dozen of them, dressed mostly in travel-stained leather. Fiona felt a sudden pang of homesickness as she saw the dark, elaborately-folded cloth over their heads, a sundrape, practical in a hot homeland, almost identical to the one her own people wore.

"Came up on a barge this morning," Campas said. "Were going to deliver their goods to Calacas on contract, and ran into the war instead. He'll try to sell them to Necias."

Fiona shook off the treacherous stab of memory. In this alien world, even a superficial familiarity could awaken a longing ache she preferred not to recognize.

"I see," she said.

"You don't know him?" Campas' voice seemed to hold out some vestige of hope.

"No." She shrugged.

"I'll tell the Abeissu." He started to step toward the tent, then hesitated. He turned back to her. "Would you like to share luncheon with me?" he asked. "I have the afternoon free—I've packed my meal in a haversack and was going to take it out in front of the lines and enjoy the sun."

Fiona nodded. "I'd be happy to."

Campas gave a quick grin. "Good. Let me speak to Necias for a moment, then I'll be out."

Campas took longer than a moment. The strangers in their sundrapes scowled at her and muttered to one another in their own language. She moved a distance off, sat down on a block that had been used to chop Necias' wood, and took out her deck, the cards flicking through her fingers.

She tried to snap a card out and it hung in the deck, a clumsy, amateurish move, and she frowned: she hadn't kept in practice.

Campas, a rucksack on his shoulder, came out of Necias' tent, and the leader of the foreign traders was allowed in amid a moving rectangle of guards. She stood, glancing automatically at the enemy towers again, her hands instinctively sorting the cards. Campas' question came as a blow.

"Why do you hate them so much?"

Her hands froze on the cards as she stared blankly ahead in shock; she recovered, not quickly enough, and turned to Campas. "Why do you ask that?"

"You look at the city with such hatred." Reasonably. "I saw you the morning after the battle, too, and I remember the expression on your face. You *hate* them. What happened to your embassy there?" He looked away, frowning uneasily. "It's not my business, of course."

"No." Tartly. "It's not."

She had told them the Igaran embassy to Neda-Calacas had been refused; she hadn't told them what had happened, fearful they'd try to recruit her for their war. She hadn't wanted to be recruited.

But she had, she knew, volunteered.

She looked at Campas again, resenting both the question and the compulsion that wanted her to answer—to clear up at least one of the misunderstandings between herself and someone else.

She turned to the city again, feeling her eyes narrow, the words, buried so long, coming out of her slowly, with deliberate anger. "They killed her," she said. "They wanted her to give—to give what she had—to them alone." She breathed out deliberately, letting the anger out with the breath. "There was threat of torture, too," she said, then looked up at Campas, seeing his steady glance, his sympathy. "That's why I'm here," she admitted. "I wanted to have—have revenge, I suppose. Not a very good reason. As my people have been telling me.''

She looked down at her hands as they busied themselves sorting the cards, then put them in her pack.

''I'm sorry, Ambassador,'' Campas said evenly. ''It's never easy to be caught in the middle of a war.'' He turned his head, looking thoughtfully at the enemy walls. ''I would have thought Tastis was more clever than that. Perhaps they were panicked, somehow.''

Oh, yes, Fiona thought with a flash of anger. It was Kira's fault, of course. She frightened them, the poor simple savages. Those dear renegades are far too unsophisticated to practice deliberate cruelty, deliberate terror, deliberate murder.

Campas turned back to her. His tone was puzzled. ''They've killed one of your ambassadors and you haven't responded?'' he asked. ''Not declared war yourselves?''

Fiona shook her head. She could feel the resentment in her tone but couldn't halt it. ''No. We're not allowed to meddle in your affairs: if we didn't hold to that firmly, you'd never trust us. We're permitted self-defense, but we can't take part in your wars. Military involvements are beyond our capabilities, anyway.'' She looked up at him. ''You've seen the announcements that I asked Necias to distribute. You know this.''

He looked at her frankly. ''Beg pardon, Ambassador, but I've learned to mistrust any announcements from diplomats.''

''You can trust this one.'' She paused, then frowned at him. ''I would appreciate it if you didn't tell Necias. He'd try to take advantage.''

''Yes. He would.'' Flatly. ''I will keep this in confidence, Ambassador.''

''Thank you.''

He fell silent for a moment, then reached for his rucksack. ''Beefsteak pies,'' he said. ''Necias' cook is a good hand with pastry. Sweet noodles for desert." He raised a bottle. "And wine. It's loot, from a country house we passed. For some reason the mercenaries didn't get to it first." He smiled in satisfaction. "I'm becoming an old campaigner. Heading for the cellars first thing."

She looked at the luncheon, then again at the enemy walls. "Shall we go to my quarters for luncheon, Campas?" she asked. "I'm not in a mood to move out forward of the lines, not if it means going closer to Calacas."

Campas did not seem surprised. "As you wish," he said briefly, and returned the bottle to its rucksack.

They walked to her tent in silence. Guarded by dozens of soldiers, it was in an area reserved for officers and diplomats, including the Government-in-Exile of Neda-Calacas, a heterogeneous, bickering group that consisted of members of purged trading houses who'd happened to be in Arrandal during the coup, plus a number of diplomatic personnel. Her tent was an anonymous cone-shaped structure, unmarked by any flag or banner to proclaim her ambassadorial status; it was larger than those used by most of the soldiery, but far smaller than Necias' grand pavilion, or the Government-in-Exile's canvas palace. She'd hired a male servant to keep it clean, and to buy fuel and food, and since she did most of the chores herself he found it easy work.

Her servant wasn't there at present; he was probably gambling his wages away with a crowd of his comrades. There were four Brodaini stools and a short folding table standing neatly by her pallet; she let the tent flap fall behind her, and gestured Campas to one of the stools.

"I'm sorry that you're not used to eating sitting up," she said.

"I've lived among Brodaini, remember," Campas reminded her. "I can digest at attention if I have to."

There were plates, cups, and knives in one of her trunks; she got them out. The wine splashed into the cups; it was a dark-red claret that the deissin made fortunes exporting abroad, and it went down well. The pastry was lovely, but as always the filling lacked spice. At least, she thought resignedly, she hadn't landed in a culture where they *boiled* things.

"Reports from the city indicate our new ships are performing well," Campas said. "The new sails can point into the wind with amazing ability." He paused. "They're called *fiono* sails, after you. The sailors gave them the feminine ending."

How would Tyson take that? she wondered. He would disapprove, she thought, as usual. She was supposed to be invisible, always the observer, never a participant.

"That's nice of them," she said.

Campas leaned back on his stool, regarding her carefully as if deciding whether or not to speak. "That sail," he said finally. "It will change everything, that's obvious. But since then you haven't . . ." He paused a moment, choosing his words. "You haven't given us anything. Just put out a list of things you can't or won't do, and spent the rest of your time visiting people, finding out about things." He fell silent again, then leaned forward and quickly took a drink of wine, as if frustrated by his inability to phrase his thoughts with the precision he demanded of himself.

"You're wondering when I'll give you more suggestions?" Fiona prompted.

He blinked. "Yes," he said. "I didn't want to sound too eager." He gave a nervous smile. "It might sound as if I—we—were ungrateful."

She shook her head. "It's an understandable question," she said. "I'm asking questions, as you put it, because we want to find out more about you before making any more suggestions. But it's not exactly my task to give you things, not as I did with the sails. That was simply to help establish my credentials. My job is more to . . . to be a kind of guide. To help your people move in a more fruitful direction. To help you to avoid dead ends.''

Campas knit his brows in thought, uncertain. Fiona searched her mind for an example. "As I did with your poetry, Campas," she said, and saw his surprise. "I didn't tell you how to write it; I didn't tell you the themes to use. You understood that you had a problem, and I offered . . . I offered a structure that helped you think about it."

"I see." Slowly, with a frown.

"I'm here more to teach a mode of thought," Fiona continued. "That things may not be assumed, that suppositons must be tested." He looked at her blankly, and she gave it up: another attempt failed. Philosophy, here including natural philosophy and what they knew of science, was a sport of gentlemen and professional rhetoricians: their tests were not whether a thing was objectively *true* but whether it followed from its premise and made a consistent philosophical whole; the premises themselves were never tested. She could teach them otherwise, she knew, given enough time, given enough practical examples. But here she'd failed: Campas simply hadn't seen her method in use often enough.

"I suppose I know what you mean," he said. She knew he was merely being polite; she sighed and told herself it didn't matter. He raised a hand. "But you *could* give us more, Ambassador," he said. "Why not simply do it? We would—we would move more quickly that way. No dead ends at all."

Fiona shook her head. "It wouldn't work, Campas. It would destroy you." She saw his surprise and spoke quickly. "Everything you've made here, all the relationships in your society—they're based on how you've adapted to your capabilities, to your environment. If you change too fast, things can crumble." He still seemed unconvinced. She took a breath and plunged on. "We could give you all our knowledge," Fiona said. "But it wouldn't turn *you* into *us*. Profitable change has to come from within, not be imposed from without—we'd be worse than conquerors, then. Making you conform to our pattern, abandon all that you know, all that you are. It's what you accused me of, once. *Making your world over*, making all that you've done and become irrelevant. It *would* destroy you, in the end.''

"So we must do it ourselves, because that's the only way it's meaningful," Campas said, frowning. She was uncertain whether he believed it, or was merely parroting her ideas.

"We Igaralla have the time," Fiona said. "We can wait for you. There's no hurry with us."

Campas shook his head. "If you say it's so, Ambassador," he said doubtfully—and then he looked up, his blue eyes challenging, forthright.

"Do you *know* this?" he asked. "Have you tried it, with others?"

Fiona felt a stab of alarm. She had forgotten how acute the man was.

Challenged this way, she could not lie. She was sick of evasion.

"Yes," she said. "Our first star ships—they caused chaos. Change happened too fast. It was like handing swords and spears to a people that have only thrown rocks at one another. There were terrible wars, and other changes—nations fell apart, vast numbers of people lost their occupations. Terrible. They recovered eventually, but it took generations. This slow way is easier."

She could not, of course, describe it fully. Instant communication on worlds that had depended on footborn messengers. Modern weapons on worlds that had depended on armored horsemen to keep the peace. Practical medicine introduced in countries that had depended on periodic epidemics to prevent overpopulation. Chaos, followed by utter demoralization; entire cultures devitalized by contact with a superior technological power that abolished their civilization virtually overnight.

As a result, a change of tactics was mandated for all interstellar embassies, resulting in the current emphasis on carefully selective interference, on suggestion, on teaching theory rather than offering practical examples. Ambassadors now were required to live among the primitive cultures, living for years as a native would live—a disciplined body of volunteers, sacrificing their own well-being so that, several hundred years in the future, the descendants of their pupils might climb out into space—and if the ambassadors, with their prolonged lifespan and the ability to freeze themselves, were lucky, and if they survived the changes they had wrought, they would be able to watch the first ships shining as new stars in the heavens.

Long centuries from now. For the moment Fiona was too discouraged to feel inspired by her work. Campas, clearly, was not convinced; she doubted he had understood anything she had tried to say. *This will happen again,* she told herself. *Over and over. I should get used to it.*

It bothered her. There was so little of her experience that she could share with Tyson, Campas, anyone. Her peers on this continent were buried in their work, showing strain but, it seemed, accomplishing so much more than she. They were stronger, perhaps.

She could feel the loneliness plucking at her. It was not worth the energy to fight it off any longer.

Kira, she thought, would have understood.

They finished their luncheon, then the wine. Watching her hand as if it were foreign to her, a part of someone else, Fiona saw it reach across the table to take his hand.

She saw that he was not surprised. *Clever boy,* she thought.

In this, at least, hands and tongues could speak without misunderstanding. The jacket and upper privy-coat came off with a shrug; his hands touched her shoulders lightly, caressed her arms, the muscles over her ribs, the small brown breasts.

What would Tyson think? she wondered, standing with her face tilted up, her eyes closed, hearing the whisper of his fingers on her skin. Tyson's opinion, she thought firmly, was not solicited.

"Your skin is so soft. I hadn't known." Campas marveled in her ear. She had herself thought she was harder. He even bathed this morning, and let her know it. Clever, clever boy.

She found herself laughing, her amusement hard to define. I shall keep this data, she thought, to mysef.

This is art, she thought, not science. Poetry.

The stanzas succeeded one another, slowly.

To myself, she thought, to myself.

Clever boy.

17

Standing in the shade of the umbrella that kept the
summer sun from his armor, Tegestu slit his eyes against
the bright summer sunlight as a long line of barges came
up the canal, strings of four or five each warped along by a
pair of mules. Supply barges mostly, bringing food and
fodder for the besieging armies. The barges flew flags to
indicate their ownership, flags of the merchant houses of
Arrandal, Acragas prominent among them with its blazon
of the god Pastas, flags of minor trading companies, house
flags of the independent bargemen who rented their hulls
to the city . . . and flags of the Brodaini kamlissi of
Arrandal, marking their own possessions.

The barge convoy meant comfort, among other things.
The siege would be a long one. Part of Necias' household
was being moved in the barges, one of which was fitted
out as his private residence, several others for servants and
functionaries, another of which was modified as a floating
partillo for the benefit of his wives, two of whom Tegestu
could see standing on the foredeck in their elaborate,
layered skirts, their faces shadowed by their parasols.

Tegestu's security people, he knew, would be thankful that Necias' barge had finally arrived—moored in one of the canals, it would be much easier to guard than his giant pavilion. One of Arrandal's deissin had been assassinated last week, an ally on the Denorru-Deissin whose absence weakened, albeit slightly, the ruling coalition . . . the prominent Abessla had suddenly gone security-mad, and it seemed that everyone above the rank of captain was suddenly demanding Brodaini bodyguards. As if Tastis cared for their foolish lives. . . .

The Brodaini barges, twelve of them, moved down the canal last of all. They were filled for the most part with Classani, some of them armed but mostly servants of the nonmartial sort: actors, singers, men and women of the Gentle Way to cater to the social and sexual needs of the soldiers—long sieges had a way of being bad for morale, and the Classani were badly needed.

It would take more than a few entertainers to cheer Tegestu, he knew. The siege would drag on for months, and every week brought several casualties. Two nights ago Tastis had unexpectedly sortied with his rowing fleet, striking by surprise against the deep-sea squadrons anchored off the roads. Arrandal's rowing fleet had come to the rescue and the attack was beaten off, but over a hundred fifty Brodaini lives had been lost, hacked or drowned when their ships, unable to make sail fast enough and not built to move under oars, were rammed or boarded. His men were being whittled away, Tegestu thought despairingly, dying in small lots—even small numbers of dead could prove tragic. This war of the cities would involve, in the end, all the Brodaini exiles, and the cities would not hesitate to ask the Brodaini to shoulder the main burden of warfare, and the main casualties as well. And why not? The Brodaini were not their own folk, and with Tastis' rebellion had proved themselves untrustworthy. Why not spend them now, in fighting one another, weakening them so they would not be a threat to anyone?

Tastis offered me the city, Tegestu thought. But that cannot be. I am Brodaini, and I cannot disobey an order given in honor. My life is my canlan's; and I knew this when I took service here.

The barges passed, the Classani on deck halting their busy movements to bow hastily in Tegestu's direction as they glided past his standard. Tegestu nodded back, acknowledging the proper respect shown by his inferiors, and then glanced out to sea at the long galley that rode just off Calacas' outer harbor, the summer sun glittering off the gold banner of kamliss Pranoth that fluttered from the maintop, just above the scarlet pendant that signified the presence of a member of the aldran.

Amasta was aboard, commanding the rowing squadron that had escorted the barges from Arrandal. It was a duty that would normally have been assigned to a subordinate, but Tegestu felt in need of Amasta's cunning, and also wanted another member of the aldran here, to welcome the commander of Prypas' Brodaini force. With himself, Grendis, Acamantu, Cascan, and now Amasta, the Arrandal aldran would now have five representatives at the siege.

The Prypas army had begun arriving two days before, the vanguard of cavalry and light foot beginning to set up their camp opposite Neda, barricading with Arrandalla aid the only safe land approach to the city, the mile-wide causeway of firm ground that stood between a treacherous salt-marsh and the river. Neda was at least much easier to besiege than Calacas, which had miles of wall to guard.

The main body was expected to arrive tomorrow, its Brodaini contingent commanded by Tanta Amandos Dantu y'Sanda, a Prypas welldran Tegestu had never met. Kamliss Sanda had been allied with Pranoth in the great war, but for geographic reasons their forces had never been able to fight side by side, and Tegestu knew very little of this Tanta's reputation. He hoped that Amasta, who had once been an emissary to the Sanda court, would be able to assist him until such time as he made his own judgements.

The last of the barges slid noiselessly past. Tegestu saw the sweeps of Amasta's galley suddenly flash sunlight as they rose in unison, then dipped water. The galley surged forward, light on the water, a bone growing in its teeth.

Tegestu heard the sound of a horse behind him and turned: it was Cascan, arriving late to Amasta's reception. Cascan dismounted from his sweating horse and bowed, then came forward, brushing dust from his surcoat. "Drandor Tegestu, I beg a word apart," he said, bowing again. Tegestu glanced at Amasta's galley and saw he had the time.

"Very well," he said. "I hope this will be brief."

"As brief as I can make it, drandor."

Tegestu signalled his umbrella-bearer to remain in place and then walked quickly away from the welcoming party, hearing the rattle of his guards' armor as they deployed themselves carefully out of earshot, yet between Tegestu and any possible attack.

"There is a new rumor in the camp," Cascan said. "Spread by Tastis' agents, no doubt—he has enough of them."

"Aye," Tegestu said. It was impossible to keep Tastis' people out, spies who attached themselves to mercenary bands, or who lived among the various unofficial military brothels and commissaries that sold their wares to the soldiers, or who posed as traders coming up and river to buy or sell—Necias had tried to keep all unlicensed persons away, but his own official commissaries were unable to keep the soldiers fully fed and happy, and infiltrations happened. It was inevitable.

"The rumor states that, in your private conference with the commander of the West Rallandas garrison, you were

offered command of the Neda-Calacas, to hold as a Brodaini
city. And that you refused.''

Tegestu felt his heart thunder at the news, but he recovered swiftly from his surprise. He looked carefully into
Cascan's impassive face, glaring at him until Cascan's
eyes fell, and when he spoke he spoke harshly. ''Why do
you ask me this, ban-demmin Cascan?'' he demanded.
''To quell the rumor, or for your own information?''

''Beg pardon if I have offended, bro-demmin Tegestu,''
Cascan said, bowing. ''I wished only to know how to
reply to this rumor.''

''Say that it is false.''

''Aye, bro-demmin. It is false.'' Cascan straightened,
licking his lips. ''It is a difficult rumor to quell, bro-
demmin.'' he said. ''It speaks to the secret wishes of so
many.''

''Those who possess such wishes are fools!'' Tegestu
snapped. ''Such wishes could never be realized,'' he
growled. ''They would lead to the destruction of all our
people. Don't they realize we have dependents in every
Elva city? Thousands of hostages to our good behavior?''

Cascan hesitated for a moment, then bowed. ''Aye,
bro-demmin,'' he said. ''Praise to your wisdom.''

''Is that all, ban-demmin?'' Tegestu asked.

''Aye, bro-demmin.''

''Very well.'' He turned on his heel and led Cascan
back to the group gathered on the canal, awaiting Amasta's
galley. *The rumor speaks to the secret wishes of so many,*
Cascan had said. True enough, he thought regretfully, and
some wishes not so secret. If only it were possible.

Tastis must have tired of waiting for his reply, he
thought. He meant to force the issue and so spread the
rumor, hoping Tegestu's own people would force him to
act. That was why Tegestu had reacted so coldly, so
angrily, hoping to squash any conspiracies before they

began. For the good of dispipline he had to enforce absolute obedience to the Elva, and do it now.

He would find it easier, however, if his heart were in it.

No matter. His heart, like the rest of him, must obey.

He returned to the shadow of his umbrella and awaited the galley.

The following night the welldrani of Arrandal played formal host to Tanta of Prypas, who proved to be a middle-aged, well-fleshed man, balding and powerfully built. "He was famous in his youth for his use of the war axe," Amasta had told Tegestu. "It is said he could wield it so dextrously that he could almost fence with it." As for his character, Amasta remembered him as a plain-spoken soldier, intelligent but scarcely a reservoir of great cunning. He was a reliable subordinate: that was why he was here, commanding on behalf of the drandor of Kamliss-Sanda-sa-Prypas, who was too elderly to take the field himself.

"We are honored, bro-demmin Tanta," Tegestu said, bowing as Tanta and his party approached, "to have as our guest a welldranu of such distinction, and of such peerless fame with the war axe. We would be honored if you would favor us soon by inspecting our forces."

Tanta flushed with pleasure as he returned the bow, clattering in his heavy formal armor, steel breast- and backplate, bracers and greaves, plumed helmet tilted back on his head. In return he praised the cunning, sagacity, and ferocity of his hosts. The dinner thereby started off on the proper note, and Tanta was offered the place of honor at the head of the table. He declined, of course; but his hosts insisted and eventually, as manners dictated, he accepted. Two Classani stood behind him, keeping his glass and plate filled, while a third held his helmet.

The dinner was out of doors, partly because no Brodaini tent was capable of holding such a gathering, but also because security was so much better out of doors, on a flat drill ground well-lit by torches, where no one could approach within two hundred yards without being seen by the cathruni. Conversation was light and inconsequential, consisting mainly of formal greetings sent from one welldran to another, or talk about relations: Tasta, through his mother, was cousin in some obscure way to Grendis. It wasn't until the meal was at an end that its real business began.

"Bro-demmin Tegestu," Tanta said, draining his cup. "I find myself needing to stretch after such a meal. I would be honored if you would accompany me for a short walk."

"The honor is mine, bro-demmin," Tegestu said, bowing. Tanta bowed to each of the welldrani in turn, thanking them, and then signalled to a Classanu for a torch as he rose. Tegestu strained upward, needing the assistance of Thesau's arm before he could rise, pain shooting through his thighs and hips. He breathed his thanks to Thesau, feeling sudden sweat popping out on his forehead, and wished the occasion hadn't demanded the formal steel armor rather than the light chain-and-leather he wore in the summer.

"Perhaps it would please you to walk this way, bro-demmin Tanta," he said as Thesau carefully coiled his braids atop his head and fixed his helmet in place, its visor raised. "The sight of Second Moon rising above that river may prove soothing." It was, of course, the path his cathruni had been guarding since noon, making certain no assassin could have hidden himself somewhere along its length.

"A profoundly stirring sight," Tanta said politely, his Classanu setting his helmet back on his head as he took the torch from another servant. "I would find it inspiring, I'm sure."

The torch in one hand, Tanta took Tegestu's arm with the other and walked with him into the night. They walked in silence until they reached the broad, silver-sheened, muttering river; they stood on a small bluff while Second Moon, scarcely brighter than a star, rose over the distant, dark horizon. Tanta broke the silence with a sigh.

"A lovely sight, bro-demmin," he said. "Thank you for showing it to me."

"It is my honor, bro-demmin."

"It reminds me of your victory poem, the one you wrote after the fight on the East Rallandas. Starlight and steel, like Second Moon on the river. And a lament for the brave dead. I have no such way with poetry."

"I am pleased the poem gave you pleasure," Tegestu said.

"The battle gave me more," Tanta said. "*Aiau*, what a victory! Tastis will be desperate for friends. He's where we need him, 'twixt hammer and anvil." He gave a feral grin. "Where we need him," he repeated, and took a scroll from his pouch.

"My lord Astapan gave me this, for you," he said. "If its contents are what I suspect, this should be burned."

Tegestu looked at Tanta in surprise. "It is not in cypher?" he asked.

"It came by a trustworthy hand," Tanta said.

Tegestu frowned, not liking the possibility of such a private message coming into unfriendly hands uncyphered, then realized that perhaps the trustworthy hand had been Tanta's own. He nodded and broke the seal.

Astapan was the Brodaini drandor in Prypas, seventy-eight now, a revered and cunning warrior unable to take the field. Tegestu broke the double seal and flattened the roll of delicate paper, squinting at the delicate writing. Tanta helpfully moved the torch to give Tegestu better light.

"Hail, bro-demmin drandor Tegestu Dellila Doren y'Pranoth," he read. "Greetings from your cousin, Astapan

Hamila Sanda y'Sanda, and from the members of our aldran.

"We send you congratulations, once again, for your victory on the Rallandas and your successful investment of Calacas. May your arm never weaken, and your cunning never fail. We hope our rebel cousin Tastis will continue frustrated in his aims.

"Word has reached our ears of a meeting at a fort on the West Rallandas, and of what may have been spoken there." Tegestu sucked in his breath in surprise, feeling his anger rise. There was only one way Astapan could have heard of this—through Tastis. Tastis is trying to drive a wedge between us, Tegestu thought as he fought down his anger. Dangling the same bait before each Brodaini drandor, hoping one will snap at it.

"This news, if true, raises possibilities that intrigue us," the message continued. "If a Brodaini aldran can achieve sovereignty, and can do so without becoming ar-demmin, then other aldrani can but praise them.

"Bro-demmin Tegestu, you are renowned for your sagacity, and all Brodaini in service to the Elva owe you a debt. We believe your actions cannot be without wisdom, and that you will not, like our unwise cousin Tastis, be tempted into rash action that will lose demmin and break hostu. Our aldran pledges to support the decisions of the drandor of Arrandal, and of your aldran; we further pledge to subordinate our forces to you in the area of Neda-Calacas. Our cousin Tanta understands this.

"Hail, cousin Tegestu, may your demmin increase. You have our confidence."

Aiau, Tegestu thought. He read the message once more, then carefully crumpled it and raised it to the torch, watching as it flared and blackened. The ashes were scuffed into the dirt, broken.

If he chose to accept Tastis' offer and take command of the city, the Prypas aldran would support him. The consequences were obvious: his actions, and that of Prypas, would signal for a general demand by the exiled Brodaini for establishing Neda-Calacas as the capital of a Brodaini state. If the Elva agreed, fine; if not there would be general revolt. And afterwards a war of extermination, with every man's hand against the rebels.

If he refused to lead this revolt, would Prypas act unilaterally? The message implied not. He had to find out.

He raised his eyes from the dust, seeing Tanta look at him expectantly, as if awaiting orders. *Careful*, his mind warned, you cannot let him think you have committed yourself to this. You cannot even imply it.

"May I ask the way in which this rumor came to you?" he asked.

"Under a flag of truce, bro-demmin. We had captured some of Tastis' people, and they wanted to exchange prisoners. There was a messenger with the party, one of Tastis' autraldi, dressed in the robes of a priest. I spoke to him privately."

"I understand," Tegestu said. He glanced northward, toward the darkness of the enemy city. "Could you favor me with the content of his message, as you remember it?" he asked.

"Aye, bro-demmin, I'll do my best," Tanta said. He frowned abstractedly, as if calling the scene to his mind, and then spoke. "I apologize for not remembering his words exactly. There was a prelude concerning how those native to this land cannot treat us with honor, as they are a different people and do not understand us. I treated the idea with the contempt it deserves, and told the man I would hear no more talk of disloyalty. He apologized, and then went on about Tastis' intentions, to create a city where Brodaini could rule Brodaini and live without misunderstanding." He spat, then smiled arrogantly. "I told him that though his city might be without misunderstanding, it was also without demmin. He seemed greatly offended. But then he said that Tastis had offered command of the city to you and to your aldran.''

"Did he say I had accepted?'' Tegestu asked sharply. Tanta hesitated, then shook his head.

"Nay, bro-demmin. He said only that you had not refused.'' Tegestu felt tension ebb from his joints: Tastis had at least told the truth. "I considered that this information, if true, would be of interest to my lord Astapan, so I left the army and posted back to Prypas, where I met with the aldran. I was given this message for you, and then returned to the army.''

"Why do you think Tastis has invited us to join in his treason, bro-demmin Tanta?'' Tegestu asked. "Could it not be to simply divide the forces against him?''

"Tastis is a traitor and a rebel, but even traitors have their uses,'' Tanta answered simply. He smiled, showing his teeth. "It does not matter to me when his head rolls, before or after the Brodaini come into their own.''

"We have dependents, bro-demmin,'' Tegestu said. "Our main force is here, not in the cities. Any action here could put them in jeopardy.''

"Should there be disturbances in Prypas, my lord Astapan can hold his citadel for a year, at least,'' Tanta said. "He is ready to seal himself in at a moment's notice. Your own quarter in Arrandal is stronger. A year is a long time—a great deal can happen in a year.''

Are you authorized to act on your own? Tegestu wanted to shout. It was clear enough that Tanta found Tastis' offer tempting, though it was less clear whether the Prypas aldran as a body agreed with him: their message seemed cautious and interested, but no more; and perhaps there was a hint that they trusted Tegestu's judgement more than Tanta's. But that was surmise: Tegestu needed to know the truth. How to find out?

"Have you received any more emissaries from Tastis?'' he asked.

"Nay, bro-demmin. The Denorru-Deissin of Prypas forbade any prisoner exchanges. They will not give back traitors."

"Very wise," Tegestu said. He hesitated a moment, trying to keep his face impassive while he thought furiously: he had to keep Tanta from communicating with Tastis on his own. Tanta seemed to be what his reputation claimed, an intelligent, vigorous, straightforward soldier, not at home in the world of intrigue, and Tastis was too clever—Tanta would be manipulated all too easily by a clever man.

"Bro-demmin welldran Tanta," he said. "I think it would be inauspicious for any—any communcations with Tastis to be conducted from the Prypas camp. I do not wish to slight you in this matter, but Tastis must not be allowed to think he can play us one against the other."

Tanta nodded, conceding the point easily. "Very well. My aldran has already given you authority in this, to speak on our behalf. Provided of course no demmin is lost—we will do nothing dishonorable." Tegestu felt relief filling his bones at Tanta's words, and he nodded.

"May your cunning never fail, bro-demmin Tanta," he said. "I believe with all my heart that this is wise."

The Prypas aldran had been more cunning, Tegestu was aware, than Tanta probably realized. On the one hand they conceded negotiating power to Tegestu, but on the other hand their stipulation meant that any resulting dishonor would accrue to Tegestu alone, Astapan having washed his hands of the talks. They were therefore in a position to enjoy the benefit from any dealings with Tastis, while being able to blame Tegestu for any disgrace and even—if the thing went totally wrong—disavowing any of Tegestu's actions and holding to their old allegiance. *Aiau*, Tegestu thought, Astapan is brilliant. Unfortunate we have never met face to face.

"Please understand this," Tegestu said. "My not giving Tastis an answer was a tactic—I wanted him to continue hoping that I would defect, so that he would not oppose our march to the city. That was all. I could not see a way to accept his proposal without becoming ar-demmin.'' He looked carefully into Tanta's face, seeing an impassive frown there.

"If you say so, bro-demmin," Tanta said. His tone seemed dubious.

"My cousin Tastis has disgraced my kamliss once, bro-demmin Tanta," Tegestu went on. "I will take no further action that will bring infamy to my family name."

"Aye, bro-demmin," Tanta said, his tone as before.

I have told the truth, Tegestu thought hopelessly, but he does not believe. What more can I do? Aiau, it is Tanta's fate not to believe the truth when it is given him. His fate and my misfortune.

"Come, bro-demmin," Tegestu said. "Let us watch the river again, and soothe our souls after this irritating discussion of treason and traitors. Afterwards, if you find it interesting, there are some actors who would be honored should you consent to view their drama. They beg permission to perform *Aspistu of the Drandor Sanda*, if it pleases you."

That was the Sanda family drama; Tanta grunted with gratified surprise. "I would find that interesting, yes," he said. "I'm sure I will be well pleased."

Throughout the moment of silence as they watched the river and the tiring walk back to the camp that left him breathless and praying for release from the heavy steel armor, Tegestu's mind churned with plans proposed and rejected. How to take advantage of this? A siege was a fact, a long and dreary fact, as solid as a stone set well in mortar; but Tastis and his attempt at conspiracy had added a certain liquidity to the situation: there was an uncertainty now, perhaps an advantage to be gained. But how to seize it?

The play was classic in style, partly in mime, partly in

poetry, partly in verse chanted to music. The story told of the drandor Sanda—one of Tanta's remote ancestors—who had been told by enemy lords, abetted by evil courtiers in his own household, of his wife's infidelity. Not entirely convinced, he put his wife to a number of imaginative and excruciating tests that convinced him of her devotion, and then, in a model act of aspistu, arranged to catch his enemies in a trap they had themselves set for the wife. At the end of the play the conspirators were tortured to death offstage, their eerie screams blending musically with the songs of adoration chanted by the happy, faithful couple.

Moral tension was provided less by the convolutions of plot than by the drandor's soliloquies, who throughout debated with himself the parts he was forced to play—he had to assume the role of a man who believed in his wife's adultery, convincing even she, while secretly laying his traps for the lying enemies. Should a lord, a successful general renowned for his truthfulness, play such a deceptive role, flattering and praising his enemies for their sagacity and wisdom in order to lure them into revealing themselves, or should he act as straightforwardly as his instincts demanded, and lead the nation to open war to avenge the suspected insult to his house?

It was after the denunciation, while the wailing conspirators were led away to the torturers, that Tegestu realized with a start his opportunity. He glanced self-consciously at Tanta in the place of honor, hoping the man hadn't seen his sudden inspiration. For the plan would betray Tanta and his house, leaving them open to the avengers of the Elva, and there would be more betrayals on top of that . . . and a betrayal of honor as well? Tegestu fervently hoped not.

He turned his eyes deliberately back to the play, shading them in order to hide the flare of triumph he felt rising in him. Amasta is here, he thought, Amasta the cunning and ruthless; and she will understand what I tell her. But there must be an instrument. . . .

He was exhausted following the play, the formal armor weighing him down, and it must have shown on his face, for Tanta, after praising the interpretation, bowed and after more compliments, withdrew with his party. Tegestu in turn complimented his own people on a hospitality worthy of their guest's status, and before they dispersed he took Cascan's arm. "A private meeting with you, ban-demmin," he said. "In an hour. Meet me at my tent."

"Aye, bro-demmin," Cascan said, his slitted eyes expressionless, and he bowed.

Grendis took his arm and they walked in silence to their tent, Tegestu leaning on her more than he would have wished. Cascan was such a perfect lord of spies, Tegestu thought as he walked. Such a perfect holder of secrets. His kamliss was too small to seize power; he must ever be a loyal follower, not a leader, for his status depended entirely on Pranoth favor: to use his knowledge against Pranoth would only be to insure his own fall from power.

Tegestu let his servants strip the heavy armor from him; then he called for tea and the masseurs. His weary body must be made ready for the meeting with Cascan, and the tea would insure alertness. Secret things had to be accomplished tonight.

When, after his massage and refreshment, he called for his light armor, Grendis' eyes widened in surprise.

"I will not be long, love," he said. "There is a piece of business that cannot wait." Her eyes filling with care, she asked if she could accompany him; he shook his head. "It will only be a matter of a few moments," he said as Thesau strapped the leather undercoat to him. "Rest easy."

Cascan was seated patiently outside the tent when he came out. "This way," he said, bowing. "My people have secured a place where we can talk."

It was not far, fortunately: even the light leather-and-chain was an unwelcome weight. In the center of a hundred-yard-diameter circle of bowmen, Cascan glanced at the disposition of his men with a critical eye, and then turned to Tegestu.

"How may I be of service, bro-demmin Tegestu?" he asked with a brief bow.

"I need a man for secret business, Cascan," Tegestu said. "He must be intelligent and discreet, preferably someone who has been attached at one time or another to an embassy, or who is familiar with diplomacy. He must be reliable and able to operate on his own, on a mission of the utmost importance. He must have a good memory, to carry information in his head. And he must be expendable—for he must die at the end of his mission, to protect the honor of our aldran."

Cascan considered for a few moments, then knelt, bowing his head. "I beg to be allowed to undertake this mission myself, bro-demmin, if you consider me worthy."

Tegestu felt his lips tighten in a smile: Aiau, what tigers this Tosta kamliss bred! "I must forbid it, bro-demmin," he said, pleased. "I shall need you for some time yet. Pick another man."

"Very well, bro-demmin," Cascan said, rising, his eyes still downcast. "May I have a few hours to consider the choice?"

"Aye. But isolate the man once you've chosen him. Put him in a tent apart—put him in quarantine, say he's got a contagious disease. No one but myself must be allowed to speak with him."

"Aye, bro-demmin."

"He'll have to be provided with passwords to get him through the lines. And the poison must always be ready—it would be best if you told him the mission was hazardous, and he should have his will made out and his death wishes recorded ahead of time, in case his death must be sudden."

"Aye, bro-demmin."

Cascan's face was shadowed by darkness, but the shadows could not entirely disguise the look of curiosity. Tegestu nodded to himself. No, my cunning Tosta, he thought; this tidbit is not for you. It is far too dangerous. There will be Pranoth men guarding the quarantine, not your own.

"Inform me of your choice in the morning," he said, bowed, and made his way back to his tent.

A messenger, Tastis' son had said, with a note under your seal will always find access to the city. Tegestu smiled grimly, pleased with his plan. This unknown, already-doomed man, he thought, will have such a seal. As he goes about my business of treachery.

18

"There," Campas said. "I thought you'd like to see it."

Leaving the landing, where it had been discharging cargo all night, was a heavy, bluff-bowed seagoing barge, ninety feet long and made for the coastal trade, clinker-built, with huge iron-strapped wooden leeboards and two masts: the first amidships, leaning slightly forward like a tipsy sailor, and the other, much smaller, aft of the tiller. Both sails, unfurled now in the light breeze to help the barge move along the placid canal, were big lugsails, slatting loudly in the uncertain puffs.

"Fiono sails," Campas said. "The first time they've been put on a big boat." He looked at her and nodded. "With the wind from a little west of south like this, other barges would have to be towed," he said.

Fiona turned her eyes from the barge to Campas. "You seem to know a lot about barges for a literary man," she said.

Campas grinned. "Most Arrandalla know about the sea, and about the river traffic," he said. "Also, my father had

264

an interest in a chandler's shop, and I apprenticed there for a time when I was twelve or so, keeping the books. Met a lot of the bargemen that way, and the deep-sea sailors as well.''

The barge passed, the two visible crewmen too occupied with steering the vessel, and with keeping the sails drawing, to pay attention to the two figures on the bank. The barge, varnished a deep brown all over, had no ornamentation except for a little red trim on the transom, on which the barge's name was picked out in gold leaf: FIONA'S BLESSING. Fiona, as she made out the lettering, felt herself flushing.

Campas' grin broadened. ''Sailors give benefactors their due,'' he nodded. ''They'll never forget you, not for what you've done for them. Every seaman who ever was trapped on a lee shore will bless you for the sail that will let them claw off it.''

''That's kind of them.'' Fiona said. ''But not necessary.'' These bargemen were people whose lives she had affected in a direct, personal way; and she hadn't even met them. The sail had been her passport into the inner circles of Arrandal, given coldly as a matter of policy: now she was being credited by sailors with a compassionate intervention she had never intended.

Well, she thought. At least her credit was good someplace.

The barge having passed, silver ripples closing easily over its wake, they walked toward her tent. Campas was cheerful, bubbling with happy conversation—now that the barges with part of Necias' household had arrived he had less work to do, and more time to spend with his poetry, and with her.

Fiona peered upward, past the brim of her sun hat, at her lover. Barring accident, she thought coldly, my life expectancy is four times his. In another fifteen years he will be an old man, his teeth going bad, rheumatism or body parasites or a host of other wasting diseases making permanent conquest of his body. There is so much we cannot share, including all my history prior to this: he couldn't hope to understand even the smallest part. We cannot share our lives; that would be a tragedy for us both. The most we can hope for is a season or two. Then I will help him find some deissu's daughter for a first wife, and make an end. That would be for the best.

He glanced at her, and she smiled up at him, contented pleasure filling her. Enough, for the moment, to enjoy his company, his wit, his laughter. Even for her, the future was uncertain enough to make her value the present, an interlude to be treasured in the memory.

Ahead she saw a Classanu in quiet livery running across the empty parade ground, raising puffs of dust, heading for the tents of one of the Brodaini encampments—and then the Classanu looked in their direction, stopped dead, and started running directly for them, his arms waving. Campas muttered something under his breath and increased his pace to meet him.

"Translator, ilean Campas!" the man said, breathless. "My lord needs a translator—there is some trouble. In the camp of Captain Pantas! Hurry, please, ilean!"

Campas cast a look back at Fiona, a look that said *stay back*, and then began to run toward the flag that marked Pantas' camp. The Classanu sketched a bow in his direction and ran for the Brodaini tents.

Pantas, Fiona thought. Bowmen, members of the city militia who used the laminated Arrandalla bow. Pantas had bought them all black wide-brimmed hats and blue neckerchiefs, and they considered themselves elite.

She began to run. She was a fast runner, having for sport or pleasure run long, dusty distances over the arid plains of her homeworld, and she settled to a fast ground-eating stride that, despite his longer legs, almost caught Campas before he arrived at the bowmen's camp.

Pantas had quartered his men in an old stone cow-barn

belonging to one of the farms that occupied the firm, fertile ground near the city—the hay had long gone to feed Tastis' animals, but the big building was a cool contrast to the midday heat, and better shelter than tents would have been. As Fiona approached she saw a roiling mass of men outside, milling in the dust, and an angry babble of voices.

She slowed, taking her gloves from her belt and pulling them on, then reaching to the back of her neck to pull the hood of her privy-coat out from beneath her Arrandalla shirt. She heard Campas' voice raised, cutting through the shouting, demanding angrily.

The crowd parted for him and Fiona saw, in the middle of a circle of the bowmen, a party of a dozen grim-faced Brodaini standing back-to-back in a defensive circle. The bowmen, she saw, had their bows strung, but as yet no arrow had been drawn from their short, decorated quivers; the Brodaini had their long, sword-bladed spears planted firmly in the ground, ready for instant use, but for the moment they were threatening no one. Coming closer, Fiona saw the Brodaini had a prisoner, one of the bowmen, forced on his knees in the center of the group.

"What's the meaning of this? Where's your captain?" Campas demanded, to be immediately answered by a dozen outraged voices. He shook his head violently and cut the air with his hands, and the noise subsided. One strangely hissing, nasal voice came rising above the throng.

"They've got one of ours, and we mean to get him back! We're not going to let them take away our corporal!"

"Treason!" It was a Brodaini-accented voice, speaking Abessas with effort. "Man speaks treason. Arrest man. Man traitor or spy."

Campas, his mouth a tight line, wheeled to speak to the Brodaini in their own tongue. Fiona thought she saw relief in their besieged faces.

"I was making an inspection with my men, ilean translator," the Brodainu said. He was a short, stocky, self-important-seeming man, his face sun-browned and brutal. "We're ordered to inspect the sanitary arrangements— these Abessla pigs don't understand about slit trenches, they just drop their trousers wherever they want, and so we have the authority to police the camp, and make them defecate like human beings." Campas' frown deepened as he heard his people so described, but he waited patiently for the man to get to the point.

"We heard this man speak treason," the Brodainu said, turning to scowl down at the captive. "We heard him say to his friends he wanted Tastis' government in Arrandal." His tone was stubborn as he recited the story, as if insisting on a point that seemed obscure even to him. "We can't have corporals talking like that to their men," he continued. "We arrested him to take him before the Judge Advocate. His friends interfered." He thumped the butt of his spear into the ground and jerked his chin up, glaring with angry pride at the bowmen. "I won't be interfered with, ilean translator!" he said. "I am Hantu Sethentha Dantu y'Dantu, son of Sapasta Hantu Pranoth y'Dantu, who was whelkran of five thousand under our lady Grendis Destu Luc y'Dantu, and a trusted advisor to our lord Tegestu. If any wish to detain me, let him state his name and lineage and I will fight him with bow, spear, and sword."

Fiona watched as Campas struggled mentally with how much of the Brodainu's message to translate, and in what spirit—Hantu's arrogant, uncompromising attitude was obvious enough to his watchers, even if they didn't speak Gostu, and Hantu seemed to understand enough Abessas to follow Campas' translation roughly.

Pulling her hood over her head and tightening it, Fiona walked into the circle. There were surprised murmurs as a few of the bowmen recognized her, and a worried glance from Campas.

"He says," Campas said, turning to the bowmen, "that

he was going about his duties when he heard your corporal
saying that he wanted Tastis' government in Arrandal.''

"That's not so!'' It was the strange hissing voice Fiona
had heard earlier; it proved to belong to an unshaven,
gangling soldier with a pair of missing front teeth. "He
didn't say anything of the sort!''

"What did he say, then?''

The soldier scratched his chin, clearly trying to decide
how much to reveal. "Many of us in this company are
bricklayers, see?'' he said finally. "Journeymen and
apprentices. Corvas was just saying that the idea of a
League of Journeymen in our Guild wasn't such a bad
idea—he'd like one in our city. He didn't say anything
about wanting that bloody Brodainu bastard Tastis in our
city.'' His voice rang with contempt. "Why the hell should
we want to be ruled by them?'' he demanded. "We don't
want a bunch of foreign mercenaries running our affairs!''

Suddenly Hantu's eyes blazed. He took a step forward
and shook his spear. "Challenge!'' he howled in his bad
Abessas. "I fight that man! Call me mercenary, spy-traitor-
money-grubbing Hostlu!''

Fiona felt herself gasp in surprise as a sudden arrow
took the Brodainu in the throat. She hadn't even seen who
had fired it. Clawing at its shaft, Hantu staggered backward into the arms of one of his men. The soldier who had
spoken seemed stunned by the sudden violence, and with
rising anger in his eyes he turned to demand who had
drawn bow . . . but one of the Brodaini was quicker,
lunging with the curved sword-blade on the end of his
spear, disembowelling the spokesman with a practiced
swipe. Fiona, her inbred reflexes taking swift charge,
struck up the spear with her arm, hearing Campas shouting,
"Down weapons! Peace here, in the Abeissu's name!'',
but there was a sudden chaos of motion as other Brodaini
spears leaped out and arrows began hissing through the air,
Hantu's armor rattling as he slipped from his man's arms

and fell kicking to the earth, with Campas in the middle of it calling for order, trying clumsily to strike up the flickering, bladed spears until an arrow clipped him and he fell. Fiona ducked between the spears, snapping her right arm in toward her chest while rotating her wrist sharply, and felt the needle snap out through her glove, protruding from the bone of her wrist.

It was meant for hurried self-defense, and was not an accurate weapon. With it she burned down the first row of bowmen, slitting her eyes against the flash. The air, outraged by the sudden release of energies, cracked like thunder. There were screams and confusion, the bowmen falling back in a yelping body; in the stunned silence that followed she barked out swift orders in Gostu. "Pick up your officer and carry him with us. Take the ilean translator. I'm the Ambassador Fiona—I'm taking command here. Now!"

Fiona saw confusion and naked fear on the Brodaini faces as they saw what her needle had done, but they responded instinctively to the chain of orders and once they began moving they moved efficiently, gathering Campas up as he clutched at his bleeding head. Fiona caught a scent of burned flesh as she pulled the hood-mask down to protect her face, then she barked orders for the Brodaini to keep on guard and draw back, with their wounded, to their own camp.

As they began to move Fiona saw that Hantu's prisoner was dead. In the first swift seconds of the fight, some practical Brodainu, not expecting to survive, had quietly prevented the corporal's escape by slitting his throat.

In the hood-mask she heard the rapid rasping of her own breath, the surge of her hammering pulse as she wondered whether the bowmen would be mad enough to pursue this fight. She began to breathe deliberately, trying to force both lungs and heart to slow, telling herself that she was not as vulnerable as she felt, her back turned to hostile bowmen. She worked her way into the middle of the Brodaini and felt them move protectively around her, shielding her with their bodies as they would one of their own officers, not knowir.₅ her armor was better than their own. She fought to control her body's instinctive reactions—she didn't want people crowding her, but it would be unsafe to force them to disperse. Through the darkened, one-way material of the face mask she could see Campas blinking through the blood that covered his face, one hand still pressed to his scalp where the arrow had scored him. The wound, though bloody like all scalp wounds, seemed superficial, and Fiona felt a breath of relief cooling her anxiety.

Three Brodaini facing back toward the bowmen, walking with their spears on guard, they passed the barn, then moved past a rubbish dump toward the parade ground. Fiona could see dust rising in the Brodaini camp as they formed to come to the rescue of their comrades, summoned by the running Classanu. Suddenly there was a cry from the rearguard as arrows hissed again from the air. Fiona felt an impact between her shoulder blades and stumbled, seeing one of Campas' bearers fall, an arrow in his side. Rage filled her, both because of the attack and because of what she knew the attack would force her to do, and she turned to see another savage flight of arrows whistling in their direction from where archers were crouching on the roof of the stone barn. She heard an answering snarl, and realized it was her own.

A Brodainu leaped in front of her to shield her body with his own, and she cursed in her own language and shouldered her way past him. She made a fist of her right hand and pulled it toward her body, increasing the power of her weapon, then fanned her arm out in the direction of the barn, her fire tearing holes in the air with the sound of lightning gone mad, blowing the barn wall away and bringing its roof down, the insect-figures of the archers falling among the rubble. Perhaps some would survive—more, anyway, than would have been the case if she'd raked the barn roof.

She heard an awed intake of breath from the Brodainu next to her as the roof came down, then she brushed past him again and shouted at them to begin moving. The Brodainu with the arrow in his side was staggering to his feet; another took his place carrying Campas, and then the group was shambling onward across the bare parade ground.

There was no more interference. Brodaini archers came pelting up, their long, powerful steel bows ready to cover the withdrawal; and they were followed by a battalion of swiftly-marching spearmen. Fiona tore her mask back, shouting out a version of the incident to their officers, making the hurried suggestion that the camp of Captain Pantas be cordoned off immediately, but that no action be taken against them until Palastinas, Necias, and Tegestu had been informed of the situation. The Brodaini officer, uncertain of his authority and hers, frowned, considered, and then acceded.

Fiona, her heart hammering, followed the Classani surgeons who were called to treat the wounded. Hantu, drowning in his own blood, was dead by the time they arrived. The other wounded Brodainu, it seemed, would survive, and so would Campas. Fiona sat cross-legged in the dust, trying to stay out of the surgeons' way, while the marching columns rushed past, and while Campas' wound was washed and bound.

Fiona pulled off her glove, seeing the bright dot of blood on her wrist that marked the place where the needle had come through her flesh. There was no pain; the nerves had been deadened when she had been modified. She rubbed her forehead, trying to decide what she would say—not just to Necias and Tegestu, but to her own people in the ship. The ships' alarms would have tripped as they detected the flow of energies she had unleashed with her needle, and her spindle, back in her tent, would be buzzing with urgent demands for communication. There was probably a team of rescuers diving into atmosphere craft, ready to ride down to her assistance.

She wondered if she could have escaped without use of the needle. She had been thoroughly protected by the privy-coat against the worst their weapons could have done; she probably could have jostled her way out of danger, pushing through the bowmen to safety.

But that would have left Campas in the middle of it all, unprotected save by his light chain shirt, amid the hacking spears and flying arrows. No, she thought, she'd had no choice; what she'd done was necessary. Her instructions gave enough amount of latitude in these situations that she felt sure she could justify her action to Tyson when the time came.

She would have to get to her spindle soon, to call the ship, and to call her rescuers off. But for the moment she sat and tried to calm herself, watching as the blood was cleaned from Campas' eyes and he looked up painfully to recognize her, and flash her a first faint smile.

19

There was no possibility that a solution would promote healing: there were too many wounds, too much anger. Necias, in the end, needed the Brodaini much more than he needed a gang of truculent bowmen. Besides, even if the Brodaini had provoked them, they had assaulted the Abessu-Denorru's personal representative *and* an ambassador—and Necias' blood still ran cold at the thought of the hellish powers Fiona had then unleashed. Fiona had been asked if she wanted to recommend punishment, with Necias dreading the possibility she'd want to exact it herself; but Necias' messengers had returned saying she considered it a matter of internal army discipline and no business of hers. So Pantas' archers were arrested—by mercenary pikemen rather than by Brodaini, which might have assuaged some feelings—disarmed, and after being held prisoner overnight in the broken remnants of the barn, an experience calculated to create as much mental unease as possible, their crimes were itemized by a herald, their standard was ceremonially burned, one out of five were flogged, and then the unit was disbanded and its men

274

broken up and assigned to other companies. Captain Pantas, who had been visiting brother officers in the Prypas camp and hadn't been within two miles of the riot, was quietly given a staff assignment.

But there was going to be bad feeling between the militia companies and the Brodaini as a result of this, and that would spoil the good feeling that had existed in the army after the victory on the East Rallandas. And Necias sensed there would be worse consequences than these.

Necias pushed away his empty luncheon plate and, wincing, tried to dislodge a piece of food from between two of his rotting teeth. Ai, Pantas and his net of souls! he thought, remembering the scene of the riot as he'd toured it, the barn blackened with its gaping wall and tumbled roof, the bodies of the dead bowmen, lying shrivelled and burnt, armor melted, some unrecognizeable. Had Fiona called down the lightning? There had been a flash and a sound of thunder, all witnesses agreed to that, and then men had died and the walls had come crashing down.

There was a lesson to be learned here, and that was the power these star people represented. If one of them could do that, what wonders, what horrors, could a company perform?

There would be a report on this sent to every city of the Elva, he thought. Unless these things were known, the Elva would be tempted to involve the star folk and their power in their own disputes. The Igaralla claimed to have no interest in local issues, but Necias knew human motivations better than that. There would have to be a convention limiting the numbers of Fiona's people allowed in the cities, and strictly regulating their neutrality. That much power, unregulated and uncontrolled, dwelling in the heart of the Elva capitals, represented a far greater danger than the Brodaini in all their numbers.

But what, he wondered, can we do to enforce the convention? If they should decide to bring more down from the sky, how could we stop them? We didn't even know Fiona was among us until she made herself known; they could move a battalion into Arrandal and be in command of the place within a day.

He had regarded Fiona as a curiosity, as a useful source of information, as an object by which he might gain prestige. Now he was compelled to regard her with apprehension and fear. How would he be known, he thought; as the man who brought otherworldly knowledge to Arrandal, knowledge to benefit the city and its inhabitants—or perhaps as an infamous figure, who first let the conquerors from the stars past the city gates?

Last night, in the timbered calm of his bedroom on his barge, he'd spoken to Brito on the subject; she had counselled, as usual, patience. "The girl was caught in a riot and defended herself," she'd said. "That's nothing to base a political judgement on. But you're right that the Igaralla's numbers should be limited—there's a lot of nonsense going on in the cities about Fiona and her people, and it ought to be contained if possible."

As for the "nonsense," he'd had reports about that as well. Fashions based on Fiona's style of dress, the sale of good-luck charms or artifacts said to have originated on Igara, the appearance of priests who claimed to spread her gospel of stellar salvation among the population. Short-lived, Necias thought, knowing exactly how long these tides of fashion would last; in another year there would be some new diversion for the mob to pursue, and for the merchants to profit from.

He wondered if he could use Campas to acquire information concerning her attitudes. Care would be required, however, since camp rumor proclaimed they were lovers. It was a rumor Necias didn't quite believe, and hoped he would never have to believe officially. He'd have to interview Campas on the subject of the riot, and try to glean what information he could.

Whatever resulted from those efforts, an official disavowal from Fiona that she had any intentions of being worshipped, or that she was in the charm business, might serve to make Arrandal that much calmer. As it was, half the population expected her to somehow conjure the gates of Calacas open and allow the allied armies to enter. . . .

Perhaps, he mused, he might be able to make use of the official dinner scheduled for this evening. Necias, Palastinas, and their respective staffs would be playing host to General Handipas of Prypas. Handipas was a difficult character by all accounts, touchy on points of precedence and honor and inclined to veto any proposal for cooperation between the two forces unless he was given the sole command. Thank the gods, Necias thought, that at least Tegestu seemed to have achieved some sort of working arrangement with his Brodainu opposite, Tanta.

Fiona, with the rest of the ambassadors, would be present at the dinner, and perhaps Necias could get a public disavowal from her of the stories circulating in the city. Necias would have preferred to have found some way of cancelling the dinner altogether, since Handipas was almost certain to object to Fiona's presence as one that would attract attention away from himself.

Damn all faction! Necias thought violently. Ah, well . . . he had handled men like Handipas before, and all it required was patience: either the man would overreach himself and be dismissed by his own employers; or Necias would wait until autumn brought the fleets from the north carrying the other allied Elva armies, at which point Necias would be able to do without him, and would then give him the choice of voluntarily accepting a subordinate position under Palastinas or of going home without having accomplished anything except a slow march along the coast and back, a humiliation he would never be able to face.

Well, the dinner would go forward. It was time to move

from the barge to his pavilion and make certain the preparations were complete. He'd dictate some correspondence while there—the pavilion was no longer a residence, but was being used as an office still—and also make his proclamation for a day of fasting for all the armies in honor of the goddess Lipanto, whose rites were celebrated two days hence.

Necias heaved himself out of his settee, put some biscuits in his pockets for later, and climbed heavily up the companion to the deck of the barge. There he blinked in the bright sun, seeing the flags of Arrandal and the house of Acragas whipping in the brisk wind, and waited while his guards were assembled by Little Necias, their captain. His bodyguards were mostly relatives, with a few trusted retainers thrown in: he didn't want Brodaini around him, and if he'd used mercenaries there would always be the worry that one of them could be bribed to allow an assassination.

As the guards formed up on the gangplank, Necias turned to the other family barge moored astern and saw, with a leap of joy, Luco's golden hair glittering on the foredeck. A lovely girl, he thought, remembering their ardent reunion and the fact that he was scheduled to sleep with her tonight. He had sent for two of his wives, letting the other four occupy themselves with household matters in Arrandal: now he had Brito for her brains and Luco for her loving, something that happily took place every second night instead of every fifth. A young wife did a man good, whatever the old saws said. She turned, seeing him on deck, and stood on tiptoe to wave, her brilliant smile warming his heart; he raised his own arm, smiling, and when his men had formed up he walked up the tilting gangplank and began his stroll to the pavilion.

His fool of a son, Listas, joined him with his pad and pencil and Necias dictated some correspondence to him as they walked, all of it routine but necessary. The guards

deployed themselves about the pavilion and Necias went
into the bright, airy main room, where a series of collapsi-
ble tables had been assembled, then covered with a long
brocade tablecloth and a vast array of silver plate. "Very
good," he nodded to his Deputy Steward—Ahastinas had
pronounced himself too elderly to accompany the army—
and lay down on his settee, adjacent to the place of honor
that Handipas would occupy.

The expressions of horror on the faces of his domestic
staff came too late for warning, so it must have been some
vague impression of movement behind him that made him
throw himself forward just as the settee shuddered to a
blow . . . and then, amid the sudden shrieking and confusion and desperate bellows from his staff, he pushed off
from the couch, kicking it back, and was crawling like a
vast insect across the table, scattering ringing silver plate
in all directions. "It is Castas all over again," he thought
with a sick and hopeless despair, remembering the brother
who had died shielding him from the assassin's dagger; but
now there was no Castas between him and the killers,
nothing but whatever inches of brocade tablecloth he could
put between himself and his assailants.

Tableware flew over his head: Listas, his popeyes almost leaping from his head as he shrieked for the guards,
was scooping up plate with both arms and flinging them
for all he was worth; and there was a metallic clang from
behind to demonstrate he'd connected with at least one of
his missiles. The Deputy Steward dashed out, seizing Necias
by his arms, and then dragged him forward across the table
by main strength; Necias, breathless, crashed to the car-
peted floor just as the table reverberated to another thud as
a blow went home.

The Deputy Steward gave a high-pitched shriek and
threw himself across Necias to the table, his dagger out,
Necias cursing him as he tried to find a path between his
legs; then Necias heard a squelching thud as a weapon

struck home and the Deputy Steward fell back, clutching at the light spear in his chest. Necias, wanting to scream himself but not having the breath for it, rolled for safety, tangled with the nerveless body of the Deputy Steward, feeling blood splattering his face with liquid warmth. At last Little Necias was there, his pike out, followed by a swarm of his people, and there were yells and clanging and in the end Necias sat up in safety, his lungs pumping desperately for air, and watched as his guards transfixed, with half a dozen pikes, his would-be assassin. There was only one attacker after all.

There was no proof—the man was a short-haired nondescript individual—but his equipment screamed *Brodaini*, and he was therefore assumed to be one of Tastis' lersri, a trained, dedicated spy and assassin who worshipped the goddess of Death and who was supposed to be ready, with the bottle of poison found on his belt, to meet her voluntarily rather than accept capture. He was armed with a heavy double-edged dagger on a thong around his neck, but his principle weapon was a short, light hollow metal spear. In his pouch there was found a digging tool: it had been attached to the other end of the spear, and with it the lersru had burrowed his way beneath the canvas walls of the pavilion, hiding in a little hole under the carpets directly behind the couch of honor, waiting with cool patience for Necias to appear. The household staff had probably been treading on him since morning.

The lersru should have succeeded with his first thrust, but Necias was not in the place of honor, which must have surprised him, and then Necias had thrown himself forward and perhaps broken the assassin's concentration; at any rate the spear had gone into the back of Necias' settee with enough force to splinter it. Having wrenched the spear free, the lersru climbed over the chair and onto the table, parrying the plate Listas had been throwing, where he'd had to kill the Deputy Steward to get to Necias, losing more seconds . . . and then Little Necias and his squad had impaled him on their long pikes that outreached his short thrusting spear, making it unnecessary for him to use his poison.

Necias, trembling, rose breathlessly to his feet, dashing the sweat out of his eyes and staring at the chaos of the canvas-walled room, the strewn array of silver plate and the bodies of the Deputy Steward and the assassin. "Are you hurt, Father?" Listas demanded, supporting his elbow; then he turned and screeched out in the pedantic, nagging voice that Necias had always disliked. "A chair for the Abessu-Denorru! Have you all gone mad?"

A chair was brought, and Necias subsided gratefully in it. His guards tore about the pavilion, anxious to prove their zeal, flinging up the carpets and looking for more enemies to kill; they found none. The bodies were quietly carried out. A drink came hastily to Necias' chair; he drank it down without tasting it, his mind slowly recovering from the attack.

"I'll write the notes calling off the dinner, don't bother yourself about it," Listas said in his ear. "Just rest yourself, and I'll take care of the arrangements."

Necias only gradually understood the words. "No!" he gasped out quickly; and then he found his mind working again, calculating swiftly the results of the near-assassination.

"No," he said, more firmly again, seeing Listas' pop-eyed surprise. "The dinner will continue—I'm not going to let that carrion interfere with matters of state." He jabbed a finger into Listas' chest, and gave him an encouraging grin. "Draft a report to the Denorru-Deissin, and make certain you urge them all to look to their own safety. And another report to the city—we don't want any rumors starting a panic." He rubbed his chin. He *had* to look undisturbed by this occurrence: otherwise people would begin saying he was so terrified he'd lost his grip. Normality had to be returned as quickly as possible.

"Clean the blood off that tablecloth: I still want to use it tonight," he said. "Replace the soiled carpets with fresh ones. *Nothing out of the ordinary*, understand?" He hauled himself out of the chair, found to his delight that his legs would support him, and then gave a laugh to his household staff. "We've got to learn to expect assassinations, hey?" he said. "I've survived two, now—Pastas Netweaver must be looking out for me. I'll give thanks tomorrow." He looked down at the bloody carpet, then rubbed his chin. He'd give an endowment to the survivors of the Deputy Steward, and add his name to the family memorials that took place on Castas' Day.

For the moment, he thought, he'd make a visit to his wives' barge. He didn't want rumors preceding him and causing a panic in the floating partillo: arriving safe and sound should scuttle rumors more thoroughly than any delivered message. And by walking to the barge he would also be showing himself to many of the army, and show he was still on his feet and making decisions.

"Captain Acragas!" he called out to Little Necias. "Form your men outside. I'm returning to the landing."

"Yes, Necias Abeissu," Little Necias said, somewhat surprised, and immediately obeyed. While Necias waited, he saw Listas looking at him hesitantly.

"You did well," he said, nodding briskly—might as well give the boy a compliment now that he'd done something right for a change. Listas seemed surprised.

"Thank you, Father," he said, and Necias wondered for a doubtful second whether his compliments had ever been so rare as to be viewed with such wonder. No, he decided, dismissing the idea; the boy was just a fool.

Necias nodded again and stepped out into the sun. A shame to have missed a day like this, he thought, enjoying the breeze on his face. That lersru's first strike had surely been foiled by the gods. Or nerves, perhaps, if Brodaini truly possessed them.

His mind buzzing thankfully with plans, Necias grinned up at the sky and paced rapidly for his barge.

That evening Handipas, followed by his staff and his Brodainu commander Tanta, walked to the pavilion through a double row of servants bearing torches and another lane of mercenaries in all their finery with lances at the salute. Handipas was dressed entirely in white from leggings to bonnet, his costume heavily embroidered with gold lace: he was a short, quick, vain man, clearly pleased with himself and his appearance. Necias welcomed him with a hug, introduced him to the officers, staff, and dignitaries present, and ushered him to the banquet and sat him down in the place of honor. He saw Handipas' eyes move slowly in a careful, sidelong examination of the room—no doubt he'd heard about the assassination attempt—but there was no sign of the fight: new carpets had been layered in place of the stained ones, the brocade tablecloth had been cleaned, and all battered tableware replaced. The roof of the tent ballooned with banners, the flags of Arrandal, Prypas, and the Elva, as well as the standards of the Brodaini.

Necias looked down at his first course already in place—pickled cold beef and onions, cut small the way he liked it, so he could chew it with his good teeth. He sipped his wine, making certain his guests were seated, then signalled Brito and Luco to come forth to be introduced; they were complimented by Handipas for their splendid gowns—particularly Luco, who was dressed in the most radical new style. It was inspired by the strange hooded undergarment the Igaralla ambassador had been observed to wear, and was therefore called the Fiono style. There was a tight-fitting black hood, embroidered in gold, that made a pale, exquisite oval of the face, and that was further complimented by a few of Luco's pale curls that had escaped the hood; the flounced skirts had been drawn in about the middle to suggest the trousers Fiona had worn

privately in her apartments, and publicly on campaign—
the rest was slashed, studded with jewels, puffed, ruffled,
and otherwise embroidered in the typical Arrandal manner,
done principally in green to reflect Luco's eyes. The affect
was unusual, and quite striking. Handipas leaned forward,
intrigued, his hand on his chin.

"What style of gown is that, stansisso Luco?" he asked.

Luco colored at being so addressed, and dropped another curtsey; under her lashes she covertly looked up at
Fiona as she answered. "It is called a Fiono gown, Handipas
cenors-efellsan," she said. "It is patterned after the dress
of Igara. I wear it in honor of the ambassador."

Necias glanced at Fiona during the answer, seeing her
surprised look. Handipas, with a grin, turned to Fiona as
well.

"Is this what the Igaralla wear at home, Ambassador?"
he asked. "Our own Igaralla ambassador hasn't spoken
much of fashion."

Fiona, taken aback, composed her reply quickly. "It
is—it is an interpretation," she said, glancing down at her
own scarlet gown, simple and plain by Arrandalla standards,
with only modest amounts of embroidery and no precious
stones at all. Necias mentally complimented her on her
diplomacy: he suspected she'd never seen anything re-
motely resembling Luco's gown before. "And quite a
becoming interpretation," Fiona added. "On behalf of my
people, stansisso Luco, I thank you for the compliment."

Luco blushed bright red and made her final curtsey and
exit. There was a partillo screen set up so that she and
Brito could eat privately, view the entertainment, and
watch the dinner without having to overstrain their delicate
sensibilities among the rude company of men.

The meal went well enough. There were some small
entertainers—as many competent jugglers, balladeers, and
comics as could be found travelling with the army, with a
Classanu troop of acrobats, about the only Brodaini enter-

tainment palatable or understandable to the Abessla, added as a compliment to Tanta. Handipas asked about the assassination attempt: Necias brushed it aside as a trifling matter, knowing Handipas had no real interest and might have welcomed Necias' removal as a threat to his own authority. He then turned the conversation to Handipas' own campaigns. Handipas was only too happy to expatiate upon his martial prowess, and his glorious career in which he'd demonstrated the might of Prypas to truculent barons and murderous river pirates.

A puppy, Necias thought. He can be managed, more easily than if he were cunning.

"Your own skill, Ambassador, is celebrated in the camp," Handipas said, turning suddenly from an anecdote of his own skill to Fiona: and for a moment Necias wondered if the puppy had more teeth than he'd thought. "You quelled that riot with a firm hand."

Necias watched carefully, wondering if Fiona could be thus surprised; but her answer was quiet and spoken without hesitation. "There were arrows flying, enventan General Handipas," she said. "I had to protect myself."

"It was most effective, Ambassador. I congratulate you," Handipas said. "Twelve men dead, a stone building brought down as if a troop of pioneers had been working on it half a day." He smiled, showing his teeth. "Are all you Igaralla so deadly, Ambassador?" he asked. "So splendid in warfare?"

Necias, with surprise, realized that the room was utterly silent; he looked at the others at the table and saw them all watching Fiona and Handipas with calculating eyes, taking their measure, Tegestu looking like an old, proud mallanto, his glowing eyes fixed on distant prey. But Fiona's own expression seemed confident in a quiet way, and the expression in her half-lidded, lazy eyes showed she knew exactly what game she was playing.

"No, we are not," Fiona said. "There are very few of

us who carry weapons at all: it's not necessary. Those who may need it are allowed weapons for their own defense."

"Such as ambassadors?" Handipas asked, his tone silky, languid. "Are all your diplomats capable of such destruction?"

"Any diplomats setting out alone to a war, certainly," Fiona said. "War is a dangerous business, and it's easy for a neutral to get caught in a dangerous situation."

"You seem to come from a dangerous place, Ambassador," Handipas continued, his fingers circling idly on the crystal rim of a goblet. "If your diplomats are capable of such destruction, how destructive can your soldiers be? Or are your diplomats soldiers as well as ambassadors?"

There was a moment of silence. Fiona smiled, then spoke, her tone confident, reassuring. "We have sent no soldiers to your world, General Handipas cenors-efellsan."

Handipas shrugged; there was still a smile on his face. "I didn't say you had, Ambassador," he said. "I was merely speculating." He pursed his lips, looking down as his finger circled the cup. A subtle ringing tone came from the cup; Necias repressed a shiver as the sound touched his nerves with delicate aural claws. "You brought down that building in a flash of lightning and thunder," Handipas said. "I imagine that with little more effort you could bring down a city wall, if you were convinced it would benefit you."

"We will not," Fiona said, "intervene in your affairs. We will never fight against you, nor will we fight with you as allies. There are very few of us and there is no possibility of our being a threat to you. But we must be allowed to defend ourselves if attacked. I regret the necessity, yesterday, but I had little choice."

"Of course, of course, so you have said," Handipas said hastily, with a complimentary smile. "I didn't mean to sound as if I were questioning your assurances, Ambassador." He took his hand from the wine cup.

"Previously your people had been known for their inquisitiveness, for their wish to gather as much information about us as possible. Now you are known to be deadly. I was praising your skill, that is all, one soldier to another." And before Fiona could reply he turned to one of the servants, holding out a purse. "Give this to the cooks, with my compliments," he said. "They've performed well, under these difficult circumstances."

Necias silently drew a breath. Handipas had been cunning, making his point with skill that no Igaralla could be trusted as long as any one of them could wield such power. Necias was glad he had seen it: Handipas was far more dangerous than he had thought.

And, for that matter, so was Fiona.

The dinner came to an end in a series of formal toasts, the company pledging eternal fidelity and friendship, undying enmity to Tastis, and vigilant cooperation; and probably meaning none of it. Luco and Brito came from behind their screen to bid farewell to the guests; Handipas bussed Necias on both cheeks and made his way out, followed by his company. Necias felt a touch on his elbow.

"Beg pardon, Abessu-Denorru." It was Tegestu, his voice pitched low. "I beg leave to speak privately, I hope this evening. It's most urgent."

Necias looked at Tegestu's face for a clue of what this might be about, seeing nothing but frowning seriousness; then he glanced at the remaining guests and calculated the amount of time it would take to empty the pavilion, compliment the staff, and detail the guards necessary to take Luco and Brito back to their barge. "Can you wait half an hour, cenors-stannan?" he asked. "It will take a while to disengage from this company."

"Aye, Abessu-Denorru," Tegestu said, bowing.

"Seat yourself, Tegestu," Necias said, throwing out an arm toward unoccupied chairs. "I'll be with you as soon as I can."

Tegestu bowed again and stepped back, his face resuming its normal arrogant scowl, and Necias made his way to where one of the Neda-Calacas Government-in-Exile seemed wrapped in ferocious argument with a junior member of the Cartenas Embassy—all of which proved not to be over policy, but rather over the relative merits of the dancing of a pair of camp followers. Necias soothed them both, called for wine, and then noticed Luco in conversation with the Ambassador Fiona. The fact of one of his family being in touch with her without his supervision made him nervous: he knew Fiona spent most of her time gathering information, and he did not want himself gathered. Besides, he thought with a shiver, she's dangerous. As Handipas has done us all the favor of pointing out.

"Ambassador," he greeted her. "I hope the evening was pleasant."

Fiona nodded with her usual self-assurance. "I enjoyed myself, Abessu-Denorru," she said. "I believe your guest of honor enjoyed himself as well."

"That horrible little man!" Luco said suddenly. Necias looked at her in surprise. Luco laughed suddenly, and then spoke, smiling; it seemed to Necias as if she gave Fiona a covert look, as if she shared a secret. "Well," she said, "we know what will happen to *him*, don't we?"

There was a slight pause before Fiona's answer. "I'm sorry, Luco stansisso. I'm not sure what you mean."

Luco smiled nervously; but Necias saw that her secret look was still there. "I mean that I've heard the Enventan. Enventan Lidrapas."

Necias saw Fiona's blank response. "Enventan Lidrapas," she repeated. "I'm not familiar with the name. A priest, I suppose? The Enventan concerns himself with what will become of General Handipas?"

"And with the others who refuse you, Ambassador Fiona," Luco said happily. "He is preaching your faith, the faith of Igara. The city is astonished by his wisdom, as well as his miracles.''

''Is it now?'' Fiona asked quietly, and the tone of her voice made Necias look at her in surprise. It was, he thought, a *dangerous* tone; he wondered if he had really heard it, or whether Handipas' suggestion had made him hear things. Fiona pursed her lips in thought for a brief moment, then looked at Luco with knitted brows. ''Please tell me what the Enventan has said regarding my faith, Luco stansisso. I would be grateful.''

''You wish a catechism now, Ambassador?'' Luco seemed startled by the request. ''I'll do my best,'' she said doubtfully, ''but I've seen the Enventan only twice, and I haven't been initiated into the mysteries.''

''Please tell me what you've heard, stansisso Luco,'' Fiona said. She smiled, Necias thought, with effort. ''Anything you can. I'd appreciate it.''

''Please oblige the Ambassador,'' Necias said grimly. Where had Luco been exposed to this charlatan? he wondered. Was his son Rinantas, looking after Acragas interests in his absence, allowing him access to the palace? If so there was going to be a stiff letter going to Arrandal by the next boat. ''I'd like to hear of this Enventan myself,'' Necias said.

Luco gave a swift glance at Necias, surprised by his wish, and then smiled. ''Of course, husband cenorsefellsan,'' she said. ''But I would have thought that you would have heard the new preaching from the Ambassador Fiona herself.''

Fiona's answer was accompanied by an ironic smile. ''I don't consider it my duty to preach, stansisso Luco,'' she said.

''Don't you? I'm sorry—I would have thought—'' Luco dissolved in confusion. ''Maybe I'm not the person to advance the preaching here. I'm not used to speaking in

front of people, and I'm sure I don't understand enough
of it.''

"That's perfectly all right," Fiona said. She reached out
to take Luco's hand, giving her encouragement. "Just tell
me what you've heard.''

"Oh. Of course," Luco said, blushing to her ears. She
gave another nervous glance to Necias, then spoke. "The
Enventan preaches that the Igaralla have come to our
world in order to offer us salvation," she said. "That you
and your people are going among us in secret, and that you
are gathering information so as to know which of us
accepts your faith, and which reject you. And that some
day soon, your star ships will come down from the skies
and take all the believers to Igara, where we will live
forever in happiness." She looked up at Fiona, her
eyes radiating worshipful awe. "And those who don't
believe, like Handipas, will have to remain here, to die
in misery." She gave a brief, nervous smile. "I hope I've
got it right, Ambassador. I'm not used to speaking like
this.''

"I'm sure you've represented the Enventan very well,"
Fiona said. She looked at Necias with a slight smile.
"Will you excuse us for a moment, Abessu-Denorru?"
she asked. "I think I would like to speak with stansisso
Luco privately.''

"Certainly, Ambassador," Necias said. Rinantas was
going to get a scorching letter, he promised himself; Lidrapas
shouldn't have even been allowed to preach in public, let
alone in the Acragas palace. He watched as Fiona and
Luco went behind the partillo screen; then he went in
search of Brito.

"Who the hell is this Lidrapas?" he demanded, after
he'd got her away from the guests. Brito looked up at him
sourly.

"A charlatan, I'm sure," she said. "I don't know where
he came from, but he's a good preacher, and he does

conjuring tricks, like the Ambassador—I'm sure he enjoys letting people think he's from Igara. He claims to preach their new religion.''

"Why hasn't he been suppressed?" Necias demanded. "Not only that—how was he allowed to preach where Luco could hear him?"

"Rinantas thought he might actually be representing the Igaralla—who could know?" Brito said, her thin face disapproving. "He thought it best to be cautious—he didn't want to offend Fiona, if she was actually behind it.''

"Pastas and Lipanto!" Necias swore. Anger raged through his limbs; he felt himself tightening his fists. "I'll smash the man! I'll have the priests draw up charges of atheism!"

Brito put a cautious hand on his arm. "Careful, Necias, you don't want to make the man a martyr—persecutions can do that." She lowered her voice. "I've been giving the matter some thought," she said. "I think it would be best to ask the Ambassador to publish a denial, and then have him arrested for fraud. With Fiona denying his preaching, he'll have no support left.''

Necias felt his rage ebbing as rapidly as it had come. Brito's advice made good sense. "Very well," he nodded. "I think that'll work.''

Brito gave him a thin, reassuring smile. Necias nodded in the direction of the partillo. "I think you'd best go comfort Luco—she's losing her faith right at this minute, if I don't miss my guess.''

"It's about time," Brito said with a grim smile. "Ever since that Lidrapas appeared, I've heard nothing else.''

Fiona came from the partillo a few moments afterwards, a self-satisfied light in her eyes. "Don't worry, Necias Abeissu," she said. "I've set Luco stansisso straight.''

"Is she very upset?"

Fiona considered, her head tilted to one side. "A little," she said with a slight smile. "But I was as gentle as I could. I don't think she'll grieve for long.''

"Acragas thanks you, Ambassador," Necias said. "Perhaps it would be possible for you to issue a denial, giving disavowal to this charlatan or any other who claims to preach on your behalf."

Fiona nodded. "If you will be so kind as to make sure it's distributed in the city—and within the army, just to head off any trouble—I can give you the text in the morning, under my seal."

Necias nodded. "Very well, Ambassador."

She took her leave then. Necias escorting her to the pavilion's entrance. He watched her scarlet gown disappearing into the darkness, inhaling deeply of the fresh, cool air, tasting the distant tang of the ocean.

Yes, he thought, I'll distribute your denial, and I'll take Lidrapas' head if I can. But I can thank Lidrapas for one thing, showing me how dangerous you are, should you choose to incite the populace against me. They are already half-inclined to believe any miracle worker that comes along, and if you and your wonders should ever strike against the Denorru-Deissin we'll be hard put to fight you.

He would have to put a stop to Fiona's going among the army and the people; it was too dangerous for her to be allowed unregulated contact. He'd simply suggest it was a matter of her own safety, after the incident the day before, and keep her in the ambassadorial compound unless he could give her escort.

Yes; and if she petitioned to bring others of her kind down from the sky he'd find some way to delay it, to keep the petition alive but never to say yes or no. He would have to keep her as isolated as possible, and try to move her back to the city and the Acragas palace as soon as possible.

Word came from the partillo that Luco and Brito were ready to leave, and he ordered their escort to stand ready, then went to bring them out. Luco seemed blotchy and distraught, as if she'd been weeping; and Brito seemed grim, as if her none-too-ample patience had been tried. He gave Brito a kiss and Luco a pat, and sent them both on their way.

He saw the other quests off, and then remembered Tegestu, sitting patiently in his chair, his stern face fixed firmly on nothing in particular. He walked back to him, airily waving him back to his seat as he tried to rise in order to kneel, then sat carelessly in the chair next to him. He looked up at the servants, each busy clearing away the remains of the feast, and called out to them. "Give the drandor Tegestu and me some privacy, boys. This won't take long, hey?"

He watched as they all left quietly, then leaned close to Tegestu and spoke quietly.

"You wished to speak with me, drandor?"

The old mallanto's eyes were expressionless. "Congratulations, Abessu-Denorru, on your timely escape from the lersru," he said. "I hope you have taken no injury."

Necias grinned. "Pastas had his finger on me," he said. "No ill effects, the Netweaver be praised."

"Among my own people," Tegestu said, "any captain of bodyguards who so failed his lord would ask permission to kill himself. If he were not invited into the Ghanaton at his lord's command."

Necias blinked. Was Tegestu offering to have Little Necias killed? He shook his head.

"That's not our way," he said firmly. "We just aren't used to fighting Brodaini. I don't think such a thing could happen again."

"I hope not, Abessu-Denorru Necias," Tegestu said. "Might I suggest you abandon the pavilion entirely now that the barges have arrived? The security here will always be difficult."

Necias nodded. "I'll take that advice, drandor Tegestu. Thank you."

"I am happy to be of service, Abessu-Denorru." Tegestu glanced behind him, then leaned closer, his voice lowering.

"I have a message from Calacas," he said. "In four nights, Tastis will launch a sortie against Handipas' army in front of Neda. He hopes that, if the sortie is successful, he can throw in the bulk of his army in support and smash the Prypas forces before we can intervene."

"How good is your information?" Necias asked automatically, while inwardly calculating the wisdom of whether or not to inform Handipas of this. A defeat for Handipas early on might make him more tractable. But no . . . he couldn't risk a rebel victory, even a limited one, that might hearten Tastis' forces. He would tell Handipas at sunset tomorrow, he thought; that would give him time enough to repel the sortie without making his preparations obvious.

"My source," Tegestu said, "is a member of Tastis' aldran, Ataman Doren Dantu y'Tosta. Ataman is a loyal Brodainu, and when Tastis empties Calacas of most of his forces in order to launch his attack, Ataman has announced his readiness to open the gates to my own people."

Necias fought the surprise, the catch at the throat and the hammering of his heart. "You—you're sure?" he gasped.

Tegestu's gaze was steady. "Aye," he said. "Ataman will do as he promises."

A grin tugged at the corners of Necias' mouth. "We'll take Calacas, then?" he asked in laughing amazement. "That'll show Handipas a thing or two, hey!"

"Ataman," Tegestu said, "will open the Inner Harbor Gate and the White Tower Gate four nights from now. But he has a condition—he wants only my own Brodaini to enter the town, to take it in the name of our aldran. Are you agreeable to this?"

Necias thought, for an instant, that he saw a strange gleam in Tegestu's eye, as if something was hanging on

Necias' assent . . . but what could hang on it but the keys of Calacas, taken from Tastis by treachery?

"Yes, Tegestu, of course!" he said, and saw the strange look fade. "Our city forces will support, and will be ready to enter the city whenever you can get the other gates open."

Tegestu, his eyes hooded, nodded slowly. "Very well, Abessu-Denorru. I beg you, inform Palastinas of this, but let it go no further."

"Oh, aye," Necias said, feeling a laugh bubbling up in him. This would show the other Elva cities that Arrandal was still head and shoulders above them all!, he thought. What a lovely coup.

"Please reward this Ataman for his loyalty," Necias said. "I'll support you in whatever you think is appropriate—I trust you in these matters."

"I thank you, Abessu-Denorru," Tegestu said. He bowed. "I will begin preparing immediately." He leaned back. "Amasta is leaving for Arrandal tomorrow," he said, speaking in a more normal tone of voice—Necias realized the secret part of the conversation was over. "I hope you will receive her before she goes."

"I will be pleased to see her," Necias said, suppressing his reaction to Amasta—a cunning, frigid bitch, he thought, as murderous as Tastis. "She leaves on the tide, I assume?" he asked. "Just after noon?"

"Aye."

"I will see her in the hour before noon, if that is convenient," Necias said.

"Aye. I will inform her. She will be honored."

"The honor is mine, old friend," Necias said, his mind still bemused by the prospect of the city delivered into his hands. That would almost force Tastis to negotiate his surrender—he'd have no hope shut up in one of the twin cities, and midsummer not even passed.

Tegestu tried to come out of his seat to kneel, but

lurched forward, his armor jingling, an expression of agony on his face. Alarmed, Necias reached out to support him and helped him to his feet. In spite of his armor, Tegestu seemed light as air.

"I am sorry, Abessu-Denorru," Tegestu said slowly, his eyes downcast. "I didn't mean to—"

"It was a little slip, Tegestu," Necias said. "Who doesn't slip from time to time?" He took Tegestu's arm and led him toward the pavilion entrance. "You'll have to take better care of yourself, drandor. Don't exhaust yourself— you're too important to us."

"Thank you, Abessu-Denorru," Tegestu said. He seemed steadier now, walking with more confidence. When he came out of the pavilion and joined his escort he could walk unaided.

Necias watched Tegestu's torchbearers disappear into the distance, feeling his heart lightening. Calacas in four nights! And without Prypas' help! It was a lovely prospect.

His own escort fell in around him and he began walking briskly toward his barge. Luco would need help getting over her upset—nothing like a lusty husband, he thought, to cheer a girl up! Calacas, four nights from now, and Luco tonight. He grinned. The population of Calacas would need feeding, he thought, and there was no organization better qualified to feed them than the House of Acragas. For, of course, a reasonable profit.

But, he thought as he saw the barges ahead, bright with lantern-light, first things first. And the first thing scheduled for tonight was his comforting of Luco. And her comforting of him.

20

Tegestu stood, contemplating his treacheries, in the approach trench outside of the White Tower Gate of Calacas, hearing the sounds of the assault columns assembling in the dark: the muffled chink of armor, the whisper of officers, the treading of feet on the duckboards. His staff were back some distance in another trench: he'd wanted a quiet look at the enemy gates himself, alone. A dark figure loomed out of the night: Tegestu recognized Cascan.

"I have placed watchers, bro-demmin," Cascan said. "They will let us know the second the bridge is lowered."

"Very well, ban-demmin," Tegestu said. He glanced nervously over his shoulder, then chastised himself for it. The night was black—only Third Moon was in the sky, the least of First Moon's husbands, and there was black, scudding high cloud—but that was no reason to assume that his guards weren't doing their job. He lowered his voice.

"Is the hermit in his cell?" he asked. "The hermit" was the code name for his messenger, the young cambranu who had been entering the city at night, carrying his words to Tastis.

"Aye, bro-demmin."

Tegestu considered for a moment, wondering if he should change his plan. The cambranu had performed well, and with discretion; it would be reassuring to have such a man on hand if needed. But no: the man knew too much that could be dangerous, a long list of betrayals and crimes. It was unfortunate, but the exchange was fair: one man for a city.

"Let the hermit drink his cup," Tegestu said. "See to it personally."

"Aye, bro-demmin." Cascan bowed. He turned, then hesitated. "A favor, bro-demmin," he said.

"Speak."

"May I inform him of the contents of the cup before he drinks it? I would regret the necessity of sending such a man into Ghanaton without his being prepared."

Tegestu considered, then shook his head. "Nay, ban-demmin," he said. "I ordered the man make his will before setting out; he should have dedicated himself to Death at that time."

"Very well, bro-demmin," Cascan said. "I understand the necessity."

"Perhaps," Tegestu said, allowing his annoyance to show at Cascan's presumption. Cascan could have guessed most of what had passed, having provided a young man with passwords to move freely among the lines, then suddenly being ordered to assist in moving the Brodaini forces to the gates of Calacas. But Cascan could not have guessed the why of it, nor the promises he had made to Tastis, or the multiple betrayals of enemies and allies. It was best that such knowledge remain only in Tegestu's mind—there and with the dead.

"See it done," Tegestu snapped.

"Aye, bro-demmin." A bow and Cascan was gone. He would see the poison in the man's evening drink, and watch while the messenger drank it. Half an hour afterwards the man would sleep with his ancestors and the blessed gods.

The death of a loyal, brave man; another treachery laid to Tegestu's account. Ah, he thought, this is an infamous thing I am doing. I am glad the night is black, to shroud my shame.

According to the emissary, Tastis had been surprised to hear that Tegestu wished command of only Calacas, rather than accepting Tastis' full offer of both the cities. But after Tegestu had assured him that he would never surrender the city to an outside overlord, Tastis had agreed swiftly enough—happy, Tegestu supposed, to retain supreme command over at least one city.

Two runners came carefully through the darkness of the trench.

"Bro-demmin drandor, a message from bro-demmin Grendis. Her party is ready at the Gate of the Outer Harbor."

"Very well."

"Bro-demmin drandor, a message from bro-demmin Acamantu. The barges are secured and await your signal."

"Very well. Thanks to you both."

Tegestu felt relief slip into him. The long line of supply barges moored along the canal were the key: with them, Tegestu could feed his army in Calacas for as long as a year, longer if Tastis actually left him part of his own supply, which was promised in their agreement but which he was inclined to doubt.

The tramp of feet in the access trenches died away. The columns were in position.

Tegestu leaned against the wall of the trench, seeking its support as he stood in the darkness and contemplated his treacheries. They were his alone; he had consulted no other, not even Grendis—all was on his head. Was he ar-demmin, as bad as Tastis? Or worse, since he was betraying a lord who had behaved toward him only with honor and decent intentions?

He shook his head, trying to clear it of self-reproach. It was too late: the decision had been made. He could always claim that he had been pushed by circumstance.

It bothered him that he would have to claim anything at all. Actions, he thought, should be clean, unambiguous, like a swordstroke—they should serve as their own justification.

He jerked his head up as he heard the sound of a distant trumpet. Then there was the booming of a drum, then more trumpets. Tastis' sortie had come crashing against the men of Prypas. He knew that the sortie would not fare well; Palastinas had "suggested" to the Prypas commanders that they stage an exercise in repelling a sortie; and Tegestu had also made a private suggestion to Tanta that he take the exercise seriously indeed—neither Handipas nor Tanta were the sort to take a suggestion like that lightly.

Another treachery, Tegestu thought; this time he had betrayed Tastis' sortie.

The distant sounds of battle did not entirely hide the sudden clack of slipping, nearby pawls, and Tegestu's heart leaped as he realized that the drawbridge of the White Tower Gate was coming down. Victory! he thought.

No, not victory, he corrected. Only the start of another war.

The scouts reported back as ordered, though their messages were redundant by the time they arrived. The drawbridge was down, the portcullis raised, and they had heard the hoofbeats as Tastis' remaining men ran for the Long Bridge to Neda. Tegestu gave heartfelt thanks to the gods, then walked down the trench to the roof dugout where his staff waited.

"Send to tell ban-demmin Grendis I will send in my assault columns," he said. "Ban-demmini, we may begin."

The first column, spearmen in light armor, began their race through the assault trenches: Tegestu could hear their drumming feet through the earth. They were under the command of Dellila Gartanu Sepestu y'Dantu, the young captain who had so distinguished himself fighting Tastis' raiders weeks ago, before the battle at the ford; they would enter the city at the run, turn left, and make a dash to raise the water gate blocking access to the barge train. There would be other obstacles as well, no doubt, cables stretched across the canal and so forth, and Dellila and his people would have to remove these.

After that, Tegestu knew, his people would be safe. For at least a year, until requisitioned food ran out.

Tegestu heard the reverberating sound of the spearmen's feet on the drawbridge. The leaders were already in the city.

The second column came dashing out of the trenches. This group, heavily armored men with rhomphaia, would secure the gate itself. After that the entire Brodaini force, every one of them, including the Classani and their Hostli men of business, all their tents and supplies and baggage animals, would begin to file into the Calacas, and Tegestu's banners would be raised from every tower.

Messengers began to come back to the bunker, reporting gates seized, towers occupied, palaces overrun. There was no resistance in the silent city: Tastis' soldiers had crossed the bridges into Neda. Any left behind would be spies, and they would not be seen, not yet. And then at last the message came that Tegestu had been waiting for:

"Ban-demmin Dellila reports the water gate has been seized, and cleared of obstacles."

Tegestu allowed himself a smile. "Order ban-demmin Acamantu to bring the barges into the city."

"Aye, bro-demmin."

"Send a message to our fleet commanders. Tell them *scarlet tide*."

"Aye, bro-demmin." *Scarlet tide* was the code word to bring the galleys under Brodaini command into the now-secure outer harbor of Calacas. Once there, they could be protected by a cable stretched across the harbor's mouth.

"You have the messengers to Amasta, Astapan, and the north standing by?" Tegestu asked.

"Awaiting your command, bro-demmin."

"Send them."

Amasta, commanding now in the Arrandal keep, would receive word of his actions before the two days were out, thanks to a fast twelve-oared dispatch galley with the new fiono sails. Amasta had already been warned, orally the night before she left, to move as many supplies as possible into the Brodaini quarter and to be prepared to cut herself off from the rest of the city; she had also been told to prepare orders informing the Brodaini forces on the islands and in all the provinces to return to garrisons and shut themselves in.

Amasta, like the others, had not been told why. No doubt she, like Cascan, had drawn her own conclusions.

Astapan, the drandor of Prypas, would also have the news, and be able to make what preparations he could. Other fast dispatch boats would be running north before the wind, carrying Tegestu's messages to the other Brodaini aldrans-in-exile. Tegestu could not command them, but he hoped they would make preparations to protect their folk if the Elva wished to make this a cause for a war of extermination.

"We will move our command post to the White Tower Gate," Tegestu said. "Leave an officer here to direct any further messages."

Tegestu felt a thrill as his foot touched the drawbridge, knowing he was stepping, though no one but he knew it, onto his own land. Sovereign Brodaini territory, here on the southern continent, subject to his own aldran, flying his own banners. For what lesser prize, he thought, would a man of demmin risk so much, and betray so many?

He climbed wearily up one of the towers that guarded the gate and then stepped into the guarded walk, seeing the slate roofs of Calacas below him. *Our city,* he thought fiercely. *To replace Pranoth, and all that we have lost. Pray the gods our betrayals will not curse it.*

"Send for a messenger," he said. "Make him one of those Cascan has trained." Cascan's scouts and spies were trained to memorize oral messages swiftly, and repeat them without flaw.

The messenger, a young woman hardly more than a girl, came onto the battlements and bowed. "A message to bro-demmin Tanta Amandos Dantu y'Sanda," he told her. "Give him salutations, and my wish that his arm never weaken. Remind him of the conversation we had while watching Second Moon, and say that it would be wise for the Brodaini of Prypas to meet the morning under arms. Say that it would be unwise to move from their camp. Say that bro-demmin Tanta would be wise if he were to obey his canlan, General Handipas, and all their commands. Say also that he is wisest of all if he does not alarm Handipas or any of the Elva men in the next few hours. Repeat this, ban-demmin."

The girl repeated it flawlessly. Tegestu smiled and sent her on her way.

Perhaps, he thought, *Tanta will forgive me this. If not, my house has made an enemy it can ill afford.*

The messages continued to come. Tegestu looked down at the drawbridge, seeing the long files entering the city, burdened down with their baggage. *How much more lightly would they step,* he thought, *if they knew they were entering their own nation?*

A messenger had come. "A message from bro-demmin Acamantu. The barges are all in the city, and the gate is down."

Slow triumph filled him. "Give ban-demmin Acamantu my thanks," he said.

"There is a herald, bro-demmin," said one of the officers. "He comes from Necias, who wishes to know if we have yet entered the city."

"Let him come."

The messenger, fortunately, was the poet Campas. He bowed, Brodaini style, and looked up with a smile he could not entirely conceal beneath his attempt at tolhostu. "I see Calacas is ours," he said. "Necias will be overjoyed."

"Aye. I have taken the city as planned," Tegestu said. "I will have a message to take to you in a few moments. Please wait in the tower, ilean poet."

Campas bowed and withdrew. Other messengers came and went: it seemed now that all the city was secure. Below Tegestu heard the hollow drumming of hooves on the bridge as the last few baggage animals came into the city.

Cascan came next. "Bro-demmin, the hermit has had his supper," he said. "His guards have his body below."

"Give him to the chiefs of his kamliss," Tegestu said. "Tell them he has gained much demmin by his death, in a service we cannot name. He should be buried with much honor."

"Aye, bro-demmin." Over Cascan's shoulder Tegestu saw the tall form of Grendis walking from the tower, and was ready for her message.

"I have three emissaries from Tastis below, with their escort," Grendis said. She leaned near Tegestu's ear. "They say they wish to discuss the merging of his aldran and ours." Her voice was emotionless. She assumed, then, as well as Cascan, that he and Tastis were now allies, and her voice carefully reserved judgement.

Tegestu gave a short, bitter laugh. Grendis looked at him with surprise. "Did they come under spear of parley?" he asked.

"Nay, bro-demmin. Their spears were not reversed."

"Our rebel cousin forgets himself," he said with another laugh. "Please discover these messengers' names, and write them down. Then separate their heads from their shoulders and give their heads to me, so I may give them to the ilean poet Campas to present to our lord Necias. Their bodies, along with a written admonition to Tastis concerning the rules of parley between enemy camps, should be thrown across the Great Bridge to the gates of Neda."

Grendis and Cascan stared, all tolhostu forgotten. Tegestu looked at them both deliberately, holding their eyes. "Did you think I was a traitor?" he demanded. "Did you think I acted without the knowledge of our lord? See that my will is carried out!"

"Aye, bro-demmin!" Grendis said with a swift bow. Her step, as she ran for the tower door, was lighter . . . she, too, had judged his treachery blacker than it was.

There was the sudden clang of weapons below, but it lasted only a few seconds. A moment thereafter Grendis was back, carrying a dripping net of heads, their eyes staring horror and suprise.

"Send for ilean Campas," Tegestu said.

The poet arrived and bowed. Tegestu saw his eyes go to the net of heads, and then swiftly away.

"Please present these heads to the Abessu-Denorru, ilean Campas," said Tegestu. "They are the heads of messengers Tastis has sent me. Their names are on this list—they are not unimportant people, I think."

Campas gave the heads another glance. He took a moment to master his distaste, then bowed. "Necias will be grateful, bro-demmin Tegestu," he said.

"I hope this may be so." Tegestu looked at the poet for a moment. He was almost the ideal messenger, he thought, and thanked the gods for sending him. He spoke.

"There is a message of great importance to be sent with these heads, ilean," he said. "Tell our lord Necias that the aldran of Arrandal thanks him for the city of Calacas, which he has given us." He saw Campas blink in surprise, and the faces of his officers suddenly fill with astonishment and joy. "Tell him," Tegestu continued, "that the Brodaini of Arrandal continue ready to make war on Tastis and all his rebel hosts." He leaned closer to Campas, emphasizing his words clearly. "Tell him," he said, "that it shall never be the Brodaini of Arrandal who break the bonds of nartil and courtesy that exist between a canlan and his subjects!" His tone softened. "We shall hold all his words in honor," he said carefully, "even if it is not possible for us to obey them all. Do you understand my words, ilean?"

Campas' eyes darted from one Brodaini to the next, and then to the heads that Grendis held in her hand. He swallowed. "Aye, bro-demmin," he said.

Tegestu smiled grimly to himself. The poet knew how to put on a brave face. "Please repeat them, ilean, I beg you," he said.

The poet repeated his words. Tegestu nodded. "Take my words to our lord," he said, and as Campas turned to go, he added, "Do not forget the heads."

The shaken messenger withdrew. "It is true, then, bro-demmin?" Grendis asked. "Is Calacas our own?"

Tegestu faced the thin edge of dawn that crept above the blackness. "It is," he said, and smiled. "If the gods bless us, it is. We must not unbraid our hair yet, ban-demmini, we must always be vigilant. If we are not watchful against all treachery, and against all who would take Calacas from us, then we shall not deserve this fine city."

"Aye, bro-demmin," Grendis said in an awed whisper as she realized what Tegestu had done: he had moved his forces into the middle position, squarely between Tastis and the Elva, where he and he alone held the balance of power.

Treachery, they would call it, and treachery it was. But

Tegestu had given them all a city where there had been nothing but landless exile, and hope where there had formerly been nothing but duty.

"The gods bless this beginning," Grendis said, and turned with Tegestu to face the dawn.

21

Necias, standing with arms akimbo on the afterdeck of his barge, looked at the Brodaini banners dotting the tops of the towers of Calacas and felt the anxiety gnawing at his heart. Tegestu's camps were abandoned, every one of them, with every stick of baggage—that superb Brodaini staff work had shown itself to advantage once again. The latest convoy of supply barges had been shepherded into the city, which would leave Necias' agents madly scrambling to find food in the countryside. The Brodaini galleys had entered the Outer Harbor and were safe behind their boom, and they'd taken with them all the Brodaini marines from the ships not directly under Brodaini command. Two attempts to enter the city, by some of Palastinas' staff, and then by Palastinas himself, had been turned away at the gates by junior officers who claimed they were not authorized to let anyone enter. And of course there had been Campas' message, which he had refused to believe until the confirming evidence had started trickling in. *The city of Calacas, which Necias has given us. . . .* Whenever

308

had he done such a mad thing as that? Hadn't he specific-
ally forbidden it? What absurd claims was Tegestu making?

He smashed a huge fist into his hand repeatedly in time
to his bursts of irritation. "What's he up to?" he barked,
seeing the frightened, uncomprehending looks from the
faces of his staff. "What in the name of the Netweaver
does Tegestu want?"

Had he joined Tastis? But he had sent Necias the heads
of some of Tastis' best advisors, including two of his
aldran. Necias even recognized one of them: one scarred
visage was unmistakably that of a grey-haired old bastard
who had headed a delegation to Arrandal a year ago.

Necias scowled at the battlements, planted his fists firmly
on his hips, and turned, seeing Palastinas sitting abstractedly on a coil of rope, stroking his little white beard and
frowning down at his boots.

"What the hell does it mean?" Necias bellowed.
Palastinas winced slightly at his volume, but otherwise
didn't change expression, didn't even look up.

"No telling, just yet," Palastinas said. "Tegestu will let
us know when he's ready." He looked up at Necias,
cocking an eye against the glare of the rising sun. "I'd like
to stand the army down. No sense in tiring them until we
know why we're doing it."

"No!" Necias barked. "Not yet!" He was keeping
thirty thousand armed men between himself and Calacas
until he understood the situation, and that was that. Tegestu's
eighteen thousand added to the twenty-five thousand or so of
Tastis' force could give the enemy a terrifying advantage—
and if Prypas' Brodaini had joined them the Arrandalla
could not count on any help from Handipas.

"He said he's ready to fight against Tastis," Palastinas
said, his gaze turning to his boots again. "He's told us he
will never be disloyal. Tegestu's a man of his word. Why
not stand the army down?"

"Because he's Brodaini, that's why! Haven't you heard

of aspistu?'' Necias demanded. ''If he's after revenge he'll hand us a hundred lies if he thinks they'll work—that's what aspistu's all about!'' Gods, he thought, what if that assassin didn't come from Tastis at all, but from Tegestu's camp? There was no way to tell. And it had been Tegestu who'd tried to suggest that Little Necias be killed for his failure—and who would that benefit but the rebels? Gods, how could he ever *know*?

He spun away from Palastinas at the sound of hoofbeats, and saw Campas pull his horse to a halt on the bank. Necias strode to meet him.

''Tanta's men are still in their lines,'' he said, smiling grimly. ''Handipas said they fought well against the sortie last night—drove Tastis right back to the moat, in fact.'' A worried look crossed his features. ''But they're under arms in their camp—standing ready.''

''Ai, gods, that does it,'' Necias said, twisting his rings in anxiety. ''I've got to tell Handipas.'' And lose every piece of cimmersan I've ever had with the man, he thought. Admitting that I've let Tegestu and his entire force get away and fort up in a situation in which he can join the enemy and outnumber us. There's no getting Handipas to accept a subordinate position now . . . no possibility in the world. And it would weaken him with the Elva as well.

Aiee, the Elva! With Tegestu protesting loyalty and claiming the city as a gift, how could he ever convince the Elva ambassadors, and their Denorrin-Deissin back home, that he hadn't intended to give the city away as part of some plot to increase his own territory by gifts to his Brodaini? They'd all lay the credit for this disaster at his door, however they chose to interpret the matter, and who could blame them? The only way to keep the Elva on his side would be to disavow Tegestu entirely, and that would mean losing him to the enemy.

Necias looked up at the grey towers of Calacas, feeling sweat popping up on his forehead as the midsummer morning heat lapped at him. Gods, he had to get the gates of the city open and quickly. He had to think. Take the first galley back to Arrandal, disassociate himself from this disaster? No, too late. He'd expected to take the credit for a victory; now all blame would be his.

Think! There had to be some escape. He pounded his fist rhythmically into his hand. He couldn't see Handipas until he had explanations for him, and as yet there were no explanations. What could he do?

He glanced up, irritated, at the sound of hoofbeats; but when he saw it was one of the mercenary officers from the outposts near the city pounding up on a sweating horse, he turned to face him. How much did the flenssin and the militia know? he wondered. They were standing to arms, facing the banners on the city wall they knew were friendly: surely they were aware that something was wrong; but did they know what? Rumors must be circulating frantically in the camp. He'd have to make them an announcement soon.

"Abeissu!" the officer called from his horse. "Messengers from Tegestu, come to see you!"

"How many? And who are they?" Necias barked, feeling relief and anxiety mixed. At last he'd find out what was happening—but how badly did he really wish to know?

"A man named Hamila. His standardbearer, and an escort of four."

Necias gnawed his nether lip. Hamila he knew, one of Tegestu's trusted commanders, but not a major figure by any means, which meant that Tegestu was not risking sending one of his welldrani lest he be taken hostage or killed in return for treachery. Necias reached into his memories about Hamila, and produced the fact that he was absolutely ignorant of Abessas. Why was Tegestu sending Necias a herald who couldn't speak his language?

"Captain Acragas!" he barked to Little Necias. "Alert all your guards! You and three of your best to be with me

at all times. Only Hamila is to be allowed on the barge—
the others are to wait on the bank.'' He turned to Campas.
"You'll greet him as he'd expect to be greeted, then escort
him below to meet me.'' he said. He jabbed Campas in the
chest with his thumb, seeing him wince, and grinned.
"We'll get to the bottom of it yet, hey?'' he said. "Hamila
can't speak Abessas—so you tell me what you think he's
thinking as well as what he's saying. He may be able to
understand what you're *doing,* but he won't understand
what you *say.* Understand?''

"Yes, Abeissu Necias!''

Little Necias put his hand on the hilt of his sword and
gave a grin as if he enjoyed the possibility of having to
give a swipe at Hamila. Necias frowned at him, hoping it
wouldn't come to that, and wishing he was wearing armor.
For a moment he considered donning his breastplate, chain
skirts, and helmet, but decided against it: it might indicate
he was afraid, and that would cost him cimmersan. At the
moment, he thought, the little he had left had become just
that much more precious.

Followed by three guards, Necias went below decks to
his receiving room, placed a Brodaini stool about ten paces
before his own massive chair, placed the three guards in
positions to intercept Hamila if he lunged out at him, and
ordered tea and cakes. He sat in his chair and drummed his
rings on the arm of his chair until Campas entered, followed by Hamila and Little Necias. Hamila stood by his
stool, knelt, then rose again. Necias looked at him carefully for a long second, locking eyes. Hamila's seemed
lively, as if he were interested, perhaps even enjoying
himself. Gradually, as Necias stared at him, the liveliness
faded, was replaced with hooded stubbornness. There was
a trace of uncertainty there as well. Good, Necias thought;
he doesn't know for certain that Tegestu holds trumps.

"Sit,'' said Necias.

Hamila was elderly, seventy or so, burly with a face

leathered by the elements. He was wearing light leather armor of the sort that was easy on the limbs of an old man, with a mantle of chain that covered his shoulders and upper chest. The chain rang lightly as he sat.

Hamila leaned forward earnestly, spoke in rapid Gostu to Campas—Necias had the impression that he was reciting a speech he'd been given—then he straightened and watched Necias with interested eyes as Campas translated. Necias watched him back. Neither of them watched Campas.

"He carries a message from lord Tegestu," Campas said. "Tegestu kneels before you as his canlan and lord and does you homage for the city you so generously have awarded to his aldran. Lord Tegestu believes that his folk will prosper in their new domain, and that he will order a ceremony which will do public homage to you as the benefactor of the Calacas Brodaini and all their dependents."

"Ah," Necias said, and held up a hand. He thrust out a finger and pointed it at Hamila. "Tell General Hamila that the Abessu-Denorru appreciates the homage that Lord Tegestu has paid us," he said. "But that the Abessu-Denorru knows that he had forbidden lord Tegestu and his people from taking Calacas for their own. The Abessu-Denorru would like to know why lord Tegestu has disobeyed his explicit command."

Hamila listened to the translation with a placid expression and no hint of surprise. His answer came back swiftly, as if, once again, it was memorized.

"General Hamila says that the lord Tegestu was surprised when you yourself reversed the order, and was so surprised to hear it that he forgot to thank you at the time, for which he apologizes." Necias snorted in disbelief. "The lord Tegestu begs you to remember," Campas continued, "the conversation after the banquet four nights ago, in which he renewed his request for you to allow him to seize the city in the name of his aldran. He says that you granted the request at that time, Abeissu.''

Necias stared at Hamila in astonishment, then anger. What in blazes had Tegestu asked him that night? He could not remember exact words—but no doubt Tegestu would be able to quote the conversation verbatim, the thin old schemer! Tegestu would not have to lie, he did not doubt; he would have been clever enough to word his request such that Necias didn't realize what favor he was granting. Necias slammed his meaty hand down on the chair arm. ''Tegestu did not make the nature of his request clear!'' he blurted.

''General Hamila is certain the lord Tegestu would not make that kind of mistake,'' Campas replied smoothly. No doubt, Necias thought, he hadn't, the cunning old white-haired bastard. And no witnesses to the conversation, either.

''The lord Tegestu is certain that you would never break hostu—that would be to create disharmony—by ignoring the bonds of nartil—that's obligation, Abeissu—between a lord and his subjects,'' Campas went on. ''He is confident you would wish nothing but harmony between his people and yourself.''

''If he wishes harmony, he will leave the city immedi-ately,'' Necias said flatly. ''As his lord, I order it. I will occupy the city with my own troops.''

He saw Campas hesitate, and then the poet turned back to Necias, looking troubled. ''Are you positive you want to give that order, Abeissu?'' he asked. ''I think that's what Tegestu is getting at with all this talk about nartil. As it stands now, the Brodaini are obligated to you, both as their lord and because they believe you've given them the city. If they think they've got a right to the city, and you order them out,'' Campas said, ''that would be the act of a bad lord. It would break nartil, and that would serve as an excuse for Tegestu's people to declare all treaties void.

They'd have the city for their own, and you wouldn't have any hold over them at all.''

Necias felt fury bubbling up his spine. "What's the point of staying their overlord if they don't obey my orders anyway?" he demanded. "Why not have it out in the open right now, if it's to be war?"

"They say they're willing to fight Tastis for you," Campas said. "That's one hold you've got over them. And another is their dependents back in the city, and out in the country and island garrisons. They're your hostages, thousands of them, and you're controlling the lines of communication between them."

Necias looked down at his hands, which always betrayed him, and saw they were gripping the chair arms with fury, the knuckles white. He relaxed them. Think! he demanded of himself. Campas was a bright boy; perhaps he knew what he was saying.

"Very well," Necias said. "Tell the lord general that Tegestu and I will disagree on this, and that I will issue a formal statement later, with which I hope the lord Tegestu will agree."

The answer was swift. "General Hamila agrees." No doubt he does, Necias thought. It's to no one's advantage but Tegestu's . . . unless I can use it to buy a little time.

"Tell the general," he went on, "that the Abessu-Denorru and the Denorru-Deissin of Arrandal will be certain to look after the welfare of such of lord Tegestu's people as are still remaining in our lands and the lands of our allies."

"General Hamila hopes that it may be arranged for these people to be moved safely to Calacas as soon as possible."

Sometime after I take my trip to the moon, Necias thought fiercely. "We will discuss this at another time," he said.

This time the answer was not as swift. "General Hamila

will agree, but hopes the time will be soon," Campas translated. Necias looked deliberately at Hamila and allowed himself a slow, predatory smile, catching a brief flash of uncertainty in return. I've got your people, you murdering bastard, Necias thought. Most of them are right in the old quarter of Arrandal, and many of the rest are on islands where they can't get away. You may have Calacas in the end, but your dependents will pay for it dearly, of that you may be certain.

Hamila leaned forward to speak to the translator again. "General Hamila," Campas reported, "begs that he be permitted to continue his message from lord Tegestu."

"Very well."

"Lord Tegestu reports that the city has been seized, but that it is far from secure." Campas opened his mouth to speak on, but Necias spoke quickly.

"Tell him that if control of the city is uncertain I will send city troops to assist lord Tegestu in securing it."

The answer was quick. "General Hamila says," Campas reported, "that the city troops will not be necessary."

"Say it will do them good. They are tired of sitting in their lines and doing nothing."

"General Hamila says it would only cause confusion."

"No doubt it would," Necias murmured, and leaned back in his chair with a frown. He caught himself tapping his rings on the arm of his chair and ceased at once. Campas wisely did not translate his remark.

"Lord Tegestu says that as the city has not been secured," the message continued, "it would not be wise for yourself to enter the city at present, as there is danger from spies, murderers, and an unruly population."

Necias nodded. He had no intention of going into the city, not as long as Tegestu controlled it alone.

"Thank the lord Tegestu for his concern," Necias said.

Hamila bowed in reply, then continued his message. "Lord Tegestu wishes to suggest that the army be united with that of General Handipas, before the city of Neda, so as to surround the rebels.''

"I will consult with Marshal Palastinas," Necias replied. "It will, of course, be necessary to maintain a force on this bank of the river, to prevent any rebels from escaping the lord Tegestu's forces in the city.''

"My lord does not believe that will be necessary.''

"I believe it will," Necias said. "The lord Tegestu admits the city is not secure, and a blockade will be necessary to prevent any of Tastis' sympathizers from moving in or out. Particularly if they hope to profit from the war by moving supplies into the city.''

Hamila listened to Campas' translation with a face of stone. There was a moment's silence in which Necias looked at Hamila again with the ghost of a smile, and then the Brodainu turned to Campas and spoke.

"Lord Tegestu believes that Tastis may have suffered a terrible blow," he said. "He may have suffered such a loss of prestige that his aldran may force him to negotiate a peace. Lord Tegestu wonders if he may approach Tastis with a message on your behalf.''

Oho! Necias thought. Here we see it. Tegestu hopes to stand between Tastis and the Elva with the intention of playing us off against one another, forcing us to make concessions, seeing who will give him the best settlement. We'll see about that, my boy, he thought.

"Tell him that the Abeissu will consider the lord Tegestu's kind offer, but will probably wish to conduct his own negotiations with the rebels," he said. He watched the effect of the translation sink into Hamila, the eyes deepening, the mouth turning down; and Necias exulted. Two, he thought, can play at this. Tegestu may find that he is not, after all, the balance of power; he may be in the scales with the rest of us.

Time, he thought, I'll have to play for time. The forces from the other Elva cities will arrive after the autumn storms, and then I'll be able to squeeze them both. In the meantime, I believe I know just how I'll handle the Elva ambassadors.

Hamila, scowling now, bowed and repeated Tegestu's thanks and praises for allowing him possession of the city; and Necias repeated his belief that Tegestu was in error. Hamila asked if Necias had any messages to carry back to Tegestu, and Necias replied that he had none at present, but would soon.

Pressure, Necias thought. Gentle pressure at first, to worry them, then increase later on. And I'll be forever busy in the background, keeping everything dancing, and ready to strike when I see my time.

The interview over, Hamila knelt once more, then was escorted out of the room by Little Necias. Necias bounced out of his chair and clapped his hands gustily. "Well, Campas?" he asked. "Have I handled him well?"

"Very well, Abeissu Necias," Campas said. "I think you're right not to make demands, now."

Necias clapped him on the back. Campas staggered a bit, his chain coat jingling. "Thanks to you, hey," he boomed. "That warning of yours was right on target." He reached down to the plate of untasted tea-cakes and swallowed two.

"I'll need the ambassadors here right away, and then alert the scribes," he said. "I've got to send some messages to all the Elva cities, and to the Denorru-Deissin." He grinned. "I'm going to have a few orders to give about the Brodaini that Tegestu was unfortunate enough to have to leave behind. There are more ways than one to apply pressure, hey?"

22

"Brilliant," Campas said. He was stretched out on Fiona's bed, his hair still wet from a recent bath, while Fiona knelt over him, her nimble magician's fingers working at the tense, knotted muscles over his ribs. He'd been crouching over his scrivener's table for too many hours, and he'd cramped.

"Necias was brilliant," Campas continued. "And afterwards with the Elva ambassadors—incredible! Here he was, faced with half a dozen angry, suspicious, confused political men, all of them half-convinced he'd connived at Tegestu's occupation of the city, with General Handipas ranting up and down about Arrandalla treachery and Brodaini double-dealing —and before the meeting was out Necias convinced them to issue the statement he'd had me draft before the meeting ever started, and furthermore he had them all thinking it was their idea. Aiee, woman! Careful of my bones!"

Fiona jabbed her thumb again into the tender place below Campas' rib, hearing him hiss in pained response. "You've got a knot there," she said. "Best we work on it.'' Fiona oiled her hands, and Campas suffered in silence while the muscle was eased. She bent down to kiss his clavicle, then looked up at him.

"What was in the draft?'' she asked.

"Hm? Oh. An announcement that Tegestu's claim on Calacas was unauthorized, and that the Elva will not recognize it. But it stopped short of ordering Tegestu out—that was what Necias had to fight longest for—since ordering him out would serve as an excuse for Tegestu to claim we were not fulfilling our obligations as his overlords, and to join Tastis.''

"Will he anyway?'' Fiona asked. With three Brodaini forces in the vicinity, the Elva forces were, perhaps, outnumbered, certainly outclassed, and furthermore divided by the river.

"I don't think so,'' Campas said. "Not right away. He's going to try to negotiate with both sides in order to get what's best for his people.'' He looked up at Fiona with a grin. "You're as good as the Brodaini masseurs,'' he said. "They were what I missed most, after I stopped living with them.''

"Mm.'' She bent over him and kissed his neck. He put his arms around her and hugged her.

"Fiona?'' he said, close to her ear. His tone made her sit up and look carefully down at him.

"Yes?''

"I think Necias knows about us.''

Fiona shrugged. "Probably half the camp knows by now. Does it matter?'' She tossed her head. "I'm past caring what people think of me. I know it should matter, as I've got to deal with them and a good opinion helps, but I don't. I can't seem to muster up any concern on that account any more.''

"It might affect me,'' Campas said. "Necias may be afraid I'd pass on any of his secret decisions to you. I think he may be wondering that already—he's been asking me questions about you."

Fiona grinned, then bent to kiss him again. "If he lets you go, I'll hire you as embassy staff. I'll be around longer than Necias, and I won't work you nearly as hard."

He looked at her sharply. "What d'you mean by that?"

"By what?"

"That you'll be around longer than Necias." She sat up again, looking at him carefully. He was looking at her with a frown creasing his brow, his eyes uncertain.

"I meant," she said, "that I'll be living longer than Necias. I'm younger. That's all."

He sighed and shook his head. "I'm sorry, love." He reached up to touch her cheek. "I just thought you might have heard something through your . . . your sources."

"No," she said simply. "I haven't."

"Forgive me. This situation has everyone on edge." She nodded, stretched out her legs, and lay down next to him, resting her head on his shoulder.

"Fiona," he said again. It was the same tone as before: something else was coming.

"Yes." Patiently.

"Don't be surprised if, in a few days, Necias requests that you stay in the ambassadorial compound. For your own safety, he'll say."

With a sudden movement Fiona propped herself up on her elbows and looked at Campas carefully. "Where did you get this?" she asked.

He frowned. "Necias mentioned it today, very casually," he said. "He said that Handipas had started him thinking, and that you're too dangerous to be at liberty in the camp. But he doesn't want to give the order right away, because it would look as if he was doing it at Handipas' suggestion."

"Damn the man!" Fiona said in her own language. Seeing Campas' baffled look, she changed back to Abessas. "If I'm confined to the compound here," she said, "I may as well go back to Arrandal. I won't be able to do any of my work.''

Campas looked grim. "I'm not sure you'll be doing any back in Arrandal, either. You'd be staying in the Acragas palace, and your movements could be restricted there as well as here. Better, perhaps.'' He reached out to stroke her hair. "I'm sorry, love,'' he said. "I wish I had more comforting news to bring you.''

He hesitated, then spoke thoughtfully. "The odd thing is, I think he *wanted* me to tell you. I got that feeling from him, the feeling I get when he's got some plot in mind.'' He shook his head. "But I've no idea what it is.''

Fiona considered, chin cupped in her hand. "What could it be?'' she wondered. "Could he be trying to see whether I'll declare for Tegestu? I won't—I couldn't—but since I helped that Brodaini patrol last week perhaps he thinks I sympathize with them.''

"Do you?'' he asked.

She shook her head. "Not politically,'' she said. "I think Tegestu's behaving like a bandit.'' She looked at him candidly. "But there's a lot to admire about the Brodaini, isn't there? They have a code of honor and stick to it. They're honest. Their women aren't treated like expensive bits of furniture, to be collected, decorated, and shown off to the neighbors.'' She gave a short, sorrowful laugh. "In a way, it's a pity they're doomed.''

Campas looked at her in surprise. "Are they?'' he asked.

"Yes,'' Fiona said. Was she giving away too much by answering that question? Possibly; but in the long run this, too, didn't matter. "Even if Tastis wins this war and keeps his city, his people are doomed in the long run. The Elva cities will win in the end. Cities like Arrandal *are* the future. The nature of power has changed: it's based on trade rather than ownership of land, and the Elva cities dominate trade. Already they control almost all the over-

seas trade in the Brodaini homelands: before they know it
the Brodaini will be dependent on them. Plus the cities
have a flexible enough system of government to be able to
respond to changing conditions. In another few hundred
years they'll have absorbed the baronies and be sending
colonies abroad.'' She looked at him. ''The Brodaini aren't
flexible enough to survive; their system is too rigid, and
it's based on land tenure, not trade. Either you'll absorb
them, or they'll have to become like you in order to
survive—and that will happen, though much more slowly,
in the Brodaini homelands as well. Either way, your people win.''

''You know this?'' Campas asked, his tone incredulous.
''You can tell what's going to happen over the next two
hundred years?''

How to answer that? she wondered. How to explain the
vast amounts of data correlated by her ship's computers,
and the long reams of probabilities they had produced?

And then, she thought, there was the cynical answer.
Your people will survive to dominate the planet because
we will be helping them.

No. Best be brief.

''We can't see into the future, no,'' she said. ''We can't
be certain. But we think that's the likely outcome.''

Campas blew his cheeks, lying back on his pillow,
overwhelmed by the idea. ''Can I tell Necias?'' he asked.

She thought for a moment. ''If you like,'' she said.
''But it won't help him. His problem is to somehow
survive the next year politically, and after that to arrange
an orderly transition of power to his heirs. What happens
in two hundred years doesn't matter to him.''

''What does your—your foresight say about his chance
of success?'' he asked.

Fiona shook her head. ''We can't make predictions of
that kind. Trends over a long period of time, yes; but there

are too many factors involved in the fate of a single individual.''

He shook his head dubiously. ''This is what you're bringing to us?'' he asked. ''This kind of magic foresight? To be able to plan our fortunes over centuries?''

''It's possible,'' Fiona said. She reached out to put a finger on his oiled sternum. ''But no person will ever know his own fate, Campas,'' she said. ''No one can ever predict that. It will always remain unknown. And most people are more interested in what they're going to eat for dinner, and where they're going to get it, than in what political power will be dominant for the next century.''

She caught a shade of wariness in his eyes as he asked his next question. ''Fiona?'' he asked, his voice hesitant. ''How old are you?''

A laugh bubbled up inside her: he'd come up with another puzzler. What would he say, she wondered, if she'd told him the truth: she had been born on Igara slightly over six hundred of his years ago. But that answer would be deceptive, as well as alarming; almost all of those six hundred years had been spent in hibernation. Counting only the years she'd been awake, she was thirty-three in her own reckoning. That would be thirty-one in Standard, used by Igara and the other advanced planets in communication with one another, and was based on the old Terran year. Or, in the slightly longer years of Echidne, she would be twenty-seven. That was what she told him.

Campas seemed relieved. ''With foresight of centuries. I thought perhaps you were an immortal, hundreds of years old. That would have been a surprise!'' He cocked his head and looked at her, his palm brushing his cheek. ''You look younger than twenty-seven,'' he said.

She gazed at him for a long moment, watching the pulse beat in his throat as she reached her own decision. It had to come sooner or later, she knew; and this night seemed made for truth.

"Campas," she said, "you're righter than you know." She propped herself on her elbows over him, looking carefully down at his expectant face. "I'm not an immortal," she said. "And right now I'm only twenty-seven. But I can live centuries, barring accident, or murder. With luck I'll live over two hundred, and be young enough in body to enjoy it."

Campas gazed back at her for a long moment, a little frown on his face, his expression fathomless. "True?" he asked, finally.

"True," Solemnly.

He turned his eyes away, gazing up at the blank roof of her tent. When he spoke his voice seemed to come from a long distance. "Is this one of the gifts you bring, Ambassador?" he asked.

"No," she said, as gently as she could. She knew that even if it were possible to begin giving the treatments to the people of this planet—and it wasn't; there was no place for long-lived people here; the population would grow to huge proportions and starvation would result—but even if it were possible, it was already too late for Campas. The treatments had to be started when very young.

Best to lie, she thought sorrowfully, wishing the realities were otherwise, that the decisions her people made were not so heartbreaking as to deny long life to so many, even with justification. But it would be too dangerous if the local rulers realized that they could demand extended life in return for their cooperation.

"My people are naturally long-lived," she said. "That's the way we're born. It isn't anything we can teach you."

"I see," he said, his voice still distant. He took a deep breath and turned toward her. "That will change things with us, won't it?" he asked. "I'll grow old, you won't."

She took his head in her hands and kissed him solemnly. "It doesn't have to change tonight," she said. "Or tomorrow night."

"No," he said. "But it will matter eventually."

"I suppose it will." She gave him a small smile. "I don't think about *eventually* very often. Like most people, I spend more time thinking of *tonight*."

His arms came around her and he held her close, his hands moving over her back, stroking her through the supple material of her privy-coat. She pressed her cheek to his neck, feeling his pulse close to her ear. He drew in a long breath, then let it out slowly, a long, ragged sigh. She sensed he had made a decision.

"Yes," he said. "You're right. You said it yourself, no one can predict his own fate. Everything could change tomorrow, not just between us, but for everyone, and possibly even you couldn't stop it from changing." He looked up at her soberly, and she nodded. "But no matter what happens tomorrow," he said, "we still have tonight. Tonight is what matters."

"Yes," she said, simply. He began to kiss her slowly, first her cheek, then the line of her chin, then lastly, gravely, her mouth. So, she thought, another barrier passed, passed only for tonight, if not forever. We have survived, she thought. Affirmed.

And accepted, with grace, the things that must be.

23

Fiona was walking from the river barge to her tent when she saw Necias' messengers waiting for her. Her busy stride slowed for a moment, then she took a breath and went on. This, she thought, was where she was asked, politely, to stay in her tent so that the Abessu-Denorru could look to her safety. And where she would demand to see Necias, make her protests, and after listening solemnly Necias would, ever so regretfully, confirm the order.

Well. She was ready, as ready as she'd ever be.

The delegation seemed to be led by Listas, Necias' popeyed son. "Beg pardon, Ambassador," Listas said, "but the Abeissu would like to see you."

"Very well." So Necias was going to do his own dirty work. Fiona looked down at her plain grey dress. She had been talking to the barge people for a long hot afternoon, and it was marked with sweat. "Have I time to change?" she asked.

"Of course. There's no hurry. Please take your time." Listas seemed to be going out of his way to be assuring. Fiona ducked into her tent, let the flap drop shut behind her, and opened her chest of clothing. She washed her face, neck, and arms in the water her servant had brought— he'd always complained that she'd wanted it boiled first— and then chose a gown of purple velvet she hadn't yet worn in Necias's company. It was plain by Abessla standards, but remarkably gaudy by her own; she topped it off with a broad-brimmed black hat trimmed with silver brocade. Always look your best, she thought, when you're going to get the chop.

"I'm ready," she said as she stepped out.

"You're looking very well, Ambassador," Listas said.

"Thank you."

They walked across two hundred yards of the busy, crowded camp on their way to Necias' barge. In the three days since Campas had warned her of her coming restriction two heavy pontoon bridges had been thrown across the river, and most of the army of Arrandal had crossed onto the narrow strip of solid land facing Tastis' city of Neda, joining Handipas' army. Tanta, the Brodaini commander from Prypas, had been ordered to withdraw his people from the siege, and was currently on a hundred-mile march to Laptillo, a minor Prypas dependency roughly halfway between Neda and Prypas. There he would camp while awaiting further orders.

Tanta, Campas told her, seemed to be cooperative enough. It was obvious that Brodaini forces could not be trusted in the siege, but likewise the government of Prypas didn't want them back in their home city, where they might threaten revolt. Having them halfway between seemed a suitable compromise, even if it meant having them squarely along their line of communications. It was better than having to live cheek-by-jowl with an armed force one didn't trust.

The united Elva forces were in a near-impregnable position, behind a breastwork thrown up behind an old green canal that had, Fiona suspected, been dug in an unsuccessful attempt to drain the vast swamp that hung off the army's left flank. There were small forts in front of the position to provide a base for patrols and a warning in case of assault, and the armies were busy throwing an earthwork up behind them, in case Tanta proved treacherous and tried to attack from behind.

Across the river, where the pontoon bridges still allowed reinforcements to move from one bank to the other, a huge earthwork had been thrown up, where most of the Elva cavalry were barracked. It was their duty to patrol the long plain in front of Calacas day and night, to prevent Tegestu from getting reinforcement or supplies.

Tegestu, Fiona thought, was going to be allowed to rot in Calacas for as long as he liked, ignored by the Elva until sufficient force came across the sea to invest him safely, and that would not be until late autumn. The day before Necias had ostentatiously sent a parley to speak to Tastis, heralds with their trumpets blowing outside the main gate of the new Broadaini citadel, and Tastis had responded with heralds of his own; so something was brewing there.

Fiona had not been paying much attention. Warned her movements might be restricted, she'd started cultivating a source of data that she could continue to work with if she were forced to return to Arrandal, and that she could even work on during the journey: she was working up a survey on Abessas' barge people—the polyglot, travelled, hardworking folk, sometimes entire families, who made their living up and down the rivers and canals of the continent. They were an interesting group: open, competent, self-assured, they were anything but the group of drunken, irresponsible louts the shore people thought them to be. They seemed to respond to her skill at sleight-of-hand with more interest than the fact she was from another planet, and hospitably offered to share their meals as soon as they'd finished their daily tasks, which mostly consisted of loading or unloading, entirely by hand, tons of food, forage, or equipment for the armies. Fiona found them fascinating, and fancied she had made some friends.

Listas led her to Necias' barge, and courteously offered her a hand on the gangplank. "Thank you, no," she said, hitched up her skirt, and went down nimbly with half the guard on deck grinning at the sight of her ankles. Guards escorted her to where Necias awaited in his audience room.

"Ambassador Fiona!" Necias roared at the sight of her, his face split by a vast grin. "I'm glad to see you!" He stood looking at her, his feet planted squarely on the deck, arms on his hips. "Can I offer you tea? Wine? Brandy?"

"Tea, thank you." Necias, she thought, was enjoying this far too much.

"Sit down, Ambassador," he said. "I have a request to make of you."

Fiona sat on the guest settee and looked up at him. The atmosphere, she thought, was wrong for what she expected him to ask her. If he were to restrict her, he would be full of soft-spoken, apologetic, and totally feigned regret—instead he was ebullient. What, she wondered, was he up to?

Necias rubbed his nose, frowned to himself for a moment, and then wandered to his own settee and sat down, the cushion under his arm. "Ambassador," he said, "the Elva will shortly be opening negotiations with Tastis for the eventual surrender of Neda."

"Congratulations, Abessu-Denorru. You must be pleased."

He glanced up at her sharply. "Yes. I am," he said. She wasn't certain whether he was telling the truth or not, or perceived her own remark as ironic. He rubbed his nose again.

"I would count it a favor if you would be present at the negotiations," he said. Fiona looked up at him in surprise. "I would very much like to have a neutral party present," he went on. "I'm told you know Gostu very well; and of

course you speak excellent Abessas. Perhaps you could
keep a third copy of the agreement in your own language,
that we could appeal to if the terms of the treaty were not
abided by. We like to have a neutral party present in these
cases, as a guarantor of our good faith.''

You cunning bastard! Fiona thought with inward delight.
He *had* wanted Campas to tell her of his intention to
restrict her movements, putting additional pressure on her
to cooperate in the matter of the negotiations.

But, she thought, exultant, none of that was necessary.
She would be delighted to play a part in the negotiations; it
was the sort of thing most likely to quickly legitimize her
presence here, as well as that of the other Igaran ambassadors. It would also, she thought, help justify her presence
at the siege to Tyson.

She frowned as if considering the invitation for a moment,
then nodded. ''Abeissu Necias, I would be honored,'' she
said.

Necias jumped to his feet and banged his hands together.
''Lovely!'' he said. ''Now all I'll have to do is convince
Tastis of it!''

She looked up at him sharply. ''He hasn't agreed?'' she
asked.

''Not yet,'' Necias said. ''But we'll make it a condition
of the negotiations—he'll go along.''

Fiona, watching his carefully, could detect nothing but
innocence, but still she wondered: had Necias found out
about Kira? Would he use Fiona's presence at the talks as
an additional form of pressure on Tastis—come to an
agreement soon or we'll unleash the Igarans on you?

This, she concluded, would require some thought. And,
perhaps, a discrete Igaran listening spike planted in Necias'
barge. Listening to private conversations was not a thing
she or her superiors normally indulged in—most of the
original spikes that had taught her the language had been
planted in public places—but if Necias wanted to use her

for his own purposes in the negotiations, she had a right to find out. She'd request the spike from Tyson as soon as she returned to her tent.

Necias grinned and clapped his hands again. "Ambassador," he said, "I'm happy you're so obliging. But I warn you, the talks will be dull, at least at first. I'm not anticipating any sudden developments. You may have to resign yourself to spending the autumn with us."

Fiona smiled. "I have no other plans, Abeissu," she said.

Necias beamed. Does he know about Kira? Fiona asked herself again. With luck, she thought, she'd know tonight.

The answer did not, she admitted, particularly interest her: she knew she was being used, and was simply curious about how.

Any pressure she could put on Tastis, she concluded, she would put there willingly.

25

The two archers standing guard in the Calacas tower were sweating as they stood at rigid attention. Tegestu let them sweat. In this late summer heat, they would not sweat alone.

With eyes narrowed against the blinding glare, Tegestu looked through the shimmering waves of heat at the treaty pavilion set carefully in the no man's land between Neda and the Elva lines. He picked up the long tube of his spyglass and braced it on the embrasure, and the picture leapt into focus: he could see parties advancing from both sides, flags of truce at their heads, heading toward the pavilion and the day's negotiation. He saw the black-hooded, scarlet-gowned figure of Fiona walking among them, her head high as she looked warily toward the other party. Why had she involved herself in this?

Ostensibly, he knew, it was to guarantee the good faith of both sides. But Tegestu also knew that she hated Tastis and his people, though he had never known why. Was Necias using her to pressure Tastis with the threat of vengeance from above? But if so, why would she agree?

Unless, of course, she had been ordered by her superiors to cooperate. Or unless she was pursuing some hidden motive of her own.

Tastis, Fiona had reported, had refused an Igaran embassy. Tegestu knew from the reports of his spies that a miracle-working woman had appeared in the town claiming to be from another world; he knew that she had been invited into the Brodaini quarter and kept secure. After that there had been no word of her whatever.

But wait—hadn't there been a report of a freak accident in one of the towers of Tastis' Keep? Some kind of lighting storm, the word had gone, with a spectacular display of lighting in the sky surrounding the city, that had also hit the tower of the Keep. . . .

Tegestu had heard of lightning once before, recently, on the day when Fiona had used her witchery against Captain Pantas' archers, and brought the old barn crashing down. Had the Igaran ambassador to Neda-Calacas been forced to defend herself against Tastis' people? Was that why Fiona was filled with such hatred?

It seemed a likely possibility. He would ask Cascan if he remembers the dispatches from those early days, and which tower had supposedly been struck. If it had been the tower used to house important prisoners, Tegestu would have his answer.

Not, of course, that the answer would seem to be worth a great deal at the moment. Tegestu blinked sweat from his eyes and peered through the long glass as the two sets of negotiators disappeared under the sun canopy they've been using for the talks.

This meeting represented the first resumption of the talks in several days. Tegestu sucked in his lips and tried to ignore the heat that enveloped him, trying to think. His mind ran hopelessly in blind alleys; he could find no answer.

The negotiations had been going on for two months,

right through the summer. In another few weeks the autumn storms would begin, beating on the coast for a month while every ship ran for a safe anchorage—and then, after the storms, would come the strong cold winds from the north, bringing Elva ships choked with soldiers and weapons.

His people in Calacas were as ready as they could be. Food had been slipping in regularly, bundled on the backs of horses and mules, all provided by contractors happy to exchange their produce for the inflated prices Tegestu was paying, and moving safely through the gates because the mercenary captains who were supposed to be patrolling the walls had proved bribable. Tanta was also sending food from his base at Laptillo, where he could buy it more legitimately. Messages moved back and forth easily enough, either by swift men on horseback or by even swifter small galleys slipping out past the blockade at night. Tegestu was well aware of developments outside his city walls—as perhaps Necias wanted him to be, since they were not encouraging.

Amasta had barracaded herself in the Brodaini quarter of Arrandal and was letting no one in or out, claiming as her reason the danger of local unrest. The forces of Arrandal had little hope of forcing her out, and she had food for a year. On the other hand, she had little chance of taking the rest of the city should the need arise, since it had been filled with a new draft of the militia, large numbers of mercenaries, and even baronial forces hired for the occasion—undisciplined men for the most part, but fighters. Amasta and the Arrandal Brodaini were, in the end, little more than hostages to Tegestu's good behavior. Elsewhere, the forces on the islands and in the countryside had withdrawn successfully into garrison and were for the moment physically safe, though isolated; but in reality they were in much the same situation as Amasta.

The exile Brodaini elsewhere in the Elva were also stalemated. They were firmly in control of their own areas, but would never leave them without permission of their overlords. None of them would be accompanying the Elva forces overseas; they would all remain in their quarters, prevented from action by swarms of newly hired native soldiers. Perhaps a revolt would be successful here or there; but it would not succeed everywhere.

The only Broadaini force free to act was Tanta's. Perhaps, with Tastis and Tegestu assaulting the Elva army from the front while Tanta cut their lines of communication and attacked from the rear, the Elva army could be smashed. But that would result in a war of extermination, perhaps ending in the death of every Brodaini in exile. It was a step Tegestu was reluctant to take—he would, he concluded bitterly, surrender first.

Seen from the tower, the two parties involved in the negotiation had arrived in the central pavilion. Tegestu had no clear idea what was on the agenda for today, but he knew the talks were proceeding slowly, in part because neither Tastis nor Necias trusted the other enough to attend in person, and instead used deputies whose actions were easy enough to disavow if they proved inconvenient. Tegestu wiped a bead of sweat from his nose and focused on the distant pavilion.

He was receiving regular, accurate reports on the state of the negotiations, principally from Tanta and Astapan, the drandor of Prypas, who had their sources within the Prypas government; there were also occasional reports from Amasta and a more irregular source within Necias' household, a servant who was occasionally in a position to overhear something, who passed on what he heard to one of Cascan's spies, and who thought he was actually working for the government of Cartenas, where the servant had relatives.

But that source had heard nothing for over two weeks, and the other sources took time. Tegestu's news was well out of date.

The negotiations, as far as Tegestu had heard, had not produced a great deal of substance. Tastis had demanded independence for himself and his Denorru-Constassin, which Necias had refused. Necias had demanded instant and unconditional surrender, which Tastis had refused. They had then sat down to negotiate what would, in the end, be a surrender, but which would, Tegestu suspected, avoid the word and stigma of "surrender" but go by another word. "Armistice," perhaps, was a word neutral enough to eventually work as a compromise.

What to do with Tastis and his aldran? Tastis wanted to return, of course, to his old allegiance, but the Neda-Calacas Government-in-Exile said no. Tastis had then hoped to take his folk out into the baronies to carve out a duchy for himself, but that proposal had been quashed quickly enough—the baronies had been settled for ten years, in part because they were more concerned with fighting old feuds than in battling Elva influence, but there was nothing more guaranteed to unite the baronies than the Elva unleashing fifty thousand homeless warriors on them. And so the current answer seemed to be to somehow split up Tastis' people, and there it hung. The Elva were less than enthusiastic about taking even small numbers of them into their service, lest the revolutionary virus infect their own Brodaini; and the alternative seemed to be to force them to become mercenaries abroad, preferably with Tastis and his aldran being sent in the opposite direction, a proposal Tastis was resisting, and which had problems of its own insofar as small wandering bands of mercenary Brodaini were going to cause trouble wherever they went.

None of this was final and the proposals changed with every session as Tastis' aldran and Necias' committee of ambassadors hewed at every proposal. And all the while, Tegestu was waiting for only one development that, if it appeared, would give him freedom to move once again. *If*, at some point in the negotiations, the Elva was willing to concede the possibility of allowing sovereign Brodaini territory *somewhere* on the continent, then Tegestu could approach Necias with his own proposals. It would mean trading Calacas for something else, but at least it would be for something real.

Thus far Tegestu had waited in vain.

He looked down from the tower, felt the sweat collecting under his armor, and tried to think. His mind could find no answers; it only spun hopelessly in old backwaters, unwilling to bring anything new to the surface.

His hope, he knew, had been that Necias would try to make a peace before autumn. Once the other Elva cities were represented by armies instead of ambassadors Necias would find it more difficult to arrive at any conclusive arrangement to end the war, and even if he did he would have to share the credit. He had thought Necias would wish, if at all possible, to arrange a peace before the autumn storms.

Apparently he had been wrong. Necias, to all appearances, seemed perfectly willing to wait until the other Elva forces arrived and strengthened his hand. Unless, of course, Necias was concealing his eagerness as a ploy to force Tastis to make concessions.

Tegestu cursed the lack of recent news. His information on the negotiations, though it was accurate, was two weeks out of date. There had been five meetings since, and Tegestu had no word of their deliberations.

Time was coming near to forcing Tegestu's hand. One problem that could not be delayed was that of his cavalry and transport horses: the city was nearly out of fodder for them, and though he had taken advantage of the main Elva force being on the other side of the river to graze his beasts outside the city walls during the daylight hours, all available grazing would be exhausted in a matter of days. He would either have to slaughter his horses or somehow get them out of the city, and he resisted the consequences of either decision. He would, he thought, try to get them out to the west and let Tanta look after them—but it would cost him in terms of his readiness here, where it was needed, and he disliked admitting such vulnerability.

That, he supposed, was a minor matter, compared with his main dilemma. Should he send his own negotiators to Tastis or not? Tastis had been utterly silent since the night Tegestu had occupied Calacas, and there was no guarantee he would not instantly retaliate by hacking off the heads of any heralds Tegestu sent, whether under a spear of parley or not. Tesestu suspected Tastis wouldn't do anything quite so drastic, simply because he didn't have the luxury of turning away someone who might offer something to his advantage, but there was no way of knowing.

No, Tegestu didn't want to send an emissary simply because it would be a confession of his own desperation, a confession Tastis would certainly use to his own advantage. Tegestu's situation, he knew, was superficially strong, here in the city with enough food to last a year, and he didn't want to dispel that illusion.

Patience, he thought. Patience is the choice of the wise leader.

It was also, he knew, the only choice that offered itself to him.

Cursing the necessity for patience, Tegestu looked out the window and hoped for inspiration. It did not come.

Two days later Tegestu had still not found his answer. He was lying in his living quarters on a massage table, a light sheet thrown over him, his eyes closed. He sensed, through the scent of perfumed oil, Grendis lying on the table next to him. The masseurs had finished and quietly left the chamber, and Tegestu listened idly to the sound of the bohau and tedec in the next chamber, behind the screens. A leather pillow lay beneath his head, and his body was perfectly relaxed; in the stillness of his mind he sought hostu, and did not find it. His mind still drifted hopelessly in its sluggish old channels, unable to find its way out.

If he had truly trapped himself here, he thought, he would suicide and hope to find hostu in the afterlife. That would give his successors a chance to negotiate with Necias on a new basis, without the embarrassment of his presence.

"Bro-demmin drandor." A soft voice, Thesau's. He had not heard his servant's quiet footsteps. "I apologize for the interruption. Bro-demmin Acamantu begs to see you on a matter of urgency."

Tegestu opened his eyes, the tranquillity he sought banished forever. He heard Grendis shift on her platform in interest. "Aye, ilean," Tegestu said, hoping his voice did not show his weariness. "Let him enter."

He heard, rather than saw, the rattle of his son's armor as he knelt in respectful greeting.

"What is it, ban-demmin?" he asked.

"Tastis has sent a herald asking to speak with you or your emissary," Acamantu said. "I've allowed him entrance."

Tegestu felt a trickle of satisfaction entering his mind. Tastis had come to *him*. Patience, he thought with contentment, always patience until the time to strike, and then move like lightning. Tastis, he thought, is brilliant, but he has never been patient. That is his weakness.

"Is it a kantu-kamliss matter, ban-demmin?" he asked.

"Nay. A full parley."

Tegestu craned his neck back, seeing his son head-downward from his reversed angle. "Did they come with spears of parley?" he asked.

"Aye, bro-demmin."

Tegestu gave a tight smile. "That is good, ban-demmin," he said. "It appears Tastis has learned manners." He saw Acamantu's answering carnivore smile; then he closed his eyes and thought for a moment. "Treat them with all courtesy, ban-demmin," he said without opening his eyes. "Tell them my emissary will meet with them in an hour. This will be in the grey meeting room—you know the one. Decorated with the moulded winged figures." The former deissu's palace he had chosen as his headquarters was huge, and even after two months Tegestu occasionally found himself lost in it, at least once he travelled outside the small well-guarded area used by his family and staff.

"Aye, bro-demmin. I know the one."

"I shall see to its preparation myself. Please send whelkran Hamila to me."

"Aye, bro-demmin. Here or in the conference chamber?"

Tegestu considered for a second. "In the conference chamber. I shall be there in half an hour."

"He shall be informed, bro-demmin." There was a pause. "Beg pardon, bro-demmin," Acamantu said hesitantly, "but do you know where ban-demmin Hamila is stationed at present?"

Tegestu smiled. "Inspecting the reserve swordsmen in the Square of the Weavers, ban-demmin," he said.

"Thank you, bro-demmin," Acamantu said, a touch of relief in his voice. He knelt, said his farewell, and was gone.

The bohau and tedec throbbed onward. Tegestu opened his eyes and turned his head toward Grendis. She had risen to a seating position, and was swinging her legs off the table. When she saw his expression she looked at him questioningly. His smile broadened.

"He has come to *us,* Grendis," he said. "His need must be great."

"I hope it may be so," she said, doubtfully. He laughed, swung off the table, and took her hands. He looked at her naked form, the trained body, still strong and limber but with the inevitable slack folds of flesh, the calluses that the weight of armor had made on her broad, swordsman's shoulders, the small breasts with their dark nipples. *I will guard your back,* she had promised, and never failed. He felt a warmth of love for her that was so extreme he felt almost frightened by it, so much did it exceed what was proper.

He took her gently by the shoulders and kissed her. "We must make a last throw of the dice, my love," he said. "And accept them, however they land."

She said nothing, but only embraced him, sensing, perhaps, the desperation beneath his light tone. He allowed himself the luxury of her nearness for a long, wordless moment, and then, reluctantly, he returned, as he must, to his duty.

The conference chamber had been expertly prepared. It was a large, airy room, with a handsome frescoed and domed ceiling, and with beautifully moulded plasterwork accenting the lovely proportions of the chamber. Tegestu had been impressed by the harmony of the room's design, and despite its un-Gostu appearance he often used it for staff meetings.

He sat concealed behind a screen in the rear of the chamber. Two Classani secretaries were with him, as well as a small writing desk, several newly-cut pens, and a ream of paper.

There was another, larger screen placed near the front of the chamber, placed behind where Hamila sat on his stool to receive Tastis' emissaries. The screen naturally attracted the eye, and if the heralds had an assassin among them he would strike first for the larger screen, thinking Tegestu would be behind it—at least that was Tegestu's hope. The spear of parley meant little in a matter of angu, and Tastis had always had an impetuous streak. It paid, Tegestu thought, to take precautions against anything an enemy was prepared to do.

Hamila adjusted his position on the stool and cleared his

throat, then nodded to the guards placed on the doors. The doors swung open, and Tastis' embassy entered.

There were long moments of formality in which the herald and Hamila proclaimed their name and lineage and presented their credentials, and then the real business of the meeting got underway.

"It is possible," Tastis' herald said, "that the negotiations currently under way between the aldran of Neda and the emissaries of the Elva may not bear fruit. My lord Tastis hopes that an embassy to bro-demmin Tegestu and his aldran may be blessed with greater success."

Tegestu sucked in his breath. *Aiau,* he thought. The talks must have collapsed entirely; the man had virtually admitted it. Tastis had no choice but to approach Tegestu and hope for an alliance. How he must have had to swallow his pride for that! To approach the man who tricked him out of a city and then hacked off the heads of two of his welldrani.

Unless, he thought cautiously, this was a trick. To lure Tegestu into negotiations, perhaps, and then reveal the fact to Necias, hoping to force Necias to declare Tegestu outlaw, thereby gaining an ally without the need for concessions. Tegestu frowned. He would have to think about that.

Hamila spoke:

"Ban-demmini," he said, "for what purposes to you wish to approach my lord Tegestu?"

"To explore the possibility of uniting our quarreling race under a single banner," the herald replied. "To explore the possibility of eventually establishing a sovereign nation for the Brodaini on this continent."

"My lord Tegestu," Hamila said, "will concede that the latter is desirable. We consent to the negotiations." Excellent, Hamila! Tegestu thought with grim satisfaction. Keep them in their place.

"My lord Tastis has a condition for the negotiations,"

the herald said. "He feels that, to guarantee the sincerity of the talks, there should be an exchange of hostages."

To keep me from chopping up any more emisaries, Tegestu smiled to himself; Tastis should have thought of that before, instead of being so greedy as to leap at my occupation of Calacas.

"On what level, ban-demmin emissary?" Hamila asked.

"The highest. My lord Tastis is prepared to offer his son, Aptan Tepesta Laches y'Pranoth, and two others."

"Their names?"

The herald gave them. Tegestu recognized them as highly-placed members of important kamlissi in Tastis' coalition, and one was a welldran. And of course, Aptan, the laughing young man of immature tolhostu who had met him at the ford of the West Rallandas. None of them were individuals Tastis would throw away lightly: even if he were inclined to sacrifice his son, which Tegestu doubted, the loss of the other two would alienate two of his most powerful clans.

"My lord Tastis," the herald continues, "intends they should be exchanged for hostages of equal rank and position."

"I will have to speak to my lord Tegestu before I can give an answer," Hamila said.

"Do not concern yourself with us, ban-demmin Hamila," the herald said. "We will be happy to wait."

Tegestu grinned at the herald's irony, then took a pen and wrote HOSTAGES AGREED—DETAILS LATER on a piece of paper, then handed it to one of his Classani. The young woman took it, bowed hastily, and slipped out the back door, presumably where the heralds would not see her. Once outside she would run around the corner, down the corridor, and emerge through a door behind the large screen in the front of the chamber. She would then slow her approach, creep out, and apologetically hand Hamila his instructions, giving all along the illusion that Tegestu was hiding himself behind the large screen at the front of the room.

"I hope, ban-demmini, that you will enjoy your tea," Hamila was saying, "It is bro-demmin Tegestu's special blend."

"The aroma is most pleasant."

Hamila was delaying until his instructions appeared. Tegestu, paying little attention, furrowed his brow and scratched his chin as his mind sped swiftly from one implication to another. The talks between Tastis and the Elva had failed, at least for the present. That put not only Tastis in a bad position, but also Necias, for Necias had lost much demmin—or cimmersan, which seemed to be demmin as the Abessla imperfectly understood it—first from allowing Tegestu to occupy Calacas against his will, secondly by failing to negotiate an end to the war before the arrival of the other Elva forces.

Was Necias as desperate as Tastis? Tegestu wondered suddenly. Would Tegestu be able to move himself into the role he desired most, a broker between Necias and Tastis?

How could he put pressure on Necias? And, if Necias finally cracked on the issue of sovereignty, what could he give the Elva in exchange?

"Ban-demmini," Hamila was saying, "I believe my lord Tegestu will agree on the exchange of hostages. But we must have some time to be able to choose hostages of suitable stature to match your own. I beg your indulgence on the matter."

"I understand," said the herald, "the need for consultation."

"I hope, ban-demmin emissary," Hamila said, "that you will favor me with an understanding of your lord Tastis' proposals for achieving his aims, so that I may have the honor of presenting them to my lord Tegestu as soon as possible."

"My lord Tastis' proposals are simple," the herald said.

"Unification of our two aldrani. An appeal to the Brodaini elsewhere in the Elva to come to our assistance. An effort made to break the seige of Neda-Calacas before autumn."

"The unification of the aldrani would indicate the choice of a new drandor," Hamila said. "Has bro-demmin Tastis reached any decision on his choice for the honor?"

Tegestu, feeling a laugh exploding inside him, tried his best to stifle it. Tears leaked from his eyes. Hamila's question reached, perhaps not tactfully, to the heart of a potential dilemma: who would lead any unified Brodaini, Tastis or Tegestu?

There was a shocked silence from the heralds' spokesman. "That will be a decision of the united aldran," he said finally, his tone flat.

Hamila began questioning the heralds concerning the details of Tastis' offer, the implementation of any unification of the Brodaini forces. Tegestu listened only with half his attention, concentrating meanwhile on his tactics. Necias, he thought, was vulnerable politically: how best to exploit it?

The talks had collapsed, he repeated to himself. Tastis can get no peace with the Elva, not on terms he's willing to accept. Necias will have to resort to military force to make any point, and that will mean uniting the Elva command under his choice of leader, which would be Palastinas. But would the others agree? The ambassadors, he thought, must be going madly from one tent to another, trying to reach a united position.

Except, he thought, for Fiona. Fiona's job of neutral observer was over.

With a start he realized that she could play a part in this, as a neutral observer in the talks. That, he thought gleefully, would serve to put pressure on Necias, letting him know of the existence of negotiations between the Brodaini factions and putting that much more pressure on him to create a peace.

Tegestu snatched up his pen and began writing, frustrated that he couldn't form his letters with the speed of thought. He finished, glanced at the letters again to make certain that they were clear enough for Hamila to read, and then handed the paper to one of the Classani. The boy took it and ducked soundlessly around the corner of the screen.

Tegestu listened for the sounds of his arrival behind the larger screen, his mind in the meantime sliding over his plan. It would work, he thought; but if he thought the better of it in the next day or so he could alter it easily enough, and no longer insist on Fiona's presence as a neutral observer at the negotiations.

It would, he thought, serve as an encouragement to courtesy, to have present a person who could call down lightnings if any rudeness occurred.

And then with a start he realized his opportunity. Perhaps a chance lurked within his first plan that, at first, he hadn't perceived. His mind slipped over it again, probing at the newly-formed idea. Fiona *hated* Tastis and his people, and that hatred could be used. He would check again with Cascan to see if the Igaran ambassador had been attacked in Tastis' Keep—that knowledge could prove important. But it was the hatred that mattered.

There were flaws in the plan, he thought, but they could be worked out. If only he could arrange for the hostages to be quartered near the Long Bridge. . . .

He bent to his desk again, his pen dashing heedlessly over the paper. He heard Hamila's words.

"Beg pardon, ban-demmini. There is another message I must read."

"Please read it, ban-demmin Hamila," the spokesman said. "Pay us no attention."

There was a silence broken only by the crackle of paper as Hamila read the message, then refolded it and put it in his belt. "Ban-demmini," he said. "I beg your pardon once again for the interruption. It was a memorandum concerning the posting of the guard this evening. It will be my duty to supervise.''

"We understand perfectly," said the spokesman agreeably, seeing easily enough through the convenient falsehood.

"It has occurred to me," Hamila said, "that my lord Tegestu may wish, to further guarantee the sincerity of any negotitions between our parties, that the Ambassador Fiona of Igara attend the talks in her capacity of neutral observer, the same capacity in which she attended the other negotiations. And my lord may further wish that she inspect the quarters granted to the hostages would be comfortable.''

"I will have to consult with my lord Tastis on this," the spokesman said. Tegestu listened closely: was there surprise in his voice? If so it could indicate that Tastis was not prepared to reveal the negotiations to Necias.

"I am afraid my lord Tegestu will insist on this," Hamila said. Tegestu returned to his writing.

He finished with a flurry, his heart pounding as he contemplated the beauty of his plan. He would consider it tonight, hoping to fill the gaps in his knowledge. He would, he knew, have to send a messenger to Necias. He must hope that Necias was as desperate for peace as he suspected.

The Classanu girl slipped out, the piece of paper clutched in her hand. Contained in it was a simple condition for the exchange of hostages, that the hostages be held in the city of Neda, rather than in the Brodaini Keep, and that they be held in a place from which they could be seen daily by a spyglass in Calacas, in order to assure Tegestu of their continuing survival and well-being. Tegestu would perform a like courtesy by parading his own hostages on the Calacas walls. It was an innocent enough condition, he thought; there was no reason why Tastis wouldn't grant it.

Yet he held his breath while Hamila announced the demand, and would not expel it until the spokesman, apparently seeing no need for consultation, agreed.

Tegestu smiled. His course, he thought, had just been set.

He would have to review the documents concerning Igaran capabilities, he thought, those prepared in the wake of the incident between the Brodaini patrol and Necias' archers. He would also have to interview each of the surviving members of the patrol personally. One of them, he knew, had seen an arrow strike Fiona squarely between her unarmored shoulders, yet bounce off as if she had been wearing proof. How certain was that witness?

The witness would have to very certain, he knew. So many lives, including Fiona's, would depend on it.

25

"Ambassador Fiona!" Fiona could hear the Gostu voice through the port on the barge's roundhouse. She turned her head to look out the port, squinting against the glare. "Ambassador Fiona, are you there?"

"Some big armored bastard out there," reported Calcas, the barge *Second Cousin's* chief mate, as he stepped into the roundhouse from the deck. "I think that's your name he's yelling."

"It is," said Fiona.

"Damned barbarian." Rubbing his chin. "I wonder what the bastard wants."

Fiona declined to guess. She finished her glass of wine and thanked her hosts, a family of the barge people with whom she'd become friendly. She decided to be cautious, and as she made her way out into the sunlight she pulled her hood over her head and drew it tight. She turned to face the bank.

"I am Fiona," she said.

The Brodainu was a huge man, made larger still by his

massive suit of plate armor. He bowed, the sun winking off his helmet.

"I am Dellila Gartanu Sepestu y'Dantu, ilean Ambassador," he said. "Bro-demmin drandor Tegestu Dellila Doren y'Pranoth has sent me to you as his emissary."

Has he, now? Fiona wondered. She raised her hand to shade her eyes and looked at the near-giant, seeing a battered, square-jawed face scarred by both disease and war, intelligent blue eyes, a red knife-cut crossing the knuckles of a massive hand. She knew she'd heard his name before, but could not recollect where or why.

She felt the *Second Cousin's* gangplank bend beneath her weight as she walked to the shore. Dellila towered over her as he straightened from another bow. There were a handful of arrow-straight Brodaini escort, including a banner-bearer with a scarlet Abessla flag of truce. They were on foot, apparently having left their horses on the river's other bank. In a half-circle about them was a troop of mercenary cavalry, Khemsinla lancers in ornate armor and elaborate ruffled clothing, their beards braided with ribbon to look as fearsome as possible, all watching the intruders carefully. Fiona looked up at Dellila, narrowing her eyes.

"I am listening, ban-demmin," she said. Brodaini manners, always abrupt and arrogant between strangers.

"I am ordered to inform you, ilean Ambassador," Dellila said, "that negotiations will shortly begin between the Brodaini of Calacas and the Brodaini of Neda. Bro-demmin Tegestu hopes that you will be able to attend the negotiations in the same capacity you served in the late talks between the Elva and the Brodaini of Neda."

Fiona felt her heart sink at the words. Tegestu and Tastis in alliance: she had always dreaded the possibility. It was one thing to know that two or three hundred years hence the Brodaini would have been absorbed by the Abessla, or become so like them there would be little or no difference; it was another to be confronted, in the *now*, with the possibility of civil war in every Elva city as the united Brodaini tried to avoid extermination, and warred to exterminate their enemies in turn.

"I shall have to consult my superiors, ban-demmin," she said. "I can give you no immediate answer." But she knew how Tyson would rule: the Igarans were attempting to establish principles of strict neutrality, which meant assisting negotiations between any governmental entity. But, Fiona thought firmly, she wasn't going into those cities without better protection than she currently possessed. Tyson knew how Kira had died: she was certain he'd agree.

"May I ask the ilean Ambassador when she will have her answer?" Dellila asked.

"Tomorrow morning," she said. That would give her time to prepare, to strengthen herself for this meeting with the enemy. She turned to him. "Part of my function in the other negotiations," she said, "was to keep a third copy of any proposals or treaties in my own language, to refer to in case of disagreement between the parties. Will you require my assistance in this fashion?"

"Bro-demmin Tegestu says, respectfully, that you will not be needed in this regard," Dellila said. "We do not have the problem in translation, you see."

"Yes. I understand."

Suddenly Fiona remembered where she'd heard Dellila's name before. He was a hero, she remembered; he'd rallied a few villagers early in the war and exterminated a whole squadron of Tastis' murdering raiders. Now, perhaps, he'd be warring on the same side as the prison scrapings Tastis had taken into his service. What would he think of that, allying with such refuse? She cocked an eye at him, seeing his stolid, scarred, arrogant face . . . damn these people, she thought angrily, they never *smile*.

"Can you present yourself at the White Tower Gate at

noon tomorrow and give us your answer, ilean Ambassador?''
Dellila asked. He had turned to face the half-circle of
mercenaries, the bearded faces with their cruel smiles; his
voice was pitched for Fiona alone. ''If your superiors give
you permission to observe the negotiations,'' he said, ''we
request that you bring clothing and anything else you may
require, as you will have to stay in the city at least one
night.''

She nodded. ''I understand.''

''Have you any questions, ilean Ambassador?'' he asked,
turning to her.

''Yes,'' she said. ''What are the negotiations about?''

She caught a tight smile tugging at the corners of his
mouth. ''I have no idea, ilean Ambassador Fiona,'' he
said. ''They wouldn't tell junior whelkran like myself. I
just obey orders.''

''I see. Well. I'll be at the White Tower Gate tomorrow,
noon, and give you your answer.''

''Thank you, ilean Ambassador.'' Dellila bowed again,
then straightened into an arrogant, iron-spined pose and
paced toward his escort. They closed in behind him as
Dellila walked toward the grim wall of cavalry, refusing to
slow his long strides. The lancers opened a way reluctantly,
then closed behind him like a living gate. They moved off
together at the walk, the lancers keeping their horses on
the heels of the Brodaini party, testing their tolerance, obviously hoping they could provoke them into a fight.

Leaving one figure behind: Campas in his mail shirt,
leading his horse. ''Necias wants to see you,'' he said.
She nodded.

''I'm not surprised.''

She began her walk down the riverbank path to Necias'
barge with Campas, leading his horse by the bridle, walking beside her. He looked at her curiously.

''What did they want?''

"They wanted me to attend some negotiations Tegestu and Tastis are conducting."

Campas blew his cheeks in surprise. "Necias won't be happy," he said. "Will you do it?"

"I have to. I'm supposed to be neutral in this war."

Campas raised his head to look toward where Necias's banners were waving above his barge. "Are Tegestu and Tastis allying against us?" he asked us.

"I don't know. I suppose they're at least talking about it."

He looked at her with slitted eyes. "Can you keep us informed of their discussions?" he asked.

She shook her head. "You know I can't." She saw his troubled frown and reached a hand out to touch his wrist. "I may be in the city for several days. Can you come see me tonight?" she said. "After midnight sometime; I'll have business until then."

"Yes," he said. "I can come."

"Good."

Necias' guards saluted her with their pikes, then escorted her to where he waited on his settee, his fingers drumming on its arm. Campas followed her into the room, not having been told to stay out.

"Ambassador," he said. His smile seemed strained. "Sit down. Have some tea. Wine if you prefer."

Necias seemed shrunken: Fiona knew he'd been under strain in recent weeks, ever since the negotiations with Neda had begun to go sour. There had been too many demands: the Neda-Calacan Government-in-Exile had wanted safety for their kinfolk in the cities, even at the expense of giving Tastis much of what he wanted; the other Elva ambassadors had insisted on a position of no compromise; Handipas had argued for one thing or another, less for reasons of conviction, Fiona suspected, than to feel himself an important part of the proceedings. In the end both sides had been far part; they had presented unreconcilable ultimata to one another and retired to their lines to wait.

To wait for what? Fiona had wondered at the time. For Tastis and Tegestu to be driven farther together, perhaps, by the Elva's inability to agree on policy.

In due course Necias asked her what the Brodainu had wanted, and Fiona, having no reason not to tell him, gave him an exact record of the conversation. Necias seemed surprised.

"They haven't cautioned you concerning secrecy?" he asked.

"No. Maybe they wanted you to know." Necias frowned as he considered that possibility, then nodded.

"That's likely," he said. "They may be trying to put pressure on me." His blunt fingers thumped several times on the arm of his settee.

"They don't realize," he said, speaking more to himself than anyone else, "my hands are tied. The Elva can't agree, and if I make any more proposals without their united backing they can refuse agreement and leave me hanging." He gave a cynical smile. "That's what they've been wanting all along, and I won't let them. I can't move in any direction without their agreement ahead of time."

"I'm sorry, Necias Abeissu," Fiona said.

He looked up at her suddenly, the smile turning sober. "Tegestu is making a mistake if he's thinking of allying with Tastis," he said. "That'll unite the Elva all right, and I won't be able to stop them from butchering every Brodainu they can find. I hope you'll find a way of telling that to Tegestu."

"If you give me a commission to tell him that, I will," Fiona said.

"You can't do it unofficially?"

She smiled. "I will, Abeissu, if I can. But as far as unofficial messages go, I can't make promises."

Necias nodded. "Your word that you'll try is good enough for me, Ambassador."

He rose ponderously from the settee, the stoutly-built furniture creaking under his weight. "Thank you, Ambassador, for your candor," he said. "I'm afraid I have business to occupy me for the rest of the afternoon."

Fiona was quick on her feet. "I understand, Necias Abeissu. I'll see myself out."

He gave her a careful embrace, as if he was afraid she might shatter in his arms; they said their farewells. Fiona returned to the sun, Campas following quietly. He turned to her, his blue eyes solemn.

"If the other Brodaini ally with Tastis, that will destroy him," he said in a quiet voice. "That's how he'll be remembered, the man who let the mad-dog Brodaini into our cities. The Elva might not be broken, but it wouldn't be *his* Elva any more." His eyes returned to the barge. "He knows that. He also knows he's run out of choices. He's got to sit here with his army and take whatever comes. And the rest of the Elva are gloating over it; he knows that, too."

"Come to my tent," Fiona said. "We'll drink a bottle of wine together. After that I'll have to talk to my superiors, and tell them what's just happened." She looked at the horizon, seeing the Brodaini flags dotting the grey walls of the cities. She took a deep breath. "And then I'll have to get ready to ride into the city tomorrow. And I don't want to."

He reached out to take her hand. "Maybe your people will say no," he said.

She shook her head, saying nothing. At least, after midnight, he might provide her a little comfort, something to remember as she journeyed toward the enemy walls of grey stone.

26

Tegestu gazed at the sculpted profile of his wife's face, silhouetted as it was in the pale radiance of the predawn light that glowed through the leaded windows of their bedchamber. He knew he would have to rise shortly: there was much to accomplish today, before the hostages took their walk to captivity across the Neda Long Bridge. The captives, with Tegestu's wife Grendis among them.

The decision had been made coldly. Tastis had offered Aptan, his son, one of his welldrani, and another important member of his coalition of clans. Tegestu, with the limited personnel available, had to make a comparable offer. Besides himself, Tegestu had two members of his family with the army: Grendis and his son Acamantu. Acamantu commanded a mixed brigade and was expendable enough in a purely military sense, but Tegestu wanted to keep him safe: he was part of the new generation, having spent most of his life in exile. He was able to deal with the Abessla on a more familiar basis than were his elders—Acamantu would, Tegestu concluded, be indispensible in the coming years, when existence would depend

on understanding the Abessla and living alongside them in
. . . in whatever new relationship came out of this war.
Tegestu did not wish to sacrifice the future to the ravenous
demands of the present.

Cascan was present, another walldran, but he was head
of the spies, assassins, and secret agents: he simply knew
too much to be risked in enemy hands.

Grendis, Tegestu had concluded, would have to be one
of the hostages. She was both family and a welldran; she
commanded the light cavalry brigade and the mounted
scouts, but the army would shortly be without its horses
and her job could in any case be handled by someone else.

One of the hostages had to be Grendis: she was the only
logical choice.

It had been a heartbreaking decision. For Tegestu's plan
to succeed, it would require, almost certainly, the sacrifice
of all the hostages.

And furthermore the hostages could not be told of their
upcoming sacrifice: they would have to walk willingly to
their deaths, and the most convincing way of walking to
certain death is not to know that death is at the end of the
path.

Tegestu watched as Grendis shifted under the coverlet, a
pleased sigh escaping her lips. At the simple, homely
sight, the sight that as boy, man, and elder he had seen on
the neighboring pillow for fifty years, Tegestu felt his
heart begin to shatter. A few lives, he admonished himself,
and the war could be over, if he had calculated aright. Any
Brodaini was committed, from birth, to sacrifice his life in
the name of his kamliss: there were no exceptions, least of
all from sentiment.

Madness, he thought.

No, not madness. Only logic. We will terminate the
war, and the Brodaini will survive in this land. What
sacrifice would not be worthy of that goal?

Silently he watched her sleep, cherishing the sight, the

curve of her cheekbone, the arch of her throat. . . . It was, perhaps, the last time he would be blessed with the sight. Impulsively he reached out to embrace Grendis and kiss her. She smiled sleepily, her hands reaching out for him, and her eyes opened drowsily, then widened as she saw his intent look.

"Yes?" she said.

He shook his head. "Nothing," he said. She touched his long unbraided hair and smiled.

"I'll be well, my love," she said. "Tastis won't dare harm me. We have both been hostages, at one time or another; this will be no different."

"If someomething goes wrong, today or tomorrow," Tegestu said, "stay with Fiona if you can. She might be able to protect you."

Her eyes narrowed, and he knew he hadn't been able to keep the urgency from his voice. She nodded. "I'll remember," she said.

Tegestu had given her all the warning he dared. He closed his eyes and committed the project to the gods. Let her be safe, he thought fiercely. Let me not be the means of her death.

You have known all along, an inner voice told him, *that this might become a possibility. That you might have to order her to her death. Why have you denied the truth so long?*

He clutched Grendis' body desperately and held her to him. She returned his embrace, her cheek against his. *Remember this,* he commanded himself. *You can never risk forgetting this.*

Long moments passed; Tegestu, at last, forced himself to relinquish her. She kissed him again and smiled. "Shall I ring for our dressers?" she asked.

"Not yet. A little while yet."

She smiled indulgently. "Of course." He took her hand,

and they watched one another in silence. The smile remained on Grendis' face and in her eyes.

The light entering the windows was brightening; Tegestu willed it to halt. What remains to be said? he thought. That you have guarded my back these long years, and that now I must refuse to protect yours? That for reasons of cold policy I must sacrifice you?

Cold policy, he thought: it has ruled our lives, both our meeting and our ending. It is the code we live by, that we all are ready to be sacrificed when policy demands. I have lived my life by that code: the gods help me, I cannot change.

The dawn, resisted hopelessly, came; and the moment of touching was over.

27

Did Kira take this path? Fiona wondered. *Did Kira's heart so thunder with fear as she rode to the gate?*

Nonsense. Kira had not ridden; she had come as Fiona had come to Arrandal, by barge. She swallowed, trying to still the fear that trembled in her limbs, and rode through the herds of Brodaini horses that were grazing outside the moated walls. She carried the Brodaini spear of parley, a short weapon with the haft painted white and the point reversed. Those of Tegestu's men who guarded the horses against a raid, heavy cavalry with their lances at the ready, had apparently been warned about her approach: they gave her stern glances but made no move to interfere.

She was dressed simply in her privy-coat with the hood pulled tight around her face, a pair of trousers and a belted tunic pulled on over it. Clipped to her belt were her recorder, her spindle, and a pistol she had asked Tyson to deliver the previous night. It was more powerful than the needle she had in her wrist; and furthermore a pistol was a weapon she could aim. It was also safe: the holster was attuned to her body and mind, as her privy-coat was tuned, and no one else could draw the weapon. She had ridden out of camp just after nightfall, heading several miles south of the perimeter to a clear area in the middle of a farmer's stubbled, harvested field; there, fully aware of the cloaked scouts that had followed her out of camp in order to make certain she wasn't meeting the Elva's enemies, she'd planted a homing device in the dry, dusty soil, retired a cautious few hundred feet, and waited for the message tube to spit out of the heavens. The tube took only a few moments to cool, then she extracted her pistol and heaved the tube up onto the saddle in front of her. Afterwards, riding back, she'd flung the tube into the flowing Neda. The scouts had made no comment. When she returned, Campas was waiting, crouched by a watchfire outside her tent.

The White Tower Gate loomed before her. She wondered why it was called that: it seemed as grey as the rest of the walls. Perhaps it had once been white, before generations of chimney soot had blackened it. The drawbridge over the moat-canal was down, the fanged portcullis raised. Through it she saw the towering form of Dellila, seated atop a huge dappled horse and surrounded by an escort of bannermen. Fiona raised the spear of parley and urged her horse to a trot.

The hooves drummed on the planking of the bridge, echoing hollowly from the brackish canal, and then the shadow of the tower fell on her and she was inside. She saw a pleased smile on Dellila's scarred face as she reined in.

"Bro-demmin Tegestu will be gratified by your presence," he said. "With your permission, ilean Ambassador, I would like to escort you to where the hostages from Neda will be quartered."

She gave a nod, Dellila turned his horse, and with the escort of bannermen following in behind they began to move off through the cobbled streets.

The buildings were tall and narrow, as they were in Arrandal, and as in Arrandal the city was composed of rings of interlocking canals edged by narrow cobbled paths that were squeezed in between the canals and the peak-roofed buildings of grey stone. There were three rings of inner walls, some showing sign of hasty repair but all as grimly functional as the current outer wall. Many of the bridges had had key parts of them removed, with a draw-bridge built to span the gap; all bridges were guarded. To take such a city by storm, she thought, would be almost an impossibility: an attacker would have to progress by short leaps across canals, under fire from the high buildings that overlooked the battle. No wonder that months ago the Elva forces had settled down to a siege rather than accept the huge casualties that would result in any storming attack.

The civilian inhabitants of the city were going about their business in large numbers, though because many had been evacuated they were not in the thronging thousands as in Arrandal; but their natural liveliness was inhibited by the presence of the cold, armored Brodaini guards that stood glowering at every major intersection, and at the sight of Dellila and his bannermen moving briskly down the towpath they ducked quickly into doorways to let them pass. Fiona, looking up, saw a few white faces peering out of the windows and doorways, almost all of them masks of hatred and fear. They were the pawns of this war and they knew it, and whatever ending was made would not be their own doing.

The party made its way to the Old City, the first Abessla settlement made across the river from Old Neda. Here Fiona was invited to dismount and inspect an old gatehouse that had been converted to the hostages' quarters. She dismounted and went up the narrow, winding stair, desighed to be held easily by any right-handed guard from above, curving in such a way that any right-handed attackers, advancing from below, were unable to swing their weapons without hitting the center post of the stair. Sunlight, reflected by the surface of the canal outside, swam crazily on the tapestries, carpets, and furniture that had been moved in. Blazing fires had been lit in the grates in order to drive out the cold and damp. One vast room had its floor scored by dozens of machicolations, through which defenders in the gatehouse could fling boiling oil and missiles on attackers trying to crash the inner gate below. Guards had been placed at the doors, and from the roof of the gatehouse, overlooked by the firing slits of the towers on the harobr wall, Fiona could see clearly across the outer harbor to the walls of Neda and the flags decorating its Old Citadel.

The hostages, Fiona concluded, would be fairly comfortable, would be able to exercise themselves daily on the roof where they could be seen by their comrades in the Old Citadel, and would have a fair measure of privacy—but they would be vulnerable to Tegestu's people, which presumably was the point. Fiona nodded.

"I'll tell the—the other people what I see," she said, not knowing what to call them. Was Tastis, in the official vocabulary of the Arrandal Broadaini, still the "rebel ardemmin Tastis," or had he become "bro-demmin drandor Tastis" once again?

Dellila seemed pleased. "Good," he said. "Let's move you down to the Long Bridge Gate. Once you've inspected the hostage quarters on the other side, we can get on with the exchange."

They moved down the narrow stairway, and then stepped out into the streets. Dellila took his horse by the bridle, and they walked the short distance to the Long Bridge Gate.

Guards were tripled here, standing ranked on the battlements above. Below was the party of hostages-to-be, the three principle hostages plus twelve escorts, bannerbearers, and servants, all standing calmly in the shade of the gate, with grooms holding their horses.

Tegestu alone was mounted. Fiona saw the old man

sitting bolt upright on his horse, wearing armor but bareheaded, his grey braids coiled around his head and pinned into place. He was standing squarely by the inner gate and Fiona's path took her past him.

She bowed as she came close, and as she rose she realized that Dellila had bowed and retired. Tegestu, it appeared, wished to speak privately with her.

His horse stepped forward a few paces; and then Tegestu twitched its reins and the horse gravely bent its forelegs and head. Fiona realized with surprise that he'd had his horse return her bow, and that Tegestu seemed to be an exceptional horseman. The horse straightened.

"I am gratified, ilean Ambassador, that you have consented to act as an observer," Tegestu said.

"The Igarans are happy to contribute to any negotiations likely to result in *peace*," Fiona said, a standard reply to be sure, but Tegestu's eyes narrowed for a moment as he caught her inflection—were these negotiations truly going to result in peace, or further bloodshed as the Elva erupted in internal war with their own Brodaini?

The horse clopped closer to her. He leaned down and for the first time she saw him up close: an aged man, his skin mottled and sagging, losing the war with gravity and the years; but with eyes that reflected fierce, burning intelligence.

"Ilean Ambassador," he said in a low voice intended only for her. "I hope this will not put you in danger. I can't *guarantee* Tastis won't resort to treachery. I hope—I hope your people have prepared you for any eventuality."

The coarse whisper sent chills flittering down her spine, and she looked up at him in surprise. Had he received a hint of treachery, then? His face was intent, hawklike; there was a hint of steely nervousness in the bunched muscles of the jaw and a throbbing vein in the forehead—he was, she realized, under ferocious pressure, and it was beginning to show.

"I am as prepared as I can be," she said cautiously. "But if you have any intelligence of Tastis' intentions I hope you can tell me."

Tegestu shook his head. "No, nothing," he said. "But Tastis is not—he is not to be trusted, understand? Take good care, Ambassador. The gods go with you."

"Thank you, bro-demmin. I'll keep your words in mind." Nodding reassuringly as she spoke, and trying with all her will to control the fear whipsawing through her—the old fear, weaponed men coming in the night, as they had come for Kira. Tegestu straightened, still looking down at her.

"Are you ready, Ambassador?" he asked.

She nodded. "Yes."

"Some of our heralds will go with you part way." Tegestu looked up and gave a signal: Classani dashed to man tackles that heaved up the massive iron-reinforced bars that held closed the inner gate, and someone in the second storey of the barbican began to work the mechanism that would raise the bar of the outer gate as well, and then lower the drawbridge to open the Neda Long Bridge.

Tegestu looked at her levelly. The vein still throbbed in his temple. "Good luck, ilean Ambassador."

"Thank you, bro-demmin."

She mounted her horse and watched the square of sunlight that was the gate brighten, and wondered whether or not to lower the mask that would give her full facial protection. No, she thought, that would be overcautious, and show them she was afraid, which might in itself invite attack.

The drawbridge thudded into place and she kneed her horse forward, her escort falling into place behind. *Did Kira take this path?* she thought again, and then cleared the thought angrily from her mind. She was protected; the ship was on alert; Tastis could not take her. She knew this; but yet the fear remained.

The Neda Long Bridge was a fantastic construction,

connecting the two cities across the base of the harbor itself; it was a good half-mile long, built of long, high stone arches standing on the bases of ancient pilings. Built along the bridge were arcades and little shops of wood, some of them hanging perilously over the brink—all deserted now, the nesting-place of birds and the eerie haunt of the wind, their bright colors already fading. She heard trumpets blaring behind her to announce her arrival.

She reached the top of the rise, the halfway point, and heard her escort reining in. Ahead she could see the drawbridge coming down on the other side as Tastis' trumpets acknowledged the parley. She raised the white spear in her hand and rode on.

Black shadow covered her as she rode through the gate, and then the high sun illuminated her waiting reception committee as the portcullis began its downward journey behind her. On her right a troop of cavalry stood in ranks, raising their lances in salute as she came through the gate. Across the way from the cavalry was another party of three: a bannerbearer, a herald with a spear of parley, and another man standing in front, dressed in heavy formal armor, his sunbrowned face framed by a coif of chain. He was a sturdily handsome man, at least fifteen years younger than Tegestu, his face split by a broad, white smile. As Fiona reined in, for a brief hallucinatory moment she fancied she saw fangs.

"I am the drandor Tastis," the man said. "Ambassador Fiona, on behalf of our aldran and denorru-constassin, I welcome you to Neda."

Tastis guided her through the hostages' quarters himself, his two assistants trooping behind him. The hostages were to be kept in a large tower that had once formed a section of Old Neda's outer wall. The city had grown up around it, and the tower had fallen into disrepair, but signs of recent work were evident, fires were blazing to drive out the damp. Like the hostage quarters in Calacas, the place was livable enough. The hostages could take their exercise on the tower roof, from which they could be seen by their friends in Calacas; and the roof, like the roof in Calacas, was overlooked by another, enemy-held structure, in this case the Old Citadel.

Tastis himself was smiling and deferent—he was trying consciously, Fiona thought, to be charming: From someone else the charm might have had its effect, but from a man she had hated for months the efforts seemed unreal, ludicrous. *Did Kira like his smile?* she wondered. *Did he smile at her this way, when he viewed her in her cell?*

She kept her face a face of stone, conscious of how her coat's protective hood pressed its oval opening against her skin: She viewed the rooms thoroughly, enjoying Tastis' sense of impatient disapproval as she searched behind tapestries and poked the repaired stonework. She turned to him.

"I think this will be satisfactory," she said. "The lodgings provided in Calacas for your folk are similar to these, perhaps even a little more comfortable." She glanced at the round, narrow room. "Larger, certainly," she said.

"I am pleased to hear it, ilean Ambassador." Again, that pleasant, sincere, un-Brodaini smile. Fiona was suddenly aware of the weight of the pistol at her hip. *One shot and I end the war,* she thought. *Who would know these three hadn't attacked me?*

No: the thought was poison. Interference of that sort, so soon after their appearance, would make impossible any more work by the Igarans. She had already jeopardized their position with her response to the archers' riot, rousing suspicions that would not easily be put to rest. A murder, even of a thoroughly deserving individual, would wreck everything she was trying to achieve.

"Shall we arrange for the transfer then, bro-demmin?" she asked.

Tastis nodded. "Certainly." He led her down the internal stairway of the tower, then out to where their horses waited by the outer canal. Fiona glanced down the canal and was surprised to see town militia guarding a bridge, until she remembered that Tastis' ruling coalition, his denorru-constassin, was composed in part of representatives from the town, and that townsmen as well as Brodaini and mercenaries had formed a part of Tastis' army at the Rallandas.

She mounted her horse and turned its head toward the Long Bridge Gate. The cavalry squadrons waited, still drawn up in their motionless lines, and as they rode up Tastis gave a signal and the double gates began to open. Fiona simply walked her horse to the inner gate and waited for it to swing clear.

There were footsteps by her side and she looked down to see Tastis standing by her stirrup, followed by a Classanu with a bundle.

"Ilean Ambassador Fiona," he said, "I wish to give you, as an Igaran ambassador, the personal possessions of Ambassador Kira. We have had them for some time, but did not know where to deliver them." He looked up at her, his face solemn. "We regret the misunderstanding that led to her death, Ambassador. We should like to petition your people to have another ambassador in residence."

Rage, blazing rage, flashed through her at his words; but her speech, when it came, was ice cold. "It was no misunderstanding that led to her death, bro-demmin Tastis," she said, glaring into his reassuring eyes. "No misunderstanding at all, nothing but your own policy."

Tastis seemed scarcely to blink at her intensity. "I assure you, it was a misunderstanding," he said blandly. "Communication was difficult—she did not understand our intent."

"Kidnapping, prison cells, and threats of torture are

difficult to misunderstand, bro-demmin,'' she said. ''The only misunderstanding was yours. You failed to understand our talents—we were talking to her the entire time, you see.'' Tastis seemed to absorb this without reaction— did he believe her? she wondered. It scarcely mattered. The sound of the drawbridge roaring downward filled the small arched tunnel beneath the gatehouse, and she raised her voice to compensate.

''As for your request for another emissary, I will relay it to my superiors,'' she said. ''I doubt they will accept—not as long as conditions remain as they are. They'll have no wish to share a siege with you, drandor. And even then, I think they'll have to insist on certain guarantees.''

Tastis' eyes had half-closed, as if to conceal the calculations behind them. Go ahead, she dared him mentally, strike at me—and then I'll have the pleasure of blowing your gate down on your head. But Tastis did nothing; he only stepped back to allow the Classanu to come forward with the bundle.

She plucked it from his hands as the drawbridge thudded into place, and then she jabbed her horse with her knees and rode into the tunnel, then out onto the bridge. She heard trumpets blaring behind her again, to be answered from the far side.

Halfway across the bridge Fiona brought her horse to a halt. She let out her breath slowly, hoping her tension, her anger, would ebb with it. She had escaped Neda, at least for the present. She would have to return, in less than an hour, with the hostages, and stay with them through tomorrow noon; and after that she'd be visiting the hostages regularly, assuring each side their people were being treated well.

She would be trotting across the Long Bridge regularly, she thought. She had better get used to it.

The bundle balanced on her saddle was wrapped in purple cloth, the Brodaini color of mourning. She touched it, feeling its silken texture, trying to detect any resonances of Kira. She could find none, and she had no time to open it.

The drawbridge ahead of her was coming down again. she reached for the spindle on her belt and transmitted a brief message, through the more powerful transmitter in her trunk, to the ship, telling them she was safe, that she would report again after delivering the hostages. As they had agreed.

She took a deep breath and urged her horse forward. It was time to be on her way.

28

Tegestu watched Necias' dark and startled eyes. "I must have your answer tonight, Abeissu Necias," he said. "Delay would not be in our interests."

Necias' fingers drummed on the arm of his settee as he listened to simultaneous translations from Campas and the Classanu scribe that Tegestu had brought with him. His eyes narrowed. "It's difficult, very difficult," he said, and then his speech faltered.

Tegestu, cloaked and hooded, had come to Necias after midnight in a small six-oared messenger craft, slipping out of Calacas' water gate with a murmur of the password. There had been no challenge as they stroked with muffled oars to the Elva camp, no challenge at all until after he and his interpreter had scrambled up the bank and walked to Necias' barge, where the interpreter had called for the captain of the guard.

"To see the Abessu-Denorru. Something to his advantage." Tegestu, hooded still, turned away from the guards' inquiring eyes.

Little Necias had been roused at the appearance of

Brodaini and had come clattering up the gangplank with a lantern and a pair of hulking, armored men with two-handed swords. "For you only, cenors-stannan," the interpreter had said, gesturing for Little Necias to come up the bank. The big man carefully obeyed, raising the lantern to meet Tegestu's frowning face, and then gasped an oath.

"We must see the Abessu-Denorru," Tegestu said. "No one but you and he must see us. A matter of urgency."

Tegestu and the Classanu were brought into the dark reception room, clanking guards posted at the doors. A lantern was lit. And then Necias, draped in a vast dressing gown that did not entirely muffle the delicate rattling of the knee-length coat of chain he wore under it, came warily into the room. His shadow bulked huge on the panelled wall, but his mouth seemed shrunken: Tegestu realized he hadn't put in his front teeth. Tegestu, making certain they were alone, pulled back his hood.

"I bring my interpreter along to make certain we do not misunderstand," he had said. "I think we can end the war, favorably for us both."

That had been an hour before. Necias had listened quietly, with a few of the nervous gestures, the rubbing of his jowls, tapping of fingers, twisting of rings, to which he was prone. And then, uncomfortably, he had raised objections. Tegestu had, he thought, dealt with them all.

"I must have an answer now, Necias Abeissu," Tegestu said.

Necias shook his head, the move amplified in grotesque shadow on the barge's beamed deckhead, then turned his head away, his eyes closed. "More time," he muttered.

"Think, Abeissu," Tegestu said. "Think until dawn, if you must. But not beyond."

And so they sat in silence, Tegestu staring intently at Necias as Necias stared into himself. The Classanu, practiced at the art of not existing when he was not wanted, sat on his heels and waited. Tegestu listened abstractedly to the sound of the river as it lapped at the barge, the faint creaking of its timbers, the sound of his own breathing. It was nearing dawn.

Necias, his eyes still closed, raised a finger. Tegestu felt his pulse leap into his throat at the gesture.

"Yes," Necias said quietly. Just the single word.

"I have the documents," Tegestu said. "In both our languages. I have already signed. It needs only your seal. You must sign as chairman of the Elva, not as Abessu-Denorru of Arrandal."

Necias brought the lantern to his side and read the papers carefully, his eyes moving slowly down the lines. It did not take long: the documents were brief. "I'll get my seal," he murmured, and returned with a pen and ink.

He signed and sealed, and handed the copies back to Tegestu.

"Remember, Abeissu," Tegestu said. "Have your forces in place by noon, outside the Old Cart Road Gate. Be there yourself, ready to send them in."

Necias gnawed worriedly on a hangnail, and nodded. "Yes," he said. "I'll announce a parade or a review." He lowered his voice, looking abstractedly at the hangnail. "Can't get too close," he murmured, "it might alarm them. The distance will call for careful judgment."

"Our forces must not fight each other," Tegestu said. "That could be a catastrophe. Let them know the passwords. The challenge will be, *The Elva,* the reply, *Victory.* They are words my people can say without much trouble."

"Elva. Victory. Very well," Necias muttered "I'll announce a change in passwords at noon. Good." He looked up, and Tegestu saw his expression had changed, his eyes full of lively curiosity and a kind of tigerish intensity. He had committed himself, and now seemed eager for the battles that would come.

Slowly, holding Necias' gaze, Tegestu lowered himself to one knee. "Canlan," he said.

Necias, knowing this to be the final time, looked down at him solemnly and nodded as if confirming something to himself. "Bro-demmin drandor Tegestu," he said. "Please rise. You are no longer mine to command."

Tegestu rose with difficulty, Necias assisting him at the end, and then threw his hood over his face again. He made his way out of the barge, then down the bank to the waiting boat. "The city," he said.

As he sped past Necias' barge he saw the vast figure of the Abeissu brooding on the foredeck, looking down at the water—and then Necias glanced up and saw him, their eyes crossing once again.

Wordlessly, they sped out of one another's sight. Necias had released the Brodaini from their oath of allegiance to Arrandal, and confirmed another relationship. They were equals now, and allies.

And fellow conspirators, whose conspiracy would hatch at noon in blood.

The boat sped swiftly down the river, entered a canal, moved through the water gate and to the Deissu's palace that Tegestu had made his headquarters. "Call Dellila and Cascan to me, and tell the staff they will meet at dawn," he ordered, throwing off his cloak. "Bring tea to me now, and breakfast in an hour."

Dellila, who had charge of the hostage guard, came stamping in full armor just seconds before Cascan arrived hastily lacing up his coat of light chain and blinking sleep from his eyes.

"Ban-demmin Dellila," Tegestu ordered. "You will call the guard together quietly at dawn. When the hostages are brought their breakfast, you will enter with the guard and kill them."

"Bro-demmin?" Dellila said in astonishment; and Cascan cried out in surprise. Tegestu fixed them with a furious stare.

"Ban-demmini," he spat, "the hostages are traitors. They deserve death, and all shall die."

Dellila swallowed hard. "Aye, bro-demmin Tegestu," he said.

"Tell your people not to strike for the face. We want them all recognizable. Afterwards, strip their bodies, wash them, and report to me."

"Aye, bro-demmin." Dellila bowed.

"Questions? Nay? You are dismissed."

The warrior bowed and turned. Cascan was still staring. "Bro-demmin, are you certain?" he asked. "Our own people—"

"Their fate is in the hands of the gods, ban-demmin," Tegestu said, and closed his eyes. *Grendis, forgive me!* he cried in his heart—and then he opened his eyes and gave the orders that would, he hoped, make good the sacrifice.

29

Alone in the darkness, Fiona woke with shrilling nerves, her lips parted and ready to cry out—or had she cried already? Gasping for breath, her pulse thudding in her ears, she listened carefully, but detected no sign that any of the hostages had heard her.

No, then, she hadn't cried out. She swung her legs out of bed, feeling an instant of vertigo as she came upright, then put her head in her hands, gulping air. She couldn't remember the dream that had brought her awake; but there was no need. She knew well enough what it was.

The vertigo faded, and she looked up at the doorway to her tiny room, one identical to the room given all the hostages, made by the assembly of small, portable screens, furnished barely, with a bed, press, and an overtasteful arrangement of flowers. Lantern-light glimmered faintly through the cracks of her door, and from not far away she heard the tread of one of the sentries.

Her head throbbed with languid, slow-motion pain. There would be no more sleep, she knew. Not in Tastis' city.

She stood up and thought the color of her privy-coat

darker, to near-black. She would wear it every moment she was among Brodaini—that was one of Tyson's orders, and one she agreed with wholeheartedly. She threw her surcoat over it, donned her belt, then took the pistol from under her pillow and clipped it to the belt. Quietly, so as not to disturb her neighbors, she slipped from her room.

The common room was to the right, and there Fiona nodded tersely to the Brodaini on watch—there were three at all times, one at each giant, heavily-barred door, another on the roof. The room was bare and clean, still well lit even at night; she passed through it quietly and walked up the winding stair to the roof.

A hot fitful wind struck her as she opened the door: the heavy stone had kept the tower's rooms cool, even here in high summer, and she gasped with the force of the heat. She could feel sweat beginning to prickle her scalp. She returned the sentry's challenge, then stepped out onto the warm flags, relieved, even if she was hot, to be out of the confining stone of the tower and under the canopy of the sky.

The southern winds had brought high scudding clouds with them, and the bright nonmoving light that was the Igaran starship was obscured. Deprived of the comfort of its sight, Fiona walked quietly to the rampart, seeing the black bulk of the Old Citadel, Tastis' threat to the hostages, rising above the tower, only a hundred yards away. She pulled herself into a crenellation, drawing up her legs and planting her back firmly against the cool stone. Then she tilted her head back to watch the stars. Unreachably high, the starship was momentarily revealed by the streaming clouds, and Fiona, unreasonably, was comforted. Her face licked by the wind, she closed her eyes.

When she woke it was past dawn. The lookout had been changed, she realized, but she hadn't heard it. The hot blast from the south still gusted through the battlements, and the entire sky was roofed by high, grey cloud. She stretched her legs out, blood returning to the cramped muscles, and then went down for breakfast.

At midmorning, in what little privacy her quarters provided, she called in a brief report to Tyson, informing him, as she put it, of her continued existence; and told him more would come later, after she'd returned to 'Calacas. Then, quietly so as not to disturb the sleep of the night guards, she asked to speak to Grendis. The Brodaini chieftain seemed pleased to have something to do: Fiona asked about her life, her ancestors, the way she had lived in Connu Keep before Pranoth had been forced into exile. She found Grendis was a soft-spoken woman, thoughtful and grave; she spoke plainly about the life she had led, the children lost to accident or war, the homes she had been forced to abandon—there was no trace of self-pity in her tone, just a dignified acceptance of her life and its turbulence. Fiona found herself admiring Grendis considerably.

And then it was noon, and time for the hostages to parade themselves on the roof, under the spyglasses of their kin in Calacas. Fiona followed Grendis up the roof, the Brodaini in their armor tramping after, followed by the Classani with their umbrellas to keep between the Brodaini and the sun.

Fiona gasped at the furnace-blast of heat from the flagstones, then stood apart from the others as Grendis was handed her long glass and began viewing the battlements. In an hour or so, when the escort came, Fiona would leave the tower and cross the bridge to Calacas, away from Tastis' city. The nightmare, for the present at least, would be over, and she would have survived. She would be visiting the hostages regularly from now on, but she would never again have to spend a night in the enemy city.

"Aiau!" Fiona looked sharply up at Grendis' startled cry, and then watched in alarm as the expression on Grendis' face turned from surprise to horror. Grendis dropped the glass and turned to her party, visibly mastering her shock in order to speak. Her voice was soft, but its tone was urgent and undeniable.

"Ban-demmini, we must leave the roof," she said. "Gather our people, and guard the doors. Capiscu, fetch your rope. We must break out of the city, and quickly."

Fiona stared at her for an instant; and then a sudden blare of trumpets from the Old Citadel spurred her limbs and she leaped for the stairway along with the rest. Tastis, she thought as her pulse began to beat about her ears, he's given the order to kill us. She pulled her hood up over her head, then slid the facemask down.

"Bro-demmin!" A voice from below, where a guard stood at the base of the stair. "The court is filling with guards!"

Fiona's heart sank. Tastis' people were moving too fast. Grendis hesitated only a second. "Make certain your door is barred, then join us," she called, then ducked into the common room, now filled with Classani strapping on their armor and snatching up their weapons. Grendis swiftly counted heads, found all present, then gave her orders.

"We'll have to try to move along the battlements toward the Old City gatehouse," she said. Her voice, amazingly, was still calm, speaking in an ordinary tone of voice but with compelling urgency. "We could be under fire from the Citadel, and we'll have to move quickly to keep the men in the gatehouse from shutting us out. If we can't get through the gatehouse we'll lower ourselves down Capiscu's rope on the opposite side of the wall, then fight our way to the Long Bridge Gatehouse. Capiscu and Sethaltin have the lead." She raised her arms swiftly, a brief and hurried blessing. "Go, cousins!" she called, and her people were in sudden motion.

A door from this second storey of the tower led to the old city wall, and from its battlements to the big gatehouse. From there, the hostages could descend to ground level, cross a canal/moat and two blocks of tenements, and then arrive at the Long Bridge Gate.

Capiscu and Sethaltin, two young, heavily armored men with rhomphaia, ran down the passage between the screened-in sleeping area, slamming gauntleted hands on the iron bolts in the door, sending them shrieking back into place. The metal-bound bar was flung aside, and then one of the Brodaini burst the door open at a run, moving with surprising speed down the battlement toward the citadel gatehouse. The rest followed: Fiona tried to stay in the middle with Grendis, thinking her coat to a stone-grey color to blend in with the wall.

The door to the second level of the gatehouse slammed in Sethaltin's face, and his rhomphaia bit at the timbers. The courtyard below was filled with milling soldiery, responding to the cry of trumpets; and then from the warriors throats came an ominous, dreadful moan as they saw the hostages above them. Fiona glanced left and right: they were trapped here on the inner wall. Arrows began whistling down from the keep, thudding into the shields the Classani held high to protect their lords. *Too late,* Fiona thought with flashing anger. *Too late.* In another few seconds those soldiers would realize the hostages' intentions and start to pour up into the gatehouse, making it impossible for the hostages to fight their way through even if they battered down the door. Others would smash their way up into the tower, and then the hostages would be cut into fragments beneath an advancing wall of steel. Her nightmare come to terrifying life.

Grendis must have realized the same thing, for she began to give swift orders for Capiscu to ready his rope so they could descend into the clear, on the other side of the wall. A Classanu lurched to the flags, a long arrow slicing into his knee as deep as the cock feather. More arrows began to come down from the gatehouse battlements, a crossfire. Fiona heard a muttered

Brodaini curse. *Too late,* she thought, and came to the inevitable decision.

"Stand back!" she shouted, her larynx burning with the force of her cry; and she drew her pistol. She shouldered her way through the milling hostages, hearing the arrows smacking solidly into the shields, trying to get a clear shot. At last she was at the front of the narrow line, seeing Capiscu, nonchalantly disregarding an arrow jutting from his shoulder, looping his line around a merlon, dropping the length to the ground below. Too slow, she thought. If we go down that way we'll be cut up one by one.

Sethaltin was still smashing at the door, hoping to convince the enemy they were still interested in making their escape that way. There was a Classanu trying frantic-eyed to shield both her and Capiscu, and she pushed him away. "Stand back!" Fiona shouted, and when Sethaltin didn't pay any attention she seized him by the collar and dragged him back, hearing him snarl. "Shield your eyes!" she commanded, feeling an arrow snap madly off her hood, and then she pointed the pistol at the door and fired.

The door was blown apart with the roar of lightnings, and before the echo died away Fiona was in motion, leaping into the dark gatehouse, stumbling over a blasted figure in blackened, half-molten armor. She looked left and right, seeing the capstan that controlled the drawbridge, its guards sprawled in stunned confusion: she fired, tearing the capstan apart, seeing the long cables slacken. No one had yet made a move to raise the drawbridge: now it was impossible.

The hostages were filling the door behind her; Fiona saw a stair to her left and ran for it, spiralling downward, her pistol outthrust. The forces in the courtyard seemed not to have realized just yet what had happened; as Fiona emerged from the stairway their eyes, blinking with the aftereffects of the flash, were still directed toward the battlements. She faced the soldiers, knowing she would have to keep them back somehow; she couldn't let them

get near her, where they could pin her down by sheer
numbers. The lead hostages reached the bottom of the
stair, behind her, and began to pelt away over the bridge.
There was a sudden snarl from the soldiers; their eyes
lowered; there was a clash as their arms were raised.
Again, they gave a unanimous, terrible moan, composed
of a hundred separate elements all giving the alarm at
once, that almost froze Fiona in place; and then they began
to dash forward.

Fiona raised her pistol. She could feel her lips curling
back in a death's head angry grin and felt a sudden flood
of angry joy, knowing Kira would have her revenge: she
burned the first rank down, hearing shrieks and wails and
claps of thunder, flagstones torn upward to clang against
shields and armor. She thought it would have discouraged
the rest; but these were Brodaini whose instincts, when
threatened, were to attack, and they kept coming, a wall of
armored figures. no one of them was a threat to her; but all
together they could knock her flat and pin her down by weight
of numbers, and then they could get her coat open and kill
her as they pleased. Fiona's madness turned to horror as she
realized what was happening; there could be no joy in this
insanity. She shrieked at them to run and save themselves,
but still they came on: Fiona fired until the courtyard was a
mass of blackened corpses and upflung flagstones, until the
surviving Brodaini were deafened and confused and running,
or praying or staggering in lunatic circles—and then, as the
last of the hostages came running from the stair behind
her, she followed them, dashing into the sunlight.

Arrows were hissing down on their backs from the
gatehouse and she could see the Classani were carrying at
least four wounded hostages, and that several others were
limping or had arrows sticking out of their armor. The
hostages were moving with painful slowness, their leaders
flashing weapons at a threatening, fleeing population. Fiona
ran to the head of the column, where Capiscu and one of

the Classani were dealing with a militiaman who had, bravely but foolishly, tried to impede their way. An arrow sped down between them, striking sparks from the cobbles. Fiona ran on, the streets clearing ahead of her.

She spun around a corner to find the Long Bridge Gate looming ahead, its battlements crowded with black, busy firures trying to determine the origin of the alarms ringing out from the citadel. The inner doors were securely shut. Above, on the battlements, war engines stood massively against the sky—they were dangerous for Fiona; her coat could not protect her against a big enough stone, or a giant arrow. Behind her she heard panting as Capiscu ran on, burdened by his armor and wounds. She raised her pistol and fired.

It took several shots to blow down the huge inner gate, militia, Brodaini, and the civilian population scattering before her fires. The hostages halted behind her, gazing in awe at the lancing thunders, the ruination of the massive gate. Fiona saw the siege engines moving on their rumbling pivots, coming to bear on her: she blew them to splinters. And then she was running, her panting breaths echoing in her closed hood, and she heard the hostages following.

She blew the outer gate off its hinges, ignoring the arrow that whistled down from the machicolations above, and then aimed at the massive iron staples that held the drawbridge cables. Two high-power blasts and they were gone, the drawbridge crashing down with a noise that rivalled her weapon's; and then she was running across, arrows whipping down around her, with her feet on the solid stone of the Neda Long Bridge.

After two hundred yards she turned to make certain the siege engines on the gatehouse had been thoroughly wrecked, and she saw the hostages scattered out behind her, moving with agonizing slowness as they bore their wounded away from the enemy city. The mad flight for safety was over: now they were conserving their strength, hoping to last long enough to cross the bridge. Capiscu was still in the lead, half a dozen arrows jabbing from his brigandine—at least one had got through, penetrating to the hamstring: he was limping badly. Triumph filled her as she saw them. It hadn't been her task to rescue them—she had done it almost by accident, while rescuing herself—but she was glad to have brought them out, fellow victims of Tastis' treachery.

She holstered her pistol and walked back, taking Capiscu's arm over her shoulder, helping him keep moving. Two Classani, bearing a burden, rushed past her, and she saw with a shock that it was Grendis, lying white-faced in their arms with a feathered shaft pinning her side, her armor penetrated. She heard Capiscu cry out as his leg gave way altogether: she bore his shocking weight until a Classanu came up on his other side, and they carried him away.

There was a clattering sound ahead, and dully she recognized the sound of the Calacas drawbridge coming down— and then there was the thunder of hooves on the bridge, and she looked up to see a moving wall of horsemen advancing. Rescuers, she thought at first, and then she saw the glitter of their lance points and knew they wouldn't stop.

"Off the road!" she called, surprised at the weakness of her voice, and she and the Classanu bore Capiscu into the shelter of one of the stalls that clung to the flanks of the bridge. Grendis was already there, her Classani bent over her, holding her head as she vomited blood onto the dusty planks. Careful of his injuries, Fiona and the Classanu laid Capiscu down, awkwardly due to the jutting arrows, and then Fiona turned toward the roadway again, and watched Tegestu's army come.

She thought she recognized Dellila and his huge horse in the lead, but he was encased entirely in steel and she could not be certain. The lancers thundered past, ignoring the ineffectural arrow fire that dribbled out of the gatehouse, and rode without stopping across the Neda bridge and into the city. They were followed by other horsemen, heavy and light and mounted archers, and then there came others, footsoldiers bearing their sword-bladed spears on high. Tegestu's entire army seemed to be on the move.

"Aiau, cousins," Grendis said, through her bubbling blood and pain. "Our master is wise. We have come out, and the city is ours."

And Fiona, far too late, realized how she had been used.

Fury struck her, her coat blackening with her thoughts, and blindly, deaf to the call of one of the Classani behind her, she stalked out into moving mass of purposeful soldiers, keeping on the edge of their column as she fought her way through them, moving always toward Calacas. She would have used her pistol if necessary, but in spite of the soldiers' hurry and the shouts of their officers, they gave way in surprise before her angry black-faced figure with its featureless mask, and those who didn't give way she easily enough shouldered aside. The column was slowing now, as if it had encountered resistance somewhere; and she could hear the clash of arms from the gate.

At last she jostled her way to the drawbridge, and fought her way across it, calling out angry curses to the soldiers who impeded her. On her way up the ramparts, she caught a glimpse through a narrow view-slit of an inner gatehouse, seeing there the butchered bodies of the hostages from Neda, the hostages Tegestu had killed to start the slaughter.

The attack in the citadel had not been treachery on the part of Tastis—it had come in answer to Tegestu's display of the dead hostages from their battlements, the naked bodies all hanging from the crenellations, easily recognizable with a long glass. Tegestu had anticipated Fiona's being embroiled in the fight, and of having to use her offworld weaponry to smash her way out.

And to smash the deafenses on which Tastis' city

depended. Neda's gates were in ruins, its drawbridge down, and Tegestu's people were pouring into the city.

A lithe light-absorbing form, the lunacy of death possessing her, she came up to the roof of the gatehouse, seeing Tegestu standing calmly at the battlements, his helmet tilted back on his head. There was a stir around him, his guards closing in; but he turned his head and saw her, then ordered them back, facing her, his arms lowered.

"If you intend to kill me, ilean, I make no objection," he said, his voice calm, accepting. "But I would like to see my wife first, if she still lives."

Fiona raised her pistol, then hesitated.

30

Fiona's clothes, her featureless mask, were the color of night, of death. Tegestu, accepting the need for his own death, stood with arms outstretched, facing the alien woman's weapon. As soon as he'd seen Fiona moving with angry purpose along the bridge, among the long column of soldiers, he had known the woman would take revenge, and he had prepared himself. His mind was at peace, yearning for vail; for the end. . . . He hoped only to see Grendis first; but it seemed that was not to be.

Tegestu stood, his arms outstretched, and waited.

The weapon, held at the end of a shadow arm, fell. Fiona's voice came clearly through her mask.

"Grendis is wounded badly," she said. "An arrow through a lung. She is on the bridge, and is being tended by her people."

A lung . . . Tegestu remembered the assassin's arrow his own lung had taken years ago, the way Grendis had nursed him through the pain and lunatic fever. He would repay her now, with all the time Fiona allowed him before her inevitable revenge. Grendis was alive: a little flame of hope kindled in Tegestu's breast. Slowly, deeply, he bowed to his death. "Thank you, ilean," Tegestu said, and gave orders for a surgeon and assistants to make their way out along the bridge to tend his wife and the other wounded hostages. And, since his death was not yet to come, he returned to his business.

Black, poised, unmoving, Fiona stood behind him at the tower entrance, watching him as he received his reports. At one point she unclipped a small object from her belt, held it to her mouth, and spoke into it in her own language—perhaps a fetish to which she was praying, he thought. His flags were already flying above the Long Bridge Gate, and the column of soldiers was still pushing into the city, though it was moving slowly. It was some hours before he received a clear notion of what was happening behind the enemy walls.

The first column of cavalry, led by Dellila, had not stopped at the gate: their orders had been to drive at the gallop for the Old Cart Road Gate, stopping for nothing. Once there, they were to seize the gate, open it, lower the bridge, and hold to the death against the counterattack that would inevitably come from the Brodaini Quarter built nearby.

Dellila had succeeded: he'd seized the gate from Tastis' people, who had thought them friendly reinforcements until it was too late. The counter attacks had come and in overwhelming numbers, but Dellila had beaten them off at the cost of half his men and, in the end, his own life. The last counterattack had been broken by Necias' mercenaries, galloping over the bridge and into the enemy city. Their route was hazardous, for the Old Cart Road was under the walls of the new-built Brodaini Quarter, but Necias and Palastinas kept their people moving in all day, running past with their shields raised high, not stopping despite the chaos and bloody ruin caused by Tastis' archers and engines.

There had been another group of cavalry following Dellila, and these had also had their orders: they were to seize every canal drawbridge they could, wrecking the mechanism that would raise the bridges, and then hold the bridges for as long as possible. Many drawbridges were dropped permanently, but few of the cavalry held them for long after Tastis' reinforcements began flooding the streets.

The rest of the battle was a mad dance of streetfighting and ambush, but the allies' weight of numbers began to tell. Tastis' Neda militia, for the most part, simply went home in hopes of protecting their families, and many of his mercenaries, concluding the war lost, forted up somewhere and began making offers of surrender with honor, which would allow them to march out with their weapons and find employment elsewhere, These were offers their enemies were swift to accept. Some Elva captain got a water-gate open and Necias began moving his people in by barge, and in the end that broke the enemy: they could hold the bridges, perhaps, but once the bargemen arrived they could create temporary bridges to span any gap of water and outflank any defense. By the end of the day Tastis' forces still held the Old Citadel and the Brodaini Quarter, but there was no effective resistance in the rest of the town.

Tegestu had won.

That news came late, however, and found him no longer in the gatehouse. The column of soldiery on the bridge had, at last, passed into Neda, and the hostages been brought back. Tegestu saw Grendis on a litter, surrounded by surgeons and guards; and he turned to Fiona and bowed. "My wife is coming," he said. "By your leave, ilean, I would see her."

Fiona, black-visaged, nodded and stood aside; Tegestu came down the tower stair and met Grendis at the gate.

Grendis was pale, her flesh waxy and the lines of her face deepened, but her eyes were open, and he saw a smile of recognition tug at the corners of her mouth as he looked down at her. He reached down to the litter and took her hand, and walked with the litter-bearers to his palace, and then to her chambers. His death followed on silent feet.

Grendis seemed not to feel any pain as she was moved from her litter to her bed; the surgeons had probably given her a narcotic. They should showed him the arrow, its long, narrow steel point forged to pierce armor. "One lung is pierced, bro-demmin," one said. "We think it has collapsed; she is breathing with the other only, and there is no air coming through the wound. There was hemorrhage at the beginning, but it ceased." The Classanu surgeon seemed strained and apprehensive: no doubt he knew that surgeons had in the past been executed for losing patients as important as Grendis. Steeling himself, he spoke on.

"It is possible she may recover, bro-demmin" he said. "But I would not hold out hope for a woman her age—if she were younger there would be a chance. My apologies, bro-demmin Tegestu."

He gazed at the Classanu levelly. "Do what you can, ilean surgeon," he said, and then walked to the bed.

Her eyes flickered as he touched her hand. A drowsy smile came across her face, and she tried to speak. Her words came as dry whispers, and he leaned close in order to hear.

"Bro-demmin," she said, her faint voice a twig dragging in the dust. "I hope we have done our duty."

Tears sprang to his eyes. He clutched her hand. "You

have given us the keys to Neda,'' he said, speaking in her ear. ''We have won the war. Aye, bro-demmin, you have done well.''

Grendis smiled; he felt her fingers squeeze his hand. And then she closed her eyes.

Somehow he knew that she would not open them again. He bent low to kiss her cheek, and let his heart crack.

31

Bitter anger spinning in her mind, Fiona watched as Tegestu bent over the quietly breathing form. Grendis was dying, Fiona thought, in the style in which she lived; quietly and with fine dignity. Tired, her legs aching from the tension with which she'd stood, Fiona leaned against the doorframe and holstered her pistol. She could not kill Tegestu now. At this instant he did not seem a bloodthirsty, cunning warlord who had thrown her to his enemies: now he was an old grieving man, bent and without majesty; he was punishing himself for his treacheries, and there was no need for her to do it. She breathed a quiet sigh. *You have your life, Tegestu,* she thought. *For her sake, not your own.*

A soft-voiced Classanu entered, an elderly man who wore his fine armor and his Pranoth blazon proudly. "Caltias Campas is here, bro-demmin Tegestu," he said. "He bears a message from the Abeissu Necias."

Tegestu gave at first no sign that he had heard; but then he slowly straightened, turned to the Classanu, and gravely nodded. Campas, in dusty riding boots, entered. His eyes flicked left and right, halting at Fiona for a second; and then he stepped forward and bowed.

"I beg your pardon, bro-demmin, for this intrusion," he said, speaking fluently in Gostu. "Necias asked me to tell you that most of the city is ours, and to give you his supreme thanks for seeing this way to victory." He gave a nervous glance toward Fiona and then continued. "He asked me to assure you that our surgeons are looking after your wounded. He will be presenting our treaty between the Elva and your people to the ambassadors later this evening. He wonders if it will be possible for you to attend."

Tegestu slowly shook his head. "I cannot come, ilean Campas. But I will send a representative."

Campas bowed. "I understand. Please allow me to convey my sorrow, and the sorrow of Abeissu Necias."

"I thank you, ilean Campas," Tegestu said; and he turned away. The inverview was at an end.

Campas bowed again, deeply, and withdrew. Fiona looked at the scene again, the old man bent over the dying woman, and then turned and followed the poet from the room. The curtain rustled shut behind her; he led her out of view of the guards and then turned to take her in his arms.

"Gods, I'm glad you're safe!" he breathed. "Aiee, I almost went mad with fear for you!"

She leaned back to tear the mask from her face, breathing in his scent, the smell of exercise, dust, his body. Numbly, she shook her head.

"I was never in great danger," she said. "He tried to warn me, that last minute before the gate . . . he put me on my guard."

"I didn't know what he'd done till this afternoon. Till the bridge came down and Necias sent in his troops. Gods! What a plan!" He touched her neck, her cheek.

"He used me," Fiona said, coldly accusing herself, her willing gullibility. "He used me, and his wife, and the others—but his plan hinged on manipulating me, and he knew just how to do it. And I let him.'' She broke from his embrace and banged a wall with her fist; the material of her glove cushioned her blow, preventing the sharp knowledge of pain she desired to inflict on herself, punishment for her stupidity.

"I'm finished here," she said bitterly. "I can't be effective here if I let myself be used this way."

"Your superiors," Campas said, "they agreed, yes? They ordered you to Neda, didn't they? Aren't they as responsible as you—more so, even?"

"I was the one on the spot," she said: "I could have refused."

"How could you have known what was in Tegestu's mind?" Campas demanded. "How could you have known he would sacrifice the hostages in such a way?" He looked at her unblinkingly. "You helped to end the war, however it was done," he said. "With the Elva at peace, you can return to your mission. Bringing us your knowledge, Fiona, and helping us to grow."

A savage laugh burst past Fiona's lips. "Do you think that's what we're *really* here for, Campas?" she asked. "Simply to help you, out of our greater goodness?" She leaned close to him, feeling her cheeks taut in a devil's relentless grin, reflecting the helpless anger roiling in her mind. "Shall I tell you what we're really here for, Campas? You'll be amused at the irony, I'm sure." She spat out a cruel, mad laugh; he reached out a hand to touch her, to calm her, but she shrugged it away. "We're recruiters, Campas!" she told him. Her voice was a painful sob. "We're here to help you to our level, so we can enlist your children in the biggest interstellar war of all! That's the sole reason we're here, my friend, so that you can help us beat our enemies!"

His hand, still outstretched to comfort her, hesitated and

then fell. His eyes were somber. "Best tell me all," he said quietly; and, hating herself, her race, she did.

The long-ago catastrophe that had destroyed the Terrans hadn't confined itself to human space: it had spread far beyond, a long wave of chaos and destruction. Far away, other beings, not human, nearer to the galactic core, had suffered from the Terrans' mistake.

But, at some distance from the center of the disaster, the effects had been lessened; their recovery had been swift. Knowing the cause of the holocaust, computing its point of origin, they had decided to take precautions against a repetition of the racial catastrophe. Their precautions were sensible and direct.

For centuries now the descendants of the Terrans, at least those who had recovered enough to scan the skies for evidence of others of their kind, had been picking up the signals of the other interplanetary species. Not all the signals were coming from planets orbiting stars. The rest were coming from a vast fleet, hundreds of ships, coming to Terran space.

The signals had been decoded. They were military in nature. The aliens were coming to sterilize human space, to prevent the Terrans from triggering another holocaust.

But they were coming slowly, at sublight speed: it would be thousands of years before they would begin to touch on human space. There was time, if the project was gone about in the right way, for the humans to recover enough to resist the assault; and that meant mobilizing as many of the human survivors as possible.

The result was the mission of starships of Igara and their ambassadors to other planets, the attempt to raise the levels of human technology in order to bring every planet within an alliance against the alien race.

Campas wasn't equipped to understand all of the truth, but Fiona told him what she could. "Don't you see the irony, Campas?" she demande. "Tegestu involved me in your war, and he found me willing enough; but what he did to me is only what my people are trying to do to your entire *planet!*'' Campas frowned inwardly, absorbing her rapid words; she looked up at him with a cynical grin. "You remember when you came to my apartments, those months ago?" she asked. "You said you didn't believe me when I told you about our disinterested, benevolent attempts to aid your people; you implied there was some less honorable motive.

"You were right. And now you know what it is."

He nodded. "Now I know," he said. He rubbed his chin, his eyes abstracted. Then he shook his head. "I don't see what else your people could do," he said. "Any war between planets is going to be up to my descendants, not to me. Right now, I've got to report to Necias."

Choking on a bitter laugh, Fiona pressed herself to Campas, her arms going around him; she wondered if he was truly opague to the irony, or did he simply not care? She stepped back, looking up at him.

"Will you tell him?" she asked.

"Probably not. Do you think I should?" He seemed irritable. "It's between yourself and my descendants. I'm sure you're capable of dealing with their questions, when they arise." He kissed her forehead and turned.

Fiona watched him walk away; then her anger ebbed and weariness took her; she leaned against the panelled wall, closing her eyes, seeing only visions of slaughter, of the brave, uncomprehending enemy falling before her other worldly fires. Lives she had taken willingly, as Tegestu had intended, rejoicing in her power. At what cost, she wondered, to her own people? Would the Elva announce restrictions on the Igarans, horrified by the destruction she'd caused? She couldn't blame them, not after the butchery she'd done.

It's between yourself and my descendants, Campas had said, and she conceded to him a certain amount of truth.

But what understanding Campas' descendents had of the Igarans depended on the ground work she was laying; and at the moment her groundwork consisted largely of blackened corpses in the courtyard of the Old Citadel, lying amid puddles of their melted armor.

Ah, Campas, she thought. You're right in a way, but what do you know about your descendants? We've chosen them to carry our message, and their future is fixed. First we'll give them the tools to conquer the planet, and then they'll do it. The Elva trading stations will be sent farther and farther abroad, garrisoned with troops brought across the water; and then there will be wars with natives and more troops, and then colonies and domination, and in the end the word the Igarans have come to your world to spread will blanket the planet, spread on a wave of Elva conquest. Your descendants will be born into the most viable culture for such a mission, and they have been chosen by us for their part, poor puppets, before they were ever birthed. Your people have a destiny to fulfill, whether they like it or not, and I am a part of their destiny.

She took a deep breath, then straightened, her head spinning. She smelled of sweat and fear, and she wished she dared have a bath, but that would mean taking off her privy-coat and that would be too dangerous—Tegestu might yet decide she was too great a threat to let her survive. She decided instead to attempt a few hours' rest, then assemble her baggage and ride to Necias' camp. It was obvious enough that her mission here had ended.

She turned and began her journey to her quarters. As she rose to its level, she saw a Classanu knocking politely on her door. He was the same dignified, armored old man she had seen in Tegestu's chamber; he turned at her footsteps and bowed.

"Ilean Ambassador," he said. "Bro-demmin Tegestu sent me to you with a message. I had hoped to find you here."

She moved past him to open the door to her sitting room. "Please enter," she said. "You are, ilean . . .?" The questioning was automatic: she tried to remember the name of everyone she encountered—it was recommended for achieving *rapport*.

"I am Thesau, Ambassador," the old man said with a bow. "I am a Classanu of the first rank, and personal servant to lord Tegestu."

Fiona summoned a polite smile. "Please sit down, ilean Thesau," she said. "I will hear your message."

"Fortive me, ilean, I do not think I should sit," Thesau said with an apologetic look. "The message is of great importance."

Fiona straightened, feeling herself scowl: she'd had quite enough of important messages from Tegestu. "Very well," she said.

The old man's face was grave. "Bro-demmin drandor Tegestu says that he is aware that he owes you a life," he said. "He hopes you will be satisfied with his, and not hold angu against his household. He is willing to surrender his life at any time, but he begs your indulgence for a few days. He has announced his intention of voluntarily drinking poison, and following bro-demmin Grendis to Ghanaton."

Fiona felt surprise strike her with almost physical force, and she looked at Thesau sharply. Why would Tegestu kill himself now, at the height of his triumph? Perhaps he was simply trying to buy himself time. Well, if that were the case, let him have his time, his schemes. Tegestu had used her as his instrument, and the knowledge was bitter to her: but she would not seek a petty revenge on his life.

"This is acceptable to me, but I will consult my superiors," she said. "They will decide these matters, not I. Bro-demmin Tegestu may do as he wishes: my duty is only obedience, as is yours." She did not relish her speech, or its effects on the bent old man holding vigil over his wife's bedside, but she suspected it would not be politically wise to let Tegestu off entirely—it would simply be an invitation for the natives to involve her people in their wars and feuds whenever they pleased—so she would let him sweat for a few hours, or days, before she informed him that her superiors did not demand his life.

Thesau's eyes widened slightly at her words, perhaps at the Brodaini-ness of it; then, without a word, he bowed and withdrew.

Fiona wandered into her bedroom and stretched herself on the soft feather mattress, feeling relief swim into her limbs. She closed her eyes, seeing again the courtyard of the Old Citadel with its dead scattered like firescorched leaves—no, there would be no sleep, not now.

She would try to compose her thoughts, and then send a full report to the ship. Let them handle it: her own reactions were too dazed, too full of immediate sensation.

Tegestu, she thought, his image floating in her mind. Damn him. He had won his damn war, hadn't he?

32

Hamila, his eyes showing no emotion, glanced at the despatch the messenger had carried from Tegestu's headquarters, then handed the message to his translator, whose eyes widened as he spoke.

"Cenors-stannin," he said. "We have received word from the rebels in the Brodaini Quarter of Neda. Tastis and his children, at the orders of his aldran, have taken poison, and the aldran is now negotiating with bro-demmin Tegestu for surrender under the terms of the Agreement."

Necias saw the ambassadors' heads turning and heard the sudden babble of voices—and felt an immediate surge of triumph. Despite the ambassadors' almost unanimous opposition to the Agreement he, as chairman of the Elva, had signed with Tegestu last night on the barge, Necias knew that it, and the Hundred-Year Peace, would prevail.

He wiped his brow. The small room on his barge smelled of sweat, of spilled drink and food gone stale. It had been a long meeting, and it had taken until hours past midnight for the balance to finally swing his way.

The Agreement possessed one giant obstacle, and for

hours Necias had been smashing at it with all the persua-
sion he could muster. Tegestu would keep Calacas, and as
head of a sovereign Brodaini government, subject to no
one. Necias had released the Arrandal Brodaini from their
vows of obligation, and with the hope that the other Elva
cities would do likewise. Tegestu's new government would
become a part of the Elva, with special functions.

The Brodaini would be obligated by treaty to maintain a
force of fifty thousand fighting men, to be deployed as the
Elva saw fit, by majority vote of the Elva's cities. It was
a vast army, forever at the Elva's disposal, able easily
enough to crush the forces of any individual city that
opposed the Elva's will, and able to swing the balance in
any war of coalitions. The ambassadors had begun to count
on their fingers, and had been appalled.

The dozen or so men composing the Neda-Calacas
Government-in-Exile had, as one, shrieked with choleric
outrage; but neither they nor the Elva ambassadors, all of
whom took their part, could suggest any remedy to the
alternative, which, as Necias pointed out, involved the
continuation of a war in which the civilian population of
Calacas would be caught in the middle—and which would
also involve war in every city in the Elva, as the Brodaini
revolted against their lords.

Gradually, without saying it in so many words, Necias
had begun asking the ambassadors whether the cause of an
native government in Calacas was worth the chance of
losing their own cities . . . and, just as gradually, Necias
had certain of them at least considering the question when
he'd made his next point.

Tegestu had informed him, just the night before, that
drandor Astapan of Prypas had placed his forces under
Tegestu's command, and that Tanta and his whole force
would soon be marching to Neda to reinforce Tegestu's
army. Since Necias' own government considered the Agreement binding until such time as the Elva ambassadors all

received instructions from their governments to vote it down, he would withdraw his own forces from the area of Neda-Calacas and go home, as he put it, to "prepare for the inevitable civil unrest that would follow a disavowal of the Agreement."

Which left them all madly counting heads once more. If Necias withdrew his forces, that would leave only General Handipas' Prypas forces present, to cope with the united forces of Tegestu, Tanta, and (presumably) Tastis' own surviving people. With such odds any dissenters would have no hope of enforcing their point of view, at least not till after the late autumn winds brought their own reinforcements, and by that time there would be civil war throughout the Elva, with Tegestu and his available Brodaini firmly holding Calacas and at least most of Neda.

Handipas leaped up to object, wincing at the pain from his bound ribs—he'd had three horses cut out from under him in the fighting—and he ranted about the desertion; but it had all been wind and everyone knew it. Necias saw the despairing looks in the eyes of the Government-in-Exile, and knew he could safely disregard them in the future—they had no force with which to dispute any conclusion come to by the rest of the Elva. He saw also the calculating looks in the Elva ambassadors' eyes; and Necias knew the ambassadors were prepared to sell Calacas for whatever silver button Necias might care to offer.

He had been about to proffer his button when the messenger had come to Hamila, who had been watching the turmoil of the meeting with his interpreter muttering in his ear, and the announcement of the last rebels' surrender filled the room. "Under terms of the Agreement," the message had concluded; and Necias thought that as the old Brodaini resumed his seat he saw a glitter of pleasure in his eyes. Necias could barely restrain himself from leaping onto the table to dance a jig. Instead he nodded profoundly, as if the news only confirmed what he had already suspected, and rapped on the table for order.

"Cenors-stannin, I'm sure this only confirms the wisdom of the Agreement, hey?" he said. "Tastis' aldran would never have ordered his suicide and started surrender talks if we hadn't shown a little flexibility." And when he saw one of the Government-in-Exile's people begin to boil over, Necias swiftly changed the subject.

"There will be some disruption, of course, and we of the Elva must unite to make things as smooth as possible," he said. "Those inhabitants of Calacas who won't wish to live under Brodaini rule will have to be settled elsewhere, and Neda can't take them all. Also, thousands of Brodaini, their dependents, and all their goods will have to be moved from the other Elva cities to Calacas, hey? The Brodaini have inherited a war fleet from Tastis, but they're all galleys good only for coastal work and they don't have any merchant vessels to speak off—so someone's going to have to rent them transport. Also, the Brodaini will be in dire need of foodstuffs for the journey, and probably until they're settled in on their new lands, and someone will have to sell them food. I propose that we should reach an agreement on this as soon as possible."

There: the silver button. Profits to be made on transport and supplies, brokerage commissions to be earned settling Calacas refugees. He saw the looks the ambassadors began giving one another, and he knew it was time to end the meeting. Necias knew he had won enormous cimmersan from this Agreement, that his momentum had slowly gathered and was now unstoppable: he had won, and the future was his.

Thank you, friend Tegestu, he thought; and he stifled a laugh at the irony of his thought, that he would ever thank such a man for such a favor.

"It's been a long night, cenors-stannin," he said, "and

a difficult day for us all. I propose we adjourn for the present, and meet again tomorrow noon. Those in favor?''

''We need to settle the matter of Calacas first,'' Handipas snapped, with a chorus of panicked assent from the Provisional Government:

Necias pursed his lips doubtfully, enjoying his charade. ''Cenors-stannin,'' he said, ''I doubt we can settle anything tonight. It's very late. Best make a fresh start in the morning.''

''Are we in principle going to support the surrender of an Elva city?'' Handipas shouted, banging his cup on the table. ''The Brodaini got it by treachery—how do we know they'll stop with conquest of the one? How do we know they're not simply uniting their forces in order to seize the whole continent? How do we know Neda isn't next?''

''Because they can't even feed themselves as it is! They'll be dependent on us for generations! If they misbehave we can starve them!'' It was the Cartenas ambassador speaking, his tone impatient—he, Necias thought, had been easy to convince: his city was in civil turmoil after the assassination of their Abeissu and the resulting scramble of merchant houses frantically putting together coalitions and purging their enemies, and Cartenas in its current fragile condition would all too easily be shattered by an assault from the Brodaini quarter. Necias could scarcely keep himself from laughing out loud—if he could adjourn the meeting now, he thought, the other Elva cities would sell out Calacas before breakfast. Even Handipas was unsupported by anyone else in the Prypas delegation.

''Adjourn! Adjourn!'' The other ambassadors were banging the table and glaring at Handipas. Handipas turned white with anger and folded his arms, his eyes burning outrage. Necias called the meeting to an end.

The delegates were quick to take their leave—eager, Necias thought, to begin to turn the new political reality to a profitable account. The Government-in-Exile left with Handipas, looking with bitter resentment over their shoulders as they left. Necias leaned back in his massive chair, stretching his spine and shoulders, then signalled to the servants to pour one last cut of wine.

"Beg pardon, Abeissu," one of the guards murmured. "Ambassador Fiona wishes to see you."

"Now?" Necias gulped wine, wondering what he should do, and how he could avoid a meeting.

"She's been waiting for some time, Abeissu. She wished a private audience."

Necias gnawed his lower lip. Fiona *had* to know that he'd had a part in throwing her to Tastis, and the woman had enormous power and an unknown capacity for revenge. He shook his head, trying to clear it. Gods, how to get rid of her? How to get rid of all her people and their danger?

He didn't know, he thought: he'd have to find out more about her. And until then he couldn't simply avoid her— she'd get through to him somehow; and if it were revenge she was after she'd get it without his permission.

Gods, he thought with a shudder, if all he'd heard was true she could burn his barge at its moorings, with all aboard her. He pictured for a terrified, fascinated moment the fireblasts mounting higher, the melting tar raining down from the rigging, his own face and hands blackening in the flames as Fiona stood on the bank, sending her lightnings down . . . .

Put the best face possible on it, he thought, feeling a desperate nausea oozing into his belly. We knew she wouldn't come to harm, didn't we? he thought, feeling sweat speckling his brow.

He took another swallow of wine. "Send her in," he said.

She entered all in black, her hood drawn tight around her face. Her eyes glittered the lamplight; they seemed fevered, not entirely human—transformed, perhaps by what they'd seen, into the eyes of a bird of prey. He rose from his seat and put on a smile.

"Ambassador!" he cried. "Please forgive the untidiness—big doings here tonight, hey?" He propped his arms on his hips, fighting joy as he watched those predator eyes with sickly fascination. She could burn me in an instant, he thought. "I'm glad to see you safe!" he boomed; and wondered if, in his nervousness, he was speaking too loudly.

"You knew," she said, levelly. He felt his mental rhythms skip a beat at the accusation. His nerves froze. Divine Pastas, he thought, help me.

Necias forced his face into a beaming, benevolent smile. "You were in no danger, I'm sure—if Tegestu had thought there was actual danger to you, I'm certain he would have—"

"You knew," she repeated. "You and Tegestu used me in your squalid, parochial little war; you deliberately compromised my neutrality, and to my cost."

"To *end* the war, Ambassador," Necias said. His muscles shrieked with the effort to keep the smile on his face. "To *end* the war, to prevent civil war in all the Elva. We need peace, Ambassador enventan, if we are to listen to your wisdom."

Fiona took a step closer, her head cocked, her eyes unblinking. "Tegestu," she said, "offered me his life in apology. What does Abeissu Necias offer me?"

Necias felt his blood freeze. It had to be the truth; Tegestu *would* offer his life like that, the cold-blooded cunning old murderer. Necias licked his lips. "Ambassador . . ." he said, and then shook his head.

"I want," Fiona said, "a building to use as an embassy. I want to be able to hire my own servants and guards—the guards will be Brodaini, I think; Tegestu's successors will be happy enough to loan them to me. I want permission to bring two more Igaralla into the city, and with the understanding that they may travel anywhere without restriction, and speak to anyone within your area of influence without interference. I also would like permission to open a school.''

Necias looked at her dully. They will come, he thought, they will come, perhaps to overwhelm us as the Brodaini threatened to overwhelm us. Impossible to stop them, as long as they have such power, holding over us their bludgeon of knowledge that none of us dares to allow others to possess alone, lest it make them too powerful. ''What sort of school?'' he asked.

''An academy of,'' she paused for a brief second, as if she were performing a difficult mental act of translation. ''Let's call it . . . practical philosophy. Teaching useful application of mathematics, philosophy, logic, rhetoric . . . similar to your academies of rhetoric, but with an emphasis on application rather than theory.''

''You will teach your own—your own system of mechanics?'' Necias asked, meaning her systems of communication, of travel . . . and of war. What demons' knowledge did she intend to bring to Arrandal?

A slight shake of the head. ''No.'' Confidently. ''We teach no new knowledge, only modes of thought suitable to discovery of new knowledge.''

And what, Necias wondered, did that mean? He sighed, lowering himself onto his settee. ''Very well,'' he said.

''I will give an agreement in writing to your people tomorrow,'' Fiona said. ''I hope it will have your signature by nightfall.''

''Of course, of course.'' Waving his hand hopelessly. He would submit to the inevitable with as much grace as possible.

For the first time Fiona allowed herself a thin smile. ''Thank you, Necias Abeissu. Perhaps some good will come out of this disaster after all.'' She bowed, Brodaini fashion, and wished him good-night.

He could not find the energy to rise at her departure. A

moment ago he had been gleeful, thinking of himself as the inventor of the future, of the Elva, of the Hundred-Year Peace . . . and how he knew differently, He was watching the future leave his cabin, small, black-garbed, confident.

He looked down at his huge, capable hands, the hands that had been unable to keep a grip on tomorrow, *I am old,* he thought, for the first time. He closed his eyes and leaned his head back against the cushions.

She has won, he thought, and clutched the table as his mind, unable to help itself, rode a long, turbulent river into a tomorrow over which he had lost all control.

33

A sweet hymns of the autraldi filled the small domed chamber, a pleasant chapel in his borrowed deissu's palace. Tegestu stood on a platform, gazing down at Grendis' body laid before the altar in full armor, the badge of kamliss Dantu blazoned on her surcoat. She had slept, growing ever weaker, two days before infection had taken her; during that time she had never regained consciousness. Below, lain at her feet, were the bodies of those she had, with her sacrifice, triumphed over: Tastis, his son Aptan, his sister and two daughters, all ordered by his aldran to drink their cups of death, that they might with a clean slate begin their negotiations for surrender.

Look what you have accomplished, he thought, looking down at Grendis.

Soon, he thought, his mind soothed by the hymn. Soon I will join you. Have patience.

He looked up at the guests: Acamantu and Cascan representing the aldran, important welldrani and staff, representatives from the kamlissi of Arrandal, autraldi to sing the rites. All had their hair unbraided, syled in the long, elaborate ringlets of the Brodaini, for the war was over. The Elva ambassadors had, in principle, accepted the Agreement over the objections of the Government-in-Exile. Within the next few years all the exiled Brodaini would be living in their new home.

The hymn ended, and the amen chorused by all. Tegestu raised his head.

"Listen, o cousins, to my testament," he said. He took the scroll handed him by Thesau, opened it, and read it into respectful silence.

It consisted of his political wishes for the future Brodaini state of Calacas, and he knew that such was his prestige now it would be obeyed to the letter. In it he admonished his successors to live in peace with the Elva, and obey the pact by which they would furnish the Elva soldiers. This, he knew, was the only way Calacas would survive its first few years.

He also made mention of the specific political ordering of the city. The Brodaini aldran would constitute the supreme authority within the state—but Tegestu knew that the tidy social structure of a homeland Brodaini kamliss would never work here. The city's population was too large, too diverse, and too ethnically polarized; and furthermore Tegestu knew that for Calacas to survive and prosper, it needed to retain most of its native population.

Necias and the rest of the Elva thought, no doubt, that Tegestu would dispose of the political machinery Tastis had set in place in his cities, and rule as dictator. Instead Tegestu proposed to use the machinery rather than abolish it.

The Denorru-Constassin, for example, the Council of the Populace. It embraced a far wider spectrum of the population than the Dennorrin-Deissin of the other Elva states, and was more suitable for conveying their needs and desires to the aldran, and in return for conveying the aldran's wishes to the population. The League of Journeymen within the guild structure was likewise useful, and would remain, though its power would be curtailed. The masters' wills would remain balanced against the journeymen; with the Brodaini aldran always standing between, holding the balance of power.

With the journeymen granted a share of power, Tegestu thought, the masters would be forced to treat them fairly, and pay them a fair wage guaranteed by the aldran. That, Tegestu thought, would attract journeymen from all over the Elva: Calacas could take its pick, choosing only the most skilled and talented. That would, in the end, raise the quality of Calacas goods.

The Brodaini, with their expertise in crafting arms and armor, were far advanced over the Elva in the arts of metallurgy. With their advantage in the working of metals combined with their attracting the finest in craftsmen, Tegestu expected Calacas would prosper under Brodaini guidance. The other Elva states, who expected Calacas to be dependent on them for decades to come, might well be surprised, Tegestu thought, at how soon Calacas recovered, and established itself as a successful rival.

"I believe that my successors will choose ·welldrani wisely, and represent all kamlissi in the new state," he said, reading from his scroll. "I hope they will choose, as their new drandor, some one of them familiar with this new land, and familiar with the new ways necessary to live here in harmony. I recommend to you my son Acamantu, who is a proven commander, and wise in the ways of the people who live in Calacas and in this land."

He heard Acamantu straighten at the mention of his name. Tegestu had drafted most of his testament with his son's consultation, as well as that of Cascan and other representatives of his coalition, but this had been a clause kept secret till now.

Acamantu would, he knew, be the new drandor, despite

his youth. The aldran would never go against his wishes in a matter of this sort.

And that, truly, was why Tegestu would drink his cup. The new Brodaini state would require new leadership, not an old man who looked always to the past, to the land he could never regain and would never see again. It would need someone raised among local conditions, who was familiar with them and who, in fact, knew nothing else. *Survival,* Tegestu thought, *survival with demmin.* That is all-important.

He would retire honorably, of his own free will, and in triumph.

"I recommend also to the aldran my servant Thesau," he read on. "Ilean Thesau has shown himself to be outstanding among those of his rank, with a full understanding of the arts of war and of demmin. My shade would be pleased were it to hear that ilean Thesau, his wife, and all his descendants be granted the rank of Brodaini, and be honored as such for their lifetimes and the lifetimes of their descendants' descendants."

He heard a gasp from Thesau and smiled to himself; Theasu would protest he was not worthy, that it was too late to begin life anew as a Brodainu. That, he thought fondly, might be true: but I do this for your children, and to honor your memory. Old friend, he thought.

His final wishes referred to his household pets. He hoped the cats would find good homes, and wished that his old hound Yellowtooth would have his final days eased by the loving attention of a new master appointed by the aldran. It was, perhaps, a little unusual to include dogs and cats among a warrior's final wishes; but Tegestu had cherished his animals and cared for them, and the thought of his pets dispersed at random among uncaring households was more than he could bear.

"Keep always the name of Brodaini, and honor the memory of our ancestors," Tegestu said, a standard admonishment but no less heartfelt for that. "Honor the gods, and seek to understand vail and demmin. Understand this land and its people, that our kind will survive. Witness this, cousins, under my hand and seal."

He signed the document with his pen, sealed it, and handed it to one of the autraldi, who received it reverently for placement in the demmis-dru. There, he suspected, it would become a holy artifact, to be brought before the aldran at moments of great decision. My words, he thought, will guide them. Gods grant my words wisdom.

"A petition, bro-demmin." This was Acamantu, coming forward to kneel with head bowed.

"Aye, ban-demmin, speak," Tegestu said. This had not been planned; he wondered what could be so important as to interrupt his ceremonious death.

"We—the aldran—" Acamantu started, then licked his lips and continued. "We beg you will accept an honorific, bro-demmin. We hope to gain your permission to call you Tegestu the Treacherous, in commemoration of your triumph."

Caught by surprise, Tegestu grinned. "I accept the appellation," he said, "though it give me too much demmin."

Acamantu bowed again and returned to the ranks. Tegestu rose to his feet, the armor weighing him down, Thesau's arm under his.

The autraldi began a hymn again, a paean to the blessed gods, and Tegestu walked down the steps of the platform to the bed where Grendis lay. He turned and held out his hand; and Thesau, his eyes brimming with tears, brought forward the silver cup. Tegestu took it and held it reverently up for the autraldi to bless; they did so, and Tegestu brought the cup to his lips.

Well, Death, he thought with a private grin. *You must be pleased to see me at last, I who have eluded you for so long.*

He took a breath, then drained the cup, feeling the narcotic numbness touching his throat with chill fingers. He gave the cup to the autraldu, who would put it in a family shrine for others of Pranoth to use at need, and then lay down on the bed next to Grendis.

He reached out for her armored hand, and took it. The poison was painless, he knew, and would take perhaps half an hour.

The hymns filled the domed chamber.

Grendis, he thought, soon I will hold you in my arms!

Patiently, as he had always waited patiently, he waited for his death.

34

"Here," Campas said. "I'd like you to read it."

He held out a thick sheaf of papers, wrapped in a thick file-holder and tied carefully with white tape. Fiona took the bundle, then raised her gaze from the papers to her lover. He must have seen the question on her face, for he nodded.

"Yes." He said. "I'm done." His word, his new poetry, written on the long months of campaign.

"It went quickly at the end," he said. "Once I'd found my way."

"Thank you." She looked down at the manuscript, touching the surface of its protective cover. He cleared his throat, uneasy.

"I'll be in my quarters," he said. "I've got work to do."

She looked after him. "Thank you," she said again; he gave an awkward wave and was gone.

Outside, through the window of the apartment she had rented in Neda, she heard the sound of marching feet as mercenary pikemen, dismissed from Necias' service, took their leave of the city, heading for the southern baronies and, they hoped, employment there. The soldiers were leaving, some on foot, others by barge; only Necias and a few thousand of the Arrandal militia remained, to keep order in Neda until its government was capable of doing the job itself.

Wind whined through her shutters, burying briefly the sound of the marching pikemen. The winds were shifting to the north; within days the autumn storms would have arrived. She was glad she was returning to the Arrandal the leisurely way, by the canals, and not by ocean-going ship.

She was waiting only for the arrival of two more of her people, the new ambassadors for Neda and Calacas, who were preparing for their tasks on the orbiting ship above. She would introduce them to the new rulers of the cities, Acamantu, who seemed almost certain to be chosen drandor of Calacas, and to whoever would be chosen as the Abessu-Denorru of Neda; she would spend a few grateful weeks with them, speaking her own language to her own kind, and then take her barge to her own post. . . .

Where Necias had guaranteed her access to the city, to all Arrandal's domains and dependencies, and, most importantly, to the minds of his people, through her academy. It was there that the future would be built, the foundations laid for the scientific investigation of their world, indeed the universe, by Arrandal's citizens. And, as well as investigation, less honorable things: exploitation, conquest, domination. The two faces of the progress she symbolized, and was here to encourage.

Fiona moved to a comfortable settee and untied the tape on the package, slipping the sheaf of manuscript out of its protective cover. The title was written in Campas' neat secretarial hand. *Songs for the Star People*.

Fiona blinked.

So, she thought, he had taken her words to heart, to write his verse not to fit the fashion of the time, but to embrace a universal audience. She set down the title page on the settee next to her, and read.

The wind howled, and the first tentative drops of rain splattered down on the shutters. She paid them no attention; she read languidly, absorbing every word, every turn of phrase, until she placed the last leaf on its pile, and then she only stared quietly ahead of her, not seeing the details of the room, her mind still resonating with the power of Campas' verse.

It was, she thought, brilliant; but brilliant seemed an inadequate description, itself a failure of the imagination.

It started with a series of short poems speculating about the inhabitants of other worlds, trying to see them in Abessla terms, describing them in terms of nature, of legend, of styles of perception and of emotion—trying to define, not simply what they were, but how they related to the Abessla, and how much they shared a common humanity.

This merged gradually into a second theme, a series of longer verses relating complex ideas. Many of them were addressed to a lover, and in addition to presenting a sophisticated picture of a loving relationship between two intelligent, independent, and very different people—from ecstacy to puzzled misunderstanding, from resentment back to ecstacy again—there was added the element of the lover's *alienness*, her estrangement from customs and values the poet had considered universal. There were jangling elements of discord introduced, the poet's resentments of the lover's accomplishments and knowledge, angry, naked jealousy as the poet, condemned to mortality, considered his lover's extended youth, and her extended old age as well, culminating an unearthly wisdom the poet could not hope to match.

The third section, long verse meditations, resolved the conflicts. The poet had learned acceptance; he had learned to seize what joy and wisdom he could from his experience; he understood that his knowledge was far from whole, far from universal, and yet he was proud of the knowledge and understanding that, in his flawed life, he *had* achieved. He understood that he would, in the end, have to let his lover go; and he had achieved acceptance of that idea, and found himself at peace with it.

The final verse was a hymn, a brief lyric that praised the gods for creating the universe in all its diversity, and for populating it with people. And lastly it praised the human race itself, for achieving knowledge, for gaining wisdom, and most importantly for being able to bridge the gaps between nations and peoples, and between the stars themselves, with a commonality of humanness.

Fiona took a breath, the conception, the scope of Campas' achievement overwhelming her. *Songs for the Star People* was a masterwork—no, not simply that, but a definitive work. It was unlike anything the Abessla poets had done before, and its publication would transform poetic thought. Future poets would either imitate, or react against it, for generations.

And when their descendants finally achieved the stars, Fiona knew, they would take this work with them, to help them speak to any they might find of the scattered children of Terra.

Fiona took up the manuscript and pressed it to her. I, in some way, have inspired this, she thought.

Whatever else she might accomplish here, whatever brilliant graduates her academy might produce, she could never feel any greater fulfillment in any of her accomplishments. Here was something she could point to with joy: an accomplishment that never hated, that did not exploit, that did not conquer, but which strove through the bridge of art to connect the diverse threads of humanity and find a common bond between them.

Wrapping the manuscript in its folder and tape, she rose from the settee to find Campas. For the first time in months she was filled with satisfaction and joy, and she wanted to tell him so.

THE END

APPENDIX: GLOSSARY OF FOREIGN TERMS

I

The Abessas language: The Abessas language is spoken over much of the great northern plain of Echidne, including the city of Arrandal as well as Cartenas and Calacas (though not, originally, in Neda, which was spared the original Abessas conquest.). "Abessas," as a political concept, exists no more than did the concept of a "Germany" prior to 1871.

Abessas is a highly inflected language, with a complex variety of case declensions and verb forms: many nouns possess gender, though a majority are neutral. Due to the Abessas conquest of an aboriginal population speaking a different language, Abessas has become polluted (or enriched, depending on one's perspective) with a variety of foreign words, particularly place-names, that do not fit into either of the two major declensions and are thus irregular. ("Arrandal" is an example of this.)

* * *

Like modern German, Abessas permits, by the seemingly random stringing together of nouns with other nouns, pronouns, and even verbs, the creation of compound nouns (Abessu-Denorru, cenors-efellsan). Abessas nouns are usually pronounced with the accent on the penultimate syllable: eFELLsan, BEGgru, AcRAGas. Exceptions have been marked with an accent.

Abeissu pl. Abeissin	Common abbreviation for Abessu-Denorru
Abessu-Denorru pl. Abessin-Denorru	Literally "Community Speaker." Chief administrative offical of a Denorru-Deissin, principal oligarch of a city. Abbreviated "Abeissu."
Amil-Deo	"Wheel of fortune." A philosophical abstract assuring the rise and fall of human societies, lords, families, fashion and so forth. An instrument of boonan.
Anildas	Acquisitiveness; desire for display and property; urge toward conspicous consumption. Considered a desirable quality.
Beggru pl. Beggrin	A merchant house, usually consisting of one extended family, headed by a Deissu.
Boonan:	Evolution, change. Boonan is considered inevitable, and usually for the better.

Boonan-re

Progress, considered as a beneficial quality necessary to human betterment.

Cenors-stannan
pl. cenors-stannin

Literally "most fortunate," a term of high respect.

Cenors-efellsan

Literally "most advantaged," a term of awed respect applied only to the very powerful.

Cenors-censto
pl. cenors-censtinno

Senior, or most favored, wife. Hostess.

Cimmersan

Advantage, initiative.

Deissu
(pl. Deissin)

Oligarch, merchant prince. Usually the head of a large trading house, or beggru.

Deo

Wealth, honor, moral advantage.

Demro

Earth. Native name for home planet.

Denorru-Deissin
pl. Denorrin-Deissin

City council, ruling board of oligarchs.

Dinessu
pl. Diné

Hustler, merchant, "little deissu." Familar term of affectionate respect.

Elfellsan

Commercial advantage.

Elva

A long-term alliance, as contrasted with Ghilta. Also, marriage as opposed to concubinage.

Elva vor Denorru-Dorsu	Literally "Alliance of/for Community of Interest." A trading federation of major cities, formed to maintain monopolies, assure political stability, and exploit unused markets.
Enventan	Gentleman of leisure. A term of respect. Also, an abbot or high-ranking priest.
Envo-Deo	Favored by fortune. "Lucky bastard."
Flenssu pl. Flenssin	Mercenary. A term often used with disrespect, not because they fight for money but rather because of a reputation for unreliability.
Ghilta pl. Ghiltin	Friendship, alliance for political or commercial gain. Assumed to be short-term, in order to secure temporary advantage, as opposed to Elva.
Klossila pl. Klossilin	"Romantics," followers of an anti-commercial, pro-agrarian philosophical and artistic movement developed by city intelligentsia.
Lariman pl. Larimin	Dotard, old fool.
Mallanto pl. Mallantinno	A large, predatory bird native to Echidne, living principally on

shellfish (for the consumption of which it possessed a hooked beak and opposed talons), but also on small animals and fish, and living principally on seacoasts. Also, the heraldric symbol for the city of Arrandal.

Ozannu pl. Ozanni	Cuckold. A vicious insult.
Partillo pl. Partillinno	Wives' quarters. Harem.
Reygran	Competition, "free enterprise" Considered morally beneficial.
Scottu pl. Scottin	Bumpkin, country clown. Used insultingly to describe feudal barons.
Stansisso pl. Stansissinno	Literally "goodwife:" A term of respect applied to a married woman.

II

The Gostu language: Gostu is spoken by the Brodaini families of the northern continent, and by their dependents. Gostu, unlike Abessas, is not a greatly inflected language: instead of cases and verb forms, Gostu depends on a wide variety of compound and pariphrastic expressions, prepositional phrases, and a syntax of word order that generally takes precedence over case. Many of the translations given here are approximate, partly because certain Gostu concepts (hostu, vail) are rather vague to begin with, but chiefly because many concepts in use among the Brodaini will not translate in all their meanings.

Gostu, like Abessas, allows the creation of compound nouns with new meanings, created by stringing other words together. The "ch" sound is hard, as in loch. Gostu words are generally accented heavily on the first syllable (not counting prefixes), with a secondary accent on the third syllable, if there is one: TEGestu, DEMmin, MENingil.

Achadan	Earth; the Gostu name for their home planet.
"Aiau!"	An exclamation of surprise or approval.
Aldran	The body of elders ruling a kamliss
An-demmina	The act of losing one's honor, becoming ar-demmin. See demmin.
An-hosta	Change, evolution, disharmony. An evil condition. See hosta.
An-vaila	Gross disharmony, satanic evil. See vail.
Angu	Blood feud.
Ar-demmin pl. ar-demmini	Honorless, outcast. See demmin.
Aspistu	Vengeance, considered as an art. Also, the religious cult of vengeance.

Autraldu pl. Autraldi	Litterally "incorruptible." Priests, usually proved warriors, appointed to guard the demmis-dru.
Ban-demmin pl. ban-demmini	"Honored," a term of polite respect. See demmin.
Bearni	Mercenaries. A term of insult, as mercenaries fight for pay rather than for the acquisition of demmin.
Bohau	A large stringed instrument, played with a plectrum. A 3-stringed, horizontal bass fiddle.
Brodainu pl. Brodaini	A member of the warrior class, the highest caste of Gostandu society. Often used incorrectly by the Abessla to describe both the Brodaini and their dependents.
Bro-demmin pl. Bro-demmini	"Most honored," a term of high respect. Use of bro-demmin, as opposed to ban-demmin, implies acknowledging the fact of higher status, or greater authority, than oneself. See demmin.
Cambranu pl. Cambrani	Spy. Among Brodaini, an honorable occupation.
Canlan pl. Canlani	Liege lord.

Cathrelku	Chief of bodyguards.
Cathrunu pl. Cathruni	Bodyguard.
Classanu pl. Classani	"Servant," a member of the second class of Gostandu society. In addition to providing personal servants to the Brodaini, Classani form an auxiliary military force.
Clattern pl. Clatterni	Kinglet, prince. A chieftain owed allegiance by more than one clan.
Clattern-y-Clatterni	"King of kings," a recently-invented title assumed by the conquering overlord of Gostandu, and not recognized by the Gostandi exiles such as the Brodaini of Arrandal.
Dai-terru	Overreaching, attempting to gain more demmin than required by the situation or by one's status.
Demmin	Honor, in its peculiarly Brodaini sense, meaning also correctness, advantage, esteem, self-worth. Required for status in warrior society. Related etymologically to demmis-dru, shemmina; see also an-demmina, ar-demmin, ban-demmin, bro-demmin, kamliss-demmin, demmin-drax.
Demmin-drax	Gaining demmin at the expense of another's demmin.

Demmis-dru

Holy place; household shrine, where wills, secret documents, treaties, etc., are kept under the protection of gods, ancestral spirits, and the autraldi.

Dentraldu

The head of the autraldi.

Drandor

Litterally "eldest." The leader of a kamliss, elected for life by the aldran.

Ghanaton

The Brodaini afterlife, a bleak, bloodless, shadowy land where status is granted the shades of the dead based on the amount of honor rendered them by the living.

Gostandu (1)

The land of the Gostu-speakers, i.e., the homeland of the Brodaini and their dependents. A recently-invented term, coined because of the need for the Clattern-y-Clatterni to describe the place he was king of. (Previous to the uniting of the continent, Gostandu rulers would have described themselves as being from a particular geographic area, or simply as being a member of a governing kamliss.)

Gostandu (2)
pl. Gostandi

A native of Gostandu.

Hostu

Stasis, perfection. An ideal earthly condition, a manifestation of vail.

Hostlu pl. Hostli	A tradesman or merchant, member of the lowest class of Gostandu society. Often used as an insult. Ar-demmin almost by definition.
Ilean	"Sir," "Madam." A term of polite respect, accorded by Brodaini to Classani, Meningli, foreigners, and others assumed to lack proper understanding of demmin.
Kamliss pl. Kamlissi	Clan, extended family, normally consisting of all four classes of Gostandu society. On their native continent a surviving kamliss has claim to territory: previous to the appearance of the Clatterni-Clatterni the territory was sovereign unless its drandor had made himself vassal to a canlan from another clan.
Kamliss-demmin	Clan honor.
Kantu-kamliss	Literally "clan-matter." Kantu-kamliss is a religious taboo invoked to guard diplomatic correspondence between a clan and its ambassadors, with the intent of its preventing despatches from being read by outsiders.
Lersru pl. Lersri	Assassin. In times of war or declared angu, an honorable occupation.

Meninglu pl. Meningli	Peasant. A member of the third rank of Gostandu society. The Meningli constitute a reserve military force used only in dire emergency; thus the term "summon the Meningli" has a colloquial meaning indicating extreme urgency.
Mardan-clannu	"Thrust of mercy," coup de grace.
Nartil	Fealty, service, obligation, respect, custom, justice, lawsuit. Usually referring to the mainstay of Gostandu society, the law of obedience, obligation, and respect.
Repinu pl. Repini	Literally "spearman." Colloquially a term of affection, like "doughboy" or "grognard." Ordinary soldiers.
Shemmina	Noticing something beneath one's notice, or killing (noticing) a person whose death cannot bring one honor because he is honorless himself. (Killing below one's station.)
Tedec	A five-stringed relative of the guitar or lute.
Tolhostu	Propriety, dignity, gravity. The Brodaini art of proper public performance.

Vail   Approximate translations include "harmony," "heaven," "tao." An ideal condition in which human and cosmic forces are in perfect alignment.

Welldran
pl. Welldrani   Literally "elder." Person, old or young, chosen to sit on the aldran by a vote of its members.

Whelkran
pl. Whelkrani   Officer commanding at least 100 soldiers. The term is usually followed by a number to indicate the precise delineation of status and authority, i.e., "a whelkran of five hundreds."